PRAISE FOR ZANE GREY

"There is a thrill on every page."
—*Boston Evening Transcript* on *Wildfire*

"Among the best of those American novelists who
have chosen the frontier as their field."
—*The New York Times*

"[Grey] knows the West."
—*The New York Herald*

THE LAST OF THE PLAINSMEN

ZANE GREY

·

LAST OF THE GREAT SCOUTS

HELEN CODY WETMORE

A TOM DOHERTY ASSOCIATES BOOK | NEW YORK

THE LAST OF THE PLAINSMEN AND LAST OF THE GREAT SCOUTS

The Last of the Plainsmen was originally published in 1908. *Last of the Great Scouts* was originally published in 1899. Zane Grey's foreword and afterword were originally published in 1918, in a later edition of the book.

A Forge Book
Published by Tom Doherty Associates, LLC
175 Fifth Avenue
New York, NY 10010

www.tor-forge.com

Forge® is a registered trademark of Tom Doherty Associates, LLC.

ISBN 978-0-7653-8149-1

Forge books may be purchased for educational, business, or promotional use. For information on bulk purchases, please contact the Macmillan Corporate and Premium Sales Department at 1-800-221-7945, extension 5442, or write to specialmarkets@macmillan.com.

First Edition: June 2015

Printed in the United States of America

0 9 8 7 6 5 4 3 2 1

CONTENTS

THE LAST OF THE PLAINSMEN

BY ZANE GREY

PREFATORY NOTE

Buffalo Jones needs no introduction to American sportsmen, but to those of my readers who are unacquainted with him a few words may not be amiss.

He was born sixty-two years ago on the Illinois prairie, and he has devoted practically all of his life to the pursuit of wild animals. It has been a pursuit which owed its unflagging energy and indomitable purpose to a singular passion, almost an obsession, to capture alive, not to kill. He has caught and broken the will of every well-known wild beast native to western North America. Killing was repulsive to him. He even disliked the sight of a sporting rifle, though for years necessity compelled him to earn his livelihood by supplying the meat of buffalo to the caravans crossing the plains. At last, seeing that the extinction of the noble beasts was inevitable, he smashed his rifle over a wagon wheel and vowed to save the species. For ten years he labored, pursing, capturing and taming buffalo, for which the West gave him fame, and the name Preserver of the American Bison.

As civilization encroached upon the plains Buffalo Jones ranged slowly westward; and to-day an isolated desert-bound plateau on the north rim of the Grand Cañon of Arizona is his home. There his buffalo browse with the mustang and deer, and are as free as ever they were on the rolling plains.

In the spring of 1907 I was the fortunate companion of

the old plainsman on a trip across the desert, and a hunt in that wonderful country of yellow crags, deep cañons and giant pines. I want to tell about it. I want to show the color and beauty of those painted cliffs and the long, brown-matted bluebell-dotted aisles in the grand forests; I want to give a suggestion of the tang of the dry, cool air; and particularly I want to throw a little light upon the life and nature of that strange character and remarkable man, Buffalo Jones.

Happily in remembrance a writer can live over his experiences, and see once more the moon-blanched silver mountain peaks against the dark blue sky; hear the lonely sough of the night-wind through the pines; feel the dance of wild expectation in the quivering pulse; the stir, the thrill, the joy of hard action in perilous moments; the mystery of man's yearning for the unattainable.

As a boy I read of Boone with a throbbing heart, and the silent moccasined, vengeful Wetzel I loved. I pored over the deeds of later men—Custer and Carson, those heroes of the plains. And as a man I came to see the wonder, the tragedy of their lives, and to write about them. It has been my destiny—what a happy fulfillment of my dreams of border spirit!—to live for a while in the fast-fading wild environment which produced these great men with the last of the great plainsmen.

ZANE GREY

CHAPTER 1

The Arizona Desert

One afternoon, far out on the sun-baked waste of sage, we made camp near a clump of withered piñon trees. The cold desert wind came down upon us with the sudden darkness. Even the Mormons, who were finding the trail for us across the drifting sands, forgot to sing and pray at sundown. We huddled round the campfire, a tired and silent little group. When out of the lonely, melancholy night some wandering Navajos stole like shadows to our fire, we hailed their advent with delight. They were good-natured Indians, willing to barter a blanket or bracelet; and one of them, a tall, gaunt fellow, with the bearing of a chief, could speak a little English.

"How," said he, in a deep chest voice.

"Hello, Noddlecoddy," greeted Jim Emmett, the Mormon guide.

"Ugh!" answered the Indian.

"Big paleface—Buffalo Jones—big chief—buffalo man," introduced Emmett, indicating Jones.

"How." The Navajo spoke with dignity, and extended a friendly hand.

"Jones big white chief—rope buffalo—tie up tight," continued Emmett, making motions with his arm, as if he were whirling a lasso.

"No big—heap small buffalo," said the Indian, holding his hand level with his knee, and smiling broadly.

Jones, erect, rugged, brawny, stood in the full light of

the campfire. He had a dark, bronzed, inscrutable face; a stern mouth and square jaw, keen eyes, half-closed from years of searching the wide plains, and deep furrows wrinkling his cheeks. A strange stillness enfolded his features—the tranquility earned from a long life of adventure.

He held up both muscular hands to the Navajo, and spread out his fingers.

"Rope buffalo—heap big buffalo—heap many—one sun."

The Indian straightened up, but kept his friendly smile.

"Me big chief," went on Jones, "me go far north—Land of Little Sticks—Naza! Naza!—rope musk-ox; rope White Manitou of Great Slaves—Naza! Naza!"

"Naza!" replied the Navajo, pointing to the North Star; "no—no."

"Yes—me big paleface—me come long way toward setting sun—go cross Big Water—go Buckskin—Siwash—chase cougar."

The cougar, or mountain lion, is a Navajo god and the Navajos hold him in as much fear and reverence as do the Great Slave Indians the musk-ox.

"No kill cougar," continued Jones, as the Indian's bold features hardened. "Run cougar horseback—run long way—dogs chase cougar long time—chase cougar up tree! Me big chief—me climb tree—climb high up—lasso cougar—rope cougar—tie cougar all tight."

The Navajo's solemn face relaxed.

"White man heap fun. No."

"Yes," cried Jones, extending his great arms. "Me strong; me rope cougar—me tie cougar; ride off wigwam, keep cougar alive."

"No," replied the savage vehemently.

"Yes," protested Jones, nodding earnestly.

"No," answered the Navajo, louder, raising his dark head.

"Yes!" shouted Jones.

"BIG LIE!" the Indian thundered.

Jones joined good-naturedly in the laugh at his expense. The Indian had crudely voiced a skepticism I had heard more delicately hinted in New York, and singularly enough, which had strengthened on our way West, as we met ranchers, prospectors and cowboys. But those few men I had fortunately met, who really knew Jones, more than overbalanced the doubt and ridicule cast upon him. I recalled a scarred old veteran of the plains, who had talked to me in true Western bluntness:

"Say, young feller, I heerd yer couldn't git acrost the cañon fer the deep snow on the north rim. Wal, ye're lucky. Now, yer hit the trail fer New York, an' keep goin'! Don't ever tackle the desert, 'specially with them Mormons. They've got water on the brain, wusser 'n religion. It's two hundred an' fifty miles from Flagstaff to Jones' range, an' only two drinks on the trail. I know this hyar Buffalo Jones. I knowed him way back in the seventies, when he was doin' them ropin' stunts thet made him famous as the preserver of the American bison. I know about that crazy trip of his'n to the Barren Lands, after musk-ox. An' I reckon I kin guess what he'll do over there in the Siwash. He'll rope cougars—sure he will—an' watch 'em jump. Jones would rope the devil, an' tie him down if the lasso didn't burn. Oh! he's hell on ropin' things. An' he's wusser 'n hell on men, an' hosses, an' dogs."

All that my well-meaning friend suggested made me, of course, only the more eager to go with Jones. Where I had once been interested in the old buffalo hunter, I was now fascinated. And now I was with him in the desert and seeing him as he was, a simple, quiet man, who fitted the mountains and the silences, and the long reaches of distance.

"It does seem hard to believe—all this about Jones," remarked Judd, one of Emmett's men. "How could a man have the strength and the nerve? And isn't it cruel to keep wild animals in captivity? Isn't it against God's word?"

Quick as speech could flow, Jones quoted: "And God said, 'Let us make man in our image, and give him dominion over the fish of the sea, the fowls of the air, over all the cattle, and over every creeping thing that creepeth upon the earth'!

"Dominion—over all the beasts of the field!" repeated Jones, his big voice rolling out. He clenched his huge fists, and spread wide his long arms. "Dominion! That was God's word!" The power and intensity of him could be felt. Then he relaxed, dropped his arms, and once more grew calm. But he had shown a glimpse of the great, strange and absorbing passion of his life. Once he had told me how, when a mere child, he had hazarded limb and neck to capture a fox squirrel, how he had held on to the vicious little animal, though it bit his hand through; how he had ever learned to play the games of boyhood: that when the youths of the little Illinois village were at play, he roamed the prairies, or the rolling, wooded hills, or watched a gopher hole. That boy was father of the man: for sixty years an enduring passion for dominion over wild animals had possessed him, and made his life an endless pursuit.

Our guests, the Navajos, departed early, and vanished silently in the gloom of the desert. We settled down again into a quiet that was broken only by the low chant-like song of a praying Mormon. Suddenly the hounds bristled, and old Moze, a surly and aggressive dog, rose and barked at some real or imaginary desert prowler. A sharp command from Jones made Moze crouch down, and the other hounds cowered close together.

"Better tie up the dogs," suggested Jones. "Like as not coyotes run down here from the hills."

The hounds were my especial delight. But Jones regarded them with considerable contempt. When all was said, this was no small wonder, for that quintet of long-eared canines would have tried the patience of a saint. Old Moze was a Missouri hound that Jones had procured in that State of uncertain qualities; and the dog had grown old over coontrails. He was black and white, grizzled and battle-scarred; and if ever a dog had an evil eye, Moze was that dog. He had a way of wagging his tail—an indeterminate, equivocal sort of wag, as if he realized his ugliness and knew he stood little chance of making friends, but was still hopeful and willing. As for me, the first time he manifested this evidence of a good heart under a rough coat, he won me forever.

To tell of Moze's derelictions up to that time would take more space than would a history of the whole trip; but the enumeration of several incidents will at once stamp him as a dog of character, and will establish the fact that even if his progenitors had never taken any blue ribbons, they had at least bequeathed him fighting blood. At Flagstaff we chained him in the yard of a livery stable. Next morning we found him hanging by his chain on the other side of an eight-foot fence. We took him down, expecting to have the sorrowful duty of burying him; but Moze shook himself, wagged his tail, and then pitched into the livery stable dog. As a matter of fact, fighting was his forte. He whipped all of the dogs in Flagstaff; and when our bloodhounds came on from California, he put three of them *hors de combat* at once, and subdued the pup with a savage growl. His crowning feat, however, made even the stoical Jones open his mouth in amaze. We had taken Moze to the El Tovar at the Grand Cañon, and finding it impossible to get over to the north rim, we left him with one of Jones's men, called Rust, who was working on the cañon trail. Rust's instructions were to bring Moze to Flagstaff in two weeks. He brought the dog a little ahead of time, and roared his appreciation of the relief it was to get the responsibility off his hands. And he related many strange things, most striking of which was how Moze had broken his chain and plunged into the raging Colorado River, and tried to swim it just above the terrible Sockdolager Rapids. Rust and his fellow-workmen watched the dog disappear in the yellow, wrestling, turbulent whirl of waters, and had heard his knell in the booming roar of the falls. Nothing but a fish could live in that current; nothing but a bird could scale those perpendicular marble walls. That night, however, when the men crossed on the tramway, Moze met them with a wag of his tail. He had crossed the river, and he had come back!

To the four reddish-brown, big-framed bloodhounds I had given the names of Don, Tige, Jude and Ranger; and by dint of persuasion, had succeeded in establishing some kind of family relation between them and Moze. This night I tied up the bloodhounds, after bathing and salving their sore feet; and I left Moze free, for he grew fretful and surly under restraint.

The Mormons, prone, dark, blanketed figures, lay on the sand. Jones was crawling into his bed. I walked a little way from the dying fire, and faced the north, where the desert stretched, mysterious and illimitable. How solemn and still it was! I drew in a great breath of the cold air, and thrilled with a nameless sensation. Something was there, away to the northward; it called to me from out of the dark and gloom; I was going to meet it.

I lay down to sleep with the great blue expanse open to

my eyes. The stars were very large, and wonderfully bright, yet they seemed so much farther off than I had ever seen them. The wind softly sifted the sand. I hearkened to the tinkle of the cowbells on the hobbled horses. The last thing I remembered was old Moze creeping close to my side, seeking the warmth of my body.

When I awakened, a long, pale line showed out of the dun-colored clouds in the east. It slowly lengthened, and tinged to red. Then the morning broke, and the slopes of snow on the San Francisco peaks behind us glowed a delicate pink. The Mormons were up and doing with the dawn. They were stalwart men, rather silent, and all workers. It was interesting to see them pack for the day's journey. They traveled with wagons and mules, in the most primitive way, which Jones assured me was exactly as their fathers had crossed the plains fifty years before, on the trail to Utah.

All morning we made good time, and as we descended into the desert, the air became warmer, the scrubby cedar growth began to fail, and the bunches of sage were few and far between. I turned often to gaze back at the San Francisco peaks. The snowcapped tips glistened and grew higher, and stood out in startling relief. Some one said they could be seen two hundred miles across the desert, and were a landmark, and a fascination to all travelers thitherward.

I never raised my eyes to the north that I did not draw my breath quickly and grow chill with awe and bewilderment with the marvel of the desert. The scaly red ground descended gradually; bare red knolls, like waves, rolled away northward; black buttes reared their flat heads; long ranges of sand flowed between them like streams, and all sloped away to merge into gray, shadowy obscurity, into wild and desolate, dreamy and misty nothingness.

"Do you see those white sand dunes there, more to the left?" asked Emmett. "The Little Colorado runs in there. How far does it look to you?"

"Thirty miles, perhaps," I replied, adding ten miles to my estimate.

"It's seventy-five. We'll get there day after tomorrow. If the snow in the mountains has begun to melt, we'll have a time getting across."

That afternoon, a hot wind blew in my face, carrying fine sand that cut and blinded. It filled my throat, sending me to the water cask till I was ashamed. When I fell into my bed at night, I never turned. The next day was hotter; the wind blew harder; the sand stung sharper.

About noon the following day, the horses whinnied, and the mules roused out of their tardy gait. "They smell water," said Emmett. And despite the heat, and the sand in my nostrils, I smelled it, too. The dogs, poor foot-sore fellows, trotted on ahead down the trail. A few more miles of hot sand and gravel and red stone brought us around a low mesa to the Little Colorado.

It was a wide stream of swiftly running, reddish-muddy water. In the channel, cut by floods, little streams trickled and meandered in all directions. The main part of the river ran in close to the bank we were on. The dogs lolled in the water; the horses and mules tried to run in, but were restrained; the men drank, and bathed their faces. According to my Flagstaff adviser, this was one of the two drinks I would get on the desert, so I availed myself heartily of the opportunity. The water was full of sand, but cold and gratefully thirst-quenching.

The Little Colorado seemed no more to me than a shallow creek; I heard nothing sullen or menacing in its musical flow.

"Doesn't look bad, eh?" queried Emmett, who read my thought. "You'd be surprised to learn how many men and Indians, horses, sheep and wagons are buried under that quicksand."

The secret was out, and I wondered no more. At once the stream and wet bars of sand took on a different color. I removed my boots, and waded out to a little bar. The sand seemed quite firm, but water oozed out around my feet; and when I stepped, the whole bar shook like jelly. I pushed my foot through the crust, and the cold, wet sand took hold, and tried to suck me down.

"How can you ford this stream with horses?" I asked Emmett.

"We must take our chances," replied he. "We'll hitch two teams to one wagon, and run the horses. I've forded here at worse stages than this. Once a team got stuck, and I had to leave it; another time the water was high, and washed me downstream."

Emmett sent his son into the stream on a mule. The rider lashed his mount, and plunging, splashing, crossed at a pace near a gallop. He returned in the same manner, and reported one bad place near the other side.

Jones and I got on the first wagon and tried to coax up the dogs, but they would not come. Emmett had to lash the four horses to start them; and other Mormons riding alongside, yelled at them, and used their whips. The wagon bowled into the water with a tremendous splash. We were wet through before we had gone twenty feet. The plunging horses were lost in yellow spray; the stream rushed through the wheels; the Mormons yelled. I wanted to see, but was lost in a veil of yellow mist. Jones yelled in my ear, but I could not hear what he said. Once the wagon wheels struck a stone or log, almost lurching us overboard. A muddy splash blinded me. I cried out in my excitement, and punched Jones in the back. Next moment, the keen exhilaration of the ride gave way to horror. We seemed to drag, and almost stop. Some one roared: "Horse down!"

One instant of painful suspense, in which imagination pictured another tragedy added to the record of this deceitful river—a moment filled with intense feeling, and sensation of splash, and yell, and fury of action; then the three able horses dragged their comrade out of the quicksand. He regained his feet, and plunged on. Spurred by fear, the horses increased their efforts, and amid clouds of spray, galloped the remaining distance to the other side.

Jones looked disgusted. Like all plainsmen, he hated water. Emmett and his men calmly unhitched. No trace of alarm, or even of excitement showed in their bronzed faces.

"We made that fine and easy," remarked Emmett.

So I sat down and wondered what Jones and Emmett, and these men would consider really hazardous. I began to have a feeling that I would find out; that experience for me was but in its infancy; that far across the desert the something which had called me would show hard, keen, perilous life. And I began to think of reserve powers of fortitude and endurance.

The other wagons were brought across without mishap; but the dogs did not come with them. Jones called and called. The dogs howled and howled. Finally I waded out over the wet bars and little streams to a point several hundred yards nearer the dogs. Moze was lying down, but the others were whining and howling in a state of great perturbation. I called and called. They answered, and even ran into the water, but did not start across.

"Hyah, Moze! hyah, you Indian!" I yelled, losing my patience. "You've already swum the Big Colorado, and this is only a brook. Come on!"

This appeal evidently touched Moze, for he barked, and plunged in. He made the water fly, and when carried off his feet, breasted the current with energy and power. He made shore almost even with me, and wagged his tail. Not to be outdone, Jude, Tige and Don followed suit, and first one and then another was swept off his feet and carried downstream. They landed below me. This left Ranger, the pup, alone on the other shore. Of all the pitiful yelps ever uttered by a frightened and lonely puppy, his were the most forlorn I had ever heard. Time after time he plunged in, and with many bitter howls of distress, went back. I kept calling, and at last, hoping to make him come by a show of indifference, I started away. This broke his heart. Putting up his head, he let out a long, melancholy wail, which for aught I knew might have been a prayer, and then consigned himself to the yellow current. Ranger swam like a boy learning. He seemed to be afraid to get wet. His forefeet were continually pawing the air in front of his nose. When he struck the swift place, he went downstream like a flash, but still kept swimming valiantly. I tried to follow along the sand-bar, but found it impossible. I encouraged him by yelling. He drifted far below, stranded on an island, crossed it, and plunged in again, to make shore almost out of my sight. And when at last I got to dry sand, there was Ranger, wet and disheveled, but consciously proud and happy.

After lunch we entered upon the seventy-mile stretch from the Little to the Big Colorado.

Imagination had pictured the desert for me as a vast, sandy plain, flat and monotonous. Reality showed me desolate mountains gleaming bare in the sun, long lines of red bluffs, white sand dunes, and hills of blue clay, areas of level ground—in all, a many-hued, boundless world in itself, wonderful and beautiful, fading all around into the purple haze of deceiving distance.

Thin, clear, sweet, dry, the desert air carried a languor, a dreaminess, tidings of far-off things, and an enthralling promise. The fragrance of flowers, the beauty and grace of women, the sweetness of music, the mystery of life—all seemed to float on that promise. It was the air breathed by the lotus-eaters, when they dreamed, and wandered no more.

Beyond the Little Colorado, we began to climb again. The sand was thick; the horses labored; the drivers shielded their faces. The dogs began to limp and lag. Ranger had to be taken into a wagon; and then, one by one, all of the other dogs except Moze. He refused to ride, and trotted along with his head down.

Far to the front the pink cliffs, the ragged mesas, the dark, volcanic spurs of the Big Colorado stood up and beckoned us onward. But they were a far hundred miles across the shifting sands, and baked clay, and ragged rocks. Always in the rear rose the San Francisco peaks, cold and pure, startlingly clear and close in the rare atmosphere.

We camped near another water hole, located in a deep, yellow-colored gorge, crumbling to pieces, a ruin of rock, and silent as the grave. In the bottom of the cañon was a pool of water, covered with green scum. My thirst was effectually quenched by the mere sight of it. I slept poorly, and lay for hours watching the great stars. The silence was painfully oppressive. If Jones had not begun to give a respectable imitation of the exhaust pipe on a steamboat, I should have been compelled to shout aloud, or get up; but this snoring would have dispelled anything. The morning came gray and cheerless. I got up stiff and sore, with a tongue like a rope.

All day long we ran the gauntlet of the hot, flying sand. Night came again, a cold, windy night. I slept well until a mule stepped on my bed, which was conducive to restlessness. At dawn cold, gray clouds tried to blot out the rosy east. I could hardly get up. My lips were cracked; my tongue swollen to twice its natural size; my eyes smarted and burned. The barrels and kegs of water were exhausted. Holes that had been dug in the dry sand of a dry stream bed the night before in the morning yielded a scant supply of muddy alkali water, which went to the horses.

Only twice that day did I rouse to anything resembling enthusiasm. We came to a stretch of country showing the wonderful diversity of the desert land. A long range of beautifully rounded clay dunes bordered the trail. So symmetrical were they that I imagined them works of sculptors. Light blue, dark blue, clay blue, marine blue, cobalt blue—every shade of blue was there, but no other color. The other time that I awoke to sensations from without was when we came to the top of a ridge. We had been passing through red-lands. Jones called the place a strong, specific word which really was illustrative of the heat amid those scaling red ridges. We came out where the red changed abruptly to gray. I seemed always to see things first, and I cried out: "Look! here are a red lake and trees!"

"No, lad, not a lake," said old Jim, smiling at me; "that's what haunts the desert traveler. It's only a mirage!"

So I awoke to the realization of that illusive thing, the mirage, a beautiful lie, false as stairs of sand. Far northward a clear rippling lake sparkled in the sunshine. Tall, stately trees, with waving green foliage, bordered the water. For a long moment it lay there, smiling in the sun, a thing almost tangible; and then it faded. I felt a sense of actual loss. So real had been the illusion that I could not believe I was not soon to drink and wade and dabble in the cool waters. Disappointment was keen. This is what maddens the prospector or sheep-herder lost in the desert. Was it not a terrible thing to be dying of thirst, to see sparkling water, almost to smell it, and then realize suddenly that all was only a lying trick of the desert, a lure, a delusion? I ceased to wonder at the Mormons, and their search for water, their talk of water. But I had not realized its true significance. I had not known what water was. I had never appreciated it. So it was my destiny to learn that water is the greatest thing on earth. I hung over a three-foot hole in a dry stream bed, and watched it ooze and seep through the sand, and fill up—oh, so slowly; and I felt it loosen my parched tongue, and steal through all my dry body with strength and life. Water is said to constitute three fourths of the universe. However that may be, on the desert it is the whole world, and all of life.

Two days passed by, all hot sand and wind and glare. The Mormons sang no more at evening; Jones was silent; the dogs were limp as rags.

At Moncaupie Wash we ran into a sandstorm. The horses turned their backs to it, and bowed their heads patiently. The Mormons covered themselves. I wrapped a blanket round my head and hid behind a sage bush. The wind, carrying the sand, made a strange hollow roar. All was enveloped in a weird yellow opacity. The sand seeped through the sage bush and swept by with a soft, rustling sound, not unlike the wind in the rye. From time to time I raised a corner of my blanket and peeped out. Where my feet had stretched was an enormous mound of sand. I felt the blanket, weighted down, slowly settle over me.

Suddenly as it had come, the sandstorm passed. It left a changed world for us. The trail was covered; the wheels hub-deep in sand; the horses, walking sand dunes. I could not close my teeth without grating harshly on sand.

We journeyed onward, and passed long lines of petrified trees, some a hundred feet in length, lying as they had fallen, thousands of years before. White ants crawled among the ruins. Slowly climbing the sandy trail, we circled a great red bluff with jagged peaks, that had seemed an interminable obstacle. A scant growth of cedar and sage again made its appearance. Here we halted to pass another night. Under a cedar I heard the plaintive, piteous bleat of an animal. I searched, and presently found a little black and white lamb, scarcely able to stand. It came readily to me, and I carried it to the wagon.

"That's a Navajo lamb," said Emmett. "It's lost. There are Navajo Indians close by."

" 'Away in the desert we heard its cry,' " quoted one of the Mormons.

Jones and I climbed the red mesa near camp to see the sunset. All the western world was ablaze in golden glory. Shafts of light shot toward the zenith, and bands of paler gold, tinging to rose, circled away from the fiery, sinking globe. Suddenly the sun sank, the gold changed to gray, then to purple, and shadows formed in the deep gorge at our feet. So sudden was the transformation that soon it was night, the solemn, impressive night of the desert. A stillness that seemed too sacred to break clasped the place; it was infinite; it held the bygone ages, and eternity.

More days, and miles, miles, miles! The last day's ride to the Big Colorado was unforgettable. We rode toward the head of a gigantic red cliff pocket, a veritable inferno, immeasurably hot, glaring, awful. It towered higher and higher above us. When we reached a point of this red barrier, we heard the dull rumbling roar of water, and we came out, at length, on a winding trail cut in the face of a bluff overhanging the Colorado River. The first sight of most famous and much-heralded wonders of nature is often disappointing; but never can this be said of the blood-hued Rio Colorado. If it had beauty, it was beauty that appalled. So riveted was my gaze that I could hardly turn it across the river, where Emmett proudly pointed out his lonely home—an oasis set down amidst beetling red cliffs. How grateful to the eye was the green of alfalfa and cottonwood! Going round the bluff trail, the wheels had only a foot of room to spare; and the sheer descent into the red, turbid, congested river was terrifying.

I saw the constricted rapids, where the Colorado took

its plunge into the box-like head of the Grand Cañon of Arizona; and the deep, reverberating boom of the river, at flood height, was a fearful thing to hear. I could not repress a shudder at the thought of crossing above that rapid.

The bronze walls widened as we proceeded, and we got down presently to a level, where a long wire cable stretched across the river. Under the cable ran a rope. On the other side was an old scow moored to the bank.

"Are we going across in that?" I asked Emmett, pointing to the boat.

"We'll all be on the other side before dark," he replied cheerily.

I felt that I would rather start back alone over the desert than trust myself in such a craft, on such a river. And it was all because I had had experience with bad rivers, and thought I was a judge of dangerous currents. The Colorado slid with a menacing roar out of a giant split in the red wall, and whirled, eddied, bulged on toward its confinement in the iron-ribbed cañon below.

In answer to shots fired, Emmett's man appeared on the other side, and rode down to the ferry landing. Here he got into a skiff, and rowed laboriously upstream for a long distance before he started across, and then swung into the current. He swept down rapidly, and twice the skiff whirled, and completely turned round; but he reached our bank safely. Taking two men aboard he rowed upstream again, close to the shore, and returned to the opposite side in much the same manner in which he had come over.

The three men pushed out the scow, and grasping the rope overhead, began to pull. The big craft ran easily. When the current struck it, the wire cable sagged, the water boiled and surged under it, raising one end, and then the other. Nevertheless, five minutes were all that were required to pull the boat over.

It was a rude, oblong affair, made of heavy planks loosely put together, and it leaked. When Jones suggested that we get the agony over as quickly as possible, I was with him, and we embarked together. Jones said he did not like the looks of the tackle; and when I thought of his by no means small mechanical skill, I had not added a cheerful idea to my consciousness. The horses of the first team had to be dragged upon the scow, and once on, they reared and plunged.

When we started, four men pulled the rope, and Emmett sat in the stern, with the tackle guys in hand. As the current hit us, he let out the guys, which maneuver caused the boat to swing stern down stream. When it pointed obliquely, he made fast the guys again. I saw that this served two purposes: the current struck, slid alongside, and over the stern, which mitigated the danger, and at the same time helped the boat across.

To look at the river was to court terror, but I had to look. It was an infernal thing. It roared in hollow, sullen voice, as a monster growling. It had a voice, this river, and one strangely changeful. It moaned as if in pain—it whined, it cried. Then at times it would seem strangely silent. The current was as complex and mutable as human life. It boiled, beat and bulged. The bulge itself was an incomprehensible thing, like a roaring lift of the waters from a submarine explosion. Then it would smooth out, and run like oil. It shifted from one channel to another, rushed to the center of the river, then swung close to one shore or the other. Again it swelled near the boat, in great, boiling, hissing eddies.

"Look! See where it breaks through the mountain!" yelled Jones in my ear.

I looked upstream to see the stupendous granite walls separated in a gigantic split that must have been made by a terrible seismic disturbance; and from this gap poured the dark, turgid, mystic flood.

I was in a cold sweat when we touched shore, and I jumped long before the boat was properly moored.

Emmett was wet to the waist where the water had surged over him. As he sat rearranging some tackle I remarked to him that of course he must be a splendid swimmer, or he would not take such risks.

"No, I can't swim a stroke," he replied; "and it wouldn't be any use if I could. Once in there a man's a goner."

"You've had bad accidents here?" I questioned.

"No, not bad. We only drowned two men last year. You see, we had to tow the boat up the river, and row across, as then we hadn't the wire. Just above, on this side, the boat hit a stone, and the current washed over her, taking off the team and two men."

"Didn't you attempt to rescue them?" I asked, after waiting a moment.

"No use. They never came up."

"Isn't the river high now?" I continued, shuddering as I glanced out at the whirling logs and drifts.

"High, and coming up. If I don't get the other teams over to-day I'll wait until she goes down. At this season she rises and lowers every day or so, until June; then comes the big flood, and we don't cross for months."

I sat for three hours watching Emmett bring over the rest of his party, which he did without accident, but at the expense of great effort. And all the time in my ears dinned the roar, the boom, the rumble of this singularly rapacious and purposeful river—a river of silt, a red river of dark, sinister meaning, a river with terrible work to perform, a river which never gave up its dead.

CHAPTER 2

The Range

After a much-needed rest at Emmett's, we bade good-by to him and his hospitable family, and under the guidance of his man once more took to the wind-swept trail. We pursued a southwesterly course now, following the lead of the craggy red wall that stretched on and on for hundreds of miles into Utah. The desert, smoky and hot, fell away to the left, and in the foreground a dark, irregular line marked the Grand Cañon cutting through the plateau.

The wind whipped in from the vast, open expanse, and meeting an obstacle in the red wall, turned north and raced past us. Jones's hat blew off, stood on its rim, and rolled. It kept on rolling, thirty miles an hour, more or less; so fast, at least, that we were a long time catching up to it with a team of horses. Possibly we never would have caught it had not a stone checked its flight. Further manifestation of the power of the desert wind surrounded us on all sides. It had hollowed out huge stones from the cliffs, and tumbled them to the plain below; and then, sweeping sand and gravel low across the desert floor, had cut them deeply, until they rested on slender pedestals, thus sculptoring grotesque and striking monuments to the marvelous persistence of this element of nature.

Late that afternoon, as we reached the height of the plateau, Jones woke up and shouted: "Ha! there's Buckskin!"

Far southward lay a long, black mountain, covered with patches of shining snow. I could follow the zigzag line of the Grand Cañon splitting the desert plateau, and saw it disappear in the haze round the end of the mountain. From this I got my first clear impression of the topography of the country surrounding our objective point. Buckskin Mountain ran its blunt end eastward to the cañon—in fact, formed a hundred miles of the north rim. As it was nine thousand feet high it still held the snow, which had occasioned our lengthy desert ride to get back of the mountain. I could see the long slopes rising out of the desert to meet the timber.

As we bowled merrily down grade I noticed that we were no longer on stony ground, and that a little scant silvery grass had made its appearance. Then little branches of green, with a blue flower, smiled out of the clayish sand.

All of a sudden Jones stood up, and let out a wild Commanche yell. I was more startled by the yell than by the great hand he smashed down on my shoulder, and for the moment I was dazed.

"There! look! look! the buffalo! Hi! Hi! Hi!"

Below us, a few miles on a rising knoll, a big herd of buffalo shone black in the gold of the evening sun. I had not Jones's incentive, but I felt enthusiasm born of the wild and beautiful picture, and added my yell to his. The huge, burly leader of the herd lifted his head, and after regarding us for a few moments calmly went on browsing.

The desert had fringed away into a grand rolling pastureland, walled in by the red cliffs, the slopes of Buckskin, and further isolated by the cañon. Here was a range of twenty-four hundred square miles without a foot of barbwire, a pasture fenced in by natural forces, with the splendid feature that the buffalo could browse on the plain in winter, and go up into the cool foothills of Buckskin in summer.

From another ridge we saw a cabin dotting the rolling plain, and in half an hour we reached it. As we climbed down from the wagon a brown and black dog came dashing out of the cabin, and promptly jumped at Moose. His selection showed poor discrimination, for Moze whipped him before I could separate them. Hearing Jones heartily greeting some one, I turned in his direction, only to be distracted by another dog fight. Don had tackled Moze for the seventh time. Memory rankled in Don, and he needed a lot of whipping, some of which he was getting when I rescued him.

Next moment I was shaking hands with Frank and Jim, Jones's ranchmen. At a glance I liked them both. Frank was short and wiry, and had a big, ferocious mustache, the effect of which was softened by his kindly brown eyes. Jim was tall, a little heavier; he had a careless, tidy look; his eyes were searching, and though he appeared a young man, his hair was white.

"I shore am glad to see you all," said Jim, in slow, soft, Southern accent.

"Get down, get down," was Frank's welcome—a typically Western one, for we had already gotten down; "an' come in. You must be worked out. Sure you've come a long way." He was quick of speech, full of nervous energy, and beamed with hospitality.

The cabin was the rudest kind of log affair, with a huge stone fireplace in one end, deer antlers and coyote skins on the wall, saddles and cowboys' traps in a corner, a nice, large, promising cupboard, and a table and chairs. Jim threw wood on a smoldering fire, that soon blazed and crackled cheerily.

I sank down into a chair with a feeling of blessed relief. Ten days of desert ride behind me! Promise of wonderful days before me, with the last of the old plainsmen! No wonder a sweet sense of ease stole over me, or that the fire seemed a live and joyously welcoming thing, or that Jim's deft maneuvers in preparation of supper roused in me a rapt admiration.

"Twenty calves this spring!" cried Jones, punching me in my sore side. "Ten thousand dollars worth of calves!"

He was now altogether a changed man; he looked almost young; his eyes danced, and he rubbed his big hands together while he plied Frank with questions. In strange surroundings—that is, away from his native wilds, Jones had been a silent man; it had been almost impossible to get anything out of him. But now I saw that I should come to know the real man. In a very few moments he had talked more than on all the desert trip, and what he said, added to the little I had already learned, put me in possession of some interesting information as to his buffalo.

Some years before he had conceived the idea of hybridizing buffalo with black Galloway cattle; and with the characteristic determination and energy of the man, he at once set about finding a suitable range. This was difficult, and took years of searching. At last the wild north rim of the Grand Cañon, a section unknown except to a few Indians and mustang hunters, was settled upon. Then the gigantic task of transporting the herd of buffalo by rail from Montana to Salt Lake was begun. The two hundred and ninety miles of desert lying between the home of the Mormons and Buckskin Mountain was an obstacle almost insurmountable. The journey was undertaken and found even more trying than had been expected. Buffalo after buffalo died on the way. Then Frank, Jones's right-hand man, put into execution a plan he had been thinking of— namely, to travel by night. It succeeded. The buffalo rested in the day and traveled by easy stages by night, with the result that the big herd was transported to the ideal range.

Here, in an environment strange to their race, but peculiarly adaptable, they thrived and multiplied. The hybrid of the Galloway cow and buffalo proved a great success. Jones called the new species "Cattalo." The cattalo took the hardiness of the buffalo, and never required artificial food or shelter. He would face the desert storm or blizzard and stand stock still in his tracks until the weather cleared. He became quite domestic, could be easily handled, and grew exceedingly fat on very little provender. The folds of his stomach were so numerous that they digested even the hardest and flintiest of corn. He had fourteen ribs on each side, while domestic cattle had only thirteen; thus he could endure rougher work and longer journeys to water. His fur was so dense and glossy that it equaled that of the unplucked beaver or otter, and was fully as valuable as the buffalo robe. And not to be overlooked by any means was the fact that his meat was delicious.

Jones had to hear every detail of all that had happened since his absence in the East, and he was particularly inquisitive to learn all about the twenty cattalo calves. He called different buffalo by name; and designated the calves by descriptive terms, such as "Whiteface" and "Crosspatch." He almost forgot to eat, and kept Frank too busy to get anything into his own mouth. After supper he calmed down.

"How about your other man—Mr. Wallace, I think you said?" asked Frank.

"We expected to meet him at Grand Cañon Station, and then at Flagstaff. But he didn't show up. Either he backed out or missed us. I'm sorry; for when we get up on Buckskin, among the wild horses and cougars, we'll be likely to need him."

"I reckon you'll need me, as well as Jim," said Frank dryly, with a twinkle in his eye. "The buffs are in good shape an' can get along without me for a while."

"That'll be fine. How about cougar sign on the mountain?"

"Plenty. I've got two spotted near Oak Spring. Comin' over two weeks ago I tracked them in the snow along the trail for miles. We'll ooze over that way, as it's goin' toward the Siwash. The Siwash breaks of the cañon—there's the place for lions. I met a wild-horse wrangler not long back, an' he was tellin' me about Old Tom an' the colts he'd killed this winter."

Naturally, I here expressed a desire to know more of Old Tom.

"He's the biggest cougar ever known of in these parts. His tracks are bigger than a horse's, an' have been seen on Buckskin for twelve years. This wrangler—his name is Clark—said he'd turned his saddle horse out to graze near camp, an' Old Tom sneaked in an' downed him. The lions over there are sure a bold bunch. Well, why shouldn't they be? No one ever hunted them. You see, the mountain is hard to get at. But now you're here, if it's big cats you want we sure can find them. Only be easy, be easy. You've all the time there is. An' any job on Buckskin will take time. We'll look the calves over, an' you must ride the range to harden up. Then we'll ooze over toward Oak. I expect it'll be boggy, an' I hope the snow melts soon."

"The snow hadn't melted on Greenland Point," replied Jones. "We saw that with a glass from the El Tovar. We wanted to cross that way, but Rust said Bright Angel Creek was breast high to a horse, and that creek is the trail."

"There's four feet of snow on Greenland," said Frank. "It was too early to come that way. There's only about three months in the year the cañon can be crossed at Greenland."

"I want to get in the snow," returned Jones. "This bunch of long-eared canines I brought never smelled a lion track. Hounds can't be trained quick without snow.

You've got to see what they're trailing, or you can't break them."

Frank looked dubious. " 'Pears to me we'll have trouble gettin' a lion without lion dogs. It takes a long time to break a hound off of deer, once he's chased them. Buckskin is full of deer, wolves, coyotes, and there's the wild horses. We couldn't go a hundred feet without crossin' trails."

"How's the hound you and Jim fetched in last year? Has he got a good nose? Here he is—I like his head. Come here, Bowser—what's his name?"

"Jim named him Sounder, because he sure has a voice. It's great to hear him on a trail. Sounder has a nose that can't be fooled, an' he'll trail anythin'; but I don't know if he ever got up a lion."

Sounds wagged his busy tail and looked up affectionately at Frank. He had a fine head, great brown eyes, very long ears and curly brownish-black hair. He was not demonstrative, looked rather askance at Jones, and avoided the other dogs.

"That dog will make a great lion-chaser," said Jones, decisively, after his study of Sounder. "He and Moze will keep us busy, once they learn we want lions."

"I don't believe any dog-trainer could teach them short of six months," replied Frank. "Sounder is no spring chicken; an' that black and dirty white cross between a cayuse an' a barb-wire fence is an old dog. You can't teach old dogs new tricks."

Jones smiled mysteriously, a smile of conscious superiority, but said nothing.

"We'll shore hev a storm to-morrow," said Jim, relinquishing his pipe long enough to speak. He had been silent, and now his meditative gaze was on the west, through the cabin window, where a dull afterglow faded under the heavy laden clouds of night and left the horizon dark.

I was very tired when I lay down, but so full of

excitement that sleep did not soon visit my eyelids. The talk about buffalo, wild-horse hunters, lions and dogs, the prospect of riding and unusual adventure; the vision of Old Tom that had already begun to haunt me, filled my mind with pictures and fancies. The other fellows dropped off to sleep, and quiet reigned. Suddenly a succession of queer, sharp barks came from the plain, close to the cabin. Coyotes were paying us a call, and judging from the chorus of yelps and howls from our dogs, it was not a welcome visit. Above the medley rose one big, deep, full voice that I knew at once belonged to Sounder. Then all was quiet again. Sleep gradually benumbed my senses. Vague phrases dreamily drifted to and fro in my mind: "Jones's wild range—Old Tom—Sounder—great name—great voice—Sounder! Sounder! Sound——"

Next morning I could hardly crawl out of my sleeping-bag. My bones ached, my muscles protested excruciatingly, my lips burned and bled, and the cold I had contracted on the desert clung to me. A good brisk walk round the corrals, and then breakfast, made me feel better.

"Of course you can ride?" queried Frank.

My answer was not given from an overwhelming desire to be truthful. Frank frowned a little, as if wondering how a man could have the nerve to start out on a jaunt with Buffalo Jones without being a good horseman. To be unable to stick on the back of a wild mustang, or a cayuse, was an unpardonable sin in Arizona. My frank admission was made relatively, with my mind on what cowboys held as a standard of horsemanship.

The mount Frank trotted out of the corral for me was a pure white, beautiful mustang, nervous, sensitive, quivering. I watched Frank put on the saddle, and when he called me I did not fail to catch a covert twinkle in his merry brown eyes. Looking away toward Buckskin Mountain, which was coincidentally in the direction of home, I said to myself: "This may be where you get on, but most certainly it is where you get off!"

Jones was already riding far beyond the corral, as I could see by a cloud of dust; and I set off after him, with the painful consciousness that I must have looked to Frank and Jim much as Central Park equestrians had often looked to me. Frank shouted after me that he would catch up with us out on the range. I was not in any great hurry to overtake Jones, but evidently my horse's inclinations differed from mine; at any rate, he made the dust fly, and jumped the little sage bushes.

Jones, who had tarried to inspect one of the pools— formed of running water from the corrals—greeted me as I came up with this cheerful observation:

"What in thunder did Frank give you that white nag for? The buffalo hate white horses—anything white. They're liable to stampede off the range, or chase you into the cañon."

I replied grimly that, as it was certain something was going to happen, the particular circumstance might as well come off quickly.

We rode over the rolling plain with a cool, bracing breeze in our faces. The sky was dull and mottled with a beautiful cloud effect that presaged wind. As we trotted along Jones pointed out to me and descanted upon the nutritive value of three different kinds of grass, one of which he called the Buffalo Pea, noteworthy for a beautiful blue blossom. Soon we passed out of sight of the cabin, and could see only the billowy plain, the red tips of the stony wall, and the black-fringed crest of Buckskin. After riding a while we made out some cattle, a few of which were on the range, browsing in the lee of a ridge. No sooner had I marked them than Jones let out another Comanche yell.

"Wolf!" he yelled; and spurring his big bay, he was off like the wind.

A single glance showed me several cows running as if bewildered, and near them a big white wolf pulling down a calf. Another white wolf stood not far off. My horse jumped as if he had been shot; and the realization darted upon me that here was where the certain something began. Spot—the mustang had one black spot in his pure white—snorted like I imagined a blooded horse might, under dire insult. Jones's bay had gotten about a hundred paces the start. I lived to learn that Spot hated to be left behind; moreover, he would not be left behind; he was the swiftest horse on the range, and proud of the distinction. I cast one unmentionable word on the breeze toward the cabin and Frank, then put mind and muscle to the sore task of remaining with Spot. Jones was born on a saddle, and had been taking his meals in a saddle for about sixty-three years, and the bay horse could run. Run is not a felicitous word—he flew. And I was rendered mentally deranged for the moment to see that hundred paces between the bay and Spot materially lessen at every jump. Spot lengthened out, seemed to go down near the ground, and cut the air like a high-geared auto. If I had not heard the fast rhythmic beat of his hoofs, and had not bounced high into the air at every jump, I would have been sure I was riding a bird. I tried to stop him. As well might I have tried to pull in the *Lusitania* with a thread. Spot was out to overhaul that bay, and in spite of me, he was doing it. The wind rushed into my face and sang in my ears. Jones seemed the nucleus of a sort of haze, and he grew larger and larger. Presently he became clearly defined in my sight; the violent commotion under me subsided; I once more felt the saddle, and then I realized that Spot had been content to stop alongside of Jones, tossing his head and champing his bit.

"Well, by George! I didn't know you were in the stretch," cried my companion. "That was a fine little brush. We must have come several miles. I'd have killed those wolves if I'd brought a gun. The big one that had the calf was a bold brute. He never let go until I was within fifty feet of him. Then I almost rode him down. I don't think the calf was much hurt. But those blood-thirsty devils will return, and like as not get the calf. That's the worst of cattle raising. Now, take the buffalo. Do you suppose those wolves could have gotten a buffalo calf out from under the mother? Never. Neither could a whole band of wolves. Buffalo stick close together, and the little ones do not stray. When danger threatens, the herd closes in and faces it and fights. That is what is grand about the buffalo and what made them once roam the prairies in countless, endless droves."

From the highest elevation in that part of the range we viewed the surrounding ridges, flats and hollows, searching for the buffalo. At length we spied a cloud of dust rising from behind an undulating mound, then big black dots hove in sight.

"Frank has rounded up the herd, and is driving it this way. We'll wait," said Jones.

Though the buffalo appeared to be moving fast, a long time elapsed before they reached the foot of our outlook. They lumbered along in a compact mass, so dense that I could not count them, but I estimated the number of seventy-five. Frank was riding zigzag behind them, swinging his lariat and yelling. When he espied us he reined in his horse and waited. Then the herd slowed down, halted and began browsing.

"Look at the cattalo calves," cried Jones, in ecstatic tones. "See how shy they are, how close they stick to their mothers."

The little dark-brown fellows were plainly frightened. I made several unsuccessful attempts to photograph them, and gave it up when Jones told me not to ride too close and that it would be better to wait till we had them in the corral.

He took my camera and instructed me to go on ahead, in the rear of the herd. I heard the click of the instrument as he snapped a picture, and then suddenly heard him shout in alarm: "Look out! look out! pull your horse!"

Thundering hoof-beats pounding the earth accompanied his words. I saw a big bull, with head down, tail raised, charging my horse. He answered Frank's yell of command with a furious grunt. I was paralyzed at the wonderfully swift action of the shaggy brute, and I sat helpless. Spot wheeled as if he were on a pivot and plunged out of the way with a celerity that was astounding. The buffalo stopped, pawed the ground, and angrily tossed his huge head. Frank rode up to him, yelled, and struck him with the lariat, whereupon he gave another toss of his horns, and then returned to the herd.

"It was that darned white nag," said Jones. "Frank, it was wrong to put an inexperienced man on Spot. For that matter, the horse should never be allowed to go near the buffalo."

"Spot knows the buffs; they'd never get to him," replied Frank. But the usual spirit was absent from his voice, and he glanced at me soberly. I knew I had turned white, for I felt the peculiar cold sensation in my face.

"Now, look at that, will you?" cried Jones. "I don't like the looks of that."

He pointed to the herd. They stopped browsing, and were uneasily shifting to and fro. The bull lifted his head; the others slowly grouped together.

"Storm! Sandstorm!" exclaimed Jones, pointing desertward. Dark yellow clouds like smoke were rolling, sweeping, bearing down upon us. They expanded, blossoming out like gigantic roses, and whirled and merged into one another, all the time rolling on and blotting out the light.

"We've got to run. That storm may last two days," yelled Frank to me. "We've had some bad ones lately. Give your horse free rein, and cover your face."

A roar, resembling an approaching storm at sea, came on puffs of wind, as the horses got into their stride. Long streaks of dust whipped up in different places; the silver-white grass bent to the ground; round bunches of sage went rolling before us. The puffs grew longer, steadier, harder. Then a shrieking blast howled on our trail, seeming to swoop down on us with a yellow, blinding pall. I shut my eyes and covered my face with a handkerchief. The sand blew so thick that it filled my gloves, pebbles struck me hard enough to sting through my coat.

Fortunately, Spot kept to an easy swinging lope, which was the most comfortable motion for me. But I began to get numb, and could hardly stick on the saddle. Almost before I had dared to hope, Spot stopped. Uncovering my face, I saw Jim in the doorway of the lee side of the cabin. The yellow, streaky, whistling clouds of sand split on the cabin and passed on, leaving a small, dusty space of light.

"Shore Spot do hate to be beat," yelled Jim, as he helped me off. I stumbled into the cabin and fell upon a buffalo robe and lay there absolutely spent. Jones and Frank came in a few minutes apart, each anathematizing the gritty, powdery sand.

All day the desert storm raged and roared. The dust sifted through the numerous cracks in the cabin, burdened our clothes, spoiled our food and blinded our eyes. Wind, snow, sleet and rainstorms are discomforting enough under trying circumstances; but all combined, they are nothing to the choking, stinging, blinding sandstorm.

"Shore it'll let up by sundown," averred Jim. And sure enough the roar died away about five o'clock, the wind abated and the sand settled.

Just before supper, a knock sounded heavily on the cabin door. Jim opened it to admit one of Emmett's sons and a very tall man whom none of us knew. He was a sand-man. All that was not sand seemed a space or two of corduroy, a big bone-handled knife, a prominent square jaw and bronzed cheek and flashing eyes.

"Get down—get down, an' come in, stranger," said Frank cordially.

"How do you do, sir," said Jones.

"Colonel Jones, I've been on your trail for twelve days," announced the stranger, with a grim smile. The sand streamed off his coat in little white streaks.

Jones appeared to be casting about in his mind.

"I'm Grant Wallace," continued the newcomer. "I missed you at the El Tovar, at Williams and at Flagstaff, where I was one day behind. Was half a day late at the Little Colorado, saw your train cross Moncaupie Wash, and missed you because of the sandstorm there. Saw you from the other side of the Big Colorado as you rode out from Emmett's along the red wall. And here I am. We've never met till now, which obviously isn't my fault."

The Colonel and I fell upon Wallace's neck. Frank manifested his usual alert excitement, and said: "Well, I guess he won't hang fire on a long cougar chase." And Jim— slow, careful Jim, dropped a plate with the exclamation: "Shore it do beat hell!" The hounds sniffed round Wallace, and welcomed him with vigorous tails.

Supper that night, even if we did grind sand with our teeth, was a joyous occasion. The biscuits were flaky and light; the bacon fragrant and crisp. I produced a jar of blackberry jam, which by subtle cunning I had been able to secrete from the Mormons on that dry desert ride, and it was greeted with acclamations of pleasure. Wallace, divested of his sand guise, beamed with the gratification of a hungry man once more in the presence of friends and food. He made large cavities in Jim's great pot of potato stew, and caused biscuits to vanish in a way that would not have shamed a Hindoo magician. The grand cañon he dug in my jar of jam, however, could not have been accomplished by legerdemain.

Talk became animated on dogs, cougars, horses and buffalo. Jones told of our experience out on the range, and concluded with some salient remarks.

"A tame wild animal is the most dangerous of beasts. My old friend, Dick Rock, a great hunter and guide out of Idaho, laughed at my advice, and got killed by one of his three-year-old bulls. I told him they knew him just well enough to kill him, and they did. My friend, A. H. Cole, of Oxford, Nebraska, tried to rope a Weetah that was too tame to be safe, and the bull killed him. Same with General Bull, a member of the Kansas Legislature, and two cowboys who went into a corral to tie up a tame elk at the wrong time. I pleaded with them not to undertake it. They had not studied animals as I had. That tame elk killed all of them. He had to be shot in order to get General Bull off his great antlers. You see, a wild animal must learn to respect a man. The way I used to teach the Yellowstone Park bears to be respectful and safe neighbors was to rope them around the front paw, swing them up on a tree clear of the ground, and whip them with a long pole. It was a dangerous business, and looks cruel, but it is the only way I could find to make the bears good. You see, they eat scraps around the hotels and get so tame they will steal everything but red-hot stoves, and will cuff the life out of those who try to shoo them off. But after a bear mother has had a licking, she not only becomes a good bear for the rest of her life, but she tells all her cubs about it with a good smack of her paw, for emphasis, and teaches them to respect peaceable citizens generation after generation.

"One of the hardest jobs I ever tackled was that of

supplying the buffalo for Bronx Park. I rounded up a magnificent 'king' buffalo bull, belligerent enough to fight a battleship. When I rode after him the cowmen said I was as good as killed. I made a lance by driving a nail into the end of a short pole and sharpening it. After he had chased me, I wheeled my broncho, and hurled the lance into his back, ripping a wound as long as my hand. That put the fear of Providence into him and took the fight all out of him. I drove him uphill and down, and across cañons at a dead run for eight miles single-handed, and loaded him on a freight car; but he came near getting me once or twice, and only quick broncho work and lance play saved me.

"In the Yellowstone Park all our buffaloes have become docile, excepting the huge bull which led them. The Indians call the buffalo leader the 'Weetah,' the master of the herd. It was sure death to go near this one. So I shipped in another Weetah, hoping that he might whip some of the fight out of old Manitou, the Mighty. They came together head on, like a railway collision, and ripped up over a square mile of landscape, fighting till night came on, and then on into the night.

"I jumped into the field with them, chasing them with my biograph, getting a series of moving pictures of that bullfight which was sure the real thing. It was a ticklish thing to do, though knowing that neither bull dared take his eyes off his adversary for a second, I felt reasonably safe. The old Weetah beat the new champion out that night, but the next morning they were at it again, and the new buffalo finally whipped the old one into submission. Since then his spirit has remained broken, and even a child can approach him safely—but the new Weetah is in turn a holy terror.

"To handle buffalo, elk and bear, you must get into sympathy with their methods of reasoning. No tenderfoot stands any show, even with the tame animals of the Yellowstone."

The old buffalo hunter's lips were no longer locked. One after another he told reminiscences of his eventful life, in a simple manner; yet so vivid and gripping were the unvarnished details that I was spellbound.

"Considering what appears the impossibility of capturing a full-grown buffalo, how did you earn the name of Preserver of the American bison?" inquired Wallace.

"It took years to learn how, and ten more to capture the fifty-eight that I was able to keep. I tried every plan under the sun. I roped hundreds, of all sizes and ages. They would not live in captivity. If they could not find an embankment over which to break their necks, they would crush their skulls on stones. Failing any means that like, they would lie down, will themselves to die, and die. Think of a savage wild nature that could will its heart to cease beating! But it's true. Finally I found I could keep only calves under three months of age. But to capture them so young entailed time and patience. For the buffalo fight for their young, and when I say fight, I mean till they drop. I almost always had to go alone, because I could neither coax nor hire any one to undertake it with me. Sometimes I would be weeks getting one calf. One day I captured eight—eight little buffalo calves! Never will I forget that day as long as I live!"

"Tell us about it," I suggested, in a matter of fact, round-the-campfire voice. Had the silent plainsman ever told a complete and full story of his adventures? I doubted it. He was not the man to eulogize himself.

A short silence ensued. The cabin was snug and warm; the ruddy embers glowed; one of Jim's pots steamed musically and fragrantly. The hounds lay curled in the cozy chimney corner.

Jones began to talk again, simply and unaffectedly, of

his famous exploit; and as he went on so modestly, passing lightly over features we recognized as wonderful, I allowed the fire of my imagination to fuse for myself all the toil, patience, endurance, skill, herculean strength and marvelous courage and unfathomable passion which he slighted in his narrative.

CHAPTER 3

The Last Herd

Over gray No-Man's-Land stole down the shadows of night. The undulating prairie shaded dark to the western horizon, rimmed with a fading streak of light. Tall figures, silhouetted sharply against the last golden glow of sunset, marked the rounded crest of a grassy knoll.

"Wild hunter!" cried a voice in sullen rage, "buffalo or no, we halt here. Did Adams and I hire to cross the Staked Plains? Two weeks in No-Man's-Land, and now we're facing the sand! We've one keg of water, yet you want to keep on. Why, man, you're crazy! You didn't tell us you wanted buffalo alive. And here you've got us looking death in the eye!"

In the grim silence that ensued the two men unhitched the team from the long, light wagon, while the buffalo hunter staked out his wiry, lithe-limbed racehorses. Soon a fluttering blaze threw a circle of light, which shone on the agitated face of Rude and Adams, and the cold, iron-set visage of their brawny leader.

"It's this way," began Jones, in a slow, cool voice; "I engaged you fellows, and you promised to stick by me. We've had no luck. But I've finally found sign—old sign, I'll admit—of the buffalo I'm looking for—the last herd on the plains. For two years I've been hunting this herd. So have other hunters. Millions of buffalo have been killed and left to rot. Soon this herd will be gone, and then the only buffalo in the world will be those I have given ten years of the hardest work in capturing. This is the last herd, I say, and my last chance to capture a calf or two. Do you imagine I'd quit? You fellows go back if you want, but I keep on."

"We can't go back. We're lost. We'll have to go with you. But, man, thirst is not the only risk we run. This is Comanche country. And if that herd is in here the Indians have it spotted."

"That worries me some," replied the plainsman, "but we'll keep on."

They slept. The night wind swished the grasses; dark storm clouds blotted out the northern stars; the prairie wolves mourned dismally.

Day broke cold, wan, threatening, under a leaden sky. The hunters traveled thirty miles by noon, and halted in a hollow where a stream flowed in wet season. Cottonwood trees were bursting into green; thickets of prickly thorn, dense and matted, showed bright spring buds.

"What is it?" suddenly whispered Rude.

The plainsman lay in strained posture, his ear against the ground.

"Hide the wagon and horses in the clump of cottonwoods," he ordered, tersely. Springing to his feet, he ran to the top of the knoll above the hollow, where he again placed his ear to the ground.

Jones's practiced ear had detected the quavering rumble of far-away, thundering hoofs. He searched the wide waste of plain with his powerful glass. To the southwest, miles distant, a cloud of dust mushroomed skyward. "Not buffalo," he muttered, "maybe wild horses." He watched and waited. The yellow cloud rolled forward, enlarging, spreading out, and drove before it a darkly indistinct, moving mass. As soon as he had one good look at this he ran back to his comrades.

"Stampede! Wild horses! Indians! Look to your rifles and hide!"

Wordless and pale, the men examined their Sharps, and made ready to follow Jones. He slipped into the thorny brake and, flat on his stomach, wormed his way like a snake far into the thickly interlaced web of branches. Rude and Adams crawled after him. Words were superfluous. Quiet, breathless, with beating hearts, the hunters pressed close to the dry grass. A long, low, steady rumble filled the air, and increased in volume till it became a roar. Moments, endless moments, passed. The roar filled out like a flood slowly released from its confines to sweep down with the sound of doom. The ground began to tremble and quake; the light faded; the smell of dust pervaded the thicket, then a continuous streaming roar, deafening as a persistent roll of thunder, pervaded the hiding place. The stampeding horses had split round the hollow. The roar lessened. Swiftly as a departing snow-squall rushing on through the pines, the thunderous thud and tramp of hoofs died away.

The trained horses hidden in the cottonwoods never stirred. "Lie low! lie low!" breathed the plainsman to his companions.

Throb of hoofs again became audible, not loud and madly pounding as those that had passed, but low, muffled, rhythmic. Jones's sharp eye, through a peephole in the thicket, saw a cream-colored mustang bob over the knoll, carrying an Indian. Another and another, then a swiftly following, close-packed throng appeared. Bright red feathers and white gleamed; weapons glinted; gaunt, bronzed savages leaned forward on racy, slender mustangs.

The plainsman shrank closer to the ground. "Apache!" he exclaimed to himself, and gripped his rifle. The band galloped down to the hollow, and slowing up, piled single file over the bank. The leader, a short, squat chief, plunged into the brake not twenty yards from the hidden men. Jones recognized the cream mustang; he knew the somber, sinister, broad face. It belonged to the Red Chief of the Apaches.

"Geronimo!" murmured the plainsman through his teeth.

Well for the Apache that no falcon savage eye discovered aught strange in the little hollow! One look at the sand of the stream bed would have cost him his life. But the Indians crossed the thicket too far up; they cantered up the slope and disappeared. The hoof-beats softened and ceased.

"Gone?" whispered Rude.

"Gone. But wait," whispered Jones. He knew the savage nature, and he knew how to wait. After a long time, he cautiously crawled out of the thicket and searched the surroundings with a plainsman's eye. He climbed the slope and saw the clouds of dust, the near one small, the far one large, which told him all he needed to know.

"Comanches?" queried Adams, with a quaver in his voice. He was new to the plains.

"Likely," said Jones, who thought it best not to tell all he knew. Then he added to himself: "We've no time to lose. There's water back here somewhere. The Indians have spotted the buffalo, and were running the horses away from the water."

The three got under way again, proceeding carefully, so as not to raise the dust, and headed due southwest. Scantier and scantier grew the grass; the hollows were washes of sand; steely gray dunes, like long, flat, ocean swells, ribbed the prairie. The gray day declined. Late into the purple night they traveled, then camped without fire.

In the gray morning Jones climbed a high rise and

scanned the southwest. Low dun-colored sand-hills waved from him down and down, in slow, deceptive descent. A solitary and remote waste reached out into gray infinitude. A pale lake, gray as the rest of that gray expanse, glimmered in the distance.

"Mirage!" he muttered, focusing his glass, which only magnified all under the dead gray, steely sky. "Water must be somewhere; but can that be it? It's too pale and elusive to be real. No life—a blasted, staked plain! Hello!"

A thin, black, wavering line of wild fowl, moving in beautiful, rapid flight, crossed the line of his vision. "Geese flying north, and low. There's water here," he said. He followed the flock with his glass, saw them circle over the lake, and vanish in the gray sheen.

"It's water." He hurried back to camp. His haggard and worn companions scorned his discovery. Adams siding with Rude, who knew the plains, said: "Mirage! the lure of the desert!" Yet dominated by a force too powerful for them to resist, they followed the buffalo-hunter. All day the gleaming lake beckoned them onward, and seemed to recede. All day the drab clouds scudded before the cold north wind. In the gray twilight, the lake suddenly lay before them, as if it had opened at their feet. The men rejoiced, the horses lifted their noses and sniffed the damp air.

The whinnies of the horses, the clank of harness, and splash of water, the whirr of ducks did not blur out of Jones's keen ear a sound that made him jump. It was the thump of hoofs, in a familiar beat, beat, beat. He saw a shadow moving up a ridge. Soon, outlined black against the yet light sky, a lone buffalo cow stood like a statue. A moment she held toward the lake, studying the danger, then went out of sight over the ridge.

Jones spurred his horse up the ascent, which was rather long and steep, but he mounted the summit in time to see the cow join eight huge, shaggy buffalo. The hunter reined in his horse, and standing high in his stirrups, held his hat at arms' length over his head. So he thrilled to a moment he had sought for two years. The last herd of American bison was near at hand. The cow would not venture far from the main herd; the eight stragglers were the old broken-down bulls that had been expelled, at this season, from the herd by younger and more vigorous bulls. The old monarchs saw the hunter at the same time his eyes were gladdened by sight of them, and lumbered away after the cow, to disappear in the gathering darkness. Frightened buffalo always make straight for their fellows; and this knowledge contented Jones to return to the lake, well satisfied that the herd would not be far away in the morning, within easy striking distance by daylight.

At dark the storm which had threatened for days, broke in a fury of rain, sleet and hail. The hunters stretched a piece of canvas over the wheels of the north side of the wagon, and wet and shivering, crawled under it to their blankets. During the night the storm raged with unabated strength.

Dawn, forbidding and raw, lightened to the whistle of the sleety gusts. Fire was out of the question. Chary of weight, the hunters had carried no wood, and the buffalo chips they used for fuel were lumps of ice. Grumbling, Adams and Rude ate a cold breakfast, while Jones, munching a biscuit, faced the biting blast from the crest of the ridge. The middle of the plain below held a ragged, circular mass, as still as stone. It was the buffalo herd, with every shaggy head to the storm. So they would stand, never budging from their tracks, till the blizzard of sleet was over.

Jones, though eager and impatient, restrained himself, for it was unwise to begin operations in the storm. There was nothing to do but wait. Ill fared the hunters that day. Food had to be eaten uncooked. The long hours dragged by with the little group huddled under icy blankets. When darkness fell, the sleet changed to drizzling rain. This blew over at midnight, and a colder wind, penetrating to the very marrow of the sleepless men, made their condition worse. In the after part of the night, the wolves howled mournfully.

With a gray, misty light appearing in the east, Jones threw off his stiff, ice-incased blanket, and crawled out. A gaunt gray wolf, the color of the day and the sand and the lake, sneaked away, looking back. While moving and threshing about to warm his frozen blood, Jones munched another biscuit. His men crawled from under the wagon, and made an unfruitful search for the whisky. Fearing it, Jones had thrown the bottle away. The men cursed. The patient horses drooped sadly, and shivered in the lee of the improvised tent. Jones kicked the inch-thick casing of ice from his saddle. Kentuck, his racer, had been spared on the whole trip for this day's work. The thoroughbred was cold, but as Jones threw the saddle over him, he showed that he knew the chase ahead, and was eager to be off. At last, after repeated efforts with his benumbed fingers, Jones got the girths tight. He tied a bunch of soft cords to the saddle and mounted.

"Follow as fast as you can," he called to his surly men. "The buffs will run north against the wind. This is the right direction for us; we'll soon leave the sand. Stick to my trail and come a-humming."

From the ridge he met the red sun, rising bright, and a keen northeasterly wind that lashed like a whip. As he had anticipated, his quarry had moved northward. Kentuck let out into a swinging stride, which in an hour had the loping herd in sight. Every jump now took him upon higher ground, where the sand failed, and the grass grew thicker and began to bend under the wind.

In the teeth of the nipping gale Jones slipped close upon the herd without alarming even a cow. More than a hundred little reddish-black calves leisurely loped in the rear. Kentuck, keen to his work, crept on like a wolf, and the hunter's great fist clenched the coiled lasso. Before him expanded a boundless plain. A situation long cherished and dreamed of had become a reality. Kentuck, fresh and strong, was good for all day. Jones gloated over the little red bulls and heifers, as a miser gloats over gold and jewels. Never before had he caught more than two in one day, and often it had taken days to capture one. This was the last herd, this the last opportunity toward perpetuating a grand race of beasts. And with born instinct he saw ahead the day of his life.

At a touch, Kentuck closed in, and the buffalo, seeing him, stampeded into the heaving roll so well known to the hunter. Racing on the right flank of the herd, Jones selected a tawny heifer and shot the lariat after her. It fell true, but being stiff and kinky from the sleet, failed to tighten, and the quick calf leaped through the loop to freedom.

Undismayed the pursuer quickly recovered his rope. Again he whirled and sent the loop. Again it circled true, and failed to close; again the agile heifer bounded through it. Jones whipped the air with the stubborn rope. To lose a chance like that was worse than boy's work.

The third whirl, running a smaller loop, tightened the coil round the frightened calf just back of its ears. A pull on the bridle brought Kentuck to a halt in his tracks, and the baby buffalo rolled over and over in the grass. Jones bounced from his seat and jerked loose a couple of the soft cords. In a twinkling his big knee crushed down on the calf, and his big hands bound it helpless.

Kentuck neighed. Jones saw his black ears go up. Danger threatened. For a moment the hunter's blood turned chill, not from fear, for he never felt fear, but because he thought the Indians were returning to ruin his work. His eye swept the plain. Only the gray forms of wolves flitted through the grass, here, there, all about him. Wolves! They were as fatal to his enterprise as savages. A trooping pack of prairie wolves had fallen in with the herd and hung close on the trail, trying to cut a calf away from its mother. The gray brutes boldly trotted to within a few yards of him, and slyly looked at him, with pale, fiery eyes. They had already scented his captive. Precious time flew by; the situation, critical and baffling, had never before been met by him. There lay his little calf tied fast, and to the north ran many others, some of which he must—he would have. To think quickly had meant the solving of many a plainsman's problem. Should he stay with his prize to save it, or leave it to be devoured?

"Ha! you old gray devils!" he yelled, shaking his fist at the wolves. "I know a trick or two." Slipping his hat between the legs of the calf, he fastened it securely. This done, he vaulted on Kentuck, and was off with never a backward glance. Certain it was that the wolves would not touch anything, alive or dead, that bore the scent of a human being.

The bison scoured away a long half-mile in the lead, sailing northward like a cloud-shadow over the plain. Kentuck, mettlesome, overeager, would have run himself out in short order, but the wary hunter, strong to restrain as well as impel, with the long day in his mind, kept the steed in his easy stride, which, springy and stretching, overhauled the herd in the course of several miles.

A dash, a whirl, a shock, a leap, horse and hunter working in perfect accord, and a fine big calf, bellowing lustily, struggled desperately for freedom under the remorseless knee. The big hands toyed with him; and then, secure in the double knots, the calf lay still, sticking out his tongue and rolling his eyes, with the coat of the hunter tucked under his bonds to keep away the wolves.

The race had but begun; the horse had but warmed to his work; the hunter had but tasted of sweet triumph. Another hopeful of a buffalo mother, negligent in danger, truant from his brothers, stumbled and fell in the enmeshing loop. The hunter's vest, slipped over the calf's neck, served as danger signal to the wolves. Before the lumbering buffalo missed their loss, another red and black baby kicked helplessly on the grass and sent up vain, weak calls, and at last lay still, with the hunter's boot tied to his cords.

Four! Jones counted them aloud, and in his mind, and kept on! Fast, hard work, covering upward of fifteen miles, had begun to tell on herd, horse and man, and all slowed down to the call for strength. The fifth time Jones closed in on his game, he encountered different circumstances such as called forth his cunning.

The herd had opened up; the mothers had fallen back to the rear; the calves hung almost out of sight under the shaggy sides of protectors. To try them out Jones darted close and threw his lasso. It struck a cow. With activity incredible in such a huge beast, she lunged at him. Kentuck, expecting just such a move, wheeled to safety. This duel, ineffectual on both sides, kept up for a while, and all the time, man and herd were jogging rapidly to the north.

Jones could not let well enough alone; he acknowledged this even as he swore he must have five. Emboldened by his marvelous luck, and yielding headlong to the passion within, he threw caution to the winds. A lame old cow with a red calf caught his eye; in he spurred his willing horse and slung his rope. It stung the haunch of the mother. The mad grunt she vented was no quicker than the velocity with which she plunged and reared. Jones had but time to swing his leg over the saddle when the hoofs beat down. Kentuck rolled on the plain, flinging his rider from him. The infuriated buffalo lowered her head for the fatal charge on the horse, when the plainsman, jerking out his heavy Colts, shot her dead in her tracks.

Kentuck got to his feet unhurt, and stood his ground, quivering but ready, showing his steadfast courage. He showed more, for his ears lay back, and his eyes had the gleam of the animal that strikes back.

The calf ran round its mother. Jones lassoed it, and tied it down, being compelled to cut a piece from his lasso, as the cords on the saddle had given out. He left his other boot with baby number five. The still heaving, smoking body of the victim called forth the stern, intrepid hunter's pity for a moment. Spill of blood he had not wanted. But he had not been able to avoid it; and mounting again with close-shut jaw and smoldering eye, he galloped to the north.

Kentuck snorted; the pursuing wolves shied off in the grass; the pale sun began to slant westward. The cold iron stirrups froze and cut the hunger's bootless feet.

When once more he came hounding the buffalo, they were considerably winded. Short-tufted tails, raised stiffly, gave warning. Snorts, like puffs of escaping steam, and deep grunts from cavernous chests evinced anger and impatience that might, at any moment, bring the herd to a defiant stand.

He whizzed the shortened noose over the head of a calf that was laboring painfully to keep up, and had slipped down, when a mighty grunt told him of peril. Never looking to see whence it came, he sprang into the saddle. Fiery Kentuck jumped into action, then hauled up with a shock that almost threw himself and rider. The lasso, fast to the horse, and its loop end round the calf, had caused the sudden check.

A maddened cow bore down on Kentuck. The gallant horse straightened in a jump, but dragging the calf pulled him in a circle, and in another moment he was running round and round the howling, kicking pivot. Then ensued a terrible race, with horse and bison describing a twenty-foot circle. Bang! Bang! The hunter fired two shots, and heard the spats of the bullets. But they only augmented the frenzy of the beast. Faster Kentuck flew, snorting in terror; closer drew the dusty, bouncing pursuer; the calf spun like a top; the lasso strung tighter than wire. Jones strained to loosen the fastening, but in vain. He swore at his carelessness in dropping his knife by the last calf he had tied. He thought of shooting the rope, yet dared not risk the shot. A hollow sound turned him again, with the Colts leveled. Bang! Dust flew from the ground beyond the bison.

The two charges left in the gun were all that stood between him and eternity. With a desperate display of strength Jones threw his weight in a backward pull, and hauled Kentuck up. Then he leaned far back in the saddle, and shoved the Colts out beyond the horse's flank. Down went the broad head, with its black, glistening horns. Bang! She slid forward with a crash, plowing the ground with hoofs and nose—spouted blood, uttered a hoarse cry, kicked and died.

Kentuck, for once completely terrorized, reared and plunged from the cow, dragging the calf. Stern command and iron arm forced him to a standstill. The calf, nearly strangled, recovered when the noose was slipped, and moaned a feeble protest against life and captivity. The remainder of Jones's lasso went to bind number six, and one of his socks went to serve as reminder to the persistent wolves.

"Six! On! On! Kentuck! On!" Weakening, but unconscious of it, with bloody hands and feet, without lasso, and with only one charge in his revolver, hatless, coatless, vestless, bootless, the wild hunter urged on the noble horse. The herd had gained miles in the interval of the fight. Game to the backbone, Kentuck lengthened out to overhaul it, and slowly the rolling gap lessened and lessened. A long hour thumped away, with the rumble growing nearer.

Once again the lagging calves dotted the grassy plain before the hunter. He dashed beside a burly calf, grasped its tail, stopped his horse, and jumped. The calf went down with him, and did not come up. The knotted, bloodstained hands, like claws of steel, bound the hind legs close and fast with a leathern belt, and left between them a torn and bloody sock.

"Seven! On! Old Faithful! We *must* have another! the last! This is your day."

The blood that flecked the hunter was not all his own.

The sun slanted westwardly toward the purpling horizon; the grassy plain gleamed like a ruffled sea of glass; the gray wolves loped on.

When next the hunter came within sight of the herd, over a wavy ridge, changes in its shape and movement met his gaze. The calves were almost done; they could run no more; their mothers faced the south, and trotted slowly to and fro; the bulls were grunting, herding, piling close. It looked as if the herd meant to stand and fight.

This mattered little to the hunter who had captured seven calves since dawn. The first limping calf he reached tried to elude the grasping hand and failed. Kentuck had been trained to wheel to the right or left, in whichever way his rider leaned; and as Jones bent over and caught an upraised tail, the horse turned to strike the calf with both front hoofs. The calf rolled; the horse plunged down; the rider sped beyond to the dust. Though the calf was tired, he still could bellow, and he filled the air with robust bawls.

Jones all at once saw twenty or more buffalo dash in at him with fast, twinkling, short legs. With the thought of it, he was in the air to the saddle. As the black, round mounds charged from every direction, Kentuck let out with all there was left in him. He leaped and whirled, pitched and swerved, in a roaring, clashing, dusty mêlée. Beating hoofs threw the turf, flying tails whipped the air, and everywhere were dusky, sharp-pointed heads, tossing low. Kentuck squeezed out unscathed. The mob of bison, bristling, turned to lumber after the main herd. Jones seized his opportunity and rode after them, yelling with all his might. He drove them so hard that soon the little fellows lagged paces behind. Only one or two old cows straggled with the calves.

Then wheeling Kentuck, he cut between the herd and a calf, and rode it down. Bewildered, the tously little bull bellowed in great affright. The hunter seized the stiff tail, and calling to his horse, leaped off. But his strength was far spent, and the buffalo, larger than his fellows, threshed about and jerked in terror. Jones threw it again and again. But it struggled up, never once ceasing its loud demands for help. Finally the hunter tripped it up and fell upon it with his knees.

Above the rumble of retreating hoofs, Jones heard the familiar short, quick, jarring pound on the turf. Kentuck neighed his alarm and raced to the right. Bearing down on the hunter, hurtling through the air, was a giant furry mass, instinct with fierce life and power—a buffalo cow robbed of her young.

With his senses almost numb, barely able to pull and raise the Colt, the plainsman willed to live, and to keep his captive. His leveled arm wavered like a leaf in a storm.

Bang! Fire, smoke, a shock, a jarring crash, and silence!

The calf stirred beneath him. He put out a hand to touch a warm, furry coat. The mother had fallen beside him. Lifting a heavy hoof, he laid it over the neck of the calf to serve as additional weight. He lay still and listened. The rumble of the herd died away in the distance.

The evening waned. Still the hunter lay quiet. From time to time the calf struggled and bellowed. Lank, gray wolves appeared on all sides; they prowled about with hungry howls, and shoved black-tipped noses through the grass. The sun sank, and the sky paled to opal blue. A star shone out, then another, and another. Over the prairie slanted the first dark shadow of night.

Suddenly the hunter laid his ear to the ground, and listened. Faint beats, like throbs of a pulsing heart, shuddered from the soft turf. Stronger they grew, till the hunter raised his head. Dark forms approached; voices broke the silence; the creaking of a wagon scared away the wolves.

"This way!" shouted the hunter weakly.

"Ha! here he is. Hurt?" cried Rude, vaulting the wheel.

"Tie up this calf. How many—did you find?" The voice grew fainter.

"Seven—alive, and in good shape, and all your clothes." But the last words fell on unconscious ears.

CHAPTER 4

The Trail

"Frank, what'll we do about horses?" asked Jones. "Jim'll want the bay, and of course you'll want to ride Spot. The rest of our nags will only do to pack the outfit."

"I've been thinkin'," replied the foreman. "You sure will need good mounts. Now it happens that a friend of mine is just at this time at House Rock Valley, an outlyin' post of one of the big Utah ranches. He is gettin' in the horses off the range, an' he has some crackin' good ones. Let's ooze over there—it's only thirty miles—an' get some horses from him."

We were all eager to act upon Frank's suggestion. So plans were made for three of us to ride over and select our mounts. Frank and Jim would follow with the pack train, and if all went well, on the following evening we would camp under the shadow of Buckskin.

Early next morning we were on our way. I tried to find a soft place on Old Baldy, one of Frank's pack horses. He was a horse that would not have raised up at the trumpet of doom. Nothing under the sun, Frank said, bothered Old Baldy but the operation of shoeing. We made the distance to the outpost by noon, and found Frank's friend a genial and obliging cowboy, who said we could have all the horses we wanted.

While Jones and Wallace strutted round the big corral, which was full of vicious, dusty, shaggy horses and mustangs, I sat high on the fence. I heard them talking about points and girth and stride, and a lot of terms that I could not understand. Wallace selected a heavy sorrel, and Jones a big bay, very like Jim's. I had observed, way over in the corner of the corral, a bunch of cayuses, and among them a clean-limbed black horse. Edging round on the fence I got a closer view, and then cried out that I had found my horse. I jumped down and caught him, much to my surprise, for the other horses were wild, and had kicked viciously. The black was beautifully built, wide-chested and powerful, but not heavy. His coat glistened like sheeny black satin, and he had a white face and white feet and a long mane.

"I don't know about giving you Satan—that's his name," said the cowboy. "The foreman rides him often. He's the fastest, the best climber, and the best dispositioned horse on the range.

"But I guess I can let you have him," he continued, when he saw my disappointed face.

"By George!" exclaimed Jones. "You've got it on us this time."

"Would you like to trade?" asked Wallace, as his sorrel tried to bite him. "That black looks sort of fierce."

I led my prize out of the corral, up to the little cabin nearby, where I tied him, and proceeded to get acquainted after a fashion of my own. Though not versed in horse-lore, I knew that half the battle was to win his confidence. I smoothed his silky coat, and patted him, and then surreptitiously slipped a lump of sugar from my pocket. This sugar, which I had purloined in Flagstaff, and carried all the way across the desert, was somewhat disreputably soiled, and Satan sniffed at it disdainfully. Evidently he had never smelled or tasted sugar. I pressed it into his mouth. He munched it, and then looked me over with some interest. I handed him another lump. He took it and rubbed his nose against me. Satan was mine!

Frank and Jim came along early in the afternoon. What with packing, changing saddles and shoeing the horses, we were all busy. Old Baldy would not be shod, so we let him off till a more opportune time. By four o'clock we were riding toward the slopes of Buckskin, now only a few miles away, standing up higher and darker.

"What's that for?" inquired Wallace, pointing to a long, rusty, wire-wrapped, double-barreled blunderbuss of a shotgun, stuck in the holster of Jones's saddle.

The Colonel, who had been having a fine time with the impatient and curious hounds, did not vouchsafe any information on that score. But very shortly we were destined to learn the use of this incongruous firearm. I was riding in advance of Wallace, and a little behind Jones. The dogs—excepting Jude, who had been kicked and lamed—were ranging along before their master. Suddenly, right before me, I saw an immense jack-rabbit; and just then Moze and Don caught sight of it. In fact, Moze bumped his blunt nose into the rabbit. When it leaped into scared action, Moze yelped, and Don followed suit. Then they were after it in wild, clamoring pursuit. Jones let out the stentorian blast, now becoming familiar, and spurred after them. He reached over, pulled the shotgun out of the holster and fired both barrels at the jumping dogs.

I expressed my amazement in strong language, and Wallace whistled.

Don came sneaking back with his tail between his legs, and Moze, who had cowered as if stung, circled round ahead of us. Jones finally succeeded in getting him back.

"Come in hyah! You measly rabbit dogs! What do you mean chasing off that way? We're after lions. Lions! understand?"

Don looked thoroughly convinced of his error, but

Moze, being more thick-headed, appeared mystified rather than hurt or frightened.

"What size shot do you use?" I asked.

"Number ten. They don't hurt much at seventy-five yards," replied our leader. "I use them as sort of a long arm. You see, the dogs must be made to know what we're after. Ordinary means would never do in a case like this. My idea is to break them off coyotes, wolves and deer, and when we cross a lion trail, let them go. I'll teach them sooner than you'd think. Only we must get where we can see what they're trailing. Then I can tell whether to call them back or not."

The sun was gilding the rim of the desert ramparts when we began the ascent of the foothills of Buckskin. A steep trail wound zigzag up the mountain. We led our horses, as it was a long, hard climb. From time to time, as I stopped to catch my breath, I gazed away across the growing void to the gorgeous Pink Cliffs, far above and beyond the red wall which had seemed so high, and then out toward the desert. The irregular ragged crack in the plain, apparently only a thread of broken ground, was the Grand Cañon. How unutterably remote, wild, grand was that world of red and brown, of purple pall, of vague outline!

Two thousand feet, probably, we mounted to what Frank called Little Buckskin. In the west a copper glow, ridged with lead-colored clouds, marked where the sun had set. The air was very thin and icy cold. At the first clump of piñon pines, we made dry camp. When I sat down it was as if I had been anchored. Frank solicitously remarked that I looked "sort of beat." Jim built a roaring fire and began getting supper. A snow squall came on the rushing wind. The air grew colder, and though I hugged the fire, I could not get warm. When I had satisfied my hunger, I rolled out my sleeping-bag and crept into it. I stretched my aching limbs and did not move again. Once I awoke, drowsily feeling the warmth of the fire, and I heard Frank say: "He's asleep, dead to the world!"

"He's all in," said Jones. "Riding's what did it. You know how a horse tears a man to pieces."

"Will he be able to stand it?" asked Frank, with as much solicitude as if he were my brother. "When you get out after anythin'—well, you're hell. An' think of the country we're goin' into. I know you've never seen the breaks of the Siwash, but I have, an' it's the worst an' roughest country I ever saw. Breaks after breaks, like the ridges on a washboard, headin' on the south slope of Buckskin, an' runnin' down, side by side miles an' miles, deeper an' deeper, till they run into that awful hole. It will be a killin' trip on men, horses an' dogs. Now, Mr. Wallace, he's been campin' an' roughin' with the Navajos for months; he's in some kind of shape, but—"

Frank concluded his remark with a doubtful pause.

"I'm some worried, too," replied Jones. "But he would come. He stood the desert well enough; even the Mormons said that."

In the ensuing silence the fire sputtered, the glare fitfully merged into dark shadows under the weird piñons, and the wind moaned through the short branches.

"Wal," drawled a slow, soft voice, "shore I reckon you're hollerin' too soon. Frank's measly trick puttin' him on Spot showed me. He rode out on Spot, an' he rode in on Spot. Shore he'll stay."

It was not all the warmth of the blankets that glowed over me then. The voices died away dreamily, and my eyelids dropped sleepily tight. Late in the night I sat up suddenly, roused by some unusual disturbance. The fire was dead; the wind swept with a rush through the piñons. From the black darkness came the staccato chorus of coyotes. Don barked his displeasure; Sounder made the welkin ring, and old Moze growled low and deep, grumbling like muttered thunder. Then all was quiet, and I slept.

Dawn, rosy red, confronted me when I opened my eyes. Breakfast was ready; Frank was packing Old Baldy; Jones talked to his horse as he saddled him; Wallace came stooping his giant figure under the piñons; the dogs, eager and soft-eyed, sat around Jim and begged. The sun peeped over the Pink Cliffs; the desert still lay asleep, tranced in a purple and golden-streaked mist.

"Come, come!" said Jones, in his big voice. "We're slow; here's the sun."

"Easy, easy," replied Frank, "we've all the time there is."

When Frank threw the saddle over Satan I interrupted him and said I would care for my horse henceforward. Soon we were under way, the horses fresh, the dogs scenting the keen, cold air.

The trail rolled over the ridges of piñon and scrubby pine. Occasionally we could see the black, ragged crest of Buckskin above us. From one of these ridges I took my last long look back at the desert, and engraved on my mind a picture of the red wall, and the many-hued ocean of sand. The trail, narrow and indistinct, mounted the last slow-rising slope; the piñons failed, and the scrubby pines became abundant. At length we reached the top, and entered the great arched aisles of Buckskin Forest. The ground was flat as a table. Magnificent pine trees, far apart, with branches high and spreading, gave the eye glad welcome. Some of these monarchs were eight feet thick at the base and two hundred feet high. Here and there one lay, gaunt and prostrate, a victim of the wind. The smell of pitch pine was sweetly overpowering.

"When I went through here two weeks ago, the snow

was a foot deep, an' I bogged in places," said Frank. "The sun has been oozin' round here some. I'm afraid Jones won't find any snow on this end of Buckskin."

Thirty miles of winding trail, brown and springy from its thick mat of pine needles, shaded always by the massive, seamy-barked trees, took us over the extremity of Buckskin. Then we faced down into the head of a ravine that ever grew deeper, stonier and rougher. I shifted from side to side, from leg to leg in my saddle, dismounted and hobbled before Satan, mounted again, and rode on. Jones called the dogs and complained to them of the lack of snow. Wallace sat his horse comfortably, taking long pulls at his pipe and long gazes at the shaggy sides of the ravine. Frank, energetic and tireless, kept the pack-horses in the trail. Jim jogged on silently. And so we rode down to Oak Spring.

The spring was pleasantly situated in a grove of oaks and piñons, under the shadow of three cliffs. Three ravines opened here into an oval valley. A rude cabin of rough-hewn logs stood near the spring.

"Get down, get down," sang out Frank. "We'll hang up here. Beyond Oak is No-Man's-Land. We take our chances on water after we leave here."

When we had unsaddled, unpacked, and got a fire roaring on the wide stone hearth of the cabin, it was once again night.

"Boys," said Jones after supper, "we're now on the edge of the lion country. Frank saw lion sign in here only two weeks ago; and though the snow is gone, we stand a show of finding tracks in the sand and dust. To-morrow morning, before the sun gets a chance at the bottom of these ravines, we'll be up and doing. We'll each take a dog and search in different directions. Keep the dog in leash, and when he opens up, examine the ground carefully for tracks. If a dog opens on any track that you are sure isn't a lion's, punish him. And when a lion track is found, hold the dog in, wait and signal. We'll use a signal I have tried and found far-reaching and easy to yell. Waa-hoo! That's it. Once yelled it means come. Twice means come quickly. Three times means come—danger!"

In one corner of the cabin was a platform of poles, covered with straw. I threw the sleeping-bag on this, and was soon stretched out. Misgivings as to my strength worried me before I closed my eyes. Once on my back, I felt I could not rise; my chest was sore; my cough deep and rasping. It seemed I had scarcely closed my eyes when Jones's impatient voice recalled me from sweet oblivion.

"Frank, Frank, it's daylight. Jim—boys!" he called.

I tumbled out in a gray, wan twilight. It was cold enough to make the fire acceptable, but nothing like the morning before on Buckskin.

"Come to the festal board," drawled Jim, almost before I had my boots laced.

"Jones," said Frank, "Jim an' I'll ooze round here to-day. There's lots to do, an' we want to have things hitched right before we strike for the Siwash. We've got to shoe Old Baldy, an' if we can't get him locoed, it'll take all of us to do it."

The light was still gray when Jones led off with Don, Wallace with Sounder and I with Moze. Jones directed us to separate, follow the dry stream beds in the ravines, and remember his instructions given the night before.

The ravine to the right, which I entered, was choked with huge stones fallen from the cliff above, and piñons growing thick; and I wondered apprehensively how a man could evade a wild animal in such a place, much less chase it.

Old Moze pulled on his chain and sniffed at coyote

and deer tracks. And every time he evinced interest in such, I cut him with a switch, which, to tell the truth, he did not notice.

I thought I heard a shout, and holding Moze tight, I waited and listened.

"Waa-hoo—waa-hoo!" floated on the air, rather deadened as if it had come from round the triangular cliff that faced into the valley. Urging and dragging Moze, I ran down the ravine as fast as I could, and soon encountered Wallace coming from the middle ravine.

"Jones," he said excitedly, "this way—there's the signal again."

We dashed in haste for the mouth of the third ravine, and came suddenly upon Jones, kneeling under a piñon tree.

"Boys, look!" he exclaimed, as he pointed to the ground. There, clearly defined in the dust, was a cat track as big as my spread hand, and the mere sight of it sent a chill up my spine. "There's a lion track for you; made by a female, a two-year-old; but I can't say if she passed here last night. Don won't take the trail. Try Moze."

I led Moze to the big, round imprint, and put his nose down into it. The old hound sniffed and sniffed, then lost interest.

"Cold!" ejaculated Jones. "No go. Try Sounder. Come, old boy, you've the nose for it."

He urged the reluctant hound forward. Sounder needed not to be shown the trail; he stuck his nose in it, and stood very quiet for a long moment; then he quivered slightly, raised his nose and sought the next track. Step by step he went slowly, doubtfully. All at once his tail wagged stiffly.

"Look at that!" cried Jones in delight. "He's caught a scent when the others couldn't. Hyah, Moze, get back. Keep Moze and Don back; give him room."

Slowly Sounder paced up the ravine, as carefully as if

he were traveling on thin ice. He passed the dusty, open trail to a scaly ground with little bits of grass, and he kept on.

We were electrified to hear him give vent to a deep bugle-blast note of eagerness.

"By George, he's got it, boys!" exclaimed Jones, as he lifted the stubborn, struggling hound off the trail. "I know that bay. It means a lion passed here this morning. And we'll get him up as sure as you're alive. Come, Sounder. Now for the horses."

As we ran pell-mell into the little glade, where Jim sat mending some saddle trapping, Frank rode up the trail with the horses.

"Well, I heard Sounder," he said with his genial smile. "Somethin's comin' off, eh? You'll have to ooze round some to keep up with that hound."

I saddled Satan with fingers that trembled in excitement, and pushed my little Remington automatic into the rifle holster.

"Boys, listen," said our leader. "We're off now in the beginning of a hunt new to you. Remember—no shooting, no blood-letting, except in self-defense. Keep as close to me as you can. Listen for the dogs, and when you fall behind or separate, yell out the signal cry. Don't forget this. We're bound to lose each other. Look out for the spikes and branches on the trees. If the dogs split, whoever follows the one that trees the lion must wait there till the rest come up. Off now! Come, Sounder; Moze, you rascal, hyah! Come, Don, come, Puppy, and take your medicine."

Except Moze, the hounds were all trembling and running eagerly to and fro. When Sounder was loosed, he led them in a bee-line to the trail, with us cantering after. Sounder worked exactly as before, only he followed the lion tracks a little farther up the ravine before he bayed. He kept going faster and faster, occasionally letting out one deep, short yelp. The other hounds did not give tongue, but eager, excited, baffled, kept at his heels. The ravine was long, and the wash at the bottom, up which the lion had proceeded, turned and twisted round bowlders large as houses, and led through dense growths of some short, rough shrub. Now and then the lion tracks showed plainly in the sand. For five miles or more Sounder led us up the ravine, which began to contract and grow steep. The dry stream bed got to be full of thickets of poplar—tall, straight, branchless saplings, about the size of a man's arm, and growing so close we had to press them aside to let our horses through.

Presently Sounder slowed up and appeared at fault. We found him puzzling over an open, grassy patch, and after nosing it for a little while, he began skirting the edge.

"Cute dog!" declared Jones. "That Sounder will make a lion chaser. Our game has gone up here somewhere."

Sure enough, Sounder directly gave tongue from the side of the ravine. It was climb for us now. Broken shale, rocks of all dimensions, piñons down and piñons up made ascending no easy problem. We had to dismount and lead the horses, thus losing ground. Jones forged ahead and reached the top of the ravine first. When Wallace and I got up, breathing heavily, Jones and the hounds were out of sight. But Sounder kept voicing his clear call, giving us our direction. Off we flew, over ground that was still rough, but enjoyable going compared to the ravine slopes. The ridge was sparsely covered with cedar and piñon, through which, far ahead, we pretty soon spied Jones. Wallace signaled, and our leader answered twice. We caught up with him on the brink of another ravine deeper and craggier than the first, full of dead, gnarled piñon and splintered rocks.

"This gulch is the largest of the three that head in at Oak Spring," said Jones. "Boys, don't forget your direction. Always keep a feeling where camp is, always sense it every time you turn. The dogs have gone down. That lion is in here somewhere. Maybe he lives down in the high cliffs near the spring and came up here last night for a kill he's buried somewhere. Lions never travel far. Hark! Hark! There's Sounder and the rest of them! They've got the scent; they've all got it! Down, boys, down, and ride!"

With that he crashed into the cedar in a way that showed me how impervious he was to slashing branches, sharp as thorns, and steep descent and peril. Wallace's big sorrel plunged after him and the rolling stones cracked. Suffering as I was by this time, with cramp in my legs, and torturing pain, I had to choose between holding my horse in or falling off; so I chose the former and accordingly got behind.

Dead cedar and piñon trees lay everywhere, with their contorted limbs reaching out like the arms of a devil-fish. Stones blocked every opening. Making the bottom of the ravine after what seemed an interminable time, I found the tracks of Jones and Wallace. A long "Waa-hoo!" drew me on; then the mellow bay of a hound floated up the ravine. Satan made up time in the sandy stream bed, but kept me busily dodging overhanging branches. I became aware, after a succession of efforts to keep from being strung on piñons, that the sand before me was clean and trackless. Hauling Satan up sharply, I waited irresolutely and listened. Then from high up the ravine side wafted down a medley of yelps and barks.

"Waa-hoo, waa-hoo!" ringing down the slope, pealed against the cliff behind me, and sent the wild echoes flying.

Satan, of his own accord, headed up the incline. Surprised at this, I gave him free rein. How he did climb! Not long did it take me to discover that he picked out easier going than I had. Once I saw Jones crossing a ledge far above me, and I yelled our signal cry. The answer returned clear and sharp; then its echo cracked under the hollow cliff, and crossing and recrossing the ravine, it died at last far away, like the muffled peal of a bell-buoy. Again I heard the blended yelping of the hounds, and closer at hand. I saw a long, low cliff above, and decided that the hounds were running at the base of it. Another chorus of yelps, quicker, wilder than the others, drew a yell from me. Instinctively I knew the dogs had jumped game of some kind. Satan knew it as well as I, for he quickened his pace and sent the stones clattering behind him.

I gained the base of the yellow cliff, but found no tracks in the dust of ages that had crumbled in its shadow, nor did I hear the dogs. Considering how close they had seemed, this was strange. I halted and listened. Silence reigned supreme. The ragged cracks in the cliff walls could have harbored many a watching lion, and I cast an apprehensive glance into their dark confines. Then I turned my horse to get round the cliff and over the ridge. When I again stopped, all I could hear was the thumping of my heart and the labored panting of Satan. I came to a break in the cliff, a steep place of weathered rock, and I put Satan to it. He went up with a will. From the narrow saddle of the ridge-crest I tried to take my bearings. Below me slanted the green of piñon, with the bleached treetops standing like spears, and uprising yellow stones. Fancying I heard a gunshot, I leaned a straining ear against the soft breeze. The proof came presently in the unmistakable report of Jones's blunderbuss. It was repeated almost instantly, giving reality to the direction, which was down the slope of what I concluded must be the third ravine. Wondering what was the meaning of the shots, and chagrined because I was out of the race, but calmer in mind, I let Satan stand.

Hardly a moment elapsed before a sharp bark tingled in my ears. It belonged to Moze. Soon I distinguished a rattling of stones and the sharp, metallic clicks of hoofs striking rocks. Then into a space below me loped a beautiful deer, so large that at first I took it for an elk. Another sharp bark, nearer this time, told the tale of Moze's dereliction. In a few moments he came in sight, running with his tongue out and his head high.

"Hyah, you old gladiator! hyah! hyah!" I yelled and yelled again. Moze passed over the saddle on the trail of the deer, and his short bark floated back to remind me how far he was from a lion dog.

Then I divined the meaning of the shotgun reports. The hounds had crossed a fresher trail than that of the lion, and our leader had discovered it. Despite a keen appreciation of Jones's task, I gave way to amusement, and repeated Wallace's paradoxical formula: "Pet the lions and shoot the hounds."

So I headed down the ravine, looking for a blunt, bold crag, which I had descried from camp. I found it before long, and profiting by past failures to judge of distance, gave my first impression a great stretch, and then decided that I was more than two miles from Oak.

Long after two miles had been covered, and I had begun to associate Jim's biscuits with a certain soft seat near a ruddy fire, I was apparently still the same distance from my landmark crag. Suddenly a slight noise brought me to a halt. I listened intently. Only an indistinct rattling of small rocks disturbed the impressive stillness. It might have been the weathering that goes on constantly, and it might have been an animal. I inclined to the former idea till I saw Satan's ears go up. Jones had told me to watch the ears of my horse, and short as had been my acquaintance with Satan, I had learned that he always discovered things more quickly than I. So I waited patiently.

From time to time a rattling roll of pebbles, almost musical, caught my ear. It came from the base of the wall of yellow cliff that barred the summit of all those ridges. Satan threw up his head and nosed the breeze. The delicate, almost stealthy sounds, the action of my horse, the waiting drove my heart to extra work. The breeze quickened and fanned my cheek, and borne upon it came the faint and far-away bay of a hound. It came again and again, each time nearer. Then on a stronger puff of wind rang the clear, deep, mellow call that had given Sounder his beautiful name. Never it seemed had I heard music so blood-stirring. Sounder was on the trail of something, and he had it headed my way. Satan heard, shot up his long ears, and tried to go ahead; but I restrained and soothed him into quiet.

Long moments I sat there, with the poignant consciousness of the wildness of the scene, of the significant rattling of the stones and of the bell-tongued hound baying incessantly, sending warm joy through my veins, the absorption in sensations new, yielding only to the hunting instinct when Satan snorted and quivered. Again the deep-toned bay rang into the silence with its stirring thrill of life. And a sharp, rattling of stones just above brought another snort from Satan.

Across an open space in the piñons a gray form flashed. I leaped off Satan and knelt to get a better view under the trees. I soon made out another deer passing along the base of the cliff. Mounting again, I rode up to the cliff to wait for Sounder.

A long time I had to wait for the hound. It proved that the atmosphere was as deceiving in regard to sound as to sight. Finally Sounder came running along the wall. I got off to intercept him. The crazy fellow—he had never responded to my overtures of friendship—uttered short, sharp yelps of delight, and actually leaped into my arms. But I could not hold him. He darted upon the trail again and paid no heed to my angry shouts. With a resolve to overhaul him, I jumped on Satan and whirled after the hound.

The black stretched out with such a stride that I was at pains to keep my seat. I dodged the jutting rocks and projecting snags; felt stinging branches in my face and the rush of sweet, dry wind. Under the crumbling walls, over slopes of weathered stone and droppings of shelving rock, round protruding noses of cliff, over and under piñons Satan thundered. He came out on the top of the ridge, at the narrow back I had called a saddle. Here I caught a glimpse of Sounder far below, going down into the ravine from which I had ascended some time before. I called to him, but I might as well have called to the wind.

Weary to the point of exhaustion, I once more turned Satan toward camp. I lay forward on his neck and let him have his will. Far down the ravine I awoke to strange sounds, and soon recognized the cracking of iron-shod hoofs against stone; then voices. Turning an abrupt bend in the sandy wash, I ran into Jones and Wallace.

"Fall in! Line up in the sad procession!" said Jones. "Tige and the pup are faithful. The rest of the dogs are somewhere between the Grand Cañon and the Utah desert."

I related my adventures, and tried to spare Moze and Sounder as much as conscience would permit.

"Hard luck!" commented Jones. "Just as the hounds jumped the cougar—Oh! they bounced him out of the rocks all right—don't you remember, just under that cliff wall where you and Wallace came up to me? Well, just as they jumped him, they ran right into fresh deer tracks. I saw one of the deer. Now that's too much for any hounds, except those trained for lions. I shot at Moze twice, but couldn't turn him. He has to be hurt, they've all got to be hurt to make them understand."

Wallace told of a wild ride somewhere in Jones's wake, and of sundry knocks and bruises he had sustained, of pieces of corduroy he had left decorating the cedars and of a most humiliating event, where a gaunt and bare piñon snag had penetrated under his belt and lifted him, mad and kicking, off his horse.

"These Western nags will hang you on a limb every chance they get," declared Jones, "and don't you overlook that. Well, there's the cabin. We'd better stay here a few day or a week and break in the dogs and horses, for this day's work was apple pie to what we'll get in the Siwash."

I groaned inwardly, and was remorselessly glad to see Wallace fall off his horse and walk on one leg to the cabin. When I got my saddle off Satan, had given him a drink and hobbled him, I crept into the cabin and dropped like a log. I felt as if every bone in my body was broken and my flesh was raw. I got gleeful gratification from Wallace's complaints, and Jones's remark that he had a stitch in his back. So ended the first chase after cougars.

CHAPTER 5

Oak Spring

Moze and Don and Sounder straggled into camp next morning, hungry, footsore and scarred; and as they limped in, Jones met them with characteristic speech: "Well, you decided to come in when you got hungry and tired? Never thought of how you fooled me, did you? Now, the first thing you get is a good licking."

He tied them in a little log pen near the cabin and whipped them soundly. And the next few days, while Wallace and I rested, he took them out separately and deliberately ran them over coyote and deer trails. Sometimes we heard his stentorian yell as a forerunner to the blast from his old shotgun. Then again we heard the shots unheralded by the yell. Wallace and I waxed warm under the collar over this peculiar method of training dogs, and each of us made dire threats. But in justice to their implacable trainer, the dogs never appeared to be hurt; never a spot of blood flecked their glossy coats, nor did they ever come home limping. Sounder grew wise, and Don gave up, but Moze appeared not to change.

"All hands ready to rustle," sang out Frank one morning. "Old Baldy's got to be shod."

This brought us all, except Jones, out of the cabin, to see the object of Frank's anxiety tied to a nearby oak. At first I failed to recognize Old Baldy. Vanished was the slow, sleepy, apathetic manner that had characterized him; his ears lay back on his head; fire flashed from his eyes. When Frank threw down a kit-bag, which emitted a metallic clanking, Old Baldy sat back on his haunches, planted his forefeet deep in the ground and plainly as a horse could speak, said "No!"

"Sometimes he's bad, and sometimes worse," growled Frank.

"Shore he's plumb bad this mornin'," replied Jim.

Frank got the three of us to hold Baldy's head and pull him up, then he ventured to lift a hind foot over his knee. Old Baldy straightened out his leg and sent Frank sprawling into the dirt. Twice again Frank patiently tried to hold a hind leg, with the same result; and then he lifted a forefoot. Baldy uttered a very intelligible snort, bit through Wallace's glove, yanked Jim off his feet, and scared me so that I let go his forelock. Then he broke the rope which held him to the tree. There was a plunge, a scattering of men, though Jim still valiantly held on to Baldy's head, and a thrashing of scrub piñon, where Baldy reached out vigorously with his hind feet. But for Jim, he would have escaped.

"What's all the row?" called Jones from the cabin. Then from the door, taking in the situation, he yelled: "Hold on, Jim! Pull down on the ornery old cayuse!"

He leaped into action with a lasso in each hand, one whirling round his head. The slender rope straightened with a whiz and whipped round Baldy's legs as he kicked viciously. Jones pulled it tight, then fastened it with nimble fingers to the tree.

"Let go! let go, Jim!" he yelled, whirling the other lasso. The loop flashed and fell over Baldy's head and tightened round his neck. Jones threw all the weight of his burly form on the lariat, and Baldy crashed to the ground, rolled, tussled, screamed, and then lay on his back, kicking the air with three free legs. "Hold this!" ordered Jones, giving the tight rope to Frank. Whereupon he grabbed my lasso from the saddle, roped Baldy's two forefeet, and pulled him down on his side. This lasso he fastened to a scrub cedar.

"He's chokin'!" said Frank.

"Likely he is," replied Jones shortly. "It'll do him good." But with his big hands he drew the coil loose and slipped it down over Baldy's nose, where he tightened it again.

"Now, go ahead," he said, taking the rope from Frank.

It had all been done in a twinkling. Baldy lay there groaning and helpless, and when Frank once again took hold of the wicked leg, he was almost passive. When the shoeing operation had been neatly and quickly attended to and Baldy released from his uncomfortable position he struggled to his feet with heavy breaths, shook himself, and looked at his master.

"How'd you like being hog-tied?" queried his conqueror, rubbing Baldy's nose. "Now, after this you'll have some manners."

Old Baldy seemed to understand, for he looked sheepish, and lapsed once more into his listless, lazy unconcern.

"Where's Jim's old cayuse, the pack-horse?" asked our leader.

"Lost. Couldn't find him this morning, an' had a deuce of a time findin' the rest of the bunch. Old Baldy was cute. He hid in a bunch of piñons an' stood quiet so his bell wouldn't ring. I had to trail him."

"Do the horses stray far when they are hobbled?" inquired Wallace.

"If they keep jumpin' all night they can cover some territory. We're now on the edge of the wild horse country, and our nags know this as well as we. They smell the mustangs, an' would break their necks to get away. Satan and the sorrel were ten miles from camp when I found them this mornin'. An' Jim's cayuse went farther, an' we never will get him. He'll wear his hobbles out, then away with the wild horses. Once with them, he'll never be caught again."

On the sixth day of our stay at Oak we had visitors, whom Frank introduced as the Stewart brothers and Lawson, wild-horse wranglers. They were still, dark men, whose facial expressions seldom varied; tall and lithe and wiry as the mustangs they rode. The Stewarts were on their way to Kanab, Utah, to arrange for the sale of a drove of horses they had captured and corraled in a narrow cañon back in the Siwash. Lawson said he was at our service, and was promptly hired to look after our horses.

"Any cougar signs back in the breaks?" asked Jones.

"Wal, there's a cougar on every deer trail," replied the elder Stewart, "an' two for every pinto in the breaks. Old Tom himself downed fifteen colts fer us this spring."

"Fifteen colts! That's wholesale murder. Why don't you kill the butcher?"

"We've tried more'n onct. It's a turrible busted up country, them brakes. No man knows it, an' the cougars do. Old Tom ranges all the ridges and brakes, even up on the slopes of Buckskin; but he lives down there in them holes, an' Lord knows, no dog I ever seen could follow him. We tracked him in the snow, an' had dogs after him, but none could stay with him, except two as never cum back. But we've nothin' agin Old Tom like Jeff Clarke, a hoss rustler, who has a string of pintos corraled north of us. Clarke swears he ain't raised a colt in two years."

"We'll put that old cougar up a tree," exclaimed Jones.

"If you kill him we'll make you all a present of a mustang, an' Clarke, he'll give you two each," replied Stewart. "We'd be gettin' rid of him cheap."

"How many wild horses on the mountain now?"

"Hard to tell. Two or three thousand, mebbe. There's almost no ketchin' them, an' they're growin' all the time.

We ain't had no luck this spring. The bunch in corral we got last year."

"Seen anythin' of the White Mustang?" inquired Frank. "Ever get a rope near him?"

"No nearer'n we hev for six years back. He can't be ketched. We seen him an' his band of blacks a few days ago, headin' fer a water-hole down where Nail Cañon runs into Kanab Cañon. He's so cunnin' he'll never water at any of our trap corrals. An' we believe he can go without water fer two weeks, unless mebbe he hes a secret hole we've never trailed him to."

"Would we have any chance to see this Whit Mustang and his band?" questioned Jones.

"See him? Why, thet'd be easy. Go down Snake Gulch, camp at singin' Cliffs, go over into Nail Cañon, an' wait. Then send someone slippin' down to the water-hole at Kanab Cañon, an' when the band cums in to drink—which I reckon will be in a few days now—hev them drive the mustangs up. Only be sure to hev them get ahead of the White Mustang, so he'll hev only one way to cum, fer he sure is knowin'. He never makes a mistake. Mebbe you'll get to see him cum by like a white streak. Why, I've heerd thet mustang's hoofs ring like bells on the rocks a mile away. His hoofs are harder'n any iron shoe as was ever made. But even if you don't get to see him, Snake Gulch is worth seein'."

I learned later from Stewart that the White Mustang was a beautiful stallion of the wildest strain of mustang blue blood. He had roamed the long reaches between the Grand Cañon and Buckskin toward its southern slope for years; he had been the most sought-for horse by all the wranglers, and had become so shy and experienced that nothing but a glimpse was ever obtained of him. A singular fact was that he never attached any of his own species to his band, unless they were coal black. He had been known to fight and kill other stallions, but he kept out of the well-wooded and watered country frequented by other bands, and ranged the brakes of the Siwash as far as he could range. The usual method, indeed the only successful way to capture wild horses, was to build corrals round the water-holes. The wranglers lay out night after night watching. When the mustangs came to drink—which was always after dark—the gates would be closed on them. But the trick had never even been tried on the White Mustang, for the simple reason that he never approached one of these traps.

"Boys," said Jones, "seeing we need breaking in, we'll give the White Mustang a little run."

This was most pleasurable news, for the wild horses fascinated me. Besides, I saw from the expression on our leader's face that an uncapturable mustang was an object of interest to him.

Wallace and I had employed the last few warm, sunny afternoons in riding up and down the valley below Oak, where there was a fine, level stretch. Here I wore out my soreness of muscle, and gradually overcame my awkwardness in the saddle, Frank's remedy of maple sugar and red pepper had rid me of my cold, and with the return of strength, and the coming of confidence, full, joyous appreciation of wild environment and life made me unspeakably happy. And I noticed that my companions were in like condition of mind, though self-contained where I was exuberant. Wallace galloped his sorrel and watched the crags; Jones talked more kindly to the dogs; Jim baked biscuit indefatigably, and smoked in contented silence; Frank said always: "We'll ooze along easy like, or we've all the time there is." Which sentiment, whether from reiterated suggestion, or increasing confidence in the practical cowboy, or charm of its free import, gradually won us all.

"Boys," said Jones, as we sat round the campfire, "I see

you're getting in shape. Well, I've worn off the wire edge myself. And I have the hounds coming fine. They mind me now, but they're mystified. For the life of them they can't understand what I mean. I don't blame them. Wait till, by good luck, we get a cougar in a tree. When Sounder and Don see that, we've lion dogs, boys! we've lion dogs! But Moze is a stubborn brute. In all my years of animal experience, I've never discovered any other way to make animals obey than by instilling fear and respect into their hearts. I've been fond of buffalo, horses and dogs, but sentiment never ruled me. When animals must obey, they must—that's all, and no mawkishness! But I never trusted a buffalo in my life. If I had I wouldn't be here to-night. You all know how many keepers of tame wild animals get killed. I could tell you dozens of tragedies. And I've often thought, since I got back from New York, of that woman I saw with her troop of African lions. I dream about those lions, and see them leaping over her head. What a grand sight that was! But the public is fooled. I read somewhere that she trained those lions by love. I don't believe it. I saw her use a whip and a steel spear. Moreover, I saw many things that escaped most observers—how she entered the cage, how she maneuvered among them, how she kept a compelling gaze on them! It was an admirable, a great piece of work. Maybe she loves those huge yellow brutes, but her life was in danger every moment while she was in that cage, and she knew it. Some day, one of her pets—likely the King of Beasts she pets the most—will rise up and kill her. That is as certain as death."

CHAPTER 6

The White Mustang

For thirty miles down Nail Cañon we marked in every dusty trail and sandy wash, the small, oval, sharply defined tracks of the White Mustang and his band.

The cañon had been well named. It was long, straight and square sided; its bare walls glared steel-gray in the sun, smooth, glistening surfaces that had been polished by wind and water. No weathered heaps of shale, no crumbled piles of stone obstructed its level floor. And, softly toning its drab austerity, here grew the white sage, waving in the breeze, the Indian Paint Brush, with vivid vermilion flower, and patches of fresh, green grass.

"The White King, as we Arizona wild-hoss wranglers call this mustang, is mighty pertickler about his feed, an' he ranged along here last night, easy like, browsin' on this white sage," said Stewart. Infected by our intense interest in the famous mustang, and ruffled slightly by Jones's manifest surprise and contempt that no one had captured him, Steward had volunteered to guide us. "Never knowed him to run in this way fer water; fact is, never knowed Nail Cañon hed a fork. It splits down here, but you'd think it was only a crack in the wall. An' thet cunnin' mustang hes been foolin' us fer years about this water-hole."

The fork of Nail Cañon, which Stewart had decided we were in, had been accidentally discovered by Frank, who, in search of our horses one morning, had crossed a ridge, to come suddenly upon the blind, box-like head of the cañon. Stewart knew the lay of the ridges and run of the cañons as well as any man could know a country where, seemingly, every rod was ridged and bisected, and he was of the opinion that we had stumbled upon one of the White Mustang's secret passages, by which he had so often eluded his pursuers.

Hard riding had been the order of the day, but still we covered ten more miles by sundown. The cañon apparently closed in on us, so camp was made for the night. The horses were staked out, and supper made ready while the shadows were dropping; and when darkness settled thick over us, we lay under our blankets.

Morning disclosed the White Mustang's secret passage. It was a narrow cleft, splitting the cañon wall, rough, uneven, tortuous and choked with fallen rocks—no more than a wonderful crack in solid stone, opening into another cañon. Above us the sky seemed a winding, flowing stream of blue. The walls were so close in places that a horse with pack would have been blocked, and a rider had to pull his legs up over the saddle. On the far side, the passage fell very suddenly for several hundred feet to the floor of the other cañon. No hunter could have seen it, or suspected it from that side.

"This is Grand Cañon country, an' nobody knows what he's goin' to find," was Frank's comment.

"Now we're in Nail Cañon proper," said Stewart, "an' I know my bearin's. I can climb out a mile below an' cut across to Kanab Cañon, an' slip up into Nail Cañon agin, ahead of the mustangs, an' drive 'em up. I can't miss 'em, fer Kanab Cañon is impassable down a little ways. The mustangs will hev to run this way. So all you need do is go below the break, where I climb out, an' wait. You're sure goin' to get a look at the White Mustang. But wait.

Don't expect him before noon, an' after thet, any time till he comes. Mebbe it'll be a couple of days, so keep a good watch."

Then taking our man Lawson, with blankets and a knapsack of food, Stewart rode off down the cañon.

We were early on the march. As we proceeded the cañon lost its regularity and smoothness; it became crooked as a rail fence, narrower, higher, rugged and broken. Pinnacled cliffs, cracked and leaning, menaced us from above. Mountains of ruined wall had tumbled into fragments.

It seemed that Jones, after much survey of different corners, angles and points in the cañon floor, chose his position with much greater care than appeared necessary for the ultimate success of our venture—which was simply to see the White Mustang, and if good fortune attended us, to snap some photographs of this wild king of horses. It flashed over me that, with his ruling passion strong within him, our leader was laying some kind of trap for that mustang, was indeed bent on his capture.

Wallace, Frank and Jim were stationed at a point below the break where Stewart had evidently gone up and out. How a horse could have climbed that streaky white slide was a mystery. Jones's instructions to the men were to wait until the mustangs were close upon them, and then yell and shout and show themselves.

He took me to a jutting corner of cliff, which hid us from the others, and here he exercised still more care in scrutinizing the lay of the ground. A wash from ten to fifteen feet wide, and as deep, ran through the cañon in a somewhat meandering course. At the corner which consumed so much of his attention, the dry ditch ran along the cliff wall about fifty feet out; between it and the wall was good level ground; on the other side huge rocks and shale made it hummocky, practically impassable for a horse. It was plain the mustangs, on their way up, would choose the inside of the wash; and here in the middle of the passage, just round the jutting corner, Jones tied our horses to good, strong bushes. His next act was significant. He threw out his lasso and, dragging every crook out of it, carefully recoiled it, and hung it loose over the pommel of his saddle.

"The White Mustang may be yours before dark," he said with the smile that came so seldom. "Now I placed our horses there for two reasons. The mustangs won't see them till they're right on them. Then you'll see a sight and have a chance for a great picture. They will halt; the stallion will prance, whistle and snort for a fight, and then they'll see the saddles and be off. We'll hide across the wash, down a little way, and at the right time we'll shout and yell to drive them up."

By piling sagebrush round a stone, we made a hiding-place. Jones was extremely cautious to arrange the bunches in natural positions. "A Rocky Mountain Big Horn is the only four-footed beast," he said, "that has a better eye than a wild horse. A cougar has an eye, too; he's used to lying high up on the cliffs and looking down for his quarry so as to stalk it at night; but even a cougar has to take second to a mustang when it comes to sight."

The hours passed slowly. The sun baked us; the stones were too hot to touch; flies buzzed behind our ears; tarantulas peeped at us from holes. The afternoon slowly waned.

At dark we returned to where we had left Wallace and the cowboys. Frank had solved the problem of water supply, for he had found a little spring trickling from a cliff, which, by skillful management, produced enough drink for the horses. We had packed our water for camp use.

"You take the first watch to-night," said Jones to me after supper. "The mustangs might try to slip by our fire in the night and we must keep a watch for them. Call Wallace when your time's up. Now, fellows, roll in."

When the pink of dawn was shading white, we were at our posts. A long, hot day—interminably long, deadening to the keenest interest—passed, and still no mustangs came. We slept and watched again, in the grateful cool of night, till the third day broke.

The hours passed; the cool breeze changed to hot; the sun blazed over the cañon wall; the stones scorched; the flies buzzed. I fell asleep in the scant shade of the sage bushes and awoke, stifled and moist. The old plainsman, never weary, leaned with his back against a stone and watched, with narrow gaze, the cañon below. The steely walls hurt my eyes; the sky was like hot copper. Though nearly wild with heat and aching bones and muscles and the long hours of wait—wait—wait, I was ashamed to complain, for there sat the old man, still and silent. I routed out a hairy tarantula from under a stone and teased him into a frenzy with my stick, and tried to get up a fight between him and a scallop-backed horned-toad that blinked wonderingly at me. Then I espied a green lizard on a stone. The beautiful reptile was about a foot in length, bright green, dotted with red, and he had diamonds for eyes. Nearby a purple flower blossomed, delicate and pale, with a bee sucking at its golden heart. I observed then that the lizard had his jewel eyes upon the bee; he slipped to the edge of the stone, flicked out a long, red tongue, and tore the insect from its honeyed perch. Here were beauty, life and death; and I had been weary for something to look at, to think about, to distract me from the wearisome wait!

"Listen!" broke in Jones's sharp voice. His neck was stretched, his eyes were closed, his ear was turned to the wind.

With thrilling, reawakened eagerness, I strained my hearing. I caught a faint sound, then lost it.

"Put your ear to the ground," said Jones.

I followed his advice, and detected the rhythmic beat of galloping horses.

"The mustangs are coming, sure as you're born!" exclaimed Jones.

"There! See the cloud of dust!" cried he a minute later.

In the first bend of the cañon below, a splintered ruin of rock now lay under a rolling cloud of dust. A white flash appeared, a line of bobbing black objects, and more dust; then with a sharp pounding of hoofs, into clear vision shot a dense black band of mustangs, and well in front swung the White King.

"Look! Look! I never saw the beat of that—never in my born days!" cried Jones. "How they move! yet that white fellow isn't half-stretched out. Get your picture before they pass. You'll never see the beat of that."

With long manes and tails flying, the mustangs came on apace and passed us in a trampling roar, the white stallion in the front. Suddenly a shrill, whistling blast, unlike any sound I had ever heard, made the cañon fairly ring. The white stallion plunged back, and his band closed in behind him. He had seen our saddle horses. Then trembling, whinnying, and with arched neck and high-poised head, bespeaking his mettle, he advanced a few paces, and again whistled his shrill note of defiance. Pure creamy white he was, and built like a racer. He pranced, struck his hoofs hard and cavorted; then, taking sudden fright, he wheeled.

It was then, when the mustangs were pivoting, with the white in the lead, that Jones jumped upon the stone, fired his pistol and roared with all his strength. Taking his cue, I did likewise. The band huddled back again, uncertain and frightened, then broke up the cañon.

Jones jumped the ditch with surprising agility, and I followed close at his heels. When we reached our plunging horses, he shouted: "Mount, and hold this passage. Keep close in by that big stone at the turn so they can't run you down, or stampede you. If they head your way, scare them back."

Satan quivered, and when I mounted, reared and plunged. I had to hold him in hard, for he was eager to run. At the cliff wall I was at some pains to check him. He kept champing his bit and stamping his feet.

From my post I could see the mustangs flying before a cloud of dust. Jones was turning in his horse behind a large rock in the middle of the cañon, where he evidently intended to hide. Presently successive yells and shots from our comrades blended in a roar which the narrow box-cañon augmented and echoed from wall to wall. High the White Mustang reared, and above the roar whistled his snort of furious terror. His band wheeled with him and charged back, their hoofs ringing like hammers on iron.

The crafty old buffalo-hunter had hemmed the mustangs in a circle and had left himself free in the center. It was a wily trick, born of his quick mind and experienced eye.

The stallion, closely crowded by his followers, moved swiftly. I saw that he must pass near the stone. Thundering, crashing, the horses came on. Away beyond them I saw Frank and Wallace. Then Jones yelled to me: "Open up! open up!"

I turned Satan into the middle of the narrow passage, screaming at the top of my voice and discharging my revolver rapidly.

But the wild horses thundered on. Jones saw that they would not now be balked, and he spurred his bay directly in their path. The big horse, courageous as his intrepid master, dove forward.

Then followed confusion for me. The pound of hoofs, the snorts, a screaming neigh that was frightful, the mad stampede of the mustangs with a whirling cloud of dust, bewildered and frightened me so that I lost sight of Jones. Danger threatened and passed me almost before I was aware of it. Out of the dust a mass of tossing manes, foam-flecked black horses, wild eyes and lifting hoofs rushed at me. Satan, with a presence of mind that shamed mine, leaped back and hugged the wall. My eyes were blinded by dust; the smell of dust choked me. I felt a strong rush of wind and a mustang grazed my stirrup. Then they had passed, on the wings of the dust-laden breeze.

But not all, for I saw that Jones had, in some inexplicable manner, cut the White Mustang and two of his blacks out of the band. He had turned them back again and was pursuing them. The bay he rode had never before appeared to much advantage, and now, with his long, lean, powerful body in splendid action, imbued with the relentless will of his rider, what a picture he presented! How he did run! With all that, the White Mustang made him look dingy and slow. Nevertheless, it was a critical time in the wild career of that king of horses. He had been penned in a space two hundred by five hundred yards, half of which was separated from him by a wide ditch, a yawning chasm that he had refused; and behind him, always keeping on the inside, wheeled the yelling hunter, who savagely spurred his bay and whirled a deadly lasso. He had been cut off and surrounded; the very nature of the rocks and trails of the cañon threatened to end his freedom or his life. Certain it was he preferred to end the latter, for he risked death from the rocks as he went over them in long leaps.

Jones could have roped either of the two blacks, but he hardly noticed them. Covered with dust and splotches of foam, they took their advantage, turned on the circle toward the passage way and galloped by me out of sight. Again Wallace, Frank and Jim let out strings of yells and volleys. The chase was narrowing down. Trapped, the White Mustang King had no chance. What a grand spirit he showed! Frenzied as I was with excitement, the thought occurred to me that this was an unfair battle, that I ought to stand aside and let him pass. But the blood and lust of primitive instinct held me fast. Jones, keeping back, met his every turn. Yet always with lithe and beautiful stride the stallion kept out of reach of the whirling lariat.

"Close in!" yelled Jones, and his voice, powerful with a note of triumph, bespoke the knell of the king's freedom.

The trap closed in. Back and forth at the upper end the White Mustang worked; then rendered desperate by the closing in, he circled round nearer to me. Fire shone in his wild eyes. The wily Jones was not to be outwitted; he kept in the middle, always on the move, and he yelled to me to open up. I lost my voice again, and fired my last shot. Then the White Mustang burst into a dash of daring, despairing speed. It was his last magnificent effort. Straight for the wash at the upper end he pointed his racy, spirited head, and his white legs stretched far apart, twinkled and stretched again. Jones galloped to cut him off, and the yells he emitted were demoniacal. It was a long, straight race for the mustang, a short curve for the bay.

That the white stallion gained was as sure as his resolve to elude capture, and he never swerved a foot from his course. Jones might have headed him, but manifestly he wanted to ride with him, as well as to meet him, so in case the lasso went true, a terrible shock might be averted.

Up went Jones's arm as the space shortened, and the lasso ringed his head. Out it shot, lengthened like a yellow, striking snake, and fell just short of the flying white tail.

The White Mustang, fulfilling his purpose in a last

heroic display of power, sailed into the air, up and up, and over the wide wash like a white streak. Free! the dust rolled in a cloud from under his hoofs, and he vanished.

Jones's superb horse, crashing down on his haunches, just escaped sliding into the hole.

I awoke to the realization that Satan had carried me, in pursuit of the thrilling chase, all the way across the circle without my knowing it.

Jones calmly wiped the sweat from his face, calmly coiled his lasso, and calmly remarked:

"In trying to capture wild animals a man must never be too sure. Now what I thought my strong point was my weak point—the wash. I made sure no horse could ever jump that hole."

CHAPTER 7

Snake Gulch

Not far from the scene of our adventures with the White Streak, as we facetiously and appreciatively named the mustang, a deep, flat cave indented the cañon wall. By reason of its sandy floor and close proximity to Frank's trickling spring, we decided to camp in it. About dark, Lawson and Stewart straggled in on spent horses, and found awaiting them a bright fire, a hot supper and cheery comrades.

"Did yu fellars git to see him?" was the tall ranger's first question.

"Did we get to see him?" echoed five lusty voices as one. "We did!"

It was after Frank, in his plain, blunt speech, had told of our experience, that the long Arizonian gazed fixedly at Jones.

"Did yu acktully tech the air of thet mustang with a rope?"

In all his days Jones never had a greater compliment. By way of reply, he moved his big hand to a button of his coat, and, fumbling over it, unwound a string of long, white hairs, then said: "I pulled these out of his tail with my lasso; it missed his left hind hoof about six inches."

There were six of the hairs, pure, glistening white, and over three feet long. Stewart examined them in expressive silence, then passed them along; and when they reached me, they stayed.

The cave, lighted up by a blazing fire, appeared to me a forbidding, uncanny place. Small, peculiar round holes, and dark cracks, suggestive of hidden vermin, gave me a creepy feeling; and although not over-sensitive on the subject of crawling, creeping things, I voiced my disgust.

"Say, I don't like the idea of sleeping in this hole. I'll bet it's full of spiders, snakes and centipedes and other poisonous things."

Whatever there was in my inoffensive declaration to rouse the usually slumbering humor of the Arizonians, and the thinly veiled ridicule of Colonel Jones, and a mixture of both in my once loyal California friend, I am not prepared to state. Maybe it was the dry, sweet, cool air of Nail Cañon; maybe my suggestion awoke ticklish associations that worked themselves off thus; maybe it was the first instance of my committing myself to a breach of camp etiquette. Be that as it may, my innocently expressed sentiment gave rise to bewildering dissertations on entomology, and most remarkable and startling tales from first-hand experience.

"Like as not," began Frank in matter-of-fact tone. "Them's tarantuler holes all right. An' scorpions, centipedes an' rattlers always rustle with tarantulers. But we never mind them—not us fellers! We're used to sleepin' with them. Why, I often wake up in the night to see a big tarantuler on my chest, an' see him wink. Ain't thet so, Jim?"

"Shore as hell," drawled faithful, slow Jim.

"Reminds me how fatal the bits of a centipede is," took up Colonel Jones, complacently. "Once I was sitting in camp with a hunter, who suddenly hissed out: 'Jones, for God's sake don't budge! There's a centipede on your arm!' He pulled his Colt, and shot the blamed centipede off as clean as a whistle. But the bullet hit a steer in the leg; and would you believe it, the bullet carried so much poison that in less than two hours the steer died of blood poisoning. Centipedes are so poisonous they leave a blue trail on flesh just by crawling over it. Look there!"

He bared his arm, and there on the brown-corded flesh was a blue trail of something, that was certain. It might have been made by a centipede.

"This is a likely place for them," put in Wallace, emitting a volume of smoke and gazing round the cave walls with the eye of a connoisseur. "My archaeological pursuits have given me great experience with centipedes, as you may imagine, considering how many old tombs, caves and cliff-dwellings I have explored. This Algonkian rock is about the right stratum for centipedes to dig in. They dig somewhat after the manner of the fluviatile long-tailed decapod crustaceans, of the genera *Thoracostraca,* the common crawfish, you know. From that, of course, you can imagine, if a centipede can bite rock, what a biter he is."

I began to grew weak, and did not wonder to see Jim's long pipe fall from his lips. Frank looked pale around the gills, so to speak, but the gaunt Stewart never batted an eye.

"I camped here two years ago," he said, "an' the cave was alive with rock-rats, mice, snakes, horned-toads, lizards an' a big Gila monster, besides bugs, scorpions, rattlers, an' as fer tarantulers an' centipedes—say! I couldn't sleep fer the noise they made fightin'."

"I seen the same," concluded Lawson, as nonchalant as a wild-horse wrangler well could be. "An' as fer me, now I allus lays perfickly still when the centipedes an' tarantulers begin to drop from their holes in the roof, same as them holes up there. An' when they light on me, I never move, nor even breathe fer about five minutes. Then they take a notion I'm dead an' crawl off. But sure, if I'd breathed I'd been a goner!"

All of this was playfully intended for the extinction of an unoffending and impressionable tenderfoot.

With an admiring glance at my tormentors, I rolled out my sleeping-bag and crawled into it, vowing I would remain there even if devil-fish, armed with pikes, invaded our cave.

Late in the night I awoke. The bottom of the cañon and the outer floor of our cave lay bathed in white, clear moonlight. A dense, gloomy black shadow veiled the opposite cañon wall. High up the pinnacles and turrets pointed toward a resplendent moon. It was a weird, wonderful scene of beauty entrancing, of breathless, dreaming silence that seemed not of life. Then a hoot-owl lamented dismally, his call fitting the scene and the dead stillness; the echoes resounded from cliff to cliff, strangely mocking and hollow, at last reverberating low and mournful in the distance.

How long I lay there enraptured with the beauty of light and mystery of shade, thrilling at the lonesome lament of the owl, I have no means to tell; but I was awakened from my trance by the touch of something crawling over me. Promptly I raised my head. The cave was as light as day. There, sitting sociably on my sleeping-bag was a great black tarantula, as large as my hand.

For one still moment, notwithstanding my contempt for Lawson's advice, I certainly acted upon it to the letter. If ever I was quiet, and if ever I was cold, the time was then. My companions snored in blissful ignorance of my plight. Slight rustling sounds attracted my wary gaze from the old black sentinel on my knee. I saw other black spiders running to and fro on the silver, sandy floor. A giant, as large as a soft-shell crab, seemed to be meditating an assault upon Jones's ear. Another, grizzled and shiny with age or moonbeams—I could not tell which—pushed long, tentative feelers into Wallace's cap. I saw black spots darting over the roof. It was not a dream; the cave was alive with tarantulas!

Not improbably my strong impression that the spider on my knee deliberately winked at me was the result of memory, enlivening imagination. But it sufficed to bring to mind, in one rapid, consoling flash, the irrevocable law of destiny—that the deeds of the wicked return unto them again.

I slipped back into my sleeping-bag, with a keen consciousness of its nature, and carefully pulled the flap in place, which almost hermetically sealed me up.

"Hey! Jones! Wallace! Frank! Jim!" I yelled, from the depths of my safe refuge.

Wondering cries gave me glad assurance that they had awakened from their dreams.

"The cave's alive with tarantulas!" I cried, trying to hide my unholy glee.

"I'll be durned if it ain't!" exclaimed Frank.

"Shore it beats hell!" added Jim, with a shake of his blanket.

"Look out, Jones, there's one on your pillow!" shouted Wallace.

Whack! A sharp blow proclaimed the opening of hostilities.

Memory stamped indelibly every word of that incident; but innate delicacy prevents the repetition of all save the old warrior's concluding remarks: "!!!—place I was ever in! Tarantulas by the million—centipedes, scorpions, bats! Rattlesnakes, too, I'll swear. Look out, Wallace! there, under your blanket!"

From the shuffling sounds which wafted sweetly into my bed, I gathered that my long friend from California must have gone through motions creditable to a contortionist. An ensuing explosion from Jones proclaimed to the listening world that Wallace had thrown a tarantula

upon him. Further fearful language suggested the thought
that Colonel Jones had passed on the inquisitive spider to
Frank. The reception accorded the unfortunate tarantula,
no doubt scared out of its wits, began with a wild yell from
Frank and ended in pandemonium.

While the confusion kept up, with whacks and blows
and threshing about, with language such as never before
had disgraced a group of old campers, I choked with rap-
ture, and reveled in the sweetness of revenge.

When quiet reigned once more in the black and white
cañon, only one sleeper lay on the moon-silvered sand of
the cave.

At dawn, when I opened sleepy eyes, Frank, Jim, Stewart and Lawson had departed, as prearranged, with the
outfit, leaving the horses belonging to us and rations for
the day. Wallace and I wanted to climb the divide at the
break, and go home by way of Snake Gulch, and the Colonel acquiesced with the remark that his sixty-three years
had taught him there was much to see in the world. Coming to undertake it, we found the climb—except for slide
of a weathered rock—no great task, and we accomplished
it in half an hour, with breath to spare and no mishap to
horses.

But descending into Snake Gulch, which was only a
mile across the sparsely cedared ridge, proved to be tedious labor. By virtue of Satan's patience and skill, I
forged ahead; which advantage, however, meant more
risk for me because of the stones set in motion above.
They rolled and bumped and cut into me, and I sustained
many a bruise trying to protect the sinewy slender legs of
my horse. The descent ended without serious mishap.

Snake Gulch had a character and sublimity which cast
Nail Cañon into the obscurity of forgetfulness. The great
contrast lay in the diversity of structure. The rock was
bright red, with parapet of yellow, that leaned, heaved,

bulged outward. These emblazoned cliff walls, two thousand feet high, were cracked from turret to base; they bowled out at such an angle that we were afraid to ride under them. Mountains of yellow rock hung balanced, ready to tumble down at the first angry breath of the gods. We rode among carved stones, pillars, obelisks and sculptured ruined walls of a fallen Babylon. Slides reaching all the way across and far up the cañon wall obstructed our passage. On every stone silent green lizards sunned themselves, gliding swiftly as we came near to their marble homes.

We came into a region of wind-worn caves, of all sizes and shapes, high and low on the cliffs; but strange to say, only on the north side of the cañon they appeared with dark mouths open and uninviting. One, vast and deep, though far off, menaced us as might the cave of a tawny-maned king of beasts; yet it impelled, fascinated and drew us on.

"It's a long, hard climb," said Wallace to the Colonel, as we dismounted.

"Boys, I'm with you," came the reply. And he was with us all the way, as we clambered over the immense blocks and threaded a passage between them and pulled weary legs up, one after the other. So steep lay the jumble of cliff fragments that we lost sight of the cave long before we got near it. Suddenly we rounded a stone, to halt and gasp at the thing looming before us.

The dark portal of death or hell might have yawned there. A gloomy hole, large enough to admit a church, had been hollowed in the cliff by ages of nature's chiseling.

"Vast sepulcher of Time's past, give up thy dead!" cried Wallace, solemnly.

"Oh! dark Stygian cave forlorn!" quoted I, as feelingly as my friend.

Jones hauled us down from the clouds.

"Now, I wonder what kind of a prehistoric animal holed in here," said he.

Forever the one absorbing interest! If he realized the sublimity of this place, he did not show it.

The floor of the cave ascended from the very threshold. Stony ridges circled from wall to wall. We climbed till we were two hundred feet from the opening, yet we were not half-way to the dome. Our horses, browsing in the sage far below, looked like ants. So steep did the ascent become that we desisted; for if one of us had slipped on the smooth incline, the result would have been terrible. Our voices rang clear and hollow from the walls. We were so high that the sky was blotted out by the overhanging square, cornice-like top of the door; and the light was weird, dim, shadowy, opaque. It was a gray tomb.

"Waa-hoo!" yelled Jones with all the power of his wide, leather lungs.

Thousands of devilish voices rushed at us, seemingly on puffs of wind. Mocking, deep echoes bellowed from the ebon shades at the back of the cave, and the walls, taking them up, hurled them on again in fiendish concatenation.

We did not again break the silence of that tomb, where the spirits of ages lay in dusty shrouds; and we crawled down as if we had invaded a sanctuary and invoked the wrath of the gods.

We all proposed names: Montezuma's Amphitheater being the only rival of Jones's selection, Echo Cave, which we finally chose.

Mounting our horses again, we made twenty miles of Snake Gulch by noon, when we rested for lunch. All the way up we had played the boy's game of spying for sights, with the honors about even. It was a question if Snake Gulch ever before had such a raking over. Despite its name, however, we discovered no snakes.

From the sandy niche of a cliff where we lunched Wallace espied a tomb, and heralded his discovery with a victorious whoop. Digging in old ruins roused in him much the same spirit that digging in old books roused in me. Before we reached him, he had a big bowie-knife buried deep in the red, sandy floor of the tomb.

This one-time sealed house of the dead had been constructed of small stones, held together by a cement, the nature of which, Wallace explained, had never become clear to civilization. It was red in color and hard as flint, harder than the rocks it glued together. The tomb was half-round in shape, and its floor was a projecting shelf of cliff rock. Wallace unearthed bits of pottery, bone and finely braided rope, all of which, to our great disappointment, crumbled to dust in our fingers. In the case of the rope, Wallace assured us, this was a sign of remarkable antiquity.

In the next mile we traversed, we found dozens of these old cells, all demolished except a few feet of the walls, all despoiled of their onetime possessions. Wallace thought these depredations were due to Indians of our own time. Suddenly we came upon Jones, standing under a cliff, with his neck craned to a desperate angle.

"Now, what's that?" demanded he, pointing upward.

High on the cliff wall appeared a small, round protuberance. It was of the unmistakably red color of the other tombs; and Wallace, more excited than he had been in the cougar chase, said it was a sepulcher, and he believed it had never been opened.

From an elevated point of rock, as high up as I could well climb, I decided both questions with my glass. The tomb resembled nothing so much as a mud-wasp's nest, high on a barn wall. The fact that it had never been broken open quite carried Wallace away with enthusiasm.

"This is no mean discovery, let me tell you that," he declared. "I am familiar with the Aztec, Toltec and Pueblo ruins, and here I find no similarity. Besides, we are out of their latitude. An ancient race of people—very ancient indeed—lived in this cañon. How long ago, it is impossible to tell."

"They must have been birds," said the practical Jones. "Now, how'd that tomb ever get there? Look at it, will you?"

As near as we could ascertain, it was three hundred feet from the ground below, five hundred from the rim wall above, and could not possibly have been approached from the top. Moreover, the cliff wall was as smooth as a wall of human make.

"There's another one," called out Jones.

"Yes, and I see another; no doubt there are many of them," replied Wallace. "In my mind, only one thing possible accounts for their position. You observe they appear to be about level with each other. Well, once the cañon floor ran along that line, and in the ages gone by it has lowered, washed away by the rains."

This conception staggered us, but it was the only one conceivable. No doubt we all thought at the same time of the little rainfall in that arid section of Arizona.

"How many years?" queried Jones.

"Years! What are years?" said Wallace. "Thousands of years, ages have passed since the race who built these tombs lived."

Some persuasion was necessary to drag our scientific friend from the spot, where obviously helpless to do anything else, he stood and gazed longingly at the isolated tombs. The cañon widened as we proceeded; and hundreds of points that invited inspection, such as overhanging shelves of rock, dark fissures, caverns and ruins had to be passed by, for lack of time.

Still, a more interesting and important discovery was

to come, and the pleasure and honor of it fell to me. My eyes were sharp and peculiarly farsighted—the Indian sight, Jones assured me; and I kept them searching the walls in such places as my companions overlooked. Presently, under a large, bulging bluff, I saw a dark spot, which took the shape of a figure. This figure, I recollected, had been presented to my sight more than once, and now it stopped me. The hard climb up the slippery stones was fatiguing, but I did not hesitate, for I was determined to know. Once upon the ledge, I let out a yell that quickly set my companions in my direction. The figure I had seen was a dark, red devil, a painted image, rude, unspeakably wild, crudely executed, but painted by the hand of man. The whole surface of the cliff wall bore figures of all shapes—men, animals, birds and strange devices, some in red paint, mostly in yellow. Some showed the wear of time; others were clear and sharp.

Wallace puffed up to me, but he had wind enough left for another whoop. Jones puffed up also, and seeing the first thing a rude sketch of what might have been a deer or a buffalo, he commented thus: "Darn me if I ever saw an animal like that! Boys, this is a find, sure as you're born. Because not even the Piutes ever spoke of these figures. I doubt if they know they're here. And the cowboys and wranglers, what few ever get by here in a hundred years, never saw these things. Beats anything I ever saw on the Mackenzie, or anywhere else."

The meaning of some devices was as mystical as that of others was clear. Two blood-red figures of men, the larger dragging the smaller by the hair, while he waved aloft a blood-red hatchet or club, left little to conjecture. Here was the old battle of men, as old as life. Another group, two figures of which resembled the foregoing in form and action, battling over a prostrate form rudely feminine in outline, attested to an age when men were as

THE LAST OF THE PLAINSMEN   101

susceptible as they are in modern times, but more force-
ful and original. An odd yellow Indian waved aloft a red
hand, which striking picture suggested the idea that he
was an ancient Macbeth, listening to the knocking at the
gate. There was a character representing a great chief,
before whom many figures lay prostrate, evidently slain
or subjugated. Large red paintings, in the shape of bats,
occupied prominent positions, and must have represented gods or devils. Armies of marching men told of
that blight of nations old and young—war. These, and
birds unnameable, and beasts unclassable, with dots and
marks and hieroglyphics, recorded the history of a bygone people. Symbols they were of an era that had gone
into the dim past, leaving only these marks, forever unintelligible; yet while they stood, century after century,
ineffaceable, reminders of the glory, the mystery, the sadness of life.

"How could paint of any kind last so long?" asked
Jones, shaking his head doubtfully.

"That is the unsolvable mystery," returned Wallace.
"But the records are there. I am absolutely sure the paintings are a least a thousand years old. I have never seen
any tombs or paintings similar to them. Snake Gulch is a
find, and I shall some day study its wonders."

Sundown caught us within sight of Oak Spring, and
we soon trotted into camp to the welcoming chorus of the
hounds. Frank and the others had reached the cabin some
hours before. Supper was steaming on the hot coals with
a delicious fragrance.

Then came the pleasantest time of the day, after a long
chase or jaunt—the silent moments, watching the glowing
embers of the fire; the speaking moments when a red-
blooded story rang clear and true; the twilight moments,
when the wood-smoke smelled sweet.

Jones seemed unusually thoughtful. I had learned that

this preoccupation in him meant the stirring of old associations, and I waited silently. By and by Lawson snored mildly in a corner; Jim and Frank crawled into their blankets, and all was still. Wallace smoked his Indian pipe and hunted in firelit dreams.

"Boys," said our leader finally, "somehow the echoes dying away in that cave reminded me of the mourn of the big white wolves in the Barren Lands."

Wallace puffed huge clouds of white smoke, and I waited, knowing that I was to hear at last the story of the Colonel's great adventure in the Northland.

CHAPTER 8

Naza! Naza! Naza!

It was a waiting day at Fort Chippewayan. The lonesome, far-northern Hudson's Bay Trading Post seldom saw such life. Tepees dotted the banks of the Slave River and lines of blanketed Indians paraded its shores. Near the boat landing a group of chiefs, grotesque in semi-barbaric, semi-civilized splendor, but black-browed, austere-eyed, stood in savage dignity with folded arms and high-held heads. Lounging on the grassy bank were white men, traders, trappers and officials of the post.

All eyes were on the distant curve of the river where, as it lost itself in a fine-fringed bend of dark green, white-glinting waves danced and fluttered. A June sky lay blue in the majestic stream; ragged, spear-topped, dense green trees massed down to the water; beyond rose bold, bald-knobbed hills, in remote purple relief.

A long Indian arm stretched south. The waiting eyes discerned a black speck on the green, and watched it grow. A flatboat, with a man standing to the oars, bore down swiftly.

Not a red hand, nor a white one, offered to help the voyager in the difficult landing. The oblong, clumsy, heavily laden boat surged with the current and passed the dock despite the boatman's efforts. He swung his craft in below upon a bar and roped it fast to a tree. The Indians crowded above him on the bank. The boatman raised his powerful form erect, lifted a bronzed face which seemed set in craggy hardness, and cast from narrow eyes a keen, cool glance on those above. The silvery gleam in his fair hair told of years.

Silence, impressive as it was ominous, broke only to the rattle of camping paraphernalia, which the voyager threw to a level, grassy bench on the bank. Evidently this unwelcome visitor had journeyed from afar, and his boat, sunk deep into the water with its load of barrels, boxes and bags, indicated that the journey had only begun. Significant, too, were a couple of long Winchester rifles shining on a tarpaulin.

The cold-faced crowd stirred and parted to permit the passage of a tall, thin, gray personage of official bearing, in a faded military coat.

"Are you the musk-ox hunter?" he asked, in tones that contained no welcome.

The boatman greeted this peremptory interlocutor with a cool laugh—a strange laugh, in which the muscles of his face appeared not to play.

"Yes, I am the man," he said.

"The chiefs of the Chippewayan and Great Slave tribes have been apprised of your coming. They have held council and are here to speak with you."

At a motion from the commandant, the line of chieftains piled down to the level bench and formed a half-circle before the voyager. To a man who had stood before grim Sitting Bull and noble Black Thunder of the Sioux, and faced the falcon-eyed Geronimo, and glanced over the sights of a rifle at gorgeous-feathered, wild, free Comanches, this semi-circle of savages—lords of the north—was a sorry comparison. Bedaubed and be-trinketed, slouch, and slovenly, these low-statured chiefs belied in appearance their scorn-bright eyes and lofty mien. They made a sad group.

One who spoke in unintelligible language, rolled out a

haughty, sonorous voice over the listening multitude. When he had finished, a half-breed interpreter, in the dress of a white man, spoke at a signal from the commandant.

"He says listen to the great orator of the Chippewayan. He has summoned all the chiefs of the tribes south of Great Slave Lake. He has held council. The cunning of the pale-face, who comes to take the musk-oxen, is well known. Let the pale-face hunter return to his own hunting-grounds; let him turn his face from the north. Never will the chiefs permit the white man to take musk-oxen alive from their country. The Ageter, the Musk-ox, is their god. He gives them food and fur. He will never come back if he is taken away, and the reindeer will follow him. The chiefs and their people would starve. They command the pale-face hunter to go back. They cry Naza! Naza! Naza!"

"Say, for a thousand miles I've heard that word Naza!" returned the hunter, with mingled curiosity and disgust. "At Edmonton Indian runners started ahead of me, and every village I struck the redskins would crowd round me and an old chief would harangue at me, and motion me back, and point north with Naza! Naza! Naza! What does it mean?"

"No white man knows; no Indian will tell," answered the interpreter. "The traders think it means the Great Slave, the North Star, the North Spirit, the North Wind, the North Lights and Ageter, the musk-ox god."

"Well, say to the chiefs to tell Ageter I have been four moons on the way after some of his little Ageters, and I'm going to keep on after them."

"Hunter, you are most unwise," broke in the commandant, in his officious voice. "The Indians will never permit you to take a musk-ox alive from the north. They worship him, pray to him. It is a wonder you have not been stopped."

"Who'll stop me?"

"The Indians. They will kill you if you do not turn back."

"Faugh! to tell an American plainsman that!" The hunter paused a steady moment, with his eyelids narrowing over slits of blue fire. "There is no law to keep me out, nothing but Indian superstition and the greed of the Hudson's Bay people. And I am an old fox, not to be fooled by pretty baits. For years the officers of this fur-trading company have tried to keep out explorers. Even Sir John Franklin, an Englishman, could not buy food of them. The policy of the company is to side with the Indians, to keep out traders and trappers. Why? So they can keep on cheating the poor savages out of clothing and food by trading a few trinkets and blankets, a little tobacco and rum for millions of dollars worth of furs. Have I failed to hire man after man, Indian after Indian, not to know why I cannot get a helper? Have I, a plainsman, come a thousand miles alone to be scared by you, or a lot of craven Indians? Have I been dreaming of musk-oxen for forty years, to slink south now, when I begin to feel the north? Not I."

Deliberately every chief, with the sound of a hissing snake, spat in the hunter's face. He stood immovable while they perpetrated the outrage, then calmly wiped his cheeks, and in his strange, cool voice, addressed the intrepreter.

"Tell them thus they show their true qualities, to insult in council. Tell them they are not chiefs, but dogs. Tell them they are not even squaws, only poor, miserable starved dogs. Tell them I turn my back on them. Tell them the pale-face has fought real chiefs, fierce, bold, like eagles, and he turns his back on dogs. Tell them he is the one who could teach them to raise the musk-oxen and the reindeer, and to keep out the cold and the wolf. But they are blinded. Tell them the hunter goes north."

Through the council of chiefs ran a low mutter, as of gathering thunder.

True to his word, the hunter turned his back on them. As he brushed by, his eye caught a gaunt savage slipping from the boat. At the hunter's stern call, the Indian leaped ashore, and started to run. He had stolen a parcel, and would have succeeded in eluding its owner but for an unforeseen obstacle, as striking as it was unexpected.

A white man of colossal stature had stepped in the thief's passage, and laid two great hands on him. Instantly the parcel flew from the Indian, and he spun in the air to fall into the river with a sounding splash. Yells signaled the surprise and alarm caused by this unexpected incident. The Indian frantically swam to the shore. Whereupon the champion of the stranger in a strange land lifted a bag, which gave forth a musical clink of steel, and throwing it with the camp articles on the grassy bench, he extended a huge, friendly hand.

"My name is Rea," he said, in deep, cavernous tones.

"Mine is Jones," replied the hunter, and right quickly did he grip the proffered hand. He saw in Rea a giant, of whom he was but a stunted shadow. Six and one-half feet Rea stood, with yard-wide shoulders, a hulk of bone and brawn. His ponderous, shaggy head rested on a bull neck. His broad face, with its low forehead, its close-shut mastiff under jaw, its big, opaque eyes, pale and cruel as those of a jaguar, marked him a man of terrible brute force.

"Free-trader!" called the commandant. "Better think twice before you join fortunes with the musk-ox hunter."

"To hell with you an' your rantin', dog-eared redskins!" cried Rea. "I've run agin a man of my own kind, a man of my own country, an' I'm goin' with him."

With this he thrust aside some encroaching, gaping Indians so unconcernedly and ungently that they sprawled upon the grass.

Slowly the crowd mounted and once more lined the bank.

Jones realized that by some late-turning stroke of fortune, he had fallen in with one of the few free-traders of the province. These free-traders, from the very nature of their calling—which was to defy the fur company, and to trap and trade on their own account—were a hardy and intrepid class of men. Rea's worth to Jones exceeded that of a dozen ordinary men. He knew the ways of the north, the language of the tribes, the habits of animals, the handling of dogs, the uses of food and fuel. Moreover, it soon appeared that he was a carpenter and blacksmith.

"There's my kit," he said, dumping the contents of his bag. It consisted of a bunch of steel traps, some tools, a broken ax, a box of miscellaneous things such as trappers used, and a few articles of flannel. "Thievin' redskins," he added, in explanation of his poverty. "Not much of an outfit. But I'm the man for you. Besides, I had a pal onct who knew you on the plains, called you 'Buff' Jones. Old Jim Bent he was."

"I recollect Jim," said Jones. "He went down in Custer's last charge. So you were Jim's pal. That'd be a recommendation if you needed one. But the way you chucked the Indian overboard got me."

Rea soon manifested himself as a man of few words and much action. With the planks Jones had on board he heightened the stern and bow of the boat to keep out the beating waves in the rapids; he fashioned a steering-gear and a less awkward set of oars, and shifted the cargo so as to make more room in the craft.

"Buff, we're in for a storm. Set up a tarpaulin an' make a fire. We'll pretend to camp to-night. These Indians won't dream we'd try to run the river after dark, and we'll slip by under cover."

The sun glazed over; clouds moved up from the north; a cold wind swept the tips of the spruces, and rain commenced to drive in gusts. By the time it was dark not an Indian showed himself. They were housed from the storm. Lights twinkled in the tepees and the big log cabins of the trading company. Jones scouted round till pitchy black night, when a freezing, pouring blast sent him back to the protection of the tarpaulin. When he got there he found that Rea had taken it down and awaited him. "Off!" said the free-trader; and with no more noise than a drifting feather the boat swung into the current and glided down till the twinkling fires no longer accentuated the darkness.

By night the river, in common with all swift rivers, had a sullen voice, and murmured its hurry, its restraint, its menace, its meaning. The two boatmen, one at the steering gear, one at the oars, faced the pelting rain and watched the dim, dark line of trees. The craft slid noiselessly onward into the gloom.

And into Jones's ears, above the storm, poured another sound, a steady, muffled rumble, like the roll of giant chariot wheels. It had come to be a familiar roar to him, and the only thing which, in his long life of hazard, had ever sent the cold, prickling, tight shudder over his warm skin. Many times on the Athabasca that rumble had presaged the dangerous and dreaded rapids.

"Hell Bend Rapids!" shouted Rea. "Bad water, but no rocks."

The rumble expanded to a roar, the roar to a boom that charged the air with heaviness, with a dreamy burr. The whole indistinct world appeared to be moving to the lash of wind, to the sound of rain, to the roar of the river. The boat shot down and sailed aloft, met shock on shock,

breasted leaping dim white waves, and in a hollow, unearthly blend of watery sounds, rode on and on, buffeted,
tossed, pitched into a black chaos that yet gleamed with
obscure shrouds of light. Then the convulsive stream
shrieked out a last defiance, changed its course abruptly
to slow down and drown the sound of rapids in muffling
distance. Once more the craft swept on smoothly, to the
drive of the wind and the rush of the rain.

By midnight the storm cleared. Murky clouds split to
show shining, blue-white stars and a fitful moon, that silvered the crests of the spruces and sometimes hid like a
gleaming, black-threaded pearl behind the dark branches.

Jones, a plainsman all his days, wonderingly watched
the moon-blanched water. He saw it shade and darken
under shadowy walls of granite, where it swelled with
hollow song and gurgle. He heard again the far-off rumble, faint on the night wind. High cliff banks appeared,
walled out the mellow light, and the river suddenly narrowed. Yawning holes, whirlpools of a second, opened
with a gurgling suck and raced with the boat.

On the craft flew. Far ahead, a long, declining plane of
jumping frosted waves played dark and white with the
moonbeams. The Slave plunged to his freedom, down his
riven, stone-spiked bed, knowing no patient eddy, and
white-wreathed his dark, shiny rocks in spume and spray.

CHAPTER 9

The Land of the Musk-Ox

A far cry it was from bright June at Port Chippewayan to dim October on Great Slave Lake.

Two long, laborious months Rea and Jones threaded the crooked shores of the great inland sea, to halt at the extreme northern end, where a plunging outlet formed the source of a river. Here they found a stone chimney and fireplace standing among the darkened, decayed ruins of a cabin.

"We mustn't lose no time," said Rea. "I feel the winter in the wind. An' see how dark the days are gettin' on us."

"I'm for hunting musk-oxen," replied Jones.

"Man, we're facin' the northern night; we're in the land of the midnight sun. Soon we'll be shut in for seven months. A cabin we want, an' wood, an' meat."

A forest of stunted spruce trees edged on the lake, and soon its dreary solitudes rang to the strokes of axes. The trees were small and uniform in size. Black stumps protruded, here and there, from the ground, showing work of the steel in time gone by. Jones observed that the living trees were no larger in diameter than the stumps, and questioned Rea in regard to the difference in age.

"Cut twenty-five, mebbe fifty years ago," said the trapper.

"But the living trees are no bigger."

"Trees an' things don't grow fast in the northland."

They erected a fifteen-foot cabin round the stone

chimney, roofed it with poles and branches of spruce, and a layer of sand. In digging near the fireplace Jones unearthed a rusty file and the head of a whisky keg, upon which was a sunken word in unintelligible letters.

"We've found the place," said Rea. "Franklin built a cabin here in 1819. An' in 1833 Captain Back wintered here when he was in search of Captain Ross of the vessel *Fury*. It was those explorin' parties thet cut the trees. I seen Indian sign out there, made last winter, I reckon; but Indians never cut down no trees."

The hunters completed the cabin, piled cords of firewood outside, stowed away the kegs of dried fish and fruits, the sacks of flour, boxes of crackers, canned meats and vegetables, sugar, salt, coffee, tobacco—all of the cargo; then took the boat apart and carried it up the bank, which labor took them less than a week.

Jones found sleeping in the cabin, despite the fire, uncomfortably cold, because of the wide chinks between the logs. It was hardly better than sleeping under the swaying spruces. When he essayed to stop up the cracks—a task by no means easy, considering the lack of material—Rea laughed his short "Ho! Ho!" and stopped him with the word, "Wait." Every morning the green ice extended farther out into the lake; the sun paled dim and dimmer; the nights grew colder. On October 8th the thermometer registered several degrees below zero; it fell a little more next night and continued to fall.

"Ho! Ho!' cried Rea. "She's struck the toboggan, an' presently she'll commence to slide. Come on, Buff, we've work to do."

He caught up a bucket, made for their hole in the ice, rebroke a six-inch layer, the freeze of a few hours, and filling his bucket, returned to the cabin. Jones had no inkling of the trapper's intention, and wonderingly he soused his bucket full of water and followed.

By the time he had reached the cabin, a matter of some thirty or forty good paces, the water no longer splashed from his pail, for a thin film of ice prevented. Rea stood fifteen feet from the cabin, his back to the wind, and threw the water. Some of it froze in the air, most of it froze on the logs. The simple plan of the trapper to incase the cabin with ice was easily divined. All day the men worked, ceasing only when the cabin resembled a glistening mound. It had not a sharp corner nor a crevice. Inside it was warm and snug, and as light as when the chinks were open.

A slight moderation of the weather brought the snow. Such snow! A blinding white flutter of great flakes, as large as feathers! All day they rustled softly; all night they swirled, sweeping, seeping, brushing against the cabin. "Ho! Ho!" roared Rea. "'Tis good; let her snow, an' the reindeer will migrate. We'll have fresh meat." The sun shone again, but not brightly. A nipping wind cut down out of the frigid north and crusted the snow. The third night following the storm, when the hunters lay snug under their blankets, a commotion outside aroused them.

"Indians," said Rea, "come north for reindeer."

Half the night, shouting and yelling, barking of dogs, hauling of sleds and cracking of dried-skin tepees murdered sleep for those in the cabin. In the morning the level plain and edge of the forest held an Indian village. Caribou hides, strung on forked poles, constituted tent-like habitations with no distinguishable doors. Fires smoked in the holes in the snow. Not till late in the day did any life manifest itself round the tepees, and then a group of children, poorly clad in ragged pieces of blankets and skins, gaped at Jones. He saw their pinched, brown faces, staring, hungry eyes, naked legs and throats, and noted particularly their dwarfish size. When he spoke they fled precipitously a little way, then turned. He called again, and all ran except one small lad. Jones went into the cabin and came out with a handful of sugar in square lumps.

"Yellow Knife Indians," said Rea. "A starved tribe! We're in for it."

Jones made motions to the lad, but he remained still, as if transfixed, and his black eyes stared wonderingly.

"Molar nasu (white man good)," said Rea.

The lad came out of his trance and looked back at his companions, who edged nearer. Jones ate a lump of sugar, then handed one to the little Indian. He took it gingerly, put it into his mouth and immediately jumped up and down.

"Hoppieshampoolie! Hoppieshampoolie!" he shouted to his brothers and sisters. They came on the run.

"Think he means sweet salt," interpreted Rea. "Of course these beggars never tasted sugar."

The band of youngster trooped round Jones, and after tasting the white lumps, shrieked in such delight that the braves and squaws shuffled out of the tepees.

In all his days Jones had never seen such miserable Indians. Dirty blankets hid all their person, except straggling black hair, hungry, wolfish eyes and moccasined feet. They crowded into the path before the cabin door and mumbled and stared and waited. No dignity, no brightness, no suggestion of friendliness marked this peculiar attitude.

"Starved!" exclaimed Rea. "They've come to the lake to invoke the Great Spirit to send the reindeer. Buff, whatever you do, don't feed them. If you do, we'll have them on our hands all winter. It's cruel, but, man, we're in the north!"

Notwithstanding the practical trapper's admonition Jones could not resist the pleading of the children. He could not stand by and see them starve. After ascertaining there was absolutely nothing to eat in the tepees, he invited the little ones into the cabin, and made a great pot of soup, into which he dropped compressed biscuits. The savage children were like wildcats. Jones had to call in Rea to assist him in keeping the famished little boys from tearing each other to pieces. When finally they were all fed, they had to be driven out of the cabin.

"That's new to me," said Jones. "Poor little beggars!"

Rea doubtfully shook his shaggy head.

Next day Jones traded with the Yellow Knives. He had a goodly supply of baubles, besides blankets, gloves and boxes of canned goods, which he had brought for such trading. He secured a dozen of the large-boned, white and black Indian dogs—huskies, Rea called them—two long sleds with harness and several pairs of snowshoes. This trade made Jones rub his hands in satisfaction, for during all the long journey north he had failed to barter for such cardinal necessities to the success of his venture.

"Better have doled out the grub to them in rations," grumbled Rea.

Twenty-four hours sufficed to show Jones the wisdom of the trapper's words, for in just that time the crazed, ignorant savages had glutted the generous store of food, which should have lasted them for weeks. The next day they were begging at the cabin door. Rea cursed and threatened them with his fists, but they returned again and again.

Days passed. All the time, in light and dark, the Indians filled the air with dismal chant and doleful incantations to the Great Spirit, and the tum! tum! tum! tum! of tomtoms, a specific feature of their wild prayer for food.

But the white monotony of the rolling land and level lake remained unbroken. The reindeer did not come. The days became shorter, dimmer, darker. The mercury kept on the slide.

Forty degrees below zero did not trouble the Indians. They stamped till they dropped, and sang till their voices vanished, and beat the tomtoms everlastingly. Jones fed the children once each day, against the trapper's advice.

One day, while Rea was absent, a dozen braves succeeded in forcing an entrance, and clamored so fiercely, and threatened so desperately, that Jones was on the point of giving them food when the door opened to admit Rea.

With a glance he saw the situation. He dropped the bucket he carried, threw the door wide open and commenced action. Because of his great bulk he seemed slow, but every blow of his sledge-hammer fist knocked a brave against the wall, or through the door into the snow. When he could reach two savages at once, by way of diversion, he swung their heads together with a crack. They dropped like dead things. Then he handled them as if they were sacks of corn, pitching them out into the snow. In two minutes the cabin was clear. He banged the door and slipped the bar in place.

"Buff, I'm goin' to get mad at these thievin' redskins some day," he said gruffly. The expanse of his chest heaved slightly, like the slow swell of a calm ocean, but there was no other indication of unusual exertion.

Jones laughed, and again gave thanks for the comradeship of this strange man.

Shortly afterward, he went out for wood, and as usual scanned the expanse of the lake. The sun shone mistier and wanner, and frost feathers floated in the air. Sky and sun and plain and lake—all were gray. Jones fancied he saw a distant moving mass of darker shade than the gray background. He called the trapper.

"Caribou,' said Rea instantly. "The vanguard of the migration. Hear the Indians! Hear their cry: 'Aton! Aton!' they mean reindeer. The idiots have scared the herd with their infernal racket, an' no meat will they get. The caribou will keep to the ice, an' man or Indian can't stalk them there."

For a few moments his companion surveyed the lake and shore with a plainsman's eye, then dashed within, to reappear with a Winchester in each hand. Through the crowd of bewailing, bemoaning Indians he sped, to the low, dying bank. The hard crust of snow upheld him. The gray cloud was a thousand yards out upon the lake and moving southeast. If the caribou did not swerve from this course they would pass close to a projecting point of land, a half-mile up the lake. So, keeping a wary eye upon them, the hunter ran swiftly. He had not hunted antelope and buffalo on the plains all his life without learning how to approach moving game. As long as the caribou were in action, they could not tell whether he moved or was motionless. In order to tell if an object was inanimate or not, they must stop to see, of which fact the keen hunter took advantage. Suddenly he saw the gray mass slow down and bunch up. He stopped running, to stand like a stump. When the reindeer moved again, he moved, and when they slackened again, he stopped and became motionless. As they kept to their course, he worked gradually closer and closer. Soon he distinguished gray, bobbing heads. When the leader showed signs of halting in his slow trot the hunter again became a statue. He saw they were easy to deceive; and, daringly confident of success, he encroached on the ice and closed up the gap till not more than two hundred yards separated him from the gray, bobbing, antlered mass.

Jones dropped on one knee. A moment only his eyes lingered admiringly on the wild and beautiful spectacle; then he swept one of the rifles to a level. Old habit made the little beaded sight cover first the stately leader. Bang! The gray monarch leaped straight forward, forehoofs up,

antlered head back, to fall dead with a crash. Then for a
few moments the Winchester spat a deadly stream of fire,
and when emptied was thrown down for the other gun,
which in the steady, sure hands of the hunter belched
death to the caribou.

The herd rushed on, leaving the white surface of the
lake gray with a struggling, kicking, bellowing heap.
When Jones reached the caribou he saw several trying to
rise on crippled legs. With his knife he killed these, not
without some hazard to himself. Most of the fallen ones
were already dead, and the others soon lay still. Beautiful
gray creatures they were, almost white, with wide-reaching,
symmetrical horns.

A medley of yells arose from the shore, and Rea appeared running with two sleds, with the whole tribe of
Yellow Knives pouring out of the forest behind him.

"Buff, you're jest what old Jim said you was," thundered Rea, as he surveyed the gray pile. "Here's winter
meat, an' I'd not have given a biscuit for all the meat I
thought you'd get."

"Thirty shots in less than thirty seconds," said Jones,
"an' I'll bet every ball I sent touched hair. How many reindeer?"

"Twenty! twenty! Buff, or I've forgot how to count. I
guess mebbe you can't handle them shootin' arms. Ho!
here comes the howlin' redskins."

Rea whipped out a bowie knife and began disembowel-
ing the reindeer. He had not proceeded far in his task
when the crazed savages were around him. Every one
carried a basket or receptacle, which he swung aloft, and
they sang, prayed, rejoiced on their knees. Jones turned
away from the sickening scenes that convinced him these
savages were little better than cannibals. Rea cursed
them, and tumbled them over, and threatened them with
the big bowie. An altercation ensued, heated on his side,

frenzied on theirs. Thinking some treachery might befall his comrade, Jones ran into the thick of the group.

"Share with them, Rea, share with them."

Whereupon the giant hauled out ten smoking carcasses. Bursting into a babel of savage glee and tumbling over one another, the Indians pulled the caribou to the shore.

"Thievin' fools!" growled Rea, wiping the sweat from his brow. "Said they'd prevailed on the Great Spirit to send the reindeer. Why, they'd never smelled warm meat but for you. Now, Buff, they'll gorge every hair, hide an' hoof of their share in less than a week. Thet's the last we do for the damned cannibals. Didn't you see them eatin' of the raw innards!—faugh! I'm calculatin' we'll see no more reindeer. It's late for the migration. The big herd has driven southward. But we're lucky, thanks to your prairie trainin'. Come on now with the sleds, or we'll have a pack of wolves to fight."

By loading three reindeer on each sled, the hunters were not long in transporting them to the cabin. "Buff, there ain't much doubt about them keepin' nice and cool," said Rea. "They'll freeze, an' we can skin them when we want."

That night the starved wolf dogs gorged themselves till they could not rise from the snow. Likewise the Yellow Knives feasted. How long the ten reindeer might have served the wasteful tribe, Rea and Jones never found out. The next day two Indians arrived with dog-trains, and their advent was hailed with another feast, and a pow-wow that lasted into the night.

"Guess we're goin' to get rid of our blasted hungry neighbors," said Rea, coming in next morning with the water pail, "an' I'll be durned, Buff, if I don't believe them crazy heathen have been told about you. Them Indians was messengers. Grab your gun, an' let's walk over and see."

The Yellow Knives were breaking camp, and the hunters were at once conscious of the difference in their bearing. Rea addressed several braves, but got no reply. He laid his broad hand on the old wrinkled chief, who repulsed him, and turned his back. With a growl, the trapper spun the Indian round, and spoke as many words of the language as he knew. He got a cold response, which ended in the ragged old chief starting up, stretching a long, dark arm northward, and with eyes fixed in fanatical subjection, shouting: "Naza! Naza! Naza!"

"Heathen!" Rea shook his gun in the faces of the messengers. "It'll go bad with you to come Nazain' any longer on our trail. Come, Buff, clear out before I get mad."

When they were once more in the cabin, Rea told Jones that the messengers had been sent to warn the Yellow Knives not to aid the white hunters in any way. That night the dogs were kept inside, and the men took turns in watching. Morning showed a broad trail southward. And with the going of the Yellow Knives the mercury dropped to fifty, and the long, twilight winter night fell.

So with this agreeable riddance and plenty of meat and fuel to cheer them, the hunters sat down in their snug cabin to wait many months for daylight.

Those few intervals when the wind did not blow were the only times Rea and Jones got out of doors. To the plainsman, new to the north, the dim gray world about him was of exceeding interest. Out of the twilight shone a wan, round, lusterless ring that Rea said was the sun. The silence and desolation were heart-numbing.

"Where are the wolves?" asked Jones of Rea.

"Wolves can't live on snow. They're farther south after caribou, or farther north after musk-ox."

In those few still intervals Jones remained out as long as he dared, with the mercury sinking to sixty degrees. He turned from the wonder of the unreal, remote sun, to the marvel in the north—Aurora borealis—ever-present, ever-changing, ever-beautiful! and he gazed in rapt attention.

"Polar lights," said Rea, as if he were speaking of biscuits. "You'll freeze. It's gettin' cold."

Cold it became, to the matter of seventy degrees. Frost covered the walls of the cabin and the roof, except just over the fire. The reindeer were harder than iron. A knife or an ax or a steel-trap burned as if it had been heated in fire, and stuck to the hand. The hunters experienced trouble in breathing; the air hurt their lungs.

The months dragged. Rea grew more silent day by day, and as he sat before the fire his wide shoulders sagged lower and lower. Jones, unaccustomed to the waiting, the restraint, the barrier of the north, worked on guns, sleds, harness, till he felt he would go mad. Then to save his mind he constructed a windmill of caribou hides and pondered over it, trying to invent, to put into practical use an idea he had once conceived.

Hour after hour he lay under his blankets unable to sleep, and listened to the north wind. Sometimes Rea mumbled in his slumbers; once his giant form started up, and he muttered a woman's name. Shadows from the fire flickered on the walls, visionary, spectral shadows, cold and gray, fitting the north. At such times he longed with all the power of his soul to be among those scenes far southward, which he called home. For days Rea never spoke a word, only gazed into the fire, ate and slept. Jones, drifting far from his real self, feared the strange mood of the trapper and sought to break it, but without avail. More and more he reproached himself, and singularly on the one fact that, as he did not smoke himself, he had brought only a small store of tobacco. Rea, inordinate and inveterate smoker, had puffed away all the weed in clouds of white, then had relapsed into gloom.

CHAPTER 10

Success and Failure

A t last the marvel in the north dimmed, the obscure gray shade lifted, the hope in the south brightened, and the mercury climbed—reluctantly, with a tyrant's hate to relinquish power.

Spring weather at twenty-five below zero! On April 12th a small band of Indians made their appearance. Of the Dog tribe were they, an off-cast of the Great Slaves, according to Rea, and as motley, staring and starved as the Yellow Knives. But they were friendly, which presupposed ignorance of the white hunters, and Rea persuaded the strongest brave to accompany them as guide northward after musk-oxen.

On April 16th, having given the Indians several caribou carcasses, and assuring them that the cabin was protected by white spirits, Rea and Jones, each with sled and train of dogs, started out after their guide, who was similarly equipped, over the glistening snow toward the north. They made sixty miles the first day, and pitched their Indian tepee on the shores of Artillery Lake. Traveling northeast, they covered its white waste of one hundred miles in two days. Then a day due north, over rolling, monotonously snowy plain, devoid of rock, tree or shrub, brought them into a country of the strangest, queerest little spruce trees, very slender, and none of them over fifteen feet in height. A primeval forest of saplings.

"Ditchen Nechila!" said the guide.

"Land of Sticks Little," translated Rea.

An occasional reindeer was seen and numerous foxes and hares trotted off into the woods, evincing more curiosity than fear. All were silver white, even the reindeer, at a distance, taking the hue of the north. Once a beautiful creature, unblemished as the snow it trod, ran up a ridge and stood watching the hunters. It resembled a monster dog, only it was inexpressibly more wild looking.

"Ho! Ho! there you are!" cried Rea, reaching for his Winchester. "Polar wolf! Them's the white devils we'll have hell with."

As if the wolf understood, he lifted his white, sharp head and uttered a bark or howl that was like nothing so much as a haunting, unearthly mourn. The animal then merged into the white, as if he were really a spirit of the world whence his cry seemed to come.

In this ancient forest of youthful appearing trees, the hunters cut firewood to the full carrying capacity of the sleds. For five days the Indian guide drove his dogs over the smooth crust, and on the sixth day, about noon, halting in a hollow, he pointed to tracks in the snow and called out: "Ageter! Ageter! Ageter!"

The hunters saw sharply defined hoof-marks, not unlike the tracks of reindeer, except that they were longer. The tepee was set up on the spot and the dogs unharnessed.

The Indian led the way with the dogs, and Rea and Jones followed, slipping over the hard crust without sinking in and traveling swiftly. Soon the guide, pointing, again let out the cry: "Ageter!" at the same moment loosing the dogs.

Some few hundred yards down the hollow, a number of large black animals, not unlike the shaggy, humpy buffalo, lumbered over the snow. Jones echoed Rea's yell, and broke into a run, easily distancing the puffing giant.

The musk-oxen squared round to the dogs, and were

soon surrounded by the yelping pack. Jones came up to find six old bulls uttering grunts of rage and shaking ram-like horns at their tormentors. Notwithstanding that for Jones this was the cumulation of years of desire, the crowning moment, the climax and fruition of long-harbored dreams, he halted before the tame and helpless beasts, with joy not unmixed with pain.

"It will be murder!" he exclaimed. "It's like shooting down sheep."

Rea came crashing up behind him and yelled: "Get busy. We need fresh meat, an' I want the skins."

The bulls succumbed to well-directed shots, and the Indian and Rea hurried back to camp with the dogs to fetch the sleds, while Jones examined with warm interest the animals he had wanted to see all his life. He found the largest bull approached within a third of the size of a buffalo. He was of a brownish-black color and very like a large, woolly ram. His head was broad, with sharp, small ears; the horns had wide and flattened bases and lay flat on the head, to run down back of the eyes, then curve forward to a sharp point. Like the bison, the musk-ox had short, heavy limbs, covered with very long hair, and small, hard hoofs with hairy tufts inside the curve of bone, which probably served as pads or checks to hold the hoof firm on ice. His legs seemed out of proportion to his body.

Two musk-oxen were loaded on a sled and hauled to camp in one trip. Skinning them was but short work for such expert hands. All the choice cuts of meat were saved. No time was lost in broiling a steak, which they found sweet and juicy, with a flavor of musk that was disagreeable.

"Now, Rea, for the calves," exclaimed Jones, "and then we're homeward bound."

"I hate to tell this redskin," replied Rea. "He'll be like

the others. But it ain't likely he'd desert us here. He's far
from his base, with nothin' but thet old musket." Rea
then commanded the attention of the brave, and began
to mangle the Great Slave and Yellow Knife languages.
Of this mixture Jones knew but few words. "Ageter nechila," which Rea kept repeating, he knew, however, meant
"musk-oxen little."

The guide stared, suddenly appeared to get Rea's
meaning, then vigorously shook his head and gazed at
Jones in fear and horror. Following this came an action
as singular as inexplicable. Slowly rising, he faced the
north, lifted his hand, and remained statuesque in his im-
mobility. Then he began deliberately packing his blankets
and traps on his sled, which had not been unhitched from
the train of dogs.

"Jackoway ditchen hula," he said, and pointèd south.

"Jackoway ditchen hula," echoed Rea. "The damned Indian says 'wife sticks none.' He's goin' to quit us. What do
you think of thet? His wife's out of wood. Jackoway out of
wood, an' here we are two days from the Arctic Ocean!
Jones, the damned heathen don't go back!"

The trapper coolly cocked his rifle. The savage, who
plainly saw and understood the action, never flinched. He
turned his breast to Rea, and there was nothing in his demeanor to suggest his relation to a craven tribe.

"Good heavens, Rea, don't kill him!" exclaimed Jones,
knocking up the leveled rifle.

"Why not, I'd like to know?" demanded Rea, as if he
were considering the fate of a threatening beast. "I reckon
it'd be a bad thing for us to let him go."

"Let him go," said Jones. "We are here on the ground.
We have dogs and meat. We'll get our calves and reach
the lake as soon as he does, and we might get there before."

"Mebbe we will," growled Rea.

No vacillation attended the Indian's mood. From a friendly guide, he had suddenly been transformed into a dark, sullen savage. He refused the musk-ox meat offered by Jones, and he pointed south and looked at the white hunters as if he asked them to go with him. Both men shook their heads in answer. The savage struck his breast a sounding blow and with his index finger pointed at the white of the north, he shouted dramatically: "Naza! Naza! Naza!"

He then leaped upon his sled, lashed his dogs into a run, and without looking back disappeared over a ridge.

The musk-ox hunters sat long silent. Finally Rea shook his shaggy locks and roared. "Ho! Ho! Jackoway out of wood! Jackoway out of wood! Jackoway out of wood!"

On the day following the desertion, Jones found tracks to the north of the camp, making a broad trail in which were numerous little imprints that sent him flying back to get Rea and the dogs. Musk-oxen in great numbers had passed in the night, and Jones and Rea had not trailed the herd a mile before they had it in sight. When the dogs burst into full cry, the musk-oxen climbed a high knoll and squared about to give battle.

"Calves! Calves! Calves!" cried Jones.

"Hold back! Hold back! Thet's a big herd, an' they'll show fight."

As good fortune would have it, the herd split up into several sections, and one part, hard pressed by the dogs, ran down the knoll, to be cornered under the lee of a bank. The hunters, seeing this small number, hurried upon them to find three cows and five badly frightened little calves backed against the bank of snow, with small red eyes fastened on the barking, snapping dogs.

To a man of Jones's experience and skill, the capturing of the calves was a ridiculously easy piece of work. The cows tossed their heads, watched the dogs, and forgot their young. The first cast of the lasso settled over the neck of a little fellow. Jones hauled him out over the slippery snow and laughed as he bound the hairy legs. In less time than he had taken to capture one buffalo calf, with half the effort, he had all the little musk-oxen bound fast. Then he signaled this feat by pealing out an Indian yell of victory.

"Buff, we've got 'em," cried Rea; "an' now for the hell of it—gettin' 'em home. I'll fetch the sleds. You might as well down thet best cow for me. I can use another skin."

Of all Jones's prizes of captured wild beasts—which numbered nearly every species common to western North America—he took greatest pride in the little musk-oxen. In truth, so great had been his passion to capture some of these rare and inaccessible mammals, that he considered the day's work the fulfillment of his life's purpose. He was happy. Never had he been so delighted as when, the very evening of their captivity, the musk-oxen, evincing no particular fear of him, began to dig with sharp hoofs into the snow for moss. And they found moss, and ate it, which solved Jones's greatest problem. He had hardly dared to think how to feed them, and here they were picking sustenance out of the frozen snow.

"Rea, will you look at that! Rea, will you look at that!" he kept repeating. "See, they're hunting feed."

And the giant, with his rare smile, watched him play with the calves. They were about two and a half feet high, and resembled long-haired sheep. The ears and horns were undiscernible, and their color considerably lighter than that of the matured beasts.

"No sense of fear of man," said the life-student of animals. "But they shrink from the dogs."

In packing for the journey south, the captives were

strapped on the sleds. This circumstance necessitated a sacrifice of meat and wood, which brought grave, doubtful shakes of Rea's great head.

Days of hastening over the icy snow, with short hours for sleep and rest, passed before the hunters awoke to the consciousness that they were lost. The meat they had packed had gone to feed themselves and the dogs. Only a few sticks of wood were left.

"Better kill a calf, an' cook meat while we've got a little wood left," suggested Rea.

"Kill one of my calves? I'd starve first!" cried Jones.

The hungry giant said no more.

They headed southwest. All about them glared the grim monotony of the arctics. No rock or bush or tree made a welcome mark upon the hoary plain Wonderland of frost, white marble desert, infinitude of gleaming silences!

Snow began to fall, making the dogs flounder, obliterating the sun by which they traveled. They camped to wait for clearing weather. Biscuits soaked in tea made their meal. At dawn Jones crawled out of the tepee. The snow had ceased. But where were the dogs? He yelled in alarm. Then little mounds of white, scattered here and there, became animated, heaved, rocked and rose to fall to pieces, exposing the dogs. Blankets of snow had been their covering.

Rea had ceased his "Jackoway out of wood," for a reiterated question: "Where are the wolves?"

"Lost," replied Jones in hollow humor.

Near the close of that day, in which they had resumed travel, from the crest of a ridge they descried a long, low, undulating dark line. It proved to be the forest of "little sticks," where, with grateful assurance of fire and of soon finding their old trail, they made camp.

"We've four biscuits left, an' enough tea for one drink

each," said Rea. "I calculate we're two hundred miles from Great Slave Lake. Where are the wolves?"

At that moment the night wind wafted through the forest a long, haunting mourn. The calves shifted uneasily; the dogs raised sharp noses to sniff the air, and Rea, settling back against a tree, cried out: "Ho! Ho!" Again the savage sound, a keen wailing note with the hunger of the northland in it, broke the cold silence. "You'll see a pack of real wolves in a minute," said Rea. Soon a swift pattering of feet down a forest slope brought him to his feet with a curse to reach a brawny hand for his rifle. White streaks crossed the black of the tree trunks; then indistinct forms, the color of snow, swept up, spread out and streaked to and fro. Jones thought the great, gaunt, pure white beasts the spectral wolves of Rea's fancy, for they were silent, and silent wolves must belong to dreams only.

"Ho! Ho!" yelled Rea. "There's green-fire eyes for you, Buff. Hell itself ain't nothin' to these white devils. Get the calves in the tepee, an' stand ready to loose the dogs, for we've got to fight."

Raising his rifle he opened fire upon the white foe. A struggling, rustling sound followed the shots. But whether it was the threshing about of wolves dying in agony, or the fighting of the fortunate ones over those shot, could not be ascertained in the confusion.

Following his example Jones also fired rapidly on the other side of the tepee. The same inarticulate, silently rustling wrestle succeeded this volley.

"Wait!" cried Rea. "Be sparin' of cartridges."

The dogs strained at their chains and bravely bayed the wolves. The hunters heaped logs and brush on the fire, which, blazing up, sent a bright light far into the woods. On the outer edge of that circle moved the white, restless, gliding forms.

"They're more afraid of fire than of us," said Jones.

So it proved. When the fire burned and crackled they kept well in the background. The hunters had a long respite from serious anxiety, during which time they collected all the available wood at hand. But at midnight, when this had been mostly consumed, the wolves grew bold again.

"Have you any shots left for the 45–90, besides what's in the magazine?" asked Rea.

"Yes, a good handful."

"Well, get busy."

With careful aim Jones emptied the magazine into the gray, gliding, groping mass. The same rustling, shuffling, almost silent strife ensued.

"Rea, there's something uncanny about those brutes. A silent pack of wolves!"

"Ho! Ho!" rolled the giant's answer through the woods.

For the present the attack appeared to have been effectually checked. The hunters, sparingly adding a little of their fast diminishing pile of fuel to the fire, decided to lie down for much needed rest, but not for sleep. How long they lay there, cramped by the calves, listening for stealthy steps, neither could tell; it might have been moments and it might have been hours. All at once came a rapid rush of pattering feet, succeeded by a chorus of angry barks, then a terrible commingling of savage snarls, growls, snaps and yelps.

"Out!" yelled Rea. "They're on the dogs!"

Jones pushed his cocked rifle ahead of him and straightened up outside the tepee. A wolf, large as a panther and white as the gleaming snow, sprang at him. Even as he discharged his rifle, right against the breast of the beast, he saw its dripping jaws, its wicked green eyes, like spurts of fire and felt its hot breath. It fell at his feet and writhed in the death struggle. Slender bodies of black and white, whirling and tussling together, sent out fiendish uproar.

Rea threw a blazing stick of wood among them, which sizzled as it met the furry coats, and brandishing another he ran into the thick of the fight. Unable to stand the proximity of fire, the wolves bolted and loped off into the woods.

"What a huge brute!" exclaimed Jones, dragging the one he had shot into the light. It was a superb animal, thin, supple, strong, with a coat of frosty fur, very long and fine. Rea began at once to skin it, remarking that he hoped to find other pelts in the morning.

Though the wolves remained in the vicinity of camp, none ventured near. The dogs moaned and whined; their restlessness increased as dawn approached, and when the gray light came, Jones found that some of them had been badly lacerated by the fangs of the wolves. Rea hunted for dead wolves and found not so much as a piece of white fur.

Soon the hunters were speeding southward. Other than a disposition to fight among themselves, the dogs showed no evil effects of the attack. They were lashed to their best speed, for Rea said the white rangers of the north would never quit their trail. All day the men listened for the wild, lonesome, haunting mourn. But it came not.

A wonderful halo of white and gold, that Rea called a sun-dog, hung in the sky all afternoon, and dazzlingly bright over the dazzling world of snow, circled and glowed a mocking sun, brother of the desert mirage, beautiful illusion, smiling cold out of the polar blue.

The first pale evening star twinkled in the east when the hunters made camp on the shore of Artillery Lake. At dusk the clear, silent air opened to the sound of a long, haunting mourn.

"Ho! Ho!" called Rea. His hoarse, deep voice rang defiance to the foe.

While he built a fire before the tepee, Jones strode up

and down, suddenly to whip out his knife and make for the tame little musk-oxen, now digging in the snow. Then he wheeled abruptly and held out the blade to Rea.

"What for?" demanded the giant.

"We've got to eat," said Jones. "And I can't kill one of them. I can't, so you do it."

"Kill one of our calves?" roared Rea. "Not till hell freezes over! I ain't commenced to get hungry. Besides, the wolves are going to eat us, calves and all."

Nothing more was said. They ate their last biscuit. Jones packed the calves away in the tepee, and turned to the dogs. All day they had worried him; something was amiss with them, and even as he went among them a fierce fight broke out. Jones saw it was unusual, for the attacked dogs showed craven fear, and the attacking ones a howling, savage intensity that surprised him. Then one of the vicious brutes rolled his eyes, frothed at the mouth, shuddered and leaped in his harness, vented a hoarse howl and fell back shaking and retching.

"My God! Rea!" cried Jones in horror. "Come here! Look! That dog is dying of rabies! Hydrophobia! The white wolves have hydrophobia!"

"If you ain't right!" exclaimed Rea. "I seen a dog die of thet onct, an' he acted like this. An' thet one ain't all. Look, Buff! look at them green eyes! Didn't I say the white wolves was hell? We'll have to kill every dog we've got."

Jones shot the dog, and soon afterward three more that manifested signs of the disease. It was an awful situation. To kill all the dogs meant simply to sacrifice his life and Rea's; it meant abandoning hope of ever reaching the cabin. Then to risk being bitten by one of the poisoned, maddened brutes, to risk the most horrible of agonizing deaths—that was even worse.

"Rea, we've one chance," cried Jones, with pale face.

"Can you hold the dogs, one by one, while I muzzle them?"

"Ho! Ho!" replied the giant. Placing his bowie knife between his teeth, with gloved hands he seized and dragged one of the dogs to the campfire. The animal whined and protested, but showed no ill spirit. Jones muzzled his jaws tightly with strong cords. Another and another were tied up, then one which tried to snap at Jones was nearly crushed by the giant's grip. The last, a surly brute, broke out into mad ravings the moment he felt the touch of Jones's hands, and writhing, frothing, he snapped Jones's sleeve. Rea jerked him loose and held him in the air with one arm, while with the other he swung the bowie. They hauled the dead dogs out on the snow, and returning to the fire sat down to await the cry they expected.

Presently, as darkness fastened down tight, it came— the same cry, wild, haunting, mourning. But for hours it was not repeated.

"Better rest some," said Rea; "I'll call you if they come."

Jones dropped to sleep as he touched his blankets. Morning dawned for him, to find the great, dark, shadowy figure of the giant nodding over the fire.

"How's this? Why didn't you call me?" demanded Jones.

"The wolves only fought a little over the dead dogs."

On the instant Jones saw a wolf skulking up the bank. Throwing up his rifle, which he had carried out of the tepee, he took a snap-shot at the beast. It ran off on three legs, to go out of sight over the bank. Jones scrambled up the steep, slippery place, and upon arriving at the ridge, which took several moments of hard work, he looked everywhere for the wolf. In a moment he saw the animal, standing still some hundred or more paces down a hollow. With the quick report of Jones's second shot, the wolf fell and rolled over. The hunter ran to the spot to find the wolf was dead. Taking hold of a front paw, he dragged the animal over the snow to camp. Rea began to skin the animal, when suddenly he exclaimed:

"This fellow's hind foot is gone!"

"That's strange. I saw it hanging by the skin as the wolf ran up the bank. I'll look for it."

By the bloody trail on the snow he returned to the place where the wolf had fallen, and thence back to the spot where its leg had been broken by the bullet. He discovered no sign of the foot.

"Didn't find it, did you?" said Rea.

"No, and it appears odd to me. The snow is so hard the foot could not have sunk."

"Well, the wolf ate his foot, thet's what," returned Rea. "Look at them teeth marks!"

"Is it possible?" Jones stared at the leg Rea held up.

"Yes, it is. These wolves are crazy at times. You've seen thet. An' the smell of blood, an' nothin' else, mind you, in my opinion, made him eat his own foot. We'll cut him open."

Impossible as the thing seemed to Jones—and he could not but believe further evidence of his own eyes—it was even stranger to drive a train of mad dogs. Yet that was what Rea and he did, and lashed them, beat them to cover many miles in the long day's journey. Rabies had broken out in several dogs so alarmingly that Jones had to kill them at the end of the run. And hardly had the sound of the shots died when faint and far away, but clear as a bell, bayed on the wind the same haunting mourn of a trailing wolf.

"Ho! Ho!' where are the wolves?" cried Rea.

A waiting, watching, sleepless night followed. Again the hunters faced the south. Hour after hour, riding, running, walking, they urged the poor, jaded, poisoned dogs.

At dark they reached the head of Artillery Lake. Rea placed the tepee between two huge stones. Then the hungry hunters, tired, grim, silent, desperate, awaited the familiar cry.

It came on the cold wind, the same haunting mourn, dreadful in its significance.

Absence of fire inspirited the wary wolves. Out of the pale gloom gaunt white forms emerged, agile and stealthy, slipping on velvet-padded feet, closer, closer, closer. The dogs wailed in terror.

"Into the tepee!" yelled Rea.

Jones plunged in after his comrade. The despairing howls of the dogs, drowned in more savage, frightful sounds, knelled one tragedy and foreboded a more terrible one. Jones looked out to see a white mass, like leaping waves of a rapid.

"Pump lead into thet!" cried Rea.

Rapidly Jones emptied his rifle into the white fray. The mass split; gaunt wolves leaped high to fall back dead; others wriggled and limped away; others dragged their hind quarters; others darted at the tepee.

"No more cartridges!" yelled Jones.

The giant grabbed the ax, and barred the door of the tepee. Crash! the heavy iron cleaved the skull of the first brute. Crash! it lamed the second. Then Rea stood in the narrow passage between the rocks, waiting with uplifted ax. A shaggy, white demon, snapping his jaws, sprang like a dog. A sodden, thudding blow met him and he slunk away without a cry. Another rabid beast launched his white body at the giant. Like a flash the ax descended. In agony the wolf fell, to spin round and round, running on his hind legs, while his head and shoulders and forelegs remained in the snow. His back was broken.

Jones crouched in the opening of the tepee, knife in hand. He doubted his senses. This was a nightmare. He saw two wolves leap at once. He heard the crash of the ax; he saw one wolf go down and the other slip under the swinging weapon to grasp the giant's hip. Jones heard the rend of cloth, and then he pounced like a cat, to drive his knife into the body of the beast. Another nimble foe lunged at Rea, to sprawl broken and limp from the iron. It was a silent fight. The giant shut the way to his comrade and the calves; he made no outcry; he needed but one blow for every beast; magnificent, he wielded death and faced it—silent. He brought the white wild dogs of the north down with lightning blows, and when no more sprang to the attack, down on the frigid silence he rolled his cry: "Ho! Ho!"

"Rea! Rea! how is it with you?" called Jones, climbing out.

"A torn coat—no more, my lad."

Three of the poor dogs were dead; the fourth and last gasped at the hunters and died.

The wintry night became a thing of half-conscious past, a dream to the hunters, manifesting its reality only by the stark, stiff bodies of wolves, white in the gray morning.

"If we can eat, we'll make the cabin," said Rea. "But the dogs an' wolves are poison."

"Shall I kill a calf?" asked Jones.

"Ho! Ho! when hell freezes over—if we must!"

Jones found one 45-90 cartridge in all the outfit, and with that in the chamber of his rifle, once more struck south. Spruce trees began to show on the barrens and caribou trails roused hope in the hearts of the hunters.

"Look! in the spruces," whispered Jones, dropping the rope of his sled. Among the black trees gray objects moved.

"Caribou!" said Rea. "Hurry! Shoot! Don't miss!"

But Jones waited. He knew the value of the last bullet.

He had a hunter's patience. When the caribou came out in an open space, Jones whistled. It was then the rifle grew set and fixed; it was then the red fire belched forth.

At four hundred yards the bullet took some fraction of time to strike. What a long time that was! Then both hunters heard the spiteful spat of the lead. The caribou fell, jumped up, ran down the slope, and fell again to rise no more.

An hour of rest, with fire and meat, changed the world to the hunters; still glistening, it yet had lost its bitter cold, its deathlike clutch.

"What's this?" cried Jones.

Moccasin tracks of different sizes, all toeing north, arrested the hunters.

"Pointed north! Wonder what thet means?" Rea plodded on, doubtfully shaking his head.

Night again, clear, cold, silver, starlit, silent night! The hunters rested, listening ever for the haunting mourn. Day again, white, passionless, monotonous, silent day! The hunters traveled on—on—on, ever listening for the haunting mourn.

Another dusk found them within thirty miles of their cabin. Only one more day now.

Rea talked of his furs, of the splendid white furs he could not bring. Jones talked of his little musk-oxen calves and joyfully watched them dig for moss in the snow.

Vigilance relaxed that night. Outworn nature rebelled, and both hunters slept.

Rea awoke first, and kicking off the blankets, went out. His terrible roar of rage made Jones fly to his side.

Under the very shadow of the tepee, where the little musk-oxen had been tethered, they lay stretched out pathetically on crimson snow—stiff, stone-cold, dead. Moccasin tracks told the story of the tragedy.

Jones leaned against his comrade.

The giant raised his huge fist.

"Jackoway out of wood! Jackoway out of wood!"

Then he choked.

The north wind, blowing through the thin, dark, weird spruce trees, moaned and seemed to sigh, "Naza! Naza! Naza!"

CHAPTER 11

On to the Siwash

"**W**ho all was doin' the talkin' last night?" asked Frank next morning, when we were having a late breakfast. "Cause I've a joke on somebody. Jim he talks in his sleep often, an' last night after you did finally get settled down, Jim he up in his sleep an' says: 'Shore he's windy as hell! Shore he's windy as hell'!"

At this cruel exposure of his subjective wanderings, Jim showed extreme humiliation; but Frank's eyes fairly snapped with the fun he got out of telling it. The genial foreman loved a joke. The week's stay at Oak, in which we all became thoroughly acquainted, had presented Jim as always the same quiet character, easy, slow, silent, lovable. In his brother cowboy, however, we had discovered in addition to his fine, frank, friendly spirit, an overwhelming fondness for playing tricks. This boyish mischievousness, distinctly Arizonian, reached its acme whenever it tended in the direction of our serious leader.

Lawson had been dispatched on some mysterious errand about which my curiosity was all in vain. The order of the day was leisurely to get in readiness, and pack for our journey to the Siwash on the morrow. I watered my horse, played with the hounds, knocked about the cliffs, returned to the cabin, and lay down on my bed. Jim's hands were white with flour. He was kneading dough, and had several low, flat pans on the table. Wallace and Jones strolled in, and later Frank, and they all took various positions before the fire. I saw Frank, with the quickness of a sleight-of-hand performer, slip one of the pans of dough on the chair Jones had placed by the table. Jim did not see the action; Jones's and Wallace's backs were turned to Frank, and he did not know I was in the cabin. The conversation continued on the subject of Jones's big bay horse, which, hobbles and all, had gotten ten miles from camp the night before.

"Better count his ribs than his tracks," said Frank, and went on talking as easily and naturally as if he had not been expecting a very entertaining situation.

But no one could ever foretell Colonel Jones's actions. He showed every intention of seating himself in the chair, then walked over to his pack to begin searching for something or other. Wallace, however, promptly took the seat; and what began to be funnier than strange, he did not get up. Not unlikely this circumstance was owing to the fact that several of the rude chairs had soft layers of old blanket tacked on them. Whatever were Frank's internal emotions, he presented a remarkably placid and commonplace exterior; but when Jim began to search for the missing pan of dough, the joker slowly sagged in his chair.

"Shore that beats hell!" said Jim. "I had three pans of dough. Could the pup have taken one?"

Wallace rose to his feet, and the bread pan clattered to the floor, with a clang and a clank, evidently protesting against the indignity it had suffered. But the dough stayed with Wallace, a great white conspicuous splotch on his corduroys. Jim, Frank and Jones all saw it at once.

"Why—Mr. Wal—lace—you set—in the dough!" exclaimed Frank, in a queer, strangled voice. Then he exploded, while Jim fell over the table.

It seemed that those two Arizona rangers, matured men though they were, would die of convulsions. I laughed with them, and so did Wallace, while he brought his bone-handled bowie knife into novel use. Buffalo Jones never cracked a smile, though he did remark about the waste of good flour.

Frank's face was a study for a psychologist when Jim actually apologized to Wallace for being so careless with his pans. I did not betray Frank, but I resolved to keep a still closer watch on him. It was partially because of this uneasy sense of his trickiness in the fringe of my mind that I made a discovery. My sleeping-bag rested on a raised platform in one corner, and at a favorable moment I examined the bag. It had not been tampered with, but I noticed a string running out through a chink between the logs. I found it came from a thick layer of straw under my bed, and had been tied to the end of a flatly coiled lasso. Leaving the thing as it was, I went outside and carelessly chased the hounds round the cabin. The string stretched along the logs to another chink, where it returned into the cabin at a point near where Frank slept. No great power of deduction was necessary to acquaint me with full details of the plot to spoil my slumbers. So I patiently awaited developments.

Lawson rode in near sundown with the carcasses of two beasts of some species hanging over his saddle. It turned out that Jones had planned a surprise for Wallace and me, and it could hardly have been a more enjoyable one, considering the time and place. We knew he had a flock of Persian sheep on the south slope of Buckskin, but had no idea it was within striking distance of Oak. Lawson had that day hunted up the shepherd and his sheep, to return to us with two sixty-pound Persian lambs. We feasted at suppertime on meat which was sweet, juicy, very tender and of as rare a flavor as that of the Rocky Mountain sheep.

My state after supper was one of huge enjoyment and

with intense interest I awaited Frank's first spar for an opening. It came presently, in a lull of the conversation.

"Saw a big rattler run under the cabin to-day," he said, as if he were speaking of one of Old Baldy's shoes. "I tried to get a whack at him, but he oozed away too quick."

"Shore I seen him often," put in Jim. Good, old, honest Jim, led away by his trickster comrade! It was very plain. So I was to be frightened by snakes.

"These old cañon beds are ideal dens for rattlesnakes," chimed in my scientific California friend. "I have found several dens, but did not molest them as this is a particularly dangerous time of the year to meddle with the reptiles. Quite likely there's a den under the cabin."

While he made this remarkable statement, he had the grace to hide his face in a huge puff of smoke. He, too, was in the plot. I waited for Jones to come out with some ridiculous theory or fact concerning the particular species of snake, but as he did not speak, I concluded they had wisely left him out of the secret. After mentally debating a moment, I decided, as it was a very harmless joke, to help Frank to the fulfillment of his enjoyment.

"Rattlesnakes!" I exclaimed. "Heavens! I'd die if I heard one, let alone seeing it. A big rattler jumped at me one day, and I've never recovered from the shock."

Plainly, Frank was delighted to hear of my antipathy and my unfortunate experience, and he proceeded to expatiate on the viciousness of rattlesnakes, particularly those of Arizona. If I had believed the succeeding stories, emanating from the fertile brains of those three fellows, I should have made certain that Arizona cañons were Brazilian jungles. Frank's parting shot, sent in a mellow, kind voice, was the best point in the whole trick. "Now, I'd be nervous if I had a sleepin'-bag like yours, because it's just the place for a rattler to ooze into."

In the confusion and dim light of bedtime I contrived

to throw the end of my lasso over the horn of a saddle hanging on the wall, with the intention of augmenting the noise I soon expected to create; and I placed my automatic rifle and .38 S. & W. Special within easy reach of my hand. Then I crawled into my bag and composed myself to listen. Frank soon began to snore, so brazenly, so fictitiously, that I wondered at the man's absorbed intensity in his joke; and I was at great pains to smother in my breast a violent burst of riotous merriment. Jones's snores, however, were real enough, and this made me enjoy the situation all the more; because if he did not show a mild surprise when the catastrophe fell, I would greatly miss my guess. I knew the three wily conspirators were wide-awake. Suddenly I felt a movement in the straw under me and a faint rustling. It was so soft, so sinuous, that if I had not known it was the lasso, I would assuredly have been frightened. I gave a little jump, such as one will make quickly in bed. Then the coil ran out from under the straw. How subtly suggestive of a snake! I made a slight outcry, a big jump, paused a moment for effectiveness—in which time Frank forgot to snore—then let out a tremendous yell, grabbed my guns, sent twelve thundering shots through the roof and pulled my lasso.

Crash! the saddle came down, to be followed by sounds not on Frank's programme and certainly not calculated upon by me. But they were all the more effective. I gathered that Lawson, who was not in the secret, and who was a nightmare sort of sleeper anyway, had knocked over Jim's table, with its array of pots and pans and then, unfortunately for Jones, had kicked that innocent person in the stomach.

As I lay there in my bag, the very happiest fellow in the wide world, the sound of my mirth was as the buzz of the wings of a fly to the mighty storm. Roar on roar filled the cabin.

When the three hypocrites recovered sufficiently from the startling climax to calm Lawson, who swore the cabin had been attacked by Indians; when Jones stopped roaring long enough to hear it was only a harmless snake that had caused the trouble, we hushed to repose once more—not, however, without hearing some trenchant remarks from the boiling Colonel anent fun and fools, and the indubitable fact that there was not a rattlesnake on Buckskin Mountain.

Long after this explosion had died away, I heard, or rather felt; a mysterious shudder or tremor of the cabin, and I knew that Frank and Jim were shaking with silent laughter. On my own score, I determined to find if Jones, in his strange make-up, had any sense of humor, or interest in life, or feeling, or love that did not center and hinge on four-footed beasts. In view of the rude awakening from what, no doubt, were pleasant dreams of wonderful white and green animals, combining the intelligence of man and strength of brutes—a new species creditable to his genius— I was perhaps unjust in my conviction as to his lack of humor. And as to the other question, whether or not he had any real human feeling for the creatures built in his own image, that was decided very soon and unexpectedly.

The following morning, as soon as Lawson got in with the horses, we packed and started. Rather sorry was I to bid good-by to Oak Spring. Taking the back trail of the Stewarts, we walked the horses all day up a slowly narrowing, ascending cañon. The hounds crossed coyote and deer trails continually, but made no break. Sounder looked up as if to say he associated painful reminiscences with certain kinds of tracks. At the head of the cañon we reached timber at about the time dust gathered, and we located for the night. Being once again nearly nine thousand feet high, we found the air bitterly cold, making a blazing fire most acceptable.

In the haste to get supper we all took a hand, and some one threw upon our tarpaulin tablecloth a tin cup of butter mixed with carbolic acid—a concoction Jones had used to bathe the sore feet of the dogs. Of course I got hold of this, spread a generous portion on my hot biscuit, placed some red-hot beans on that, and began to eat like a hungry hunter. At first I thought I was only burned. Then I recognized the taste and burn of the acid and knew something was wrong. Picking up the tin, I examined it, smelled the pungent odor, and felt a strange, numb sense of fear. This lasted only for a moment, as I well knew the use and power of the acid, and had not swallowed enough to hurt me. I was about to make known my mistake in a matter-of-fact way, when it flashed over me the accident could be made to serve a turn.

"Jones!" I cried hoarsely. "What's in this butter?"

"Lord! you haven't eaten any of that. Why, I put carbolic acid in it."

"Oh—oh—oh—I'm poisoned! I ate nearly all of it! Oh—I'm burning up! I'm dying!" With that I began to moan and rock to and fro and hold my stomach.

Consternation preceded shock. But in the excitement of the moment, Wallace—who, though badly scared, retained his wits—made for me with a can of condensed milk. He threw me back with no gentle hand, and was squeezing the life out of me to make me open my mouth, when I gave him a jab in his side. I imagined his surprise, as this peculiar reception of his first-aid-to-the-injured made him hold off to take a look at me, and in this interval I contrived to whisper to him: "Joke! Joke! you idiot! I'm only shamming. I want to see if I can scare Jones and get even with Frank. Help me out! Cry! Get tragic!"

From that moment I shall always believe that the stage lost a great tragedian in Wallace. With a magnificent gesture he threw the can of condensed milk at Jones, who was so stunned he did not try to dodge. "Thoughtless man! Murderer! it's too late!" cried Wallace, laying me back across his knees. "It's too late. His teeth are locked. He's far gone. Poor boy! poor boy! Who's to tell his mother?"

I could see from under my hat-brim that the solemn, hollow voice had penetrated the cold exterior of the plainsman. He could not speak; he clasped and un-clasped his big hands in helpless fashion. Frank was as white as a sheet. This was simply delightful to me. But the expression of miserable, impotent distress on old Jim's sun-browned face was more than I could stand, and I could no longer keep up the deception. Just as Wallace cried out to Jones to pray—I wished then I had not weak-ened so soon—I got up and walked to the fire.

"Jim, I'll have another biscuit, please."

His under jaw dropped, then he nervously shoveled biscuits at me. Jones grabbed my hand and cried out with a voice that was new to me: "You can eat? You're better? You'll get over it?"

"Sure. Why, carbolic acid never phases me. I've often used it for rattlesnake bites. I did not tell you, but that rat-tler at the cabin last night actually bit me, and I used car-bolic to cure the poison."

Frank mumbled something about horses, and faded into the gloom. As for Jones, he looked at me rather in-credulously, and the absolute, almost childish gladness he manifested because I had been snatched from the grave, made me regret my deceit, and satisfied me forever on one score.

On awakening in the morning I found frost half an inch thick covered my sleeping-bag, whitened the ground, and made the beautiful silver spruce trees silver in hue as well as in name.

We were getting ready for an early start, when two rid-ers, with pack-horses jogging after them, came down the trail from the direction of Oak Spring. They proved to be Jeff Clarke, the wild-horse wrangler mentioned by the Stewarts, and his helper. They were on the way into the breaks for a string of pintos. Clarke was a short, heavily bearded man, of jovial aspect. He said he had met the Stewarts going into Fredonia, and being advised of our destination, had hurried to come up with us. As we did not know, except in a general way, where we were making for, the meeting was a fortunate event.

Our camping site had been close to the divide made by one of the long, wooded ridges sent off by Buckskin Mountain, and soon we were descending again. We rode half a mile down a timbered slope, and then out into a beautiful, flat forest of gigantic pines. Clarke informed us it was a level bench some ten miles long, running out from the slopes of Buckskin to face the Grand Cañon on the south, and the breaks of the Siwash on the west. For two hours we rode between the stately lines of trees, and the hoofs of the horses gave forth no sound. A long, silvery grass, sprinkled with smiling bluebells, covered the ground, except close under the pines, where soft red mats invited lounging and rest. We saw numerous deer, great gray mule deer, almost as large as elk. Jones said they had been crossed with elk once, which accounted for their size. I did not see a stump, or a burned tree, or a windfall during the ride.

Clarke led us to the rim of the cañon. Without any preparation—for the giant trees hid the open sky—we rode right out to the edge of the tremendous chasm. At first I did not seem to think; my faculties were benumbed; only the pure sensorial instinct of the savage who sees, but does not feel, made me take note of the abyss. Not one of our party had ever seen the cañon from this side, and not one of us said a word. But Clarke kept talking.

"Wild place this is hyar," he said. "Seldom any one but

horse wranglers gits over this far. I've hed a bunch of wild pintos down in a cañon below fer two years. I reckon you can't find no better place fer camp than right hyar. Listen. Do you hear thet rumble? Thet's Thunder Falls. You can only see it from one place, an' thet far off, but thar's brooks you can git at to water the hosses. Fer thet matter, you can ride up the slopes an' git snow. If you can git snow close, it'd be better, fer thet's an all-fired bad trail down fer water."

"Is this the cougar country the Stewarts talked about?" asked Jones.

"Reckon it is. Cougars is as thick in hyar as rabbits in a spring-hole cañon. I'm on the way now to bring up my pintos. The cougars hev cost me hundreds—I might say thousands of dollars. I lose hosses all the time; an' damn me, gentlemen, I've never raised a colt. This is the greatest cougar country in the West. Look at those yellow crags! Thar's where the cougars stay. No one ever hunted 'em. It seems to me they can't be hunted. Deer and wild hosses by the thousand browse hyar on the mountain in summer, an' down in the breaks in winter. The cougars live fat. You'll find deer and wild-hoss carcasses all over this country. You'll find lions's dens full of bones. You'll find warm deer left for the coyotes. But whether you'll find the cougars, I can't say. I fetched dogs in hyar, an' tried to ketch Old Tom. I've put them on his trail an' never saw hide nor hair of them again. Jones, it's no easy huntin' hyar."

"Well, I can see that," replied our leader. "I never hunted lions in such a country, and never knew any one who had. We'll have to learn how. We've the time and the dogs, all we need is the stuff in us."

"I hope you fellars git some cougars, an' I believe you will. Whatever you do, kill Old Tom."

"We'll catch him alive. We're not on a hunt to kill cougars," said Jones.

"What!" exclaimed Clarke, looking from Jones to us. His rugged face wore a half-smile.

"Jones ropes cougars, an' ties them up," replied Frank.

"I'll be damned if he'll ever rope Old Tom," burst out Clarke, ejecting a huge quid of tobacco. "Why, man alive! it'd be the death of you to git near thet old villain. I never seen him, but I've seen his tracks fer five years. They're larger than any hoss tracks you ever seen. He'll weigh over three hundred, thet old cougar. Hyar, take a look at my man's hoss. Look at his back. See them marks? Wal, Old Tom made them, an' he made them right in camp last fall, when we were down in the cañon."

The mustang to which Clarke called our attention was a sleek cream and white pinto. Upon his side and back were long regular scars, some an inch wide, and bare of hair.

"How on earth did he get rid of the cougar?" asked Jones.

"I don't know. Perhaps he got scared of the dogs. It took thet pinto a year to git well. Old Tom is a real lion. He'll kill a full-grown hoss when he wants, but a yearlin' colt is his especial likin'. You're sure to run acrost his trail, an' you'll never miss it. Wal, if I find any cougar sign down in the cañon, I'll build two fires so as to let you know. Though no hunter, I'm tolerably acquainted with the varmints. The deer an' hosses are rangin' the forest slopes now, an' I think the cougars come up over the rim rock at night an' go back in the mornin'. Anyway, if your dogs can follow the trails, you've got sport, an' more'n sport comin' to you. But take it from me—don't try to rope Old Tom."

After all our disappointments in the beginning of the expedition, our hardship on the desert, our trials with the dogs and horses, it was real pleasure to make permanent camp with wood, water and feed at hand, a soul-stirring, ever-changing picture before us, and the certainty that we were in the wild lairs of the lions—among the Lords of the Crags!

While we were unpacking, every now and then I would straighten up and gaze out beyond. I knew the outlook was magnificent and sublime beyond words, but as yet I had not begun to understand it. The great pine trees, growing to the very edge of the rim, received their full quota of appreciation from me, as did the smooth, flower-decked aisles leading back into the forest.

The location we selected for camp was a large glade, fifty paces or more from the precipice—far enough, the cowboys averred, to keep our traps from being sucked down by some of the whirlpool winds, native to the spot. In the center of this glade stood a huge gnarled and blasted old pine, that certainly by virtue of hoary locks and bent shoulders had earned the right to stand aloof from his younger companions. Under this tree we placed all our belongings, and then, as Frank so felicitously expressed it, we were free to "ooze round an' see things."

I believe I had a sort of subconscious, selfish idea that some one would steal the cañon away from me if I did not hurry to make it mine forever; so I sneaked off, and sat under a pine growing on the very rim. At first glance, I saw below me, seemingly miles away, a wild chaos of red and buff mesas rising out of dark purple clefts. Beyond these reared a long, irregular tableland, running south almost to the extent of my vision, which I remembered Clarke had called Powell's Plateau. I remembered, also, that he had said it was twenty miles distant, was almost that many miles long, was connected to the mainland of Buckskin Mountain by a very narrow wooded dip of land called the Saddle, and that it practically shut us out of a view of the Grand Cañon proper. If that was true, what, then, could be the name of the cañon at my feet? Suddenly, as my gaze wandered from point to point, it was arrested by a dark, conical mountain, white-tipped, which rose in the notch of the Saddle. What could it mean? Were there such things as cañon mirages? Then the dim purple of its color told of its great distance from me; and then its familiar shape told I had come into my own again—I had found my old friend once more. For in all that plateau there was only one snow-capped mountain—the San Francisco Peak; and there, a hundred and fifty, perhaps two hundred miles away, far beyond the Grand Cañon, it smiled brightly at me, as it had for days and days across the desert.

Hearing Jones yelling for somebody or everybody, I jumped up to find a procession heading for a point farther down the rim wall, where our leader stood waving his arms. The excitement proved to have been caused by cougar signs at the head of the trail where Clarke had started down.

"They're here, boys, they're here," Jones kept repeating, as he showed us different tracks. "This sign is not so old. Boys, tomorrow we'll get up a lion, sure as you're born. And if we do, and Sounder sees him, then we've got a lion-dog! I'm afraid of Don. He has a fine nose; he can run and fight, but he's been trained to deer, and maybe I can't break him. Moze is still uncertain. If old Jude only hadn't been lamed! She would be the best of the lot. But Sounder is our hope. I'm almost ready to swear by him."

All this was too much for me, so I slipped off again to be alone, and this time headed for the forest. Warm patches of sunlight, like gold, brightened the ground; dark patches of sky, like ocean blue, gleamed between the treetops. Hardly a rustle of wind in the fine-toothed green branches disturbed the quiet. When I got fully out of sight of camp, I started to run as if I were a wild Indian. My running had no aim; just sheer mad joy of the grand old forest, the smell of pine, the wild silence and beauty loosed the spirit in me so it had to run, and I ran with it till the physical being failed.

While resting on a fragrant bed of pine needles, endeavoring to regain control over a truant mind, trying to subdue the encroaching of the natural man on the civilized man, I saw gray objects moving under the trees. I lost them, then saw them, and presently so plainly that, with delight on delight, I counted seventeen deer pass through an open arch of dark green. Rising to my feet, I ran to get round a low mound. They saw me and bounded away with prodigiously long leaps. Bringing their forefeet together, stiff-legged under them, they bounced high, like rubber balls, yet they were graceful.

The forest was so open that I could watch them for a long way; and as I circled with my gaze, a glimpse of something white arrested my attention. A light, grayish animal appeared to be tearing at an old stump. Upon nearer view, I recognized a wolf, and he scented or sighted me at the same moment, and loped off into the shadows of the trees. Approaching the spot where I had marked him I found he had been feeding from the carcass of a horse. The remains had been only partly eaten, and were of an animal of the mustang build that had evidently been recently killed. Frightful lacerations under the throat showed where a lion had taken fatal hold. Deep furrows in the ground proved how the mustang had sunk his hoofs, reared and shaken himself. I traced roughly defined tracks fifty paces to the lee of a little bank, from which I concluded the lion had sprung.

I gave free rein to my imagination and saw the forest dark, silent, peopled by none but its savage denizens. The lion crept like a shadow, crouched noiselessly down, then leaped on his sleeping or browsing prey. The lonely night stillness split to a frantic snort and scream of terror, and the stricken mustang with his mortal enemy upon his back, dashed off with fierce, wild love of life. As he went he felt his foe crawl toward his neck on claws of fire; he saw the tawny body and the gleaming eyes; then the cruel teeth snapped with the sudden bite, and the woodland tragedy ended.

On the spot I conceived an antipathy toward lions. It was born of the frightful spectacle of what had once been a glossy, prancing mustang, of the mute, sickening proof of the survival of the fittest, of the law that levels life.

Upon telling my camp-fellows about my discovery, Jones and Wallace walked out to see it, while Jim told me the wolf I had seen was a "lofer," one of the giant buffalo wolves of Buckskin; and if I would watch the carcass in the mornings and evenings, I would "shore as hell get a plunk at him."

White pine burned in a beautiful, clear blue flame, with no smoke; and in the center of the campfire left a golden heart. But Jones would not have any sitting up, and hustled us off to bed, saying we would be "blamed" glad of it in about fifteen hours. I crawled into my sleeping-bag, made a hood of my Navajo blanket, and peeping from under it, watched the fire and the flickering shadows. The blaze burned down rapidly. Then the stars blinked. Arizona stars would be moons in any other State! How serene, peaceful, august, infinite and wonderfully bright! No breeze stirred the pines. The clear tinkle of the cowbells on the hobbled horses rang from near and distant parts of the forest. The prosaic bell of the meadow and the pasture brook, here, in this environment, jingled out different notes, as clear, sweet, musical as silver bells.

CHAPTER 12

Old Tom

At daybreak our leader routed us out. The frost man-
tled the ground so heavily that it looked like snow,
and the rare atmosphere bit like the breath of winter. The
forest stood solemn and gray; the cañon lay wrapped in
vapory slumber.

Hot biscuits and coffee, with a chop or two of the delicious Persian lamb meat, put a less Spartan tinge on the
morning, and gave Wallace and me more strength—we
needed not incentive—to leave the fire, hustle our saddles
on the horses and get in line with our impatient leader.
The hounds scampered over the frost, shoving their noses
at the tufts of grass and bluebells. Lawson and Jim remained in camp; the rest of us trooped southwest.

A mile or so in that direction, the forest of pine ended
abruptly, and a wide belt of low, scrubby oak trees, breast
high to a horse, fringed the rim of the cañon and appeared
to broaden out and grow wavy southward. The edge of
the forest was as dark and regular as if a band of wood-
choppers had trimmed it. We threaded our way through
this thicket, all peering into the bisecting deer trails for
cougar tracks in the dust.

"Bring the dogs! Hurry!" suddenly called Jones from a
thicket.

We lost no time complying, and found him standing in
a trail, with his eyes on the sand. "Take a look, boys. A

good-sized male cougar passed here last night. Hyar, Sounder, Don, Moze, come on!"

It was a nervous, excited pack of hounds. Old Jude got to Jones first, and she sang out; then Sounder opened with his ringing bay, and before Jones could mount, a string of yelping dogs sailed straight for the forest.

"Ooze along, boys!" yelled Frank, wheeling Spot.

With the cowboy leading, we strung into the pines, and I found myself behind. Presently even Wallace disappeared. I almost threw the reins at Satan, and yelled for him to go. The result enlightened me. Like an arrow from a bow, the black shot forward. Frank had told me of his speed, that when he found his stride it was like riding a flying feather to be on him. Jones, fearing he would kill me, had cautioned me always to hold him in, which I had done. Satan stretched out with long, graceful motions; he did not turn aside for logs, but cleared them with easy and powerful spring, and he swerved only slightly for the trees. This latter, I saw at once, made the danger for me. It became a matter of saving my legs, and dodging branches. The imperative need of this came to me with convincing force. I dodged a branch on one tree, only to be caught square in the middle by a snag on another. Crack! If the snag had not broken, Satan would have gone on riderless, and I would have been left hanging, a pathetic and drooping monition to the risks of the hunt. I kept ducking my head, now and then falling flat over the pommel to avoid a limb that would have brushed me off, and hugging the flanks of my horse with my knees. Soon I was at Wallace's heels, and had Jones in sight. Now and then glimpses of Frank's white horse gleamed through the trees.

We began to circle toward the south, to go up and down shallow hollows, to find the pines thinning out;

then we shot out of the forest into the scrubby oak. Riding through this brush was the cruelest kind of work, but Satan kept on close to the sorrel. The hollows began to get deeper, and the ridges between them narrower. No longer could we keep a straight course.

On the crest of one of the ridges we found Jones awaiting us. Jude, Tige and Don lay panting at his feet. Plainly the Colonel appeared vexed.

"Listen," he said, when we reined in.

We complied, but did not hear a sound.

"Frank's beyond there some place," continued Jones, "but I can't see him, nor hear the hounds any more. Don and Tige split again on deer trails. Old Jude hung on the lion track, but I stopped her here. There's something I can't figure. Moze held a beeline southwest, and he yelled seldom. Sounder gradually stopped baying. Maybe Frank can tell us something."

Jones's long drawn-out signal was answered from the direction he expected, and after a little time, Frank's white horse shone out of the gray-green of a ridge a mile away.

This drew my attention to our position. We were on a high ridge out in the open, and I could see fifty miles of the shaggy slopes of Buckskin. Southward the gray, ragged line seemed to stop suddenly, and beyond it purple haze hung over a void I knew to be the cañon. And facing west, I came, at last, to understand perfectly the meaning of the breaks in the Siwash. They were nothing more than ravines that headed up on the slopes and ran down, getting deeper and steeper, though scarcely wider, to break into the cañon. Knife-crested ridges rolled westward, wave on wave, like the billows of a sea. I appreciated that these breaks were, at their sources, little washes easy to jump across, and at their mouths a mile deep and impassable. Huge pine trees shaded these gullies, to give way to the gray growth of stunted oak, which in turn merged into the dark green of piñon. A wonderful country for deer and lions, it seemed to me, but impassable, all but impossible for a hunter.

Frank soon appeared, brushing through the bending oaks, and Sounder trotted along behind him.

"Where's Moze?" inquired Jones.

"The last I heard of Moze he was out of the brush, goin' across the piñon flat, right for the cañon. He had a hot trail."

"Well, we're certain of one thing; if it was a deer, he won't come back soon, and if it was a lion, he'll tree it, lose the scent, and come back. We've got to show the hounds a lion in a tree. They'd run a hot trail, bump into a tree, and then be at fault. What was wrong with Sounder?"

"I don't know. He came back to me."

"We can't trust him, or any of them yet. Still, maybe they're doing better than we know."

The outcome of the chase, so favorably started, was a disappointment, which we all felt keenly. After some discussion, we turned south, intending to ride down to the rim wall and follow it back to camp. I happened to turn once, perhaps to look again at the far-distant pink cliffs of Utah, or the wave-like dome of Trumbull Mountain, when I saw Moze trailing close behind me. My yell halted the Colonel.

"Well, I'll be darned!" exclaimed he, as Moze hove in sight. "Come hyar, you rascal!"

He was a tired dog, but had no sheepish air about him, such as he had worn when lagging in from deer chases. He wagged his tail, and flopped down to pant and pant, as if to say: "What's wrong with you guys?"

"Boys, for two cents I'd go back and put Jude on that trail. It's just possible that Moze treed a lion. But—well, I expect there's more likelihood of his chasing the lion over the rim; so we may as well keep on. The strange thing is that Sounder wasn't with Moze. There may have been two lions. You see we are up a tree ourselves. I have known lions to run in pairs, and also a mother keep four two-year-olds with her. But such cases are rare. Here, in this country, though, maybe they run round and have parties."

As we left the breaks behind we got out upon a level piñon flat. A few cedars grew with the piñons. Deer runways and trails were thick.

"Boys, look at that," said Jones. "This is great lion country, the best I ever saw."

He pointed to the sunken, red, shapeless remains of two horses, and near them a ghastly scattering of bleached bones. "A lion-lair right here on the flat. Those two horses were killed early this spring, and I see no signs of their carcasses having been covered with brush and dirt. I've got to learn lion lore over again, that's certain."

As we paused at the head of a depression, which appeared to be a gap in the rim wall, filled with massed piñons and splintered piles of yellow stone, I caught Sounder going through some interesting moves. He stopped to smell a bush. Then he lifted his head, and electrified me with a great, deep-sounding bay.

"Hi! there, listen to that!" yelled Jones. "What's Sounder got? Give him room—don't run him down. Easy now, old dog, easy, easy!"

Sounder suddenly broke down a trail. Moze howled, Don barked, and Tige let out his staccato yelp. They ran through the brush here, there, everywhere. Then all at once old Jude chimed in with her mellow voice, and Jones tumbled off his horse.

"By the Lord Harry! There's something here."

"Here, Colonel, here's the bush Sounder smelt, and there's a sandy trail under it," I called.

"There go Dan an' Tige down into the break," cried Frank. "They've got a hot scent!"

Jones stooped over the place I designated, to jerk up with reddening face, and as he flung himself into the saddle roared out: "After Sounder! Old Tom! Old Tom! Old Tom!"

We all heard Sounder, and at the moment of Jones's discovery, Moze got the scent and plunged ahead of us.

"Hi! Hi! Hi! Hi!" yelled the Colonel. Frank sent Spot forward like a white streak. Sounder called to us in irresistible bays, which Moze answered, and then crippled Jude bayed in baffled, impotent distress.

The atmosphere was charged with that lion. As if by magic, the excitation communicated itself to all, and men, horses and dogs acted in accord. The ride through the forest had been a jaunt. This was a steeplechase, a mad, heedless, perilous, glorious race. And we had for a pace-maker a cowboy mounted on a tireless mustang.

Always it seemed to me, while the wind rushed, the brush whipped, I saw Frank far ahead, sitting his saddle as if glued there, holding his reins loosely forward. To see him ride so was a beautiful sight. Jones let out his Comanche yell at every dozen jumps, and Wallace sent back a thrilling "Waa-hoo-o!" In the excitement I had again checked my horse, and when I remembered, and loosed the bridle, how the noble animal responded! The pace he settled into dazed me; I could hardly distinguish the deer trail down which he was thundering. I lost my comrades ahead; the piñon blurred in my sight; I only faintly heard the hounds. It occurred to me we were making for the breaks, but I did not think of checking Satan. I thought only of flying on faster and faster.

"On! On! old fellow! Stretch out! Never lose this race! We've got to be there at the finish!" I called to Satan, and he seemed to understand and stretched lower, farther, quicker.

The brush pounded my legs and clutched and tore my clothes; the wind whistled; the piñon branches cut and whipped my face. Once I dodged to the left, as Satan swerved to the right, with the result that I flew out of the saddle, and crashed into a piñon tree, which marvelously brushed me back into the saddle. The wild yells and deep bays sounded nearer. Satan tripped and plunged down, throwing me as gracefully as an aërial tumbler wings his flight. I alighted in a bush, without feeling of scratch or pain. As Satan recovered and ran past, I did not seek to make him stop, but getting a good grip on the pommel, I vaulted up again. Once more he raced like a wild mustang. And from nearer and nearer in front pealed the alluring sounds of the chase.

Satan was creeping close to Wallace and Jones, with Frank looming white through the occasional piñons. Then all dropped out of sight, to appear again suddenly. They had reached the first break. Soon I was upon it. Two deer ran out of the ravine, almost brushing my horse in the haste. Satan went down and up in a few giant strides. Only the narrow ridge separated us from another break. It was up and down then for Satan, a work to which he manfully set himself. Occasionally I saw Wallace and Jones, but heard them oftener. All the time the breaks grew deeper, till finally Satan had to zigzag his way down and up. Discouragement fastened on me, when from the summit of the next ridge I saw Frank far down the break, with Jones and Wallace not a quarter of a mile away from him. I sent out a long, exultant yell as Satan crashed into the hard, dry wash in the bottom of the break.

I knew from the way he quickened under me that he intended to overhaul somebody. Perhaps because of the clear going, or because my frenzy had cooled to a thrilling excitement which permitted detail, I saw clearly and distinctly the speeding horsemen down the ravine. I picked out the smooth pieces of ground ahead, and with the slightest touch of the rein on his neck, guided Satan into them. How he ran! The light, quick beats of his hoofs were regular, pounding. Seeing Jones and Wallace sail high into the air, I knew they had jumped a ditch. Thus prepared, I managed to stick on when it yawned before me; and Satan, never slackening, leaped up and up, giving me a new swing.

Dust began to settle in little clouds before me; Frank, far ahead, had turned his mustang up the side of the break; Wallace, within hailing distance, now turned to wave me a hand. The rushing wind fairly sang in my ears; the walls of the break were confused blurs of yellow and green; at every stride Satan seemed to swallow a rod of the white trail.

Jones began to scale the ravine, heading up obliquely far on the side of where Frank had vanished, and as Wallace followed suit, I turned Satan. I caught Wallace at the summit, and we raced together out upon another flat of piñon. We heard Frank and Jones yelling in a way that caused us to spur our horses frantically. Spot, gleaming white near a clump of green piñons, was our guiding star. That last quarter of a mile was a ringing run, a ride to remember.

As our mounts crashed back with stiff forelegs and haunches, Wallace and I leaped off and darted into the clump of piñons, whence issued a hair-raising medley of yells and barks. I saw Jones, then Frank, both waving their arms, then Moze and Sounder running wildly, aimlessly about.

"Look there!" rang in my ear, and Jones smashed me on the back with a blow, which at any ordinary time would have laid me flat.

In a low, stubby piñon tree, scarce twenty feet from us, was a tawny form. An enormous mountain lion, as large as an African lioness, stood planted with huge, round legs on two branches; and he faced us gloomily, neither frightened nor fierce. He watched the running dogs with pale, yellow eyes, waved his massive head and switched a long, black-tufted tail.

"It's Old Tom! sure as you're born! It's Old Tom!" yelled Jones. "There's no two lions like that in one country. Hold still now. Jude is here, and she'll see him—she'll show him to the other hounds. Hold still!"

We heard Jude coming at a fast pace for a lame dog, and we saw her presently, running with her nose down for a moment, then up. She entered the clump of trees, and bumped her nose against the piñon Old Tom was in, and looked up like a dog that knew her business. The series of wild howls she broke into quickly brought Sounder and Moze to her side. They, too, saw the big lion, not fifteen feet over their heads.

We were all yelling and trying to talk at once, some such state as the dogs.

"Hyar, Moze! Come down out of that!" hoarsely shouted Jones.

Moze had begun to climb the thick, many-branched, low piñon tree. He paid not the slightest attention to Jones, who screamed and raged at him.

"Cover the lion!" cried he to me. "Don't shoot unless he crouches to jump on me."

The little beaded front-sight wavered slightly as I held my rifle leveled at the grim, snarling face, and out of the corner of my eye, as it were, I saw Jones dash in under the lion and grasp Moze by the hind leg and haul him down. He broke from Jones and leaped again to the first low branch. His master then grasped his collar and carried him to where we stood and held him choking.

"Boys, we can't keep Tom up there. When he jumps, keep out of his way. Maybe we can chase him up a better tree."

Old Tom suddenly left the branches, swinging violently; and hitting the ground like a huge cat on springs, he bounded off, tail up, in a most ludicrous manner. His running, however, did not lack speed, for he quickly outdistanced the bursting hounds.

A stampede for horses succeeded this move. I had difficulty in closing my camera, which I had forgotten until the last moment, and got behind the others. Satan sent the dust flying and the piñon branches crashing. Hardly had I time to bewail my ill-luck in being left, when I dashed out of a thick growth of trees to come upon my companions, all dismounted on the rim of the Grand Cañon.

"He's gone down! He's gone down!" raged Jones, stamping the ground. "What luck! What miserable luck! But don't quit; spread along the rim, boys, and look for him. Cougars can't fly. There's a break in the rim somewhere."

The rock wall, on which we dizzily stood, dropped straight down for a thousand feet, to meet a long, piñon-covered slope, which graded a mile to cut off into what must have been the second wall. We were far west of Clarke's trail now, and faced a point above where Kanab Cañon, a red gorge a mile deep, met the great cañon. As I ran along the rim, looking for a fissure or break, my gaze seemed impellingly drawn by the immensity of this thing I could not name, and for which I had as yet no intelligible emotion.

Two "Waa-hoos" in the rear turned me back in double-quick time, and hastening by the horses, I found the three men grouped at the head of a narrow break.

"He went down here. Wallace saw him round the base of that tottering crag."

The break was wedge-shaped, with the sharp end toward the rim, and it descended so rapidly as to appear almost perpendicular. It was a long, steep slide of small, weathered shale, and a place that no man in his right senses would ever have considered going down. But Jones, designating Frank and me, said in his cool, quick voice:

"You fellows go down. Take Jude and Sounder in leash. If you find his trail below along the wall, yell for us. Meanwhile, Wallace and I will hang over the rim and watch for him."

Going down, in one sense, was much easier than had appeared, for the reason that once started we moved on sliding beds of weathered stone. Each of us now had an avalanche for a steed. Frank forged ahead with a roar, and then seeing danger below, tried to get out of the mass. But the stones were like quicksand; every step he took sunk him in deeper. He grasped the smooth cliff, to find holding impossible. The slide poured over a fall like so much water. He reached and caught a branch of a piñon, and lifting his feet up, hung on till the treacherous area of moving stones had passed.

While I had been absorbed in his predicament, my avalanche augmented itself by slide on slide, perhaps loosened by his; and before I knew it, I was sailing down with ever-increasing momentum. The sensation was distinctly pleasant, and a certain spirit, before restrained in me, at last ran riot. The slide narrowed at the drop where Frank had jumped, and the stones poured over in a stream. I jumped also, but having a rifle in one hand, failed to hold, and plunged down into the slide again. My feet were held this time, as in a vise. I kept myself upright and waited. Fortunately, the jumble of loose stone slowed and stopped, enabling me to crawl over to one side where there was comparatively good footing. Below us, for fifty

yards, was a sheet of rough stone, as bare as washed granite well could be. We slid down this in regular schoolboy
fashion, and had reached another restricted neck in the
fissure, when a sliding crash above warned us that the
avalanches had decided to move of their own free will.
Only a fraction of a moment had we to find footing along
the yellow cliff, when, with a cracking roar, the mass
struck the slippery granite. If we had been on that slope,
our lives would not have been worth a grain of the dust flying in clouds above us. Huge stones, that had formed the
bottom of the slides, shot ahead, and rolling, leaping,
whizzed by us with frightful velocity, and the remainder
groaned and growled its way down, to thunder over the
second fall and die out in a distant rumble.

The hounds had hung back, and were not easily coaxed
down to us. From there on, down to the base of the gigantic cliff, we descended with little difficulty.

"We might meet the old gray cat anywheres along
here," said Frank.

The wall of yellow limestone had shelves, ledges, fissures and cracks, any one of which might have concealed
a lion. On these places I turned dark, uneasy glances. It
seemed to me events succeeded one another so rapidly that
I had no time to think, to examine, to prepare. We were
rushed from one sensation to another.

"Gee! look here," said Frank; "here's his tracks. Did
you ever see the like of that?"

Certainly I had never fixed my eyes on such enormous
cat-tracks as appeared in the yellow dust at the base of the
rim wall. The mere sight of them was sufficient to make
a man tremble.

"Hold in the dogs, Frank," I called. "Listen. I think I
heard a yell."

From far above came a yell, which, though thinned out
by distance, was easily recognized as Jones's. We returned

to the opening of the break, and throwing our heads back, looked up the slide to see him coming down.

"Wait for me! Wait for me! I saw the lion go in a cave. Wait for me!"

With the same roar and crack and slide of rocks as had attended our descent, Jones bore down on us. For an old man it was a marvelous performance. He walked on the avalanches as though he wore seven-league boots, and presently, as we began to dodge whizzing bowlders, he stepped down to us, whirling his coiled lasso. His jaw bulged out; a flash made fire in his cold eyes.

"Boys, we've got Old Tom in a corner. I worked along the rim north and looked over every place I could. Now, maybe you won't believe it, but I heard him pant. Yes, sir, he panted like the tired lion he is. Well, presently I saw him lying along the base of the rim wall. His tongue was hanging out. You see, he's a heavy lion, and not used to running long distances. Come on, now. It's not far. Hold in the dogs. You there with the rifle, lead off, and keep your eyes peeled."

Single file, we passed along in the shadow of the great cliff. A wide trail had been worn in the dust.

"A lion run-way," said Jones. "Don't you smell the cat?"

Indeed, the strong odor of cat was very pronounced; and that, without the big fresh tracks, made the skin on my face tighten and chill. As we turned a jutting point in the wall, a number of animals, which I did not recognize, plunged helter-skelter down the cañon slope.

"Rocky Mountain sheep!" exclaimed Jones. "Look! Well, this is a discovery. I never heard of a bighorn in the cañon."

It was indicative of the strong grip Old Tom had on us that we at once forgot the remarkable fact of coming upon those rare sheep in such a place.

Jones halted us presently before a deep curve described by the rim-wall, the extreme end of which terminated across the slope in an impassable projecting corner.

"See across there, boys. See that black hole. Old Tom's in there."

"What's your plan?" queried the cowboy sharply.

"Wait. We'll slip up to get better lay of the land."

We worked our way noiselessly along the rim-wall curve for several hundred yards and came to a halt again, this time with a splendid command of the situation. The trail ended abruptly at the dark cave, so menacingly staring at us, and the corner of the cliff had curled back upon itself. It was a box-trap, with a drop at the end, too great for any beast, a narrow slide of weathered stone running down, and the rim-wall trail. Old Tom would plainly be compelled to choose one of these directions if he left his cave.

"Frank, you and I will keep to the wall and stop near that scrub piñon, this side of the hole. If I rope him, I can use that tree."

Then he turned to me:

"Are you to be depended on here?"

"I? What do you want me to do?" I demanded, and my whole breast seemed to sink in.

"You cut across the head of this slope and take up your position in the slide below the cave, say just by that big stone. From there you can command the cave, our position and your own. Now, if it is necessary to kill this lion to save me or Frank, or, of course, yourself, can you be depended upon to kill him?"

I felt a strange sensation around my heart and a tightening of the skin upon my face! What a position for me to be placed in! For one instant I shook like a quivering aspen leaf. Then because of the pride of a man, or perhaps inherited instincts cropping out at this perilous moment, I looked up and answered quietly:

"Yes. I will kill him!"

"Old Tom is cornered, and he'll come out. He can run only two ways: along this trail, or down that slide. I'll take my stand by the scrub piñon there so I can get a hitch if I rope him. Frank, when I give the word, let the dogs go. Grey, you block the slide. If he makes at us, even if I do get my rope on him, kill him! Most likely he'll jump down hill—then you'll *have* to kill him! Be quick. Now loose the hounds. Hi! Hi! Hi! Hi!"

I jumped into the narrow slide of weathered stone and looked up. Jones's stentorian yell rose high above the clamor of the hounds. He whirled his lasso.

A huge yellow form shot over the trail and hit the top of the slide with a crash. The lasso streaked out with arrowy swiftness, circled, and snapped viciously close to Old Tom's head. "Kill him! Kill him!" roared Jones. Then the lion leaped, seemingly into the air above me. Instinctively I raised my little automatic rifle. I seemed to hear a million bellowing reports. The tawny body, with its grim, snarling face, blurred in my sight. I heard a roar of sliding stones at my feet. I felt a rush of wind. I caught a confused glimpse of a whirling wheel of fur, rolling down the slide.

Then Jones and Frank were pounding me, and yelling I know not what. From far above came floating down a long "Waa-hoo!" I saw Wallace silhouetted against the blue sky. I felt the hot barrel of my rifle, and shuddered at the bloody stones below me—then, and then only, did I realize, with weakening legs, that Old Tom had jumped at me, and had jumped to his death.

CHAPTER 13

Singing Cliffs

Old Tom had rolled two hundred yards down the cañon, leaving a red trail and bits of fur behind him.
When I had clambered down to the steep slide where he
had lodged, Sounder and Jude had just decided he was no
longer worth biting, and were wagging their tails. Frank
was shaking his head, and Jones, standing above the lion,
lasso in hand, wore a disconsolate face.

"How I wish I had got the rope on him!"

"I reckon we'd be gatherin' up the pieces of you if you
had," said Frank, dryly.

We skinned the old king on the rocky slope of his
mighty throne, and then, beginning to feel the effects of
severe exertion, we cut across the slope for the foot of the
break. Once there, we gazed up in dismay. That break
resembled a walk of life—how easy to slip down, how
hard to climb! Even Frank, inured as he was to strenuous
toil, began to swear and wipe his sweaty brow before we
had made one-tenth of the ascent. It was particularly
exasperating, not to mention the danger of it, to work a
few feet up a slide, and then feel it start to move. We had
to climb in single file, which jeopardized the safety of
those behind the leader. Sometimes we were all sliding
at once, like boys on a pond, with the difference that we
were in danger. Frank forged ahead, turning to yell now
and then for us to dodge a cracking stone. Faithful old
Jude could not get up in some places, so laying aside my

rifle, I carried her, and returned for the weapon. It became necessary, presently, to hide behind cliff projections to escape the avalanches started by Frank, and to wait till he had surmounted the break. Jones gave out completely several times, saying the exertion affected his heart. What with my rifle, my camera and Jude, I could offer him no assistance, and was really in need of that myself. When it seemed as if one more step would kill us, we reached the rim, and fell panting with labored chests and dripping skins. We could not speak. Jones had worn a pair of ordinary shoes without thick soles and nails, and it seemed well to speak of them in the past tense. They were split into ribbons and hung on by the laces. His feet were cut and bruised.

On the way back to camp, we encountered Moze and Don coming out of the break where we had started Sounder on the trail. The paws of both hounds were yellow with dust, which proved they had been down under the rim wall. Jones doubted not in the least that they had chased a lion.

Upon examination, this break proved to be one of the two which Clarke used for trails to his wild horse corral in the cañon. According to him, the distance separating them was five miles by the rim wall, and less than half that in a straight line. Therefore, we made for the point of the forest where it ended abruptly in the scrub oak. We got into camp, a fatigued lot of men, horses and dogs. Jones appeared particularly happy, and his first move, after dismounting, was to stretch out the lion skin and measure it.

"Ten feet, three inches and a half!" he sang out.

"Shore it do beat hell!" exclaimed Jim in tones nearer to excitement than any I had ever heard him use.

"Old Tom beats, by two inches, any cougar I ever saw," continued Jones. "He must have weighed more than three hundred. We'll set about curing the hide. Jim, stretch it well on a tree, and we'll take a hand in peeling off the fat."

All of the party worked on the cougar skin that afternoon. The gristle at the base of the neck, where it met the shoulders, was so tough and thick we could not scrape it thin. Jones said this particular spot was so well protected because in fighting, cougars were most likely to bite and claw there. For that matter, the whole skin was tough, tougher than leather; and when it dried, it pulled all the horseshoe nails out of the pine tree upon which we had it stretched.

About time for the sun to set, I strolled along the rim wall to look into the cañon. I was beginning to feel something of its character and had growing impressions. Dark purple smoke veiled the clefts deep down between the mesas. I walked along to where points of cliff ran out like capes and peninsulas, all seamed, cracked, wrinkled, scarred and yellow with age, with shattered, toppling ruins of rocks ready at a touch to go thundering down. I could not resist the temptation to crawl out to the farthest point, even though I shuddered over the yard-wide ridges; and when once seated on a bare promontory, two hundred feet from the regular rim wall, I felt isolated, marooned.

The sun, a liquid red globe, had just touched its under side to the pink cliffs of Utah, and fired a crimson flood of light over the wonderful mountains, plateaus, escarpments, mesas, domes and turrets of the gorge. The rim wall of Powell's Plateau was a thin streak of fire; the timber above like grass of gold; and the long slopes below shaded from bright to dark. Point Sublime, bold and bare, ran out toward the plateau, jealously reaching for the sun. Bass's Tomb peeped over the Saddle. The Temple of Vishnu lay bathed in vapory shading clouds, and the Shinumo Altar shone with rays of glory.

The beginning of the wondrous transformation, the dropping of the day's curtain, was for me a rare and perfect moment. As the golden splendor of sunset sought out a peak or mesa or escarpment, I gave it a name to suit my fancy; and as flushing, fading, its glory changed, sometimes I rechristened it. Jupiter's Chariot, brazen wheeled, stood ready to roll into the clouds. Semiramis's Bed, all gold, shone from a tower of Babylon. Castor and Pollux clasped hands over a Stygian river. The Spur of Doom, a mountain shaft as red as hell, and inaccessible, insurmountable, lured with strange light. Dusk, a bold, black dome, was shrouded by the shadow of a giant mesa. The Star of Bethlehem glittered from the brow of Point Sublime. The Wraith, fleecy, feathered curtain of mist, floated down among the ruins of castles and palaces, like the ghost of a goddess. Vales of Twilight, dim, dark ravines, mystic homes of specters, led into the awful Valley of the Shadow, clothed in purple night.

Suddenly, as the first puff of the night wind fanned my cheek, a strange, sweet, low moaning and sighing came to my ears. I almost thought I was in a dream. But the cañon, now blood-red, was there in overwhelming reality, a profound, solemn, gloomy thing, but real. The wind blew stronger, and then I was listening to a sad, sweet song, which lulled as the wind lulled. I realized at once that the sound was caused by the wind blowing into the peculiar formations of the cliffs. It changed, softened, shaded, mellowed, but it was always sad. It rose from low, tremulous, sweetly quavering sighs, to a sound like the last woeful, despairing wail of a woman. It was the song of the sea sirens and the music of the waves; it had the soft sough of the night wind in the trees, and the haunting moan of lost spirits.

With reluctance I turned my back to the gorgeously changing spectacle of the cañon and crawled in to the rim wall. At the narrow neck of stone I peered over to look down into misty blue nothingness.

That night Jones told stories of frightened hunters, and assuaged my mortification by saying "buck-fever" was pardonable after the danger had passed, and especially so in my case, because of the great size and fame of Old Tom.

"The worst case of buck-fever I ever saw was on a buffalo hunt I had with a fellow named Williams," went on Jones. "I was one of the scouts leading a wagon-train west on the old Santa Fé trail. This fellow said he was a big hunter, and wanted to kill a buffalo, so I took him out. I saw a herd making over the prairie for a hollow where a brook ran, and by hard work, got in ahead of them. I picked out a position just below the edge of the bank, and we lay quiet, waiting. From the direction of the buffalo, I calculated we'd be just about right to get a shot at no very long range. As it was, I suddenly heard thumps on the ground, and cautiously raising my head, saw a huge buffalo bull just over us, not fifteen feet up the bank. I whispered to Williams: 'For God's sake, don't shoot, don't move!' The bull's little fiery eyes snapped, and he reared. I thought we were goners, for when a bull comes down on anything with his forefeet, it's done for. But he slowly settled back, perhaps doubtful. Then, as another buffalo came to the edge of the bank, luckily a little way from us, the bull turned broadside, presenting a splendid target. Then I whispered to Williams: 'Now's your chance. Shoot!' I waited for the shot, but none came. Looking at Williams, I saw he was white and trembling. Big drops of sweat stood out on his brow; his teeth chattered, and his hands shook. He had forgotten he carried a rifle."

"That reminds me," said Frank. "They tell a story over at Kanab on a Dutchman named Schmitt. He was very fond of huntin', an' I guess had pretty good success after deer an' small game. One winter he was out in the Pink Cliffs with a Mormon named Shoonover, an' they run into a lammin' big grizzly track, fresh an' wet. They trailed him to a clump of chaparral, an' on goin' clear round it, found no tracks leadin' out. Shoonover said Schmitt commenced to sweat. They went back to the place where the trail led in, an' there they were, great big silver-tip tracks, bigger'n hoss-tracks, so fresh the water was oozin' out of 'em. Schmitt said: 'Zake, you go in und ged him. I hef took sick righdt now.'"

Happy as we were over the chase of Old Tom, and our prospects—for Sounder, Jude and Moze had seen a lion in a tree—we sought our blankets early. I lay watching the bright stars, and listening to the roar of the wind in the pines. At intervals it lulled to a whisper, and then swelled to a roar, and then died away. Far off in the forest a coyote barked once. Time and time again, as I was gradually sinking into slumber, the sudden roar of the wind startled me. I imagined it was the crash of rolling, weathered stone, and I saw again that huge outspread flying lion above me.

I awoke sometime later to find Moze had sought the warmth of my side, and he lay so near my arm that I reached out and covered him with an end of the blanket I used to break the wind. It was very cold and the time must have been very late, for the wind had died down, and I heard not a tinkle from the hobbled horses. The absence of the cowbell music gave me a sense of loneliness, for without it the silence of the great forest was a thing to be felt.

This oppressiveness, however, was broken by a far-distant cry, unlike any sound I had ever heard. Not sure of myself, I freed my ears from the blanketed hood and listened. It came again, a wild cry, that made me think first of a lost child, and then of the mourning wolf of the north. It must have been a long distance off in the forest. An interval of some moments passed, then it pealed out again, nearer this time, and so human that it startled me. Moze raised his head and growled low in his throat and sniffed the keen air.

"Jones, Jones," I called, reaching over to touch the old hunter.

He awoke at once, with the clear-headedness of the light sleeper.

"I heard the cry of some beast," I said, "and it was so weird, so strange. I want to know what it was."

Such a long silence ensued that I began to despair of hearing the cry again, when, with a suddenness which straightened the hair on my head, a wailing shriek, exactly like a despairing woman might give in death agony, split the night silence. It seemed right on us.

"Cougar! Cougar! Cougar!" exclaimed Jones.

"What's up?" queried Frank, awakened by the dogs.

Their howling roused the rest of the party, and no doubt scared the cougar, for his womanish scream was not repeated. Then Jones got up and gathered his blankets in a roll.

"Where you oozin' for now?" asked Frank sleepily.

"I think that cougar just came up over the rim on a scouting hunt, and I'm going to go down to the head of the trail and stay there till morning. If he returns that way, I'll put him up a tree."

With this, he unchained Sounder and Don, and stalked off under the trees, looking like an Indian. Once the deep bay of Sounder rang out; Jones's sharp command followed, and then the familiar silence encompassed the forest and was broken no more.

When I awoke all was gray, except toward the cañon, where the little bit of sky I saw through the pines glowed a delicate pink. I crawled out on the instant, got into my boots and coat, and kicked up the smoldering fire. Jim heard me, and said:

"Shore you're up early."

"I'm going to see the sunrise from the north rim of the Grand Cañon," I said, and knew when I spoke that very few men, out of all the millions of travelers, had ever seen this, probably the most surpassingly beautiful pageant in the world. At most, only a few geologists, scientists, perhaps an artist or two, and horse wranglers, hunters and prospectors have ever reached the rim on the north side; and these men, crossing from Bright Angel or Mystic Spring trails on the south rim, seldom or never get beyond Powell's Plateau.

The frost cracked under my boots like frail ice, and the bluebells peeped warily from the white. When I reached the head of Clarke's trail it was just daylight; and there, under a pine, I found Jones rolled in his blankets, with Sounder and Moze asleep beside him. I turned without disturbing him, and went along the edge of the forest, but back a little distance from the rim wall.

I saw deer off in the woods, and tarrying, watched them throw up graceful heads, and look and listen. The soft pink glow through the pines deepened to rose, and suddenly I caught a point of red fire. Then I hurried to the place I had named Singing Cliffs, and keeping my eyes fast on the stone beneath me, crawled out to the very farthest point, drew a long, deep breath, and looked eastward.

The awfulness of sudden death and the glory of heaven stunned me! The thing that had been mystery at twilight, lay clear, pure, open in the rosy hue of dawn. Out of the gates of the morning poured a light which glorified the palaces and pyramids, purged and purified the afternoon's inscrutable clefts, swept away the shadows of the mesas, and bathed that broad, deep world of mighty mountains, stately spars of rock, sculptured cathedrals and alabaster terraces in an artist's dream of color. A pearl from heaven had burst, flinging its heart of fire into this chasm. A stream of opal flowed out of the sun, to touch each peak, mesa, dome, parapet, temple and tower, cliff and cleft into the newborn life of another day.

I sat there for a long time and knew that every second the scene changed, yet I could not tell how. I knew I sat high over a hole of broken, splintered, barren mountains; I knew I could see a hundred miles of the length of it, and eighteen miles of the width of it, and a mile of the depth of it, and the shafts and rays of rose light on a million glancing, many-hued surfaces at once; but that knowledge was no help to me. I repeated a lot of meaningless superlatives to myself, and I found words inadequate and superfluous. The spectacle was too elusive and too great. It was life and death, heaven and hell.

I tried to call up former favorite views of mountain and sea, so as to compare them with this; but the memory pictures refused to come, even with my eyes closed. Then I returned to camp, with unsettled, troubled mind, and was silent, wondering at the strange feeling burning within me.

Jones talked about our visitor of the night before, and said the trail near where he had slept showed only one cougar track, and that led down into the cañon. It had surely been made, he thought, by the beast we had heard. Jones signified his intention of chaining several of the hounds for the next few nights at the head of this trail; so if the cougar came up, they would scent him and let us know. From which it was evident that to chase a lion bound into the cañon and one bound out were two different things.

The day passed lazily, with all of us resting on the warm, fragrant pine-needle beds, or mending a rent in a coat, or working on some camp task impossible of commission on exciting days.

About four o'clock, I took my little rifle and walked off through the woods in the direction of the carcass where I had seen the gray wolf. Thinking it best to make a wide detour, so as to face the wind, I circled till I felt the breeze was favorable to my enterprise, and then cautiously approached the hollow where the dead horse lay. Indian fashion, I slipped from tree to tree, a mode of forest travel not without its fascination and effectiveness, till I reached the height of a knoll beyond which I made sure was my objective point. On peeping out from behind the last pine, I found I had calculated pretty well, for there was the hollow, the big windfall, with its round, starfish-shaped roots exposed to the bright sun, and near that, the carcass. Sure enough, pulling hard at it, was the gray-white wolf I recognized as my "lofer."

But he presented an exceedingly difficult shot. Backing down the ridge, I ran a little way to come up behind another tree, from which I soon shifted to a fallen pine. Over this I peeped, to get a splendid view of the wolf. He had stopped tugging at the horse, and stood with his nose in the air. Surely he could not have scented me, for the wind was strong from him to me; neither could he have heard my soft footfalls on the pine needles; nevertheless, he was suspicious. Loth to spoil the picture he made, I risked a chance, and waited. Besides, though I prided myself on being able to take a fair aim, I had no great hope that I could hit him at such a distance. Presently he returned to his feeding, but not for long. Soon he raised his long, fine-pointed head, and trotted away a few yards, stopped to sniff again, then went back to his grewsome work.

At this juncture, I noiselessly projected my rifled barrel over the log. I had not, however, gotten the sights in line with him, when he trotted away reluctantly, and ascended the knoll on his side of the hollow. I lost him, and had just

THE LAST OF THE PLAINSMEN   179

begun sourly to call myself a mollycoddle hunter, when
he reappeared. He halted in an open glade, on the very
crest of the knoll, and stood still as a statue wolf, a white,
inspiriting target, against a dark green background. I could
not stifle a rush of feeling, for I was a lover of the beautiful first, and a hunter secondly; but I steadied down as the
front sight moved into the notch through which I saw the
black and white of his shoulder.

Spang! How the little Remington sang! I watched
closely, ready to send five more missiles after the gray
beast. He jumped spasmodically, in a half-curve, high in
the air, with loosely hanging head, then dropped in a
heap. I yelled like a boy, ran down the hill, up the other
side of the hollow, to find him stretched out dead, a small
hole in his shoulder where the bullet had entered, a great
one where it had come out.

The job I made of skinning him lacked some hundred
degrees the perfection of my shot, but I accomplished it,
and returned to camp in triumph.

"Shore I knowed you'd plunk him," said Jim, very much
pleased. "I shot one the other day same way, when he was
feedin' off a dead horse. Now thet's a fine skin. Shore you
cut through once or twice. But he's only half lofer, the
other half is plain coyote. That accounts fer his feedin' on
dead meat."

My naturalist host and my scientific friend both remarked somewhat grumpily that I seemed to get the best
of all the good things. I might have retaliated that I certainly had gotten the worst of all the bad jokes; but, being
generously happy over my prize, merely remarked: "If you
want fame or wealth or wolves, go out and hunt for them."

Five o'clock supper left a good margin of day, in which
my thoughts reverted to the cañon. I watched the purple
shadows stealing out of their caverns and rolling up about
the base of the mesas. Jones came over to where I stood,

and I persuaded him to walk with me along the rim wall. Twilight had stealthily advanced when we reached the Singing Cliffs, and we did not go out upon my promontory, but chose a more comfortable one nearer the wall.

The night breeze had not sprung up yet, so the music of the cliffs was hushed.

"You cannot accept the theory of erosion to account for this chasm?" I asked my companion, referring to a former conversation.

"I can for this part of it. But what stumps me is the mountain range three thousand feet high, crossing the desert and the cañon just above where we crossed the river. How did the river cut through that without the help of a split or earthquake?"

"I'll admit that is a poser to me as well as to you. But I suppose Wallace could explain it as erosion. He claims this whole western country was once under water, except the tips of the Sierra Nevada mountains. There came an uplift of the earth's crust, and the great inland sea began to run out, presumably by way of the Colorado. In so doing it cut out the upper cañon, this gorge eighteen miles wide. Then came a second uplift, giving the river a much greater impetus toward the sea, which cut out the second, or marble cañon. Now as to the mountain range crossing the cañon at right angles. It must have come with the second uplift. If so, did it dam the river back into another inland sea, and then wear down into that red perpendicular gorge we remember so well? Or was there a great break in the fold of granite, which let the river continue on its way? Or was there, at that particular point, a softer stone, like this limestone here, which erodes easily?"

"You must ask somebody wiser than I."

"Well, let's not perplex our minds with its origin. It is, and that's enough for any mind. Ah! listen! Now you will hear my Singing Cliffs."

From out of the darkening shadows murmurs rose on the softly rising wind. This strange music had a depressing influence; but it did not fill the heart with sorrow, only touched it lightly. And when, with the dying breeze, the song died away, it left the lonely crags lonelier for its death.

The last rosy gleam faded from the tip of Point Sublime; and as if that were a signal, in all the clefts and cañons below, purple, shadowy clouds marshaled their forces and began to sweep upon the battlements, to swing colossal wings into amphitheaters where gods might have warred, slowly to enclose the magical sentinels. Night intervened, and a moving, changing, silent chaos pulsated under the bright stars.

"How infinite all this is! How impossible to understand!" I exclaimed.

"To me it is very simple," replied my comrade. "The world is strange. But this cañon—why, we can see it all! I can't make out why people fuss so over it. I only feel peace. It's only bold and beautiful, serene and silent."

With the words of this quiet old plainsman, my sentimental passion shrank to the true appreciation of the scene. Self passed out to the recurring, soft strains of cliff song. I had been reveling in a species of indulgence, imagining I was a great lover of nature, building poetical illusions over storm-beaten peaks. The truth, told by one who had lived fifty years in the solitudes, among the rugged mountains, under the dark trees, and by the sides of the lonely streams, was the simple interpretation of a spirit in harmony with the bold, the beautiful, the serene, the silent.

He meant the Grand Cañon was only a mood of nature, a bold promise, a beautiful record. He meant that mountains had sifted away in its dust, yet the cañon was young. Man was nothing, so let him be humble. This cataclysm of the earth, this playground of a river was not inscrutable; it was only inevitable—as inevitable as nature herself. Millions of years in the bygone ages it had lain serene under a live moon; it would bask silent under a rayless sun, in the onward edge of time.

It taught simplicity, serenity, peace. The eye that saw only the strife, the war, the decay, the ruin, or only the glory and the tragedy, saw not all the truth. It spoke simply, though its words were grand: "My spirit is the Spirit of Time, of Eternity, of God. Man is little, vain, vaunting. Listen. To-morrow he shall be gone. Peace! Peace!"

CHAPTER 14

All Heroes but One

As we rode up the slope of Buckskin, the sunrise glinted red-gold through the aisles of frosted pines, giving us a hunter's glad greeting.

With all due respect to, and appreciation of, the breaks of the Siwash, we unanimously decided that if cougars inhabited any other section of cañon country, we preferred it, and were going to find it. We had often speculated on the appearance of the rim wall directly across the neck of the cañon upon which we were located. It showed a long stretch of breaks, fissures, caves, yellow crags, crumbled ruins and clefts green with piñon pine. As a crow flies, it was only a mile or two straight across from camp, but to reach it, we had to ascend the mountain and head the cañon which deeply indented the slope.

A thousand feet or more above the level bench, the character of the forest changed; the pines grew thicker, and interspersed among them were silver spruces and balsams. Here in the clumps of small trees and underbrush, we began to jump deer, and in a few moments a greater number that I had ever seen in all my hunting experiences loped within range of my eye. I could not look out into the forest, where an aisle or lane or glade stretched to any distance, without seeing a big gray deer cross it. Jones said the herds had recently come up from the breaks, where they had wintered. These deer were twice the size of the Eastern species, and as fat as well-fed cattle. They were almost as tame, too. A big herd ran out of one glade, leaving behind several curious does, which watched us intently for a moment, then bounded off with the stiff, springy bounce that so amused me.

Sounder crossed fresh trails one after another; Jude, Tige and Ranger followed him, but hesitated often, barked and whined; Don started off once, to come sneaking back at Jones's stern call. But surly old Moze either would not or could not obey, and away he dashed. Bang! Jones sent a charge of fine shot after him. He yelped, doubled up as if stung, and returned as quickly as he had gone.

"Hyar, you white and black coon dog," said Jones, "get in behind, and stay there."

We turned to the right after a while and got among shallow ravines. Gigantic pines grew on the ridges and in the hollows, and everywhere bluebells shone blue from the white frost. Why the frost did not kill these beautiful flowers was a mystery to me. The horses could not step without crushing them.

Before long, the ravines became so deep that we had to zigzag up and down their sides, and to force our horses through the aspen thickets in the hollows. Once from a ridge I saw a troop of deer, and stopped to watch them. Twenty-seven I counted outright, but there must have been three times that number. I saw the herd break across a glade, and watched them until they were lost in the forest. My companions having disappeared, I pushed on, and while working out of a wide, deep hollow, I noticed the sunny patches fade from the bright slopes, and the golden streaks vanish among the pines. The sky had become overcast, and the forest was darkening. The "Waa-hoo" I cried out returned in echo only. The wind blew hard in my face, and the pines began to bend and roar. An immense black cloud enveloped Buckskin.

Satan had carried me no farther than the next ridge, when the forest frowned dark as twilight, and on the wind whirled flakes of snow. Over the next hollow, a white pall roared through the trees toward me. Hardly had I time to get the direction of the trail, and its relation to the trees nearby, when the storm enfolded me. Of his own accord Satan stopped in the lee of a bushy spruce. The roar in the pines equaled that of the cave under Niagara, and the bewildering, whirling mass of snow was as difficult to see through as the tumbling, seething waterfall.

I was confronted by the possibility of passing the night there, and calming my fears as best I could, hastily felt for my matches and knife. The prospect of being lost the next day in a white forest was also appalling, but I soon reassured myself that the storm was only a snow squall, and would not last long. Then I gave myself up to the pleasure and beauty of it. I could only faintly discern the dim trees; the limbs of the spruce, which partially protected me, sagged down to my head with their burden; I had but to reach out my hand for a snowball. Both the wind and snow seemed warm. The great flakes were like swan feathers on a summer breeze. There was something joyous in the whirl of snow and roar of wind. While I bent over to shake my holster, the storm passed as suddenly as it had come. When I looked up, there were the pines, like pillars of Parian marble, and a white shadow, a vanishing cloud fled, with receding roar, on the wings of the wind. Fast on this retreat burst the warm, bright sun.

I faced my course, and was delighted to see, through an opening where the ravine cut out of the forest, the red-tipped peaks of the cañon, and the vaulted dome I had named St. Marks. As I started, a new and unexpected after-feature of the storm began to manifest itself. The sun being warm, even hot, began to melt the snow, and under the trees a heavy rain fell, and in the glades and hollows a fine mist blew. Exquisite rainbows hung from white-tipped branches and curved over the hollows. Glistening patches of snow fell from the pines, and broke the showers.

In a quarter of an hour, I rode out of the forest to the rim wall on dry ground. Against the green piñons Frank's white horse stood out conspicuously, and near him browsed the mounts of Jim and Wallace. The boys were not in evidence. Concluding they had gone down over the rim, I dismounted and kicked off my chaps, and taking my rifle and camera, hurried to look the place over.

To my surprise and interest, I found a long section of rim wall in ruins. It lay in a great curve between the two giant capes; and many short, sharp, projecting promontories, like the teeth of a saw, overhung the cañon. The slopes between these points of cliff were covered with a deep growth of piñon, and in these places descent would be easy. Everywhere in the corrugated wall were rents and rifts; cliffs stood detached like islands near a shore; yellow crags rose out of green clefts; jumbles of rocks, and slides of rim wall, broken into blocks, massed under the promontories.

The singular raggedness and wildness of the scene took hold of me, and was not dispelled until the baying of Sounder and Don roused action in me. Apparently the hounds were widely separated. Then I heard Jim's yell. But it ceased when the wind lulled, and I heard it no more. Running back from the point, I began to go down. The way was steep, almost perpendicular; but because of the great stones and the absence of slides, was easy. I took long strides and jumps, and slid over rocks, and swung on piñon branches, and covered distance like a rolling stone. At the foot of the rim wall, or at a line where it would have reached had it extended regularly, the slope became less pronounced. I could stand up without holding on to a support. The largest piñons I had seen made a forest that almost stood on end. These trees grew up, down, and out, and twisted in curves, and many were two feet in thickness. During my descent, I halted at intervals to listen, and always heard one of the hounds, sometimes several. But as I descended for a long time, and did not get anywhere or approach the dogs, I began to grow impatient.

A large piñon, with a dead top, suggested a good outlook, so I climbed it, and saw I could sweep a large section of the slope. It was a strange thing to look down hill, over the tips of green trees. Below, perhaps four hundred yards, was a slide open for a long way; all the rest was green incline, with many dead branches sticking up like spars, and an occasional crag. From this perch I heard the hounds; then followed a yell I thought was Jim's, and after it the bellowing of Wallace's rifle. Then all was silent. The shots had effectually checked the yelping of the hounds. I let out a yell. Another cougar that Jones would not lasso! All at once I heard a familiar sliding of small rocks below me, and I watched the open slope with greedy eyes.

Not a bit surprised was I to see a cougar break out of the green, and go tearing down the slide. In less than six seconds, I had sent six steel-jacketed bullets after him. Puffs of dust rose closer and closer to him as each bullet went nearer the mark and the last showered him with gravel and turned him straight down the cañon slope.

I slid down the dead piñon and jumped nearly twenty feet to the soft sand below, and after putting a loaded clip in my rifle, began kangaroo leaps down the slope. When I reached the point where the cougar had entered the slide, I called the hounds, but they did not come nor answer me. Notwithstanding my excitement, I appreciated the distance to the bottom of the slope before I reached it. In my haste, I ran upon the verge of a precipice twice as deep as the first rim wall, but one glance down sent me shudderingly backward.

With all the breath I had left I yelled: "Waa-hoo! Waa-hoo!" From the echoes flung at me, I imagined at first that my friends were right on my ears. But no real answer came. The cougar had probably passed along this second rim wall to a break, and had gone down. His trail could easily be taken by any of the hounds. Vexed and anxious, I signaled again and again. Once, long after the echo had gone to sleep in some hollow cañon, I caught a faint "Waa-ho-o-o!" But it might have come from the clouds. I did not hear a hound barking above me on the slope; but suddenly, to my amazement, Sounder's deep bay rose from the abyss below. I ran along the rim, called till I was hoarse, leaned over so far that the blood rushed to my head, and then sat down. I concluded this cañon hunting could bear some sustained attention and thought, as well as frenzied action.

Examination of my position showed how impossible it was to arrive at any clear idea of the depth or size, or condition of the cañon slopes from the main rim wall above. The second wall—a stupendous, yellow-faced cliff two thousand feet high—curved to my left round to a point in front of me. The intervening cañon might have been a half-mile wide, and it might have been ten miles. I had become disgusted with judging distance. The slope above this second wall facing me ran up far above my head; it fairly towered, and this routed all my former judgments, because I remembered distinctly that from the rim this yellow and green mountain had appeared an insignificant little ridge. But it was when I turned to gaze up behind me that I fully grasped the immensity of the place. This wall and slope were the first two steps down the long stairway of the Grand Cañon, and they towered over me, straight up a half-mile in dizzy height. To think of climbing it took my breath away.

Then again Sounder's bay floated distinctly to me, but it seemed to come from a different point. I turned my ear to the wind, and in the succeeding moments I was more and more baffled. One bay sounded from below, and next from far to the right; another from the left. I could not distinguish voice from echo. The acoustic properties of the amphitheater beneath me were too wonderful for my comprehension.

As the bay grew sharper, and correspondingly more significant, I became distracted, and focused a strained vision on the cañon deeps. I looked along the slope to the notch where the wall curved and followed the base line of the yellow cliff. Quite suddenly I saw a very small black object moving with snail-like slowness. Although it seemed impossible for Sounder to be so small, I knew it was he. Having something now to judge distance from, I conceived it to be a mile, without the drop. If I could hear Sounder, he could hear me, so I yelled encouragement. The echoes clapped back at me like so many slaps in the face. I watched the hound until he disappeared among broken heaps of stone, and long after that his bay floated to me.

Having rested, I essayed the discovery of some of my lost companions or the hounds, and began to climb. Before I started, however, I was wise enough to study the rim wall above, to familiarize myself with the break so I would have a landmark. Like horns and spurs of gold the pinnacles loomed up. Massed closely together, they were not unlike an astounding pipe-organ. I had a feeling of my littleness, that I was lost, and should devote every moment and effort to the saving of my life. It did not seem possible I could be hunting. Though I climbed diagonally,

and rested often, my heart pumped so hard I could hear it.
A yellow crag, with a round head like an old man's cane,
appealed to me as near the place where I last heard from
Jim, and toward it I labored. Every time I glanced up,
the distance seemed the same. A climb which I decided
would not take more than fifteen minutes, required an
hour.

While resting at the foot of the crag, I heard more baying of hounds, but for my life I could not tell whether the
sound came from up or down, and I commenced to feel
that I did not much care. Having signaled till I was
hoarse, and receiving none but mock answers, I decided
that if my companions had not toppled over a cliff, they
were wisely withholding their breath.

Another stiff pull up the slope brought me under the
rim wall, and there I groaned, because the wall was
smooth and shiny, without a break. I plodded slowly
along the base, with my rifle ready. Cougar tracks were so
numerous I got tired of looking at them, but I did not forget that I might meet a tawny fellow or two among those
narrow passes of shattered rock, and under the thick,
dark piñons. Going on in this way, I ran point-blank into a
pile of bleached bones before a cave. I had stumbled on
the lair of a lion and from the looks of it one like that of
Old Tom. I flinched twice before I threw a stone into the
dark-mouthed cave. What impressed me as soon as I found
I was in no danger of being pawed and clawed round the
gloomy spot, was the fact of the bones being there. How
did they come on a slope where a man could hardly walk?
Only one answer seemed feasible. The lion had made his
kill one thousand feet above, had pulled his quarry to the
rim and pushed it over. In view of the theory that he might
have had to drag his victim from the forest, and that very
seldom two lions worked together, the fact of the location
of the bones was startling. Skulls of wild horses and deer,

antlers and countless bones, all crushed into shapelessness, furnished indubitable proof that the carcasses had fallen from a great height. Most remarkable of all was the skeleton of a cougar lying across that of a horse. I believed—I could not help but believe that the cougar had fallen with his last victim.

Not many rods beyond the lion den, the rim wall split into towers, crags and pinnacles. I thought I had found my pipe organ, and began to climb toward a narrow opening in the rim. But I lost it. The extraordinarily cut-up condition of the wall made holding to one direction impossible. Soon I realized I was lost in a labyrinth. I tried to find my way down again, but the best I could do was to reach the verge of a cliff, from which I could see the cañon. Then I knew where I was, yet I did not know, so I plodded wearily back. Many a blind cleft did I ascend in the maze of crags. I could hardly crawl along, still I kept at it, for the place was conducive to dire thoughts. A tower of Babel menaced me with tons of loose shale. A tower that leaned more frightfully than the Tower of Pisa threatened to build my tomb. Many a lighthouse-shaped crag sent down little scattering rocks in ominous notice.

After toiling in and out of passageways under the shadows of these strangely formed cliffs, and coming again and again to the same point, a blind pocket, I grew desperate. I named the baffling place Deception Pass, and then ran down a slide. I knew if I could keep my feet I could beat the avalanche. More by good luck than management I outran the roaring stones and landed safely. Then rounding the cliff below, I found myself on a narrow ledge, with a wall to my left, and to the right the tips of piñon trees level with my feet.

Innocently and wearily I passed round a pillar-like corner of wall, to come face to face with an old lioness and cubs. I heard the mother snarl, and at the same time her ears went back flat, and she crouched. The same fire of yellow eyes, the same grim snarling expression so familiar in my mind since Old Tom had leaped at me, faced me here.

My recent vow of extermination was entirely forgotten and one frantic spring carried me over the ledge.

Crash! I felt the brushing and scratching of branches, and saw a green blur. I went down straddling limbs and hit the ground with a thump. Fortunately, I landed mostly on my feet, in sand, and suffered no serious bruise. But I was stunned, and my right arm was numb for a moment. When I gathered myself together, instead of being grateful the ledge had not been on the face of Point Sublime—from which I would most assuredly have leaped—I was the angriest man ever let loose in the Grand Cañon.

Of course the cougars were far on their way by that time, and were telling neighbors about the brave hunter's leap for life; so I devoted myself to further efforts to find an outlet. The niche I had jumped into opened below, as did most of the breaks, and I worked out of it to the base of the rim wall, and tramped a long, long mile before I reached my own trail leading down. Resting every five steps, I climbed and climbed. My rifle grew to weigh a ton; my feet were lead; the camera strapped to my shoulder was the world. Soon climbing meant trapeze work—long reach of arm, and pull of weight, high step of foot, and spring of body. Where I had slid down with ease, I had to strain and raise myself by sheer muscle. I wore my left glove to tatters and threw it away to put the right one on my left hand. I thought many times I could not make another move; I thought my lungs would burst, but I kept on. When at last I surmounted the rim, I saw Jones, and flopped down beside him, and lay panting, dripping, boiling, with scorched feet, aching limbs and numb chest.

"I've been here two hours," he said, "and I knew things

were happening below; but to climb up that slide would kill me. I am not young any more, and a steep climb like this takes a young heart. As it was I had enough work. Look!" He called my attention to his trousers. They had been cut to shreds, and the right trouser leg was missing from the knee down. His shin was bloody. "Moze took a lion along the rim, and I went after him with all my horse could do. I yelled for the boys, but they didn't come. Right here it is easy to go down, but below, where Moze started this lion, it was impossible to get over the rim. The lion lit straight out of the piñons. I lost ground because of the thick brush and numerous trees. Then Moze doesn't bark often enough. He treed the lion twice. I could tell by the way he opened up and bayed. The rascal coon-dog climbed the trees and chased the lion out. That's what Moze did! I got to an open space and saw him, and was coming up fine when he went down over a hollow which ran into the cañon. My horse tripped and fell, turning clear over with me before he threw me into the brush. I tore my clothes, and got this bruise, but wasn't much hurt. My horse is pretty lame."

I began a recital of my experience, modestly omitting the incident where I bravely faced an old lioness. Upon consulting my watch, I found I had been almost four hours climbing out. At that moment, Frank poked a red face over the rim. He was in his shirt sleeves, sweating freely, and wore a frown I had never seen before. He puffed like a porpoise, and at first could hardly speak.

"Where—were—you—all?" he panted. "Say! but mebbe this hasn't been a chase! Jim an' Wallace an' me went tumblin' down after the dogs, each one lookin' out for his perticular dog, an' darn me if I don't believe his lion, too. Don took one oozin' down the cañon, with me hot-footin' it after him. An' somewhere he treed thet lion, right below me, in a box cañon, sort of an offshoot of the second rim, an' I couldn't locate him. I blamed near killed myself more'n once. Look at my knuckles! Barked 'em slidin' about a mile down a smooth wall. I thought once the lion had jumped Don, but soon I heard him barkin' again. All thet time I heard Sounder, an' once I heard the pup. Jim yelled, an' somebody was shootin'. But I couldn't find nobody, or make nobody hear me. Thet cañon is a mighty deceivin' place. You'd never think so till you go down. I wouldn't climb up it again for all the lions in Buckskin. Hello, there comes Jim oozin' up."

Jim appeared just over the rim, and when he got up to us, dusty, torn and fagged out, with Don, Tige and Ranger showing signs of collapse, we all blurted out questions. But Jim took his time.

"Shore that cañon is one hell of a place," he began finally. "Where was everybody? Tige and the pup went down with me an' treed a cougar. Yes, they did, an' I set under a piñon holdin' the pup, while Tige kept the cougar treed. I yelled an' yelled. After about an hour or two, Wallace came poundin' down like a giant. It was a sure thing we'd get the cougar; an' Wallace was takin' his picture when the blamed cat jumped. It was embarrassin', because he wasn't polite about how he jumped. We scattered some, an' when Wallace got his gun, the cougar was humpin' down the slope, an' he was goin' so fast an' the piñons was so thick thet Wallace couldn't get a fair shot, an' missed. Tige an' the pup was so scared by the shots they wouldn't take the trail again. I heard some one shoot about a million times, an' shore thought the cougar was done for. Wallace went plungin' down the slope an' I followed. I couldn't keep up with him—he shore takes long steps—an' I lost him. I'm reckonin' he went over the second wall. Then I made tracks for the top. Boys, the way you can see an' hear things down in thet cañon, an' the way you can't hear an' see things is pretty funny."

"If Wallace went over the second rim wall, will he get back to-day?" we all asked.

"Shore, there's no tellin'."

We waited, lounged, and slept for three hours, and were beginning to worry about our comrade when he hove in sight eastward, along the rim. He walked like a man whose next step would be his last. When he reached us, he fell flat, and lay breathing heavily for a while.

"Somebody once mentioned Israel Putnam's ascent of a hill," he said slowly. "With all respect to history and a patriot, I wish to say Putnam never saw a hill!"

"Ooze for camp," called out Frank.

Five o'clock found us round a bright fire, all casting ravenous eyes at a smoking supper. The smell of the Persian meat would have made a wolf of a vegetarian. I devoured four chops, and could not have been counted in the running. Jim opened a can of maple sirup which he had been saving for a grand occasion, and Frank went him one better with two cans of peaches. How glorious to be hungry—to feel the craving for food, and to be grateful for it, to realize that the best of life lies in the daily needs of existence, and to battle for them!

Nothing could be stronger than the simple enumeration and statement of the facts of Wallace's experience after he left Jim. He chased the cougar, and kept it in sight, until it went over the second rim wall. Here he dropped over a precipice twenty feet high, to alight on a fan-shaped slide which spread toward the bottom. It began to slip and move by jerks, and then started off steadily, with an increasing roar. He rode an avalanche for one thousand feet. The jar loosened bowlders from the walls. When the slide stopped, Wallace extricated his feet and began to dodge the bowlders. He had only time to jump over the large ones or dart to one side out of their way. He dared not run. He had to watch them coming. One huge stone hurtled over his head and smashed a piñon tree below.

When these had ceased rolling, and he had passed down to the red shale, he heard Sounder baying near, and knew a cougar had been treed or cornered. Hurdling the stones and dead piñons, Wallace ran a mile down the slope, only to find he had been deceived in the direction. He sheered off to the left. Sounder's illusive bay came up from a deep cleft. Wallace plunged into a piñon, climbed to the ground, skidded down a solid slide, to come upon an impassable obstacle in the form of a solid wall of red granite. Sounder appeared and came to him, evidently having given up the chase.

Wallace consumed four hours in making the ascent. In the notch of the curve of the second rim wall, he climbed the slippery steps of a waterfall. At one point, if he had not been six feet five inches tall, he would have been compelled to attempt retracing his trail—an impossible task. But his height enabled him to reach a root, by which he pulled himself up. Sounder he lassoed *à la* Jones, and hauled up. At another spot, which Sounder climbed, he lassoed a piñon above, and walked up with his feet slipping from under him at every step. The knees of his corduroy trousers were holes, as were the elbows of his coat. The sole of his left boot—which he used most in climbing—was gone, and so was his hat.

CHAPTER 15

Jones on Cougars

The mountain lion, or cougar, of our Rocky Mountain region, is nothing more nor less than the panther. He is a little different in shape, color and size, which vary according to his environment. The panther of the Rockies is usually light, taking the grayish hue of the rocks. He is stockier and heavier of build, and stronger of limb than the Eastern species, which difference comes from climbing mountains and springing down the cliffs after his prey.

In regions accessible to man, or where man is encountered even rarely, the cougar is exceedingly shy, seldom or never venturing from cover during the day. He spends the hours of daylight high on the most rugged cliffs, sleeping and basking in the sunshine, and watching with wonderfully keen sight the valleys below. His hearing equals his sight, and if danger threatens, he always hears it in time to skulk away unseen. At night he steals down the mountain side toward deer or elk he has located during the day. Keeping to the lowest ravines and thickets, he creeps upon his prey. His cunning and ferocity are keener and more savage in proportion to the length of time he has been without food. As he grows hungrier and thinner, his skill and fierce strategy correspondingly increase. A well-fed cougar will creep upon and secure only about one in seven of the deer, elk, antelope or mountain sheep that he stalks. But a starving cougar is another animal.

He creeps like a snake, is as sure on the scent as a vulture, makes no more noise than a shadow, and he hides behind a stone or bush that would scarcely conceal a rabbit. Then he springs with terrific force, and intensity of purpose, and seldom fails to reach his victim, and once the claws of a starved lion touch flesh, they never let go.

A cougar seldom pursue his quarry after he has leaped and missed, either from disgust or failure, or knowledge that a second attempt would be futile. The animal making the easiest prey for the cougar is the elk. About every other elk attacked falls a victim. Deer are more fortunate, the ratio being one dead to five leaped at. The antelope, living on the lowlands or upland meadows, escapes nine times out of ten; and the mountain sheep, or bighorn, seldom falls to the onslaught of his enemy.

Once the lion gets a hold with the great forepaw, every movement of the struggling prey sinks the sharp, hooked claws deeper. Then as quickly as is possible, the lion fastens his teeth in the throat of his prey and grips till it is dead. In this way elk have carried lions for many rods. The lion seldom tears the skin of the neck, and never, as is generally supposed, sucks the blood of its victim; but he cuts into the side, just behind the foreshoulder, and eats the liver first. He rolls the skin back as neatly and tightly as a person could do it. When he has gorged himself, he drags the carcass into a ravine or dense thicket, and rakes leaves, sticks or dirt over it to hide it from other animals. Usually he returns to his cache on the second night, and after that the frequency of his visits depends on the supply of fresh prey. In remote regions, unfrequented by man, the lion will guard his cache from coyote and buzzards.

In sex there are about five female lions to one male. This is caused by the jealous and vicious disposition of the male. It is a fact that the old Toms kill every young

lion they can catch. Both male and female of the litter
suffer alike until after weaning time, and then only the
males. In this matter wise animal logic is displayed by
the Toms. The domestic cat, to some extent, possesses the
same trait. If the litter is destroyed, the mating time is
sure to come about regardless of the season. Thus this savage trait of the lions prevents overproduction, and breeds
a hardy and intrepid race. If by chance or that cardinal
feature of animal life—the survival of the fittest—a young
male lion escapes to the weaning time, even after that he is
persecuted. Young male lions have been killed and found
to have had their flesh beaten until it was a mass of bruises
and undoubtedly it had been the work of an old Tom.
Moreover, old males and females have been killed, and
found to be in the same bruised condition. A feature, and
a conclusive one, is the fact that invariably the female is
suckling her young at this period, and sustains the bruises
in desperately defending her litter.

It is astonishing how cunning, wise and faithful an old
lioness is. She seldom leaves her kittens. From the time
they are six weeks old she takes them out to train them for
the battles of life, and the struggle continues from birth
to death. A lion hardly ever dies naturally. As soon as night
descends, the lioness stealthily stalks forth, and because
of her little ones, takes very short steps. The cubs follow,
stepping in their mother's tracks. When she crouches for
game, each little lion crouches also, and each one remains perfectly still until she springs, or signals them to
come. If she secures the prey, they all gorge themselves.
After the feast the mother takes her back trail, stepping
in the tracks she made coming down the mountain. And
the cubs are very careful to follow suit, and not to leave
marks of their trail in the soft snow. No doubt this habit
is practiced to keep their deadly enemies in ignorance of
their existence. The old Toms and white hunters are their

only foes. Indians never kill a lion. This trick of the lions has fooled many a hunter, concerning not only the direction, but particularly the number.

The only successful way to hunt lions is with trained dogs. A good hound can trail them for several hours after the tracks have been made, and on a cloudy or wet day can hold the scent much longer. In snow the hound can trail for three or four days after the track has been made.

When Jones was game warden of the Yellowstone National Park, he had unexampled opportunities to hunt cougars and learn their habits. All the cougars in that region of the Rockies made a rendezvous of the game preserve. Jones soon procured a pack of hounds, but as they had been trained to run deer, foxes and coyotes he had great trouble. They would break on the trail of these animals, and also on elk and antelope just when this was farthest from his wish. He soon realized that to train the hounds was a sore task. When they refused to come back at his call, he stung them with fine shot, and in this manner taught obedience. But obedience was not enough; the hounds must know how to follow and tree a lion. With this in mind, Jones decided to catch a lion alive and give his dogs practical lessons.

A few days after reaching this decision, he discovered the tracks of two lions in the neighborhood of Mt. Everett. The hounds were put on the trail and followed it into an abandoned coal shaft. Jones recognized this as his opportunity, and taking his lasso and an extra rope, he crawled into the hole. Not fifteen feet from the opening sat one of the cougars, snarling and spitting. Jones promptly lassoed it, passed his end of the lasso round a side prop of the shaft, and out to the soldiers who had followed him. Instructing them not to pull till he called, he cautiously began to crawl by the cougar, with the intention of getting farther back and roping its hind leg, so as to prevent disaster when the soldiers pulled it out. He accomplished this, not without some uneasiness in regard to the second lion, and giving the word to his companions, soon had his captive hauled from the shaft and tied so tightly it could not move.

Jones took the cougar and his hounds to an open place in the park, where there were trees, and prepared for a chase. Loosing the lion, he held his hounds back a moment, then let them go. Within one hundred yards the cougar climbed a tree, and the dogs saw the performance. Taking a forked stick, Jones mounted up to the cougar, caught it under the jaw with the stick, and pushed it out. There was a fight, a scramble, and the cougar dashed off to run up another tree. In this manner, he soon trained his hounds to the pink of perfection.

Jones discovered, while in the park, that the cougar is king of all the beasts of North America. Even a grizzly dashed away in great haste when a cougar made his appearance. At the road camp, near Mt. Washburn, during the fall of 1904, the bears, grizzlies and others, were always hanging round the cook tent. There were cougars also, and almost every evening, about dusk, a big fellow would come parading past the tent. The bears would grunt furiously and scamper in every direction. It was easy to tell when a cougar was in the neighborhood, by the peculiar grunts and snorts of the bears, and the sharp, distinct, alarmed yelps of coyotes. A lion would just as lief kill a coyote as any other animal and he would devour it, too. As to the fighting of cougars and grizzlies, that was a mooted question, with the credit on the side of the former.

The story of the doings of cougars, as told in the snow, was intensely fascinating and tragical. How they stalked deer and elk, crept to within springing distance, then crouched flat to leap, was as easy to read as if it had been told in print. The leaps and bounds were beyond belief. The longest leap on a level measured eighteen and one-half feet. Jones trailed a half-grown cougar, which in turn was trailing a big elk. He found where the cougar had struck his game, had clung for many rods, to be dashed off by the low limb of a spruce tree. The imprint of the body of the cougar was a foot deep in the snow; blood and tufts of hair covered the place. But there was no sign of the cougar renewing the chase.

In rare cases cougars would refuse to run, or take to trees. One day Jones followed the hounds, eight in number, to come on a huge Tom holding the whole pack at bay. He walked to and fro, lashing his tail from side to side, and when Jones dashed up, he coolly climbed a tree. Jones shot the cougar, which, in falling, struck one of the hounds, crippling him. This hound would never approach a tree after this incident, believing probably that the cougar had sprung upon him.

Usually the hounds chased their quarry into a tree long before Jones rode up. It was always desirable to kill the animal with the first shot. If the cougar was wounded, and fell or jumped among the dogs, there was sure to be a terrible fight, and the best dogs always received serious injuries, if they were not killed outright. The lion would seize a hound, pull him close, and bite him in the brain.

Jones asserted that a cougar would usually run from a hunter, but that this feature was not to be relied upon. And a wounded cougar was as dangerous as a tiger. In his hunts Jones carried a shotgun, and shells loaded with ball for the cougar, and others loaded with fine shot for the hounds. One day, about ten miles from the camp, the hounds took a trail and ran rapidly, as there were only a few inches of snow. Jones found a large lion had taken refuge in a tree that had fallen against another, and aiming at the shoulder of the beast, he fired both barrels. The cougar made no sign he had been hit. Jones reloaded and fired at the head. The old fellow growled fiercely, turned in the tree and walked down head first, something he would not have been able to do had the tree been upright. The hounds were ready for him, but wisely attacked in the rear. Realizing he had been shooting fine shot at the animal, Jones began a hurried search for a shell loaded with ball. The lion made for him, compelling him to dodge behind trees. Even though the hounds kept nipping the cougar, the persistent fellow still pursued the hunter. At last Jones found the right shell, just as the cougar reached for him. Major, the leader of the hounds, darted bravely in, and grasped the leg of the beast just in the nick of time. This enabled Jones to take aim and fire at close range, which ended the fight. Upon examination, it was discovered the cougar had been half-blinded by the fine shot, which accounted for the ineffectual attempts he had made to catch Jones.

The mountain lion rarely attacks a human being for the purpose of eating. When hungry he will often follow the tracks of people, and under favorable circumstances may ambush them. In the park where game is plentiful, no one has ever known a cougar to follow the trail of a person; but outside the park lions have been known to follow hunters, and particularly stalk little children. The Davis family, living a few miles north of the park, have had children pursued to the very doors of their cabin. And other families relate similar experiences. Jones heard of only one fatality, but he believes that if the children were left alone in the woods, the cougars would creep closer and closer, and when assured there was no danger, would spring to kill.

Jones never heard the cry of a cougar in the National Park, which strange circumstance, considering the great number of the animals there, he believed to be on account of the abundance of game. But he had heard it when a boy in Illinois, and when a man all over the West, and the cry was always the same, weird and wild, like the scream of a terrified woman. He did not understand the significance of the cry, unless it meant hunger, or the wailing mourn of a lioness for her murdered cubs.

The destructiveness of this savage species was murderous. Jones came upon one old Tom's den, where there was a pile of nineteen elk, mostly yearlings. Only five or six had been eaten. Jones hunted this old fellow for months, and found that the lion killed on the average three animals a week. The hounds got him up at length, and chased him to the Yellowstone River, which he swam at a point impassable for man or horse. One of the dogs, a giant bloodhound named Jack, swam the swift channel, kept on after the lion, but never returned. All cougars have their peculiar traits and habits, the same as other creatures, and all old Toms have strongly marked characteristics, but this one was the most destructive cougar Jones ever knew.

During Jones's short sojourn as warden in the park, he captured numerous cougars alive, and killed seventy-two.

CHAPTER 16

Kitty

It seemed my eyelids had scarcely touched when Jones's exasperating, yet stimulating, yell aroused me. Day was breaking. The moon and stars shone with wan luster. A white, snowy frost silvered the forest. Old Moze had curled close beside me, and now he gazed at me reproachfully and shivered. Lawson came hustling in with the horses. Jim busied himself around the campfire. My fingers nearly froze while I saddled my horse.

At five o'clock we were trotting up the slope of Buckskin, bound for the section of ruined rim wall where we had encountered the convention of cougars. Hoping to save time, we took a short cut, and were soon crossing deep ravines.

The sunrise coloring the purple curtain of cloud over the cañon was too much for me, and I lagged on a high ridge to watch it, thus falling behind my more practical companions. A far-off "Waa-hoo!" brought me to a realization of the day's stern duty, and I hurried Satan forward on the trail.

I came suddenly upon our leader, leading his horse through the scrub piñon on the edge of the cañon, and I knew at once something had happened, for he was closely scrutinizing the ground.

"I declare this beats me all hollow!" began Jones. "We might be hunting rabbits instead of the wildest animals on the continent. We jumped a bunch of lions in this clump of piñon. There must have been at least four. I thought first we'd run upon an old lioness with cubs, but all the trails were made by full-grown lions. Moze took one north along the rim, same as the other day, but the lion got away quick. Frank saw one lion. Wallace is following Sounder down into the first hollow. Jim has gone over the rim wall after Don. There you are! Four lions playing tag in broad daylight on top of this wall! I'm inclined to believe Clarke didn't exaggerate. But confound the luck! the hounds have split again. They're doing their best, of course, and it's up to us to stay with them. I'm afraid we'll lose some of them. Hello! I hear a signal. That's from Wallace. Waa-hoo! Waa-hoo! There he is, coming out of the hollow."

The tall Californian reached us presently with Sounder beside him. He reported that the hound had chased a lion into an impassable break. We then joined Frank on a jutting crag of the cañon wall.

"Waa-hoo!" yelled Jones. There was no answer except the echo, and it rolled up out of the chasm with strange, hollow mockery.

"Don took a cougar down this slide," said Frank. "I saw the brute, an' Don was makin' him hump. A—ha! There! Listen to thet!"

From the green and yellow depths soared the faint yelp of a hound.

"That's Don! that's Don!" cried Jones. "He's hot on something. Where's Sounder? Hyar, Sounder! By George! there he goes down the slide. Hear him! He's opened up! Hi! Hi! Hi!"

The deep, full mellow bay of the hound came ringing on the clear air.

"Wallace, you go down. Frank and I will climb out on that pointed crag. Grey, you stay here. Then we'll have the slide between us. Listen and watch!"

From my promontory I watched Wallace go down with his gigantic strides, sending the rocks rolling and cracking; and then I saw Jones and Frank crawl out to the end of a crumbling ruin of yellow wall which threatened to go splintering and thundering down into the abyss.

I thought, as I listened to the penetrating voice of the hound, that nowhere on earth could there be a grander scene for wild action, wild life. My position afforded a commanding view over a hundred miles of the noblest and most sublime work of nature. The rim wall where I stood sheered down a thousand feet, to meet a long wooded slope which cut abruptly off into another giant precipice; a second long slope descended, and jumped off into what seemed the grave of the world. Most striking in that vast void were the long, irregular points of rim wall, protruding into the Grand Cañon. From Point Sublime to the Pink Cliffs of Utah there were twelve of these colossal capes, miles apart, some sharp, some round, some blunt, all rugged and bold. The great chasm in the middle was full of purple smoke. It seemed a mighty sepulcher from which misty fumes rolled upward. The turrets, mesas, domes, parapets and escarpments of yellow and red rock gave the appearance of an architectural work of giant hands. The wonderful river of silt, the blood-red, mystic and sullen Rio Colorado, lay hidden except in one place far away, where it glimmered wanly. Thousands of colors were blended before my rapt gaze. Yellow predominated, as the walls and crags lorded it over the lower cliffs and tables; red glared in the sunlight; green softened these two, and then purple and violet, gray, blue and the darker hues shaded away into dim and distinct obscurity.

Excited yells from my companions on the other crag recalled me to the living aspect of the scene. Jones was leaning far down in a niche, at seeming great hazard of life, yelling with all the power of his strong lungs. Frank stood still farther out on a cracked point that made me tremble, and his yell reënforced Jones's. From far below rolled up a chorus of thrilling bays and yelps, and Jim's call, faint, but distinct on that wonderfully thin air, with its unmistakable note of warning.

Then on the slide I saw a lion headed for the rim wall and climbing fast. I added my exultant cry to the medley, and I stretched my arms wide to that illimitable void and gloried in a moment full to the brim of the tingling joy of existence. I did not consider how painful it must have been to the toiling lion. It was only the spell of wild environment, of perilous yellow crags, of thin, dry air, of voice of man and dog, of the stinging expectation of sharp action, of life.

I watched the lion growing bigger and bigger. I saw Don and Sounder run from the piñon into the open slide, and heard their impetuous burst of wild yelps as they saw their game. Then Jones's clarion yell made me bound for my horse. I reached him, was about to mount, when Moze came trotting toward me. I caught the old gladiator. When he heard the chorus from below, he plunged like a mad bull. With both arms round him I held on. I vowed never to let him get down that slide. He howled and tore, but I held on. My big black horse with ears laid back stood like a rock.

I heard the pattering of little sliding rocks below; stealthy padded footsteps and hard panting breaths, almost like coughs; then the lion passed out of the slide not twenty feet away. He saw us, and sprang into the piñon scrub with the leap of a scared deer.

Samson himself could no longer have held Moze. Away he darted with his sharp, angry bark. I flung myself upon Satan and rode out to see Jones ahead and Frank flashing through the green on the white horse.

At the end of the piñon thicket Satan overhauled Jones's bay, and we entered the open forest together. We saw Frank glinting across the dark pines.

"Hi! Hi!" yelled the Colonel.

No need was there to whip or spur those magnificent horses. They were fresh; the course was open, and smooth as a racetrack, and the impelling chorus of the hounds was in full blast. I gave Satan a loose rein, and he stayed neck and neck with the bay. There was not a log, nor a stone, nor a gully. The hollows grew wider and shallower as we raced along, and presently disappeared altogether. The lion was running straight from the cañon, and the certainty that he must sooner or later take to a tree, brought from me a yell of irresistible wild joy.

"Hi! Hi! Hi!" answered Jones.

The whipping wind with its pine-scented fragrance, warm as the breath of summer, was intoxicating as wine. The huge pines, too kingly for close communion with their kind, made wide arches under which the horses stretched out long and low, with supple, springy, powerful strides. Frank's yell rang clear as a bell. We saw him curve to the right, and took his yell as a signal for us to cut across. Then we began to close in on him, and to hear more distinctly the baying of the hounds.

"Hi! Hi! Hi! Hi!" bawled Jones, and his great trumpet voice rolled down the forest glades.

"Hi! Hi! Hi! Hi!" I screeched, in wild recognition of the spirit of the moment.

Fast as they were flying, the bay and the black responded to our cries, and quickened, strained and lengthened under us till the trees sped by in blurs.

There, plainly in sight ahead ran the hounds, Don leading, Sounder next, and Moze not fifty yards behind a desperately running lion.

There are all-satisfying moments of life. That chase

through the open forest, under the stately pines, with the wild, tawny quarry in plain sight and the glad staccato yelps of the hounds filling my ears and swelling my heart, with the splendid action of my horse carrying me on the wings of the wind, was glorious answer and fullness to the call and hunger of a hunter's blood.

But as such moments must be, they were brief. The lion leaped gracefully into the air, splintering the bark from a pine fifteen feet up, and crouched on a limb. The hounds tore madly round the tree.

"Full-grown female," said Jones calmly, as we dismounted, "and she's ours. We'll call her Kitty."

Kitty was a beautiful creature, long, slender, glossy, with white belly and black-tipped ears and tail. She did not resemble the heavy, grimfaced brute that always hung in the air of my dreams. A low, brooding menacing murmur, that was not a snarl nor a growl, came from her. She watched the dogs with bright, steady eyes, and never so much as looked at us.

The dogs were worth attention, even from us, who certainly did not need to regard them from her personally hostile point of view. Don stood straight up, with his forepaws beating the air; he walked on his hind legs like the trained dog in the circus; he yelped continuously, as if it agonized him to see the lion safe out of his reach. Sounder had lost his identity. Joy had unhinged his mind and had made him a dog of double personality. He had always been unsociable with me, never responding to my attempts to caress him, but now he leaped into my arms and licked my face. He had always hated Jones till that moment, when he raised his paws to his master's breast. And perhaps more remarkable, time and time again he sprang up at Satan's nose, whether to bite him or kiss him, I could not tell. Then old Moze, he of Grand Cañon fame, made the delirious antics of his canine fellows look cheap. There was a small, dead pine that had fallen against a drooping branch of the tree Kitty had taken refuge in, and up this narrow ladder Moze began to climb. He was fifteen feet up, and Kitty had begun to shift uneasily, when Jones saw him.

"Hyar! you wild coon-chaser! Git out of that! Come down! Come down!"

But Jones might have been in the bottom of the cañon for all Moze heard or cared. Jones removed his coat, carefully coiled his lasso, and began to go hand and knee up the leaning pine.

"Hyar! dod-blast you, git down!" yelled Jones, and he kicked Moze off. The persistent hound returned, and followed Jones to a height of twenty feet, where again he was thrust off.

"Hold him, one of you!" called Jones.

"Not me," said Frank, "I'm lookin' out for myself."

"Same here," I cried, with a camera in one hand and a rifle in the other. "Let Moze climb if he likes."

Climb he did, to be kicked off again. But he went back. It was a way he had. Jones at last recognized either his own waste of time or Moze's greatness, for he desisted, allowing the hound to keep close after him.

The cougar, becoming uneasy, stood up, reached for another limb, climbed out upon it, and peering down, spat hissingly at Jones. But he kept steadily on with Moze close on his heels. I snapped my camera on them when Kitty was not more than fifteen feet above them. As Jones reached the snag which upheld the leaning tree, she ran out on her branch, and leaped into an adjoining pine. It was a good long jump, and the weight of the animal bent the limb alarmingly.

Jones backed down, and laboriously began to climb the other tree. As there were no branches low down, he had to hug the trunk with arms and legs as a boy climbs. His lasso hampered his progress. When the slow ascent was accomplished up to the first branch, Kitty leaped back into her first perch. Strange to say Jones did not grumble; none of his characteristic impatience manifested itself here. I supposed with him all the exasperating waits and vexatious obstacles were little things preliminary to the real work, to which he had now come. He was calm and deliberate, and slid down the pine, walked back to the leaning tree, and while resting a moment, shook his lasso at Kitty. This action fitted him, somehow; it was so compatible with his grim assurance.

To me, and to Frank, also, for that matter, it was all new and startling, and we were as excited as the dogs. We kept continually moving about, Frank mounted, and I afoot, to get good views of the cougar. When she crouched as if to leap, it was almost impossible to remain under the tree, and we kept moving.

Once more Jones crept up on hands and knees. Moze walked the slanting pine like a rope performer. Kitty began to grow restless. This time she showed both anger and impatience, but did not yet appear frightened. She growled low and deep, opened her mouth and hissed, and swung her tufted tail faster and faster.

"Look out, Jones! look out!" yelled Frank warningly.

Jones, who had reached the trunk of the tree, halted and slipped round it, placing it between him and Kitty. She had advanced on her limb, a few feet above Jones, and threateningly hung over. Jones backed down a little till she crossed to another branch, then he resumed his former position.

"Watch below," called he.

Hardly any doubt was there as to how we watched. Frank and I were all eyes, except very high and throbbing hearts. When Jones thrashed the lasso at Kitty we both yelled. She ran out on the branch and jumped. This time she fell short of her point, clutched a dead snag, which broke, letting her through a bushy branch from where she hung head downward. For a second she swung free, then reaching toward the tree caught it with front paws, ran down like a squirrel, and leaped off when thirty feet from the ground. The action was as rapid as it was astonishing.

Like a yellow rubber ball she bounded up, and fled with the yelping hounds at her heels. The chase was short. At the end of a hundred yards Moze caught up with her and nipped her. She whirled with savage suddenness, and lunged at Moze, but he cunningly eluded the vicious paws. Then she sought safety in another pine.

Frank, who was as quick as the hounds, almost rode them down in his eagerness. While Jones descended from his perch, I led the two horses down the forest.

This time the cougar was well out on a low spreading branch. Jones conceived the idea of raising the loop of his lasso on a long pole, but as no pole of sufficient length could be found, he tried from the back of his horse. The bay walked forward well enough; when, however, he got under the beast and heard her growl, he reared and almost threw Jones. Frank's horse could not be persuaded to go near the tree. Satan evinced no fear of the cougar, and without flinching carried Jones directly beneath the limb, and stood with ears back and forelegs stiff.

"Look at that! look at that!" cried Jones, as the wary cougar pawed the loop aside. Three successive times did Jones have the lasso just ready to drop over her neck, when she flashed a yellow paw and knocked the noose awry. Then she leaped far out over the waiting dogs, struck the ground with a light, sharp thud, and began to run with the speed of a deer. Frank's cowboy training now stood us in good stead. He was off like a shot and turned the cougar from the direction of the cañon. Jones lost not a moment in pursuit, and I, left with Jones's badly frightened bay, got going in time to see the race, but not to assist. For several hundred yards Kitty made the hounds appear slow. Don, being swiftest, gained on her steadily toward the close of the dash, and presently was running under her upraised tail. On the next jump he nipped her. She turned and sent him reeling. Sounder came flying up to bite her flank, and at the same moment fierce old Moze closed in on her. The next instant a struggling mass whirled on the ground. Jones and Frank, yelling like demons, almost rode over it. The cougar broke from her assailants, and dashing away leaped on the first tree. It was a half-dead pine with short snags low down and a big branch extending out over a ravine.

"I think we can hold her now," said Jones. The tree proved to be a most difficult one to climb. Jones made several ineffectual attempts before he reached the first limb, which broke, giving him a hard fall. This calmed me enough to make me take notice of Jones's condition. He was wet with sweat and covered with the black pitch from the pines; his shirt was slit down the arm, and there was blood on his temple and his hand. The next attempt began by placing a good-sized log against the tree, and proved to be the necessary help. Jones got hold of the second limb and pulled himself up.

As he kept on, Kitty crouched low as if to spring upon him. Again Frank and I sent warning calls to him, but he paid no attention to us or to the cougar, and continued to climb. This worried Kitty as much as it did us. She began to move on the snags, stepping from one to the other, every moment snarling at Jones, and then she crawled up. The big branch evidently took her eye. She tried several times to climb up to it, but small snags close together made her distrustful. She walked uneasily out upon two limbs, and as they bent with her weight she hurried back. Twice she did this, each time looking up, showing her desire to leap to the big branch. Her distress became plainly evident; a child could have seen that she feared she would fall. At length, in desperation, she spat at Jones, then ran out and leaped. She all but missed the branch, but succeeded in holding to it and swinging to safety. Then she turned to her tormentor, and gave utterance to most savage sounds. As she did not intimidate her pursuer, she retreated out on the branch, which sloped down at a deep angle, and crouched on a network of small limbs.

When Jones had worked up a little farther, he commanded a splendid position for his operations. Kitty was somewhat below him in a desirable place, yet the branch she was on joined the tree considerably above his head. Jones cast his lasso. It caught on a snag. Throw after throw he made with like result. He recoiled and recast nineteen times, to my count, when Frank made a suggestion.

"Rope those dead snags an' break them off."

This practical idea Jones soon carried out, which left him a clear path. The next fling of the lariat caused the cougar angrily to shake her head. Again Jones sent the noose flying. She pulled it off her back and bit it savagely.

Though very much excited, I tried hard to keep sharp, keen faculties alert so as not to miss a single detail of the thrilling scene. But I must have failed, for all of a sudden I saw how Jones was standing in the tree, something I had not before appreciated. He had one hand hold, which he could not use while recoiling the lasso, and his feet rested upon a precariously frail-appearing, dead snag. He made eleven casts of the lasso, all of which bothered Kitty, but did not catch her. The twelfth caught her front paw. Jones jerked so quickly and hard that he almost lost his balance, and he pulled the noose off. Patiently he recoiled the lasso.

"That's what I want. If I can get her front paw she's

ours. My idea is to pull her off the limb, let her hang there, and then lasso her hind legs."

Another cast, the unlucky thirteenth, settled the loop perfectly round her neck. She chewed on the rope with her front teeth and appeared to have difficulty in holding it.

"Easy! Easy! Ooze thet rope! Easy!" yelled the cowboy.

Cautiously Jones took up the slack and slowly tightened the nose, then with a quick jerk, fastened it close round her neck.

We heralded this achievement with yells of triumph that made the forest ring.

Our triumph was short-lived. Jones had hardly moved when the cougar shot straight out into the air. The lasso caught on a branch, hauling her up short, and there she hung in mid air, writhing, struggling and giving utterance to sounds terribly human. For several seconds she swung, slowly descending, in which frenzied time I, with ruling passion uppermost, endeavored to snap a picture of her.

The unintelligible commands Jones was yelling to Frank and me ceased suddenly with a sharp crack of breaking wood. Then crash! Jones fell out of the tree. The lasso streaked up, ran over the limb, while the cougar dropped pell-mell into the bunch of waiting, howling dogs.

The next few moments it was impossible for me to distinguish what actually transpired. A great flutter of leaves whirled round a swiftly changing ball of brown and black and yellow, from which came a fiendish clamor.

Then I saw Jones plunge down the ravine and bounce here and there in mad efforts to catch the whipping lasso. He was roaring in a way that made all his former yells merely whispers. Starting to run, I tripped on a root, fell prone on my face into the ravine, and rolled over and over until I brought up with a bump against a rock.

What a tableau riveted my gaze! It staggered me so I did not think of my camera. I stood transfixed not fifteen feet from the cougar. She sat on her haunches with body well drawn back by the taut lasso to which Jones held tightly. Don was standing up with her, upheld by the hooked claws in his head. The cougar had her paws outstretched; her mouth open wide, showing long, cruel, white fangs; she was trying to pull the head of the dog to her. Don held back with all his power, and so did Jones. Moze and Sounder were tussling round her body. Suddenly both ears of the dog pulled out, slit into ribbons. Don had never uttered a sound, and once free, he made at her again with open jaws. One blow sent him reeling and stunned. Then began again that wrestling whirl.

"Beat off the dogs! Beat off the dogs!" roared Jones. "She'll kill them! She'll kill them!"

Frank and I seized clubs and ran in upon the confused furry mass, forgetful of peril to ourselves. In the wild contagion of such a savage moment the minds of men revert wholly to primitive instincts. We swung our clubs and yelled; we fought all over the bottom of the ravine, crashing through the bushes, over logs and stones. I actually felt the soft fur of the cougar at one fleeting instant. The dogs had the strength born of insane fighting spirit. At last we pulled them to where Don lay, half-stunned, and with an arm tight round each, I held them while Frank turned to help Jones.

The disheveled Jones, bloody, grim as death, his heavy jaw locked, stood holding to the lasso. The cougar, her sides shaking with short, quick pants, crouched low on the ground with eyes of purple fire.

"For God's sake, get a half-hitch on the saplin'!" called the cowboy.

His quick grasp of the situation averted a tragedy. Jones was nearly exhausted, even as he was beyond thinking for himself or giving up. The cougar sprang, a yellow, frightful flash. Even as she was in the air, Jones took a quick step to one side and dodged as he threw his lasso round the sapling. She missed him, but one alarmingly outstretched paw grazed his shoulder. A twist of Jones's big hand fastened the lasso—and Kitty was a prisoner. While she fought, rolled, twisted, bounded, whirled, writhed with hissing, snarling fury, Jones sat mopping the sweat and blood from his face.

Kitty's efforts were futile; she began to weaken from the choking. Jones took another rope, and tightening a noose around her back paws, which he lassoed as she rolled over, he stretched her out. She began to contract her supple body, gave a savage, convulsive spring, which pulled Jones flat on the ground, then the terrible wrestling started again. The lasso slipped over her back paws. She leaped the whole length of the other lasso. Jones caught it and fastened it more securely; but this precaution proved unnecessary, for she suddenly sank down either exhausted or choked, and gasped with her tongue hanging out. Frank slipped the second noose over her back paws, and Jones did likewise with a third lasso over her right front paw. These lassoes Jones tied to different saplings.

"Now you are a good Kitty," said Jones, kneeling by her. He took a pair of clippers from his hip pocket, and grasping a paw in his powerful fist he calmly clipped the points of the dangerous claws. This done, he called to me to get the collar and chain that were tied to his saddle. I procured them and hurried back. Then the old buffalo hunter loosened the lasso which was round her neck, and as soon as she could move her head, he teased her to bite a club. She broke two good sticks with her sharp teeth, but the third, being solid, did not break. While she was chewing it Jones forced her head back and placed his heavy knee on the club. In a twinkling he had strapped the collar round her neck. The chain he made fast to the sapling. After removing the club from her mouth he placed his knee on her neck, and while her head was in this helpless position he dexterously slipped a loop of thick copper wire over her nose, pushed it back and twisted it tight. Following this, all done with speed and precision, he took from his pocket a piece of steel rod, perhaps one-quarter of an inch thick, and five inches long. He pushed this between Kitty's jaws, just back of her great white fangs, and in front of the copper wire. She had been shorn of her sharp weapons; she was muzzled, bound, helpless, an object to pity.

Lastly Jones removed the three lassoes. Kitty slowly gathered her lissom body in a ball and lay panting, with the same brave wildfire in her eyes. Jones stroked her black-tipped ears and ran his hand down her glossy fur. All the time he had kept up a low monotone, talking to her in the strange language he used toward animals. Then he rose to his feet.

"We'll go back to camp now, and get a pack-saddle and horse," he said. "She'll be safe here. We'll rope her again, tie her up, throw her over a pack-saddle, and take her to camp."

To my utter bewilderment the hounds suddenly commenced fighting among themselves. Of all the vicious bloody dog-fights I ever saw that was the worst. I began to belabor them with a club, and Frank sprang to my assistance. Beating had no apparent effect. We broke a dozen sticks, and then Frank grappled with Moze and I with Sounder. Don kept on fighting either one till Jones secured him. Then we all took a rest, panting and weary.

"What's it mean?" I exclaimed, appealing to Jones.

"Jealous, that's all. Jealous over the lion."

We all remained seated, men and hounds, a sweaty, dirty, bloody, ragged group. I discovered I was sorry for Kitty. I forgot all the carcasses of deer and horses, the brutality of this species of cat; and even forgot the grim, snarling yellow devil that had leaped at me. Kitty was beautiful and helpless. How brave she was, too! No sign of fear shone in her wonderful eyes, only hate, defiance, watchfulness.

On the ride back to camp Jones expressed himself thus: "How happy I am that I can keep this lion and the others we are going to capture, for my own! When I was in the Yellowstone Park I did not get to keep one of the many I captured. The military officials took them from me."

When we reached camp Lawson was absent, but fortunately Old Baldy browsed near at hand, and was easily caught. Frank said he would rather take Old Baldy for the cougar than any other horse we had. Leaving me in camp, he and Jones rode off to fetch Kitty.

About five o'clock they came trotting up through the forest with Jim, who had fallen in with them on the way. Old Baldy had remained true to his fame—nothing, not even a cougar bothered him. Kitty, evidently no worse for her experience, was chained to a pine tree about fifty feet from the campfire.

Wallace came riding wearily in, and when he saw the captive, he greeted us with an exultant yell. He got there just in time to see the first special features of Kitty's captivity. The hounds surrounded her, and could not be called off. We had to beat them. Whereupon the six jealous canines fell to fighting among themselves, and fought so savagely as to be deaf to our cries and insensible to blows. They had to be torn apart and chained.

About six o'clock Lawson loped in with the horses. Of course he did not know we had a cougar, and no one seemed interested enough to inform him. Perhaps only Frank and I thought of it; but I saw a merry snap in Frank's eyes, and kept silent. Kitty had hidden behind the pine tree. Lawson, astride Jim's pack-horse, a crochety animal, reined in just abreast of the tree, and leisurely threw his leg over the saddle. Kitty leaped out to the extent of her chain, and fairly exploded in a frightful cat-spit.

Lawson had stated some time before that he was afraid of cougars, which was a weakness he need not have divulged in view of what happened. The horse plunged, throwing him ten feet, and snorting in terror, stampeded with the rest of the bunch and disappeared among the pines.

"Why the hell didn't you tell a feller?" reproachfully growled the Arizonian. Frank and Jim held each other upright, and the rest of us gave way to as hearty if not as violent mirth.

We had supper, during which Kitty sat by her pine and watched our every movement.

"We'll rest up for a day or two," said Jones. "Things have commenced to come our way. If I'm not mistaken we'll bring an old Tom alive into camp. But it would never do for us to get a big Tom in the fix we had Kitty to-day. You see, I wanted to lasso her front paw, pull her off the limb, tie my end of the lasso to the tree, and while she hung I'd go down and rope her hind paws. It all went wrong to-day, and was as tough a job as I ever handled."

Not until late next morning did Lawson corral all the horses. That day we lounged in camp mending broken bridles, saddles, stirrups, lassoes, boots, trousers, leggins, shirts and even broken skins.

During this time I found Kitty a most interesting study. She reminded me of an enormous yellow kitten. She did not appear wild or untamed until approached. Then she slowly sank down, laid back her ears, opened her mouth and hissed and spat, at the same time throwing both paws out viciously. Kitty may have rested, but did not sleep. At times she fought her chain, tugging and straining at it, and trying to bite it through. Everything in reach she clawed, particularly the bark of the tree. Once she tried to hang herself by leaping over a low limb. When any one walked by her she crouched low, evidently imagining herself unseen. If one of us walked toward her, or looked at her, she did not crouch. At other times, noticeably when no one was near, she would roll on her back and extend all four paws in the air. Her actions were beautiful, soft, noiseless, quick and subtle.

The day passed, as all days pass in camp, swiftly and pleasantly, and twilight stole down upon us round the ruddy fire. The wind roared in the pines and lulled to repose; the lonesome, friendly coyote barked; the bells on the hobbled horses jingled sweetly; the great watch stars blinked out of the blue.

The red glow of the burning logs lighted up Jones's calm, cold face. Tranquil, unalterable and peaceful it seemed; yet beneath the peace I thought I saw a suggestion of wild restraint, of mystery, of unslaked life.

Strangely enough, his next words confirmed my last thought.

"For forty years I've had an ambition. It's to get possession of an island in the Pacific, somewhere between Vancouver and Alaska, and then go to Siberia and capture a lot of Russian sables. I'd put them on the island and cross them with our silver foxes. I'm going to try it next year if I can find the time."

The ruling passion and character determine our lives. Jones was sixty-three years old, yet the thing that had ruled and absorbed his mind was still as strong as the longing for freedom in Kitty's wild heart.

Hours after I had crawled into my sleeping-bag, in the

silence of night I heard her working to get free. In darkness she was most active, restless, intense. I heard the clink of her chain, the crack of her teeth, the scrape of her claws. How tireless she was. I recalled the wistful light in her eyes that saw, no doubt, far beyond the campfire to the yellow crags, to the great downward slopes, to freedom. I slipped my elbow out of the bag and raised myself. Dark shadows were hovering under the pines. I saw Kitty's eyes gleam like sparks, and I seemed to see in them the hate, the fear, the terror she had of the clanking thing that bound her.

I shivered, perhaps from the cold night wind which moaned through the pines; I saw the stars glittering pale and far off, and under their wan light the still, set face of Jones, and blanketed forms of my other companions.

The last thing I remembered before dropping into dreamless slumber was hearing a bell tinkle in the forest, which I recognized as the one I had placed on Satan.

CHAPTER 17

Conclusion

Kitty was not the only cougar brought into camp alive. The ensuing days were fruitful of cougars and adventure. There were more wild rides to the music of the baying hounds, and more heart-breaking cañon slopes to conquer, and more swinging, tufted tails and snarling savage faces in the piñons. Once again, I am sorry to relate, I had to glance down the sights of the little Remington, and I saw blood on the stones. Those eventful days sped by all too soon.

When the time for parting came it took no little discussion to decide on the quickest way of getting me to a railroad. I never fully appreciated the inaccessibility of the Siwash until the question arose of finding a way out. To return on our back trail would require two weeks, and to go out by the trail north to Utah meant half as much time over the same kind of desert. Lawson came to our help, however, with the information that an occasional prospector or horse hunter crossed the cañon from the Saddle, where a trail led down to the river.

"I've heard the trail is a bad one," said Lawson, "an' though I never seen it, I reckon it could be found. After we get to the Saddle we'll build two fires on one of the high points an' keep them burnin' well after dark. If Mr. Bass, who lives on the other side, sees the fires he'll come down his trail next mornin' an' meet us at the river. He keeps a boat there. This is takin' a chance, but I reckon it's worth while."

So it was decided that Lawson and Frank would try to get me out by way of the cañon; Wallace intended to go by the Utah route, and Jones was to return at once to his range and his buffalo.

That night round the campfire we talked over the many incidents of the hunt. Jones stated he had never in his life come so near getting his "everlasting" as when the big bay horse tripped on a cañon slope and rolled over him. Notwithstanding the respect with which we regarded his statement we held different opinions. Then, with the unfailing optimism of hunters, we planned another hunt for the next year.

"I'll tell you what," said Jones. "Up in Utah there's a wild region called Pink Cliffs. A few poor sheep-herders try to raise sheep in the valleys. They wouldn't be so poor if it was not for the grizzly and black bears that live on the sheep. We'll go up there, find a place where grass and water can be had, and camp. We'll notify the sheep-herders we are there for business. They'll be only too glad to hustle in with news of a bear, and we can get the hounds on the trail by sun-up. I'll have a dozen hounds then, maybe twenty, and all trained. We'll put every black bear we chase up a tree, and we'll rope and tie him. As to grizzlies—well, I'm not saying so much. They can't climb trees, and they are not afraid of a pack of hounds. If we rounded up a grizzly, got him cornered, and threw a rope on him—there'd be some fun, eh, Jim?"

"Shore there would," Jim replied.

On the strength of this I stored up food for future thought and thus reconciled myself to bidding farewell to the purple cañons and shaggy slopes of Buckskin Mountain.

At five o'clock next morning we were all stirring. Jones yelled at the hounds and untangled Kitty's chain. Jim was already busy with the biscuit dough. Frank shook the frost off the saddles. Wallace was packing. The merry jangle of bells came from the forest, and presently Lawson appeared driving in the horses. I caught my black and saddled him, then realizing we were soon to part I could not resist giving him a hug.

An hour later we all stood at the head of the trail leading down into the chasm. The east gleamed rosy red. Powell's Plateau loomed up in the distance, and under it showed the dark-fringed dip in the rim called the Saddle. Blue mist floated round the mesas and domes.

Lawson led the way down the trail. Frank started Old Baldy with the pack.

"Come," he called, "be oozin' along."

I spoke the last good-by and turned Satan into the narrow trail. When I looked back Jones stood on the rim with the fresh glow of dawn shining on his face. The trail was steep, and claimed my attention and care, but time and time again I gazed back. Jones waved his hand till a huge jutting cliff walled him from view. Then I cast my eyes on the rough descent and the wonderful void beneath me. In my mind lingered a pleasing consciousness of my last sight of the old plainsman. He fitted the scene; he belonged there among the silent pines and the yellow crags.

THE END

LAST OF THE GREAT SCOUTS

BY HELEN CODY WETMORE

To the memory of a mother
whose Christian character still lives
a hallowed influence

FOREWORD

By Zane Grey

It is an honor and a pleasure for me to add a few words to this splendid book, "The Last of the Great Scouts," by Colonel Cody's sister, Mrs. Helen Cody Wetmore.

When the history of our western frontier is at last written, the name of Buffalo Bill will stand out perhaps as no other. He was symbolical of the heroic west. He inspired the pioneer, guided the soldier, and helped the builders of the railroad. And his life was more thrilling than any wild, adventurous and moving romance. Facts may not be so strange as fiction, but they are more convincing. And some facts, if written as fiction, would be unbelievable.

The early West bred men of heroic mould. The like of Buffalo Bill, Wild Bill, Buffalo Jones, and many other famous frontiersmen will never be met with again in this world. The time needed them, and they developed. These three types of the West were singularly unlike—Buffalo Bill was the scout and pathfinder and hunter; Wild Bill was the gunman, the killer, the foe of the rampant desperado class; Buffalo Jones was the preserver.

And so a narrative of Buffalo Bill's life, by a relative, written simply and truthfully from first-hand facts, is an absorbingly interesting story as well as a valuable adjunct to history.

It will show a man growing great through the life of the times—an outdoor life of swift action, of various service, of perilous adventure, of unselfish devotion of an ideal, of magnificent effrontery in the face of death, of steadfast friendship, of inexplicable hardihood and endurance through heat, storm, cold, desert thirst and mountain loneliness—all that some day men might have free, happy homes in the boundless West.

—ZANE GREY

GENEALOGY OF BUFFALO BILL

The following genealogical sketch was compiled in 1897:

It is not generally known that genuine royal blood courses in Colonel Cody's veins. He is a lineal descendant of Milesius, king of Spain, that famous monarch whose three sons, Heber, Heremon, and Ir, founded the first dynasty in Ireland, about the beginning of the Christian era. The Cody family comes through the line of Heremon. The original name was Tireach, which signifies "The Rocks." Muiredach Tireach, one of the first of this line, and son of Fiacha Straivetine, was crowned king of Ireland, Anno Domini 320. Another of the line became king of Connaught, Anno Domini 701. The possessions of the Sept were located in the present counties of Clare, Galway, and Mayo. The names Connaught-Gallway, after centuries, gradually contracted to Connallway, Connellway, Connelly, Conly, Cory, Coddy, Coidy, and Cody, and is clearly shown by ancient indentures still traceable among existing records. On the maternal side, Colonel Cody can, without difficulty, follow his lineage to the best blood of England. Several of the Cody family emigrated to America in 1747, settling in Maryland, Pennsylvania, and Virginia. The name is frequently mentioned in Revolutionary history. Colonel Cody is a member of the Cody family of Revolutionary fame. Like the other Spanish-Irish families, the Codys have their proof of ancestry in the form of a crest. The lion signifies Spanish origin. It is the same figure that forms a part of the royal coat-of-arms of Spain to this day—Castile and Leon. The arm and cross denote that the descent is through the line of Heremon, whose posterity were among the first to follow the cross, as a symbol of their adherence to the Christian faith.

PREFACE TO THE FIRST EDITION

In presenting this volume to the public, the writer has a twofold purpose. For a number of years there has been an increasing demand for an authentic biography of "Buffalo Bill," and in response many books of varying value have been submitted; yet no one of them has borne the hallmark of veracious history. Naturally, there were incidents in Colonel Cody's life—more especially in the earlier years—that could be given only by those with whom he had grown up from childhood. For many incidents of his later life I am indebted to his own and others' accounts. I desire to acknowledge obligation to General P. H. Sheridan, Colonel Inman, Colonel Ingraham, and my brother for valuable assistance furnished by Sheridan's Memoirs, "The Santa Fé Trail," "The Great Salt Lake Trail," "Buffalo Bill's Autobiography," and "Stories from the Life of Buffalo Bill."

A second reason that prompted the writing of my brother's life-story is purely personal. The sobriquet of "Buffalo Bill" has conveyed to many people an impression of his personality that is far removed from the facts. They have pictured in fancy a rough frontier character, without tenderness and true nobility. But in very truth has the poet sung:

> "The bravest are the tenderest—
> The loving are the daring."

The public knows my brother as boy Indian-slayer, a champion buffalo-hunter, a brave soldier, a daring scout, an intrepid frontiersman, and a famous exhibitor. It is only fair to him that a glimpse be given of the parts he played behind the scenes—devotion to a widowed mother, that pushed the boy so early upon a stage of ceaseless action, continued care and tenderness displayed in later years, and the generous thoughtfulness of manhood's prime.

Thus a part of my pleasant task has been to enable the public to see my brother through his sister's eyes—eyes that have seen truly if kindly. If I have been tempted into praise where simple narrative might to the reader seem all that was required, if I have seemed to exaggerate in any of my history's details, I may say that I am not conscious of having set down more than "a plain, unvarnished tale." Embarrassed with riches of fact, I have had no thought of fiction.

—H.C.W.
Codyview
Duluth, Minnesota
February 26, 1899

CHAPTER 1

The Old Homestead in Iowa

A pleasant, roomy farm-house, set in the sunlight against a background of cool, green wood and mottled meadow—this is the picture that my earliest memories frame for me. To this home my parents, Isaac and Mary Cody, had moved soon after their marriage.

The place was known as the Scott farm, and was situated in Scott County, Iowa, near the historic little town of Le Clair, where, but a few years before, a village of the Fox Indians had been located; where Black Hawk and his thousand warriors had assembled for their last war-dance; where the marquee of General Scott was erected, and the treaty with the Sacs and Foxes drawn up; and where, in obedience to the Sac chief's terms, Antoine Le Clair, the famous half-breed Indian scholar and interpreter, had built his cabin, and given to the place his name. Here, in this atmosphere of pioneer struggle and Indian warfare—in the farm-house in the dancing sunshine, with the background of wood and meadow—my brother, William Frederick Cody, was born, on the 26th day of February, 1846.

Of the good, old-fashioned sort was our family, numbering five daughters and two sons—Martha, Samuel, Julia, William, Eliza, Helen, and May. Samuel, a lad of unusual beauty of face and nature, was killed through an unhappy accident before he was yet fourteen.

He was riding "Betsy Baker," a mare well known among

old settlers in Iowa as one of speed and pedigree, yet displaying at times a most malevolent temper, accompanied by Will, who, though only seven years at age, yet sat his pony with the ease and grace that distinguished the veteran rider of the future. Presently Betsy Baker became fractious and sought to throw her rider. In vain did she rear and plunge; he kept his saddle. Then, seemingly, she gave up the fight, and Samuel cried, in boyish exultation:

"Ah, Betsy Baker, you didn't quite come it that time!"

His last words! As if she knew her rider was a careless victor off his guard, the mare reared suddenly and flung herself upon her back, crushing the daring boy beneath her.

Though to us younger children our brother Samuel was but a shadowy memory, in him had centered our parents' fondest hopes and aims. These, naturally, were transferred to the younger, now the only son, and the hope that mother, especially, held for him was strangely stimulated by the remembrance of the mystic divination of a soothsayer in the years agone. My mother was a woman of too much intelligence and force of character to nourish an average superstition; but prophecies fulfilled will temper, though they may not shake, the smiling unbelief of the most hard-headed skeptic. Mother's moderate skepticism was not proof against the strange fulfillment of one prophecy, which fell out in this wise:

To a Southern city, which my mother visited when a girl, there came a celebrated fortune-teller, and led by curiosity, my mother and my aunt one day made two of the crowd that thronged the sibyl's drawing-rooms.

Both received with laughing incredulity the prophecy that my aunt and the two children with her would be dead in a fortnight; but the dread augury was fulfilled to the letter. All three were stricken with yellow fever, and died within less than the time set. This startling confirmation of the soothsayer's divining powers not unnaturally affected my mother's belief in that part of the prophecy relating to herself: that "she would meet her future husband on the steamboat by which she expected to return home; that she would be married to him in a year, and bear three sons, of whom only the second would live, but that the name of this son would be known all over the world, and would one day be that of the President of the United States." The first part of this prophecy was verified, and Samuel's death was another link in the curious chain of circumstances. Was it, then, strange that mother looked with unusual hope upon her second son?

That 'tis good fortune for a boy to be only brother to five sisters is open to question. The older girls petted Will; the younger regarded him as a superior being; while to all it seemed so fit and proper that the promise of the stars concerning his future should be fulfilled that never for a moment did we weaken in our belief that great things were in store for our only brother. We looked for the prophecy's complete fulfillment, and with childish veneration regarded Will as one destined to sit in the executive's chair.

My mother, always somewhat delicate, was so affected in health by the shock of Samuel's death that a change of scene was advised. The California gold craze was then at its height, and father caught the fever, though in a mild form; for he had prospered as a farmer, and we not only had a comfortable home, but were in easy circumstances. Influenced in part by a desire to improve mother's health, and in part, no doubt, by the golden daydreams that lured so many Argonauts Pacificward, he disposed of his farm, and bade us prepare for a Western journey. Before his plans were completed he fell in with certain disappointed gold-seekers returning from the coast, and impressed by their representations, decided in favor of Kansas instead of California.

Father had very extravagant ideas regarding vehicles and horses, and such a passion for equestrian display that we often found ourselves with a stable full of thoroughbreds and an empty cupboard. For our Western migration we had, in addition to three prairie-schooners, a large family carriage, drawn by a span of fine horses in silver-mounted harness. This carriage had been made to order in the East, upholstered in the finest leather, polished and varnished as though for a royal progress. Mother and we girls found it more comfortable riding than the springless prairie-schooners.

Brother Will constituted himself an armed escort, and rode proudly alongside on his pony, his gun slung across the pommel of his saddle, and the dog Turk bringing up the rear.

To him this Western trip thrilled with possible Indian skirmishes and other stirring adventures, though of the real dangers that lay in our path he did not dream. For him, therefore, the first week of our travels held no great interest, for we were constantly chancing upon settlers and farm-houses, in which the night might be passed; but with every mile the settlers grew fewer and farther between, until one day Will whispered to us, in great glee: "I heard father tell mother that he expected we should have to camp to-night. Now we'll have some fun!"

Will's hope was well founded. Shortly before nightfall we reached a stream that demanded a ferry-boat for its crossing, and as the nearest dwelling was a dozen miles away, it was decided that we should camp by the streamside. The family was first sent across the ferry, and upon the eight-year-old lad of the house father placed the responsibility of selecting the ground on which to pitch the tents.

My brother's career forcibly illustrates the fact that environment plays as large a part as heredity in shaping character. Perhaps his love for the free life of the plains is a heritage derived from some long-gone ancestor; but there can be no doubt that to the earlier experiences of which I am writing he owed his ability as a scout. The faculty for obtaining water, striking trails, and finding desirable camping-grounds in him seemed almost instinct.

The tents being pitched upon a satisfactory site, Will called to Turk, the dog, and rifle in hand, set forth in search of game for supper. He was successful beyond his fondest hopes. He had looked only for small game, but scarcely had he put the camp behind him when Turk gave a signaling yelp, and one of the bushes bounded a magnificent deer. Nearly every hunter will confess to "buck fever" at sight of his first deer, so it is not strange that a boy of Will's age should have stood immovable, staring dazedly at the graceful animal until it vanished from sight. Turk gave chase, but soon trotted back, and barked reproachfully at his young master. But Will presently had an opportunity to recover Turk's good opinion, for the dog, after darting away, with another signaling yelp fetched another fine stag within gun range. This time the young hunter, mastering his nerves, took aim with steady hand, and brought down his first deer.

On the following Sabbath we were encamped by another deep, swift-running stream. After being wearied and overheated by a rabbit chase, Turk attempted to swim across this little river, but was chilled, and would have perished had not Will rushed to the rescue. The ferryman saw the boy struggling with the dog in the water, and started after him with his boat. But Will reached the bank without assistance.

"I've hearn of dogs saving children, but this is the first time I ever hearn of a child saving a dog from drowning," ejaculated the ferryman. "How old be you?"

"Eight, going on nine," answered Will.

"You're a big boy for your age," said the man. "But it's a wonder you didn't sink with that load; he's a big old fellow," referring to Turk, who, standing on three feet, was vigorously shaking the water from his coat. Will at once knelt down beside him, and taking the uplifted foot in his hands, remarked: "He must have sprained one of his legs when he fell over that log; he doesn't whine like your common curs when they get hurt."

"He's blooded stock, then," said the man. "What kind of a dog do you call him?"

"He's an Ulm dog," said Will.

"I never heard tell of that kind of dog before."

"Did you ever hear of a tiger-mastiff, German mastiff, boar-hound, great Dane? Turk's all of them together."

"Well," said the ferryman, "you're a pretty smart little fellow, and got lots of grit. You ought to make your mark in the world. But right now you had better get into some dry clothes." And on the invitation of the ferryman, Will and the limping dog got into the boat, and were taken back to camp.

Turk played so conspicuous and important a part in our early lives that he deserves a brief description. He was a large and powerful animal of the breed of dogs anciently used in Germany in hunting the wild boars. Later the dogs were imported into England, where they were particularly valued by people desiring a strong, brave watch-dog. When specially trained, they are more fierce and active than the English mastiff. Naturally they are not as fond of the water as the spaniel, the stag-hound, or the Newfoundland, though they are the king of dogs on land. Not alone Will, but the rest of the family, regarded Turk as the best of his kind, and he well deserved the veneration he inspired. His fidelity and almost human intelligence were time and again the means of saving life and property; ever faithful, loyal, and ready to lay down his life, if need be, in our service.

Outlaws and desperadoes were always to be met with on Western trails in those rugged days and more than once Turk's constant vigilance warned father in time to prevent attacks from suspicious night prowlers. The attachment which had grown up between Turk and his young master was but the natural love of boys for their dogs intensified. Will at that time estimated dogs as in later years he did men, the qualities which he found to admire in Turk being vigilance, strength, courage, and constancy. With men, as with dogs, he is not lavishly demonstrative; rarely pats them on the back. But deeds of merit do not escape his notice or want his appreciation. The patience, unselfishness, and true nobility observed in this faithful canine friend of his boyhood days have many times proved to be lacking in creatures endowed with a soul; yet he has never lost faith in mankind, or in the ultimate destiny of his race. This I conceive to be a characteristic of all great men.

This trip was memorable for all of us, perhaps especially so for brother Will, for it comprehended not only his first deer, but his first negro.

As we drew near the Missouri line we came upon a comfortable farm-house, at which father made inquiry concerning a lodging for the night. A widow lived there, and the information that father was brother to Elijah Cody, of Platte County, Missouri, won us a cordial welcome and the hospitality of her home.

We were yet in the road, waiting father's report, when our startled vision and childish imagination took in a seeming apparition, which glided from the bushes by the wayside.

It proved a full-blooded African, with thick lips, woolly

hair, enormous feet, and scant attire. To all except mother this was a new revelation of humanity, and we stared in wild-eyed wonder; even Turk was surprised into silence. At this point father rejoined us, to share in mother's amusement and to break the spell for us by pleasantly addressing the negro, who returned a respectful answer, accompanied by an ample grin. He was a slave on the widow's plantation.

Reassured by the grin, Will offered his hand, and tasted the joy of being addressed as "Massa" in the talk that followed. It was with difficulty that we prevailed upon "Massa" to come to supper.

After a refreshing night's sleep we went on our way, and in a few days reached my uncle's home. A rest was welcome, as the journey had been long and toilsome, despite the fact that it had been enlivened by many interesting incidents, and was thoroughly enjoyed by all of the family.

CHAPTER 2

Will's First Indian

My uncle's home was in Weston, Platte County, Missouri, at that time the large city of the West. As father desired to get settled again as soon as possible, he left us at Weston, and crossed the Missouri River on a prospecting tour, accompanied by Will and a guide. More than one day went by in the quest for a desirable location, and one morning Will, wearied in the reconnaissance, was left asleep at the night's camping-place, while father and the guide rode away for the day's exploring.

When Will opened his eyes, they fell upon the most interesting object that the world just then could offer him—an Indian!"

The "noble red man," as he has been poetically termed by people who have but known him from afar, was in the act of mounting Will's horse, while near by stood his own, a miserable, scrawny beast.

Will's boyish dreams were now a reality; he looked upon his first Indian. Here, too, was a "buck"—not a graceful, vanishing deer, but a dirty redskin, who seemingly was in some hurry to be gone. Without a trace of "buck fever," Will jumped up, rifle in hand, and demanded:

"Here, what are you doing with my horse?"

The Indian regarded the lad with contemptuous composure.

"Me swap horses with paleface boy," said he.

The red man was fully armed, and Will did not know whether his father and the guide were within call or not; but to suffer the Indian to ride away with Uncle Elijah's fine horse was to forfeit his father's confidence and shake his mother's and sister's belief in the family hero; so he put a bold face upon the matter, and remarked carelessly, as if discussing a genuine transaction:

"No; I won't swap."

"Paleface boy fool" returned the Indian serenely.

Now this was scarcely the main point at issue, so Will contented himself with replying, quietly but firmly:

"You cannot take my horse."

The Indian condescended to temporize. "Paleface horse no good," said he.

"Good enough for me," replied Will, smiling despite the gravity of the situation. The Indian shone rather as a liar than a judge of horseflesh. "Good enough for me; so you can take your old rack of bones and go."

Much to Will's surprise, the red man dropped the rein, flung himself upon his own pony, and made off. And down fell "Lo the poor Indian" from the exalted niche that he had filled in Will's esteem, for while it was bad in a copper hero to steal horses, it was worse to flee from a boy not yet in his teens. But a few moments later Lo went back to his lofty pedestal, for Will heard the guide's voice, and realized that it was the sight of a man, and not the threats of a boy, that had sent the Indian about his business—if he had any.

The guide had returned to escort Will to the spot which father, after a search of nearly a week, had discovered, and where he had decided to locate our home. It was in Salt Creek Valley, a fertile bluegrass region, sheltered by an amphitheater range of hills. The old Salt Lake trail traversed this valley. There were at this time two great highways of Western travel, the Santa Fé and the Salt Lake trails; later the Oregon trail came into prominence. Of these the oldest and most historic was the Santa Fé trail, the route followed by explorers three hundred years ago. It had been used by Indian tribes from time, to white men, immemorial. At the beginning of this century it was first used as an artery of commerce. Over it Zebulon Pike made his well-known Western trip, and from it radiated his explorations. The trail lay some distance south of Leavenworth. It ran westward, dipping slightly to the south until the Arkansas River was reached; then, following the course of this stream to Bent's Fort, it crossed the river and turned sharply to the south. It went through Raton Pass, and below Las Vegas it turned west to Santa Fé.

Exploration along the line of the Salt Lake trail began also with this century. It became a beaten highway at the time of the Mormon exodus from Nauvoo to their present place of abode. The trail crossed the Missouri River at Leavenworth, and ran northerly to the Platte, touching that stream at Fort Kearney. With a few variations it paralleled the Platte to its junction with the Sweetwater, and left this river valley to run through South Pass to big Sandy Creek, turning south to follow this little stream. At Fort Bridger it turned westward again, passed Echo Cañon, and a few miles farther on ran into Salt Lake City. Over this trail journeyed thousands of gold-hunters toward California, hopeful and high-spirited on the westerly way, disappointed and depressed, the large majority of them, on the back track. Freighting outfits, cattle trains, emigrants— nearly all the western travel—followed this track across the new land. A man named Rively, with the gift of grasping the advantage of location, had obtained permission to establish a trading-post on this trail three miles beyond the

Missouri, and as proximity to this depot of supplies was a manifest convenience, father's selection of a claim only two miles distant was a wise one.

The Kansas-Nebraska Bill, which provided for the organizing of those two territories and opened them for settlement, was passed in May, 1854. This bill directly opposed the Missouri Compromise, which restricted slavery to all territory south of 36° 30″ north latitude. A clause in the new bill provided that the settlers should decide for themselves whether the new territories were to be free or slave states. Already hundreds of settlers were camped upon the banks of the Missouri, waiting the passage of the bill before entering and acquiring possession of the land. Across the curtain of the night ran a broad ribbon of dancing camp-fires, stretching for miles along the bank of the river.

None too soon had father fixed upon his claim. The act allowing settlers to enter was passed in less than a week afterward. Besides the pioneers intending actual settlement, a great rush was made into the territories by members of both political parties. These became the gladiators, with Kansas the arena, for a bitter, bloody contest between those desiring and those opposing the extension of slave territory.

Having already decided upon his location, father was among the first, after the bill was passed, to file a claim and procure the necessary papers, and shortly afterward he had a transient abiding-place prepared for us. Whatever mother may have thought of the one-roomed cabin, whose chinks let in the sun by day and the moon and stars by night, and whose carpet was nature's greenest velvet, life in it was a perennial picnic for the children. Meantime, father was at work on our permanent home, and before the summer fled we were domiciled in a large double-log house—rough and primitive, but solid and comfort-breeding.

This same autumn held an episode so deeply graven in my memory that time has not blurred a line of it. Jane, our faithful maid of all work, who went with us to our Western home, had little time to play the governess. Household duties claimed her every waking hour, as mother was delicate, and the family a large one; so Turk officiated as both guardian and playmate of the children.

One golden September day Eliza and I set out after wild flowers, accompanied by Turk and mother's caution not to stray too far, as wild beasts, 'twas said, lurked in the neighboring forest; but the prettiest flowers were always just beyond, and we wandered afield until we reached a fringe of timber half a mile from the house, where we tarried under the trees. Meantime, mother grew alarmed, and Will was dispatched after the absent tots.

Turk, as we recalled, had sought to put a check upon our wanderings, and when we entered the woods his restlessness increased. Suddenly he began to paw up the carpet of dry leaves, and a few moments later the shrill scream of a panther echoed through the forest aisles.

Eliza was barely six years old, and I was not yet four. We clung to each other in voiceless terror. Then from afar came a familiar whistle—Will's call to his dog. That heartened us, babes as we were, for was not our brother our reliance in every emergency? Rescue was at hand; but Turk continued tearing up the leaves, after signaling his master with a loud bark. Then, pulling at our dresses, he indicated the refuge he had dug for us. Here we lay down, and the dog covered us with the leaves, dragging to the heap, as a further screen, a large dead branch. Then, with the heart of a lion, he put himself on guard.

From our leafy covert we could see the panther's tawny form come gliding through the brush. He saw Turk, and crouched for a spring. This came as an arrow, but Turk dodged it; and then, with a scream such as I never heard from dog before or since, our defender hurled himself upon the foe.

Turk was powerful, and his courage was flawless, but he was no match for the panther. In a few moments the faithful dog lay stunned and bleeding from one stroke of the forest-rover's steel-shod paw. The cruel beast had scented other prey, and dismissing Turk, he paced to and fro, seeking to locate us. We scarcely dared to breath, and every throb of our frightened little hearts was a prayer that Will would come to us in time.

At last the panther's roving eyes rested upon our inadequate hiding-place, and as he crouched for the deadly leap we hid our faces.

But Turk had arisen. Wounded as he was, he yet made one last heroic effort to save us by again directing the panther's attention to himself.

The helpless, hopeless ordeal of agony was broken by a rifle's sharp report. The panther fell, shot through the heart, and out from the screen of leaves rushed two hysterical little girls, with pallid faces drowned in tears, who clung about a brother's neck and were shielded in his arms.

Will, himself but a child, caressed and soothed us in a most paternal fashion; and when the storm of sobs was passed we turned to Turk. Happily his injuries were not fatal, and he whined feebly when his master reached him.

"Bravo! Good dog!" cried Will. "You saved them, Turk! You saved them!" And kneeling beside our faithful friend, he put his arms about the shaggy neck.

Dear old Turk! If there be a land beyond the sky for such as thou, may the snuggest corner and best of bones be thy reward!

CHAPTER 3

The Shadow of Partisan Strife

Owing to the conditions, already spoken of, under which Kansas was settled, all classes were represented in its population. Honest, thrifty farmers and well-to-do traders leavened a lump of shiftless ne'er-do-wells, lawless adventurers, and vagabonds of all sorts and conditions. If father at times questioned the wisdom of coming to this new and untried land, he kept his own counsel, and set a brave face against the future.

He had been prominent in political circles in Iowa, and had filled positions of public trust; but he had no wish to become involved in the partisan strife that raged in Kansas. He was a Free Soil man, and there were but two others in that section who did not believe in slavery. For a year he kept his political views to himself; but it became rumored about that he was an able public speaker, and the pro-slavery men naturally ascribed to him the same opinions as those held by his brother Elijah, a pronounced pro-slavery man; so they regarded father as a promising leader in their cause. He had avoided the issue, and had skilfully contrived to escape declaring for one side or the other, but on the scroll of his destiny it was written that he should be one of the first victims offered on the sacrificial altar of the struggle for human liberty.

The post-trader's was a popular rendezvous for all the settlers round. It was a day in the summer of '55 that father visited the store, accompanied, as usual, by Will and Turk. Among the crowd, which was noisy and excited, he noted a number of desperadoes in the pro-slavery faction, and noted, too, that Uncle Elijah and our two Free Soil neighbors, Mr. Hathaway and Mr. Lawrence, were present.

Father's appearance was greeted by a clamor for a speech. To speak before that audience was to take his life in his hands; yet in spite of his excuses he was forced to the chair.

It was written! There was no escape! Father walked steadily to the dry-goods box which served as a rostrum. As he passed Mr. Hathaway, the good old man plucked him by the sleeve and begged him to serve out platitudes to the crowd, and to screen his real sentiments.

But father was not a man that dealt in platitudes.

"Friends," said he quietly, as he faced his audience and drew himself to his full height,—"friends, you are mistaken in your man. I am sorry to disappoint you. I have no wish to quarrel with you. But you have forced me to speak, and I can do no less than declare my real convictions. I am, and always have been, opposed to slavery. It is an institution that not only degrades the slave, but brutalizes the slave-holder, and I pledge you my word that I shall use my best endeavors—yes, that I shall lay down my life, if need be—to keep this curse from finding lodgment upon Kansas soil. It is enough that the fairest portions of our land are already infected with this blight. May it spread no farther. All my energy and my ability shall swell the effort to bring in Kansas as a Free Soil state."

Up to this point the crowd had been so dumfounded by his temerity that they kept an astonished silence. Now the storm broke. The rumble of angry voices swelled into a roar of fury. An angry mob surrounded the speaker. Several desperadoes leaped forward with deadly intent, and one, Charles Dunn by name, drove his knife to the hilt into the body of the brave man who dared thus openly to avow his principles.

As father fell, Will sprang to him, and turning to the murderous assailant, cried out in boyhood's fury:

"You have killed my father! When I'm a man I'll kill you!"

The crowd slunk away, believing father dead. The deed appalled them; they were not yet hardened to the lawlessness that was so soon to put the state to blush.

Mr. Hathaway and Will then carried father to a hiding-place in the long grass by the wayside. The crowd dispersed so slowly that dusk came on before the coast was clear. At length, supported by Will, father dragged his way home-ward, marking his tortured progress with a trail of blood.

This path was afterward referred to in the early history of Kansas as "The Cody Bloody Trail."

It was such wild scenes as these that left their impress on the youth and fashioned the Cody of later years— cool in emergency, fertile in resource, swift in decision, dashing and intrepid when the time for action came.

Our troubles were but begun. Father's convalescence was long and tedious; he never recovered fully. His ene-mies believed him dead, and for a while we kept the secret guarded; but as soon as he was able to be about persecu-tion began.

About a month after the tragedy at Rively's, Will ran in one evening with the warning that a band of horsemen were approaching. Suspecting trouble, mother put some of her own clothes about father, gave him a pail, and bade him hide in the cornfield. He walked boldly from the house, and, sheltered by the gathering dusk, succeeded in passing the horsemen unchallenged. The latter rode up to the house and dismounted.

"Where's Cody?" asked the leader. He was informed that father was not at home.

"Lucky for him!" was the frankly brutal rejoinder. "We'll make sure work of the killing next time!"

Disappointed in their main intention, the marauders revenged themselves in their own peculiar way by looting the house of every article that took their fancy; then they sat down with the announced purpose of waiting the return of their prospective victim.

Fearing the effect of the night air upon father, though it was yet summer, mother made a sign to Will, who slipped from the room, and guided by Turk, carried blankets to the cornfield, returning before his absence had been remarked. The ruffians soon tired of waiting, and rode away, after warning mother of the brave deed they purposed to perform. Father came in for the night, returning to his covert with the dawn.

In expectation of some such raid, we had secreted a good stock of provisions; but as soon as the day was up Will was dispatched to Rively's store to reconnoiter, under pretext of buying groceries. Keeping eyes and ears open, he learned that father's enemies were on the watch for him; so the cornfield must remain his screen. After several days the exposure and anxiety told on his strength. He decided to leave home and go to Fort Leavenworth, four miles distant. When night fell he returned to the house, packed a few needed articles, and bade us farewell. Will urged that he ride Prince, but he regarded his journey as safer afoot. It was a sad parting. None of us knew whether we should ever again see our father.

"I hope," he said to mother, "that these clouds will soon pass away, and that we may have a happy home once more." Then, placing his hands on Will's head, "You will have to be the man of the house until my return," he said. "But I know I can trust my boy to watch over his mother and sisters."

With such responsibilities placed upon his shoulders,

such confidence reposed in him, small wonder that Will should grow a man in thought and feeling before he grew to be one in years.

Father reached Fort Leavenworth in safety, but the quarrel between the pro-slavery party and the Free Soilers waxed more bitter, and he decided that security lay farther on; so he took passage on an up-river boat to Doniphan, twenty miles distant. This was then a mere landing-place, but he found a small band of men in camp cooking supper. They were part of Colonel Jim Lane's command, some three hundred strong, on their way West from Indiana.

Colonel Lane was an interesting character. He had been a friend to Elijah Lovejoy, who was killed, in 1836, for maintaining an anti-slavery newspaper in Illinois. The Kansas contest speedily developed the fact that the actual settlers sent from the North by the emigrant-aid societies would enable the Free State party to outnumber the ruffians sent in by the Southerners; and when the pro-slavery men were driven to substituting bullets for ballots, Colonel Lane recruited a band of hardy men to protect the anti-slavery settlers, and incidentally to avenge the murder of Lovejoy.

The meeting of father and Lane's men was a meeting of friends, and he chose to cast his lot with theirs. Shortly afterward he took part in "The Battle of Hickory Point," in which the pro-slavery men were defeated with heavy loss; and thenceforward the name of Jim Lane was a terror to the lawless and a wall of protection to our family.

The storm and stress of battle had drawn heavily on what little strength was left to father, and relying for safety upon the proximity of Colonel Lane and his men, he returned to us secretly by night, and was at once prostrated on a bed of sickness.

This proved a serious strain upon our delicate mother,

for during father's absence a little brother had been added to our home, and not only had she, in addition to the care of Baby Charlie, the nursing of a sick man, but she was constantly harassed by apprehensions for his safety as well.

CHAPTER 4

Persecution Continues

Mother's fears were well grounded. A few days after father had returned home, a man named Sharpe, who disgraced the small office of justice of the peace, rode up to our house, very much the worse for liquor, and informed mother that his errand was to "search the house for that abolition husband of yours." The intoxicated ruffian then demanded something to eat. While mother, with a show of hospitality, was preparing supper for him, the amiable Mr. Sharpe killed time in sharpening his bowie-knife on the sole of his shoe.

"That," said he to Will, who stood watching him, "that's to cut the heart out of that Free State father of yours!" And he tested the edge with brutally suggestive care.

Will's comment was to take down his rifle and place himself on the staircase leading up to father's room. There was trouble in that quarter for Mr. Sharpe if he attempted to ascend those stairs.

But the justice, as mother surmised, had no notion that father was at home, else he would not have come alone. He ate heartily of the supper, which Will hoped would choke him, and passing from drowsiness to drunken slumber, soon tumbled from his chair. This so confused him that he forgot his pretended errand, and shambled out of the house. He was not so drunk that he could not tell a good bit of horseflesh, and he straightway took a fancy to Prince, the pet pony of the family. An unwritten plank in the platform of the pro-slavery men was that the Free Soil party had no rights they were bound to respect, and Sharpe remarked to Will, with a malicious grin:

"That's a nice pony of yours, sonny. Guess I'll take him along with me." And he proceeded to exchange the saddle from the back of his own horse to that of Prince.

"You old coward!" muttered Will, bursting with wrath. "I'll get even with you some day."

The justice was a tall, burly fellow, and he cut so ridiculous a figure as he rode away on Prince's back, his heels almost touching the ground, that Will laughed outright as he thought of a plan to save his pony.

A shrill whistle brought Turk to the scene, and receiving his cue, the dog proceeded to give Sharpe a very bad five minutes. He would nip at one of the dangling legs, spring back out of reach of the whip with a triumphant bark, then repeat the performance with the other leg. This little comedy had a delighted spectator in Will, who had followed at a safe distance. Just as Sharpe made one extra effort to reach Turk, the boy whistled a signal to Prince, who responded with a bound that dumped his rider in the dust. Here Turk stood over him and showed his teeth.

"Call off your dog, bub!" the justice shouted to Will, "and you may keep your little sheep, for he's no good, anyway."

"That's a bargain!" cried Will, restored to good humor; and helping the vanquished foe upon his own steed, he assured him that he need not fear Turk so long as he kept his word. Sharpe departed, but we were far from being rid of him.

About a fortnight later we were enjoying an evening with father, who was now able to come downstairs. He was seated in a big arm-chair before the open fire, with his family gathered round him, by his side our frail, beautiful mother, with Baby Charlie on her knee, Martha and Julia, with their sewing, and Will, back of mother's chair, tenderly smoothing the hair from her brow, while he related spiritedly some new escapade of Turk. Suddenly he checked his narrative, listened for a space, and announced:

"There are some men riding on the road toward the house. We'd better be ready for trouble."

Mother, equal to every emergency, hurriedly disposed her slender forces for defense. Martha and Julia were directed to help father to bed; that done, to repair to the unfurnished front room above stairs; Will was instructed to call the hired man and Jane, who was almost as large and quite as strong as the average man; and the three were armed and given their cue. They were all handy with their weapons, but mother sought to win by strategy, if possible. She bade the older girls don heavy boots, and gave them further instructions. By this time the horsemen had reached the gate. Their leader was the redoubtable Justice Sharpe. He rode up to the door, and rapped with the butt of his riding-whip. Mother threw up the window overhead.

"Who's there, and what do you want?" she demanded.

"We want that old abolition husband of yours, and, dead or alive, we mean to have him!"

"All right, Mr. Sharpe," was the steady answer. "I'll ask Colonel Lane and his men to wait on you."

The hired man, who had served in the Mexican War, here gave a sharp word of command, which was responded to by trampling of heavy boots upon the bare floor. Then, calling a halt, the pretended Colonel Lane advanced to the window and shouted to the horsemen:

"Set foot inside that gate and my men will fire on you!"

Sharpe, an arrant coward, had retreated at the first

sound of a man's voice, and after a short parley with his non-plused companions he led them away—outwitted by a woman.

As a sort of consolation prize, Sharpe again made off with Prince; but Will's sorrow in the morning was short-lived, for the sagacious little creature slipped his halter and came flying home before the forenoon was half spent.

After this experience father decided that, for our sakes as well as for his own, he must again leave home, and as soon as he recovered a measure of his strength he went to Grasshopper Falls, thirty-five miles west of Leaven-worth. Here he erected a sawmill, and hoped that he had put so many miles between him and his enemies that he might be allowed to pursue a peaceful occupation. He made us occasional visits, so timing his journey that he reached home after nightfall, and left again before the sun was up.

One day when we were looking forward to one of these visits, our good friend Mr. Hathaway made his appearance about eleven o'clock.

"It is too bad to be the bearer of ill tidings," said he, "but the news of your husband's expected visit has been noised about in some way, and another plot to kill him is afoot. Some of his enemies are camped at Big Stranger's Creek, and intend to shoot him as he passes there."

Then followed a long and anxious consultation, which ended without any plan of rescue.

All of which had been overheard by Will, who was confined to his bed with an attack of ague. In him, he decided, lay the only hope for father's safety; so, dressing, he presented his fever-flushed face to mother. As he held out a handkerchief, "Tie it tight around my head, mother," said he; "then it won't ache so hard."

A remonstrance against his getting out of bed brought out the fact that he contemplated riding to Grasshopper Falls!

He was almost too weak to stand, a storm threatened, and thirty miles lay between him and father; yet he was not to be dissuaded from his undertaking. So Julia and Martha saddled Prince and helped the ague-racked courier to his saddle.

The plunge into the open air and the excitement of the start encouraged Will to believe that he could hold out. As he settled down to his long, hard ride he reflected that it was not yet noon, and that father would not set out until late in the day. Prince seemed to discern that something extraordinary was afoot, and swung along at a swift, steady gait.

Big Stranger's Creek cut the road halfway to the Falls, and Will approached it before the afternoon was half gone. The lowering sky darkened the highway, and he hoped to pass the ambush unrecognized; but as he came up to the stream he made out a camp and campers, one of whom called out carelessly to him as he passed:

"Are you all right on the goose?"—the cant phrase of the pro-slavery men.

"Never rode a goose in my life, gentlemen," was the reply.

"That's Cody's boy!" shouted another voice; and the word "Halt!" rang out just as Will had galloped safely past the camp.

Will's answer was to drive the spurs into Prince and dart ahead, followed by a rain of bullets. He was now well out of range, and the pony still strong and fleet.

The chase was on, and in the thrill of it Will forgot his weakness. A new strength came with the rush of air and the ring of hoofs, and "I'll reach the Falls in time!" was his heartening thought, as pursuer and pursued sped through the forests, clattered over bridges, and galloped up hill and down.

Then broke the long-impending storm, and the hard road became the bed of a muddy stream. The pursuit was abandoned, and this stimulus removed, Will felt the chills and weakness coming on again. He was drenched to the skin, and it was an effort to keep his saddle, but he set his teeth firmly in his resolve to accomplish his heroic purpose.

At last! A welcome light gleamed between the crystal bars of the rain. His mission was accomplished.

His ride had been longer by ten miles than that famous gallop of the friend of his after years—Phil Sheridan. Like Sheridan, he reached the goal in time, for father was just mounting his horse.

But the ride proved too much for his strength, and Will collapsed. Father started with him, a few days later, for Topeka, which was headquarters for the Free State party.

Father acquainted mother of their safety, and explained that he had gone to Topeka because he feared his life was no longer safe at Grasshopper Falls.

Party strife in Kansas was now at its height. Thousands came into the territory from adjacent slave states simply to vote, and the pro-slavery party elected a legislature, whose first meeting was held at Le Compton. This election the Free Soilers declared illegal, because of fraudulent voting, and assembling at Topeka in the winter of 1855–56, they framed a constitution excluding slavery, and organized a rival government. Of this first Free-Soil Legislature father was a member.

Thenceforth war was the order of the day, and in the fall of 1856 a military governor was appointed, with full authority to maintain law and order in Kansas.

Recognizing the good work effected by the emigrant-aid societies, and realizing that in a still larger Northern emigration to Kansas lay the only hope of its admission as a free state, father went to Ohio in the following spring, to labor for the salvation of the territory he had chosen for his home. Here his natural gift of oratory had free play, and as the result of his work on the stump he brought back to Kansas sixty families, the most of whom settled in the vicinity of Grasshopper Falls, now Valley Falls.

This meant busy times for us, for with that magnificent disregard for practical matters that characterizes many men of otherwise great gifts, father had invited each separate family to make headquarters at his home until other arrangements could be perfected. As a result, our house overflowed, while the land about us was dotted with tents; but these melted away, as one by one the families selected claims and put up cabins.

Among the other settlers was Judge Delahay, who, with his family, located at Leavenworth, and began the publishing of the first abolition newspaper in Kansas. The appointing of the military governor was the means of restoring comparative tranquillity; but hundreds of outrages were committed, and the judge and his newspaper came in for a share of suffering. The printing-office was broken into, and the type and press thrown into the Missouri River. Undaunted, the judge procured a new press, and the paper continued.

A semi-quiet now reigned in the territory; father resumed work at the sawmill, and we looked forward to a peaceful home and the joy of being once more permanently united. But it was not to be. The knife wound had injured father's lung. With care and nursing it might have healed, but constant suffering attended on the life that persecution had led him, and in the spring of '57 he again came home, and took to his bed for the last time.

All that could be was done, but nothing availed. After a very short illness he passed away—one of the first martyrs in the cause of freedom in Kansas.

The land of his adoption became his last, long resting-place. His remains now lie on Pilot Knob, which overlooks the beautiful city of Leavenworth. His death was regretted even by his enemies, who could not help but grant a tribute of respect to a man who had been upright, just, and generous to friend and foe.

CHAPTER 5

The "Boy Extra"

At this sorrowful period mother was herself almost at death's door with consumption, but far from sinking under the blow, she faced the new conditions with a steadfast calm, realizing that should she, too, be taken, her children would be left without a protector, and at the mercy of the enemies whose malignity had brought their father to an untimely end. Her indomitable will opposed her bodily weakness. "I will not die," she told herself, "until the welfare of my children is assured." She was needed, for our persecution continued.

Hardly was the funeral over when a trumped-up claim for a thousand dollars, for lumber and supplies, was entered against our estate. Mother knew the claim was fictitious, as all the bills had been settled, but the business had been transacted through the agency of Uncle Elijah, and father had neglected to secure the receipts. In those bitter, troublous days it too often happened that brother turned against brother, and Elijah retained his fealty to his party at the expense of his dead brother's family.

This fresh affliction but added fuel to the flame of mother's energy. Our home was paid for, but father's business had been made so broken and irregular that our financial resources were of the slenderest, and should this unjust claim for a thousand dollars be allowed, we would be homeless.

The result of mother's study of the situation was, "If I had the ready money, I should fight the claim."

"You fight the claim, and I'll get the money," Will replied.

Mother smiled, but Will continued:

"Russell, Majors & Waddell will give me work. Jim Willis says I am capable of filling the position of 'extra.' If you'll go with me and ask Mr. Majors for a job, I'm sure he'll give me one."

Russel, Majors & Waddell was overland freighters and contractors, with headquarters at Leavenworth. To Will's suggestion mother entered a demurrer, but finally yielded before his insistence. Mr. Majors had known father, and was more than willing to aid us, but Will's youth was an objection not lightly overridden.

"What can a boy of your age do?" he asked kindly.

"I can ride, shoot, and herd cattle," said Will; "but I'd rather be an 'extra' on one of your trains."

"But that is a man's work, and is dangerous besides." Mr. Majors hesitated. "But I'll let you try it one trip, and if you do a man's work, I'll give you a man's pay."

So Will's name was put on the company roll, and he signed a pledge that illustrates better than a description the character and disposition of Mr. Majors.

"I, William F. Cody," it read, "do hereby solemnly swear, before the great and living God, that during my engagement with, and while I am in the employ of, Russell, Majors & Waddell, I will, under no circumstances, use profane language, that I will not quarrel or fight with any other employee of the firm, and that in every respect I will conduct myself honestly, be faithful to my duties, and so direct all my acts as to win the confidence of my employers. So help me God!"

Mr. Majors employed many wild and reckless men, but the language of the pledge penetrated to the better nature of them all. They endeavored, with varying success, to live up to its conditions, although most of them held that driving a bull-team constituted extenuating circumstances for an occasional expletive.

The pledge lightened mother's heart; she knew that Will would keep his word; she felt, too, that a man that required such a pledge of his employees was worthy of their confidence and esteem.

The train was to start in a day, and all of us were busy with the preparations for Will's two months' trip. The moment of parting came, and it was a trying ordeal for mother, so recently bereaved of husband. Will sought to soothe her, but the younger sisters had better success, for with tears in our eyes we crowded about him, imploring him to "run if he saw any Indians."

'Tis but a step from tears to smiles; the situation was relieved, and Will launched his life bark amid adieus of hope and confidence and love. His fortitude lasted only till he was out of sight of the house; but youth is elastic, the plains lay before him, and mother and sisters were to be helped; so he presented a cheerful face to his employers.

That night the bed of the "boy extra" was a blanket under a wagon; but he slept soundly, and was ready when the train started with the dawn.

The "bull-train" took its name from the fact that each of the thirty-five wagons making up a full train was hauled by several yoke of oxen, driven by one man, known as a bullwhacker. This functionary's whip cracked like a rifle, and could be heard about as far. The wagons resembled the ordinary prairie-schooner, but were larger and more strongly built; they were protected from the weather by a double covering of heavy canvas, and had a freight capacity of seven thousand pounds.

Besides the bullwhackers there were cavallard drivers (who cared for the loose cattle), night herders, and sundry extra hands, all under the charge of a chief wagon-master, termed the wagon-boss, his lieutenants being the boss of the cattle train and the assistant wagon-master. The men were disposed in messes, each providing its own wood and water, doing its own cooking, and washing up its own tin dinner service, while one man in each division stood guard. Special duties were assigned to the "extras," and Will's was to ride up and down the train delivering orders. This suited his fancy to a dot, for the oxen were snail-gaited, and to plod at their heels was dull work. Kipling tells us it is quite impossible to "hustle the East"; it was as easy, as Will discovered, to hustle a bull-train.

From the outset the "boy extra" was a favorite with the men. They liked his pluck in undertaking such work, and when it was seen that he took pride in executing orders promptly, he became a favorite with the bosses as well. In part, his work was play to him; he welcomed an order as a break in the monotony of the daily march, and hailed the opportunity of a gallop on a good horse.

The world of Will's fancy was bounded by the hazy rim where plain and sky converge, and when the first day's journey was done, and he had staked out and cared for his horse, he watched with fascinated eyes the strange and striking picture limned against the black hills and sweeping stretch of darkening prairie. Everything was animation; the bullwhackers unhitching and disposing of their teams, the herders staking out the cattle, and—not the least interesting—the mess cooks preparing the evening meal at the crackling camp-fires, with the huge, canvas-covered wagons encircling them like ghostly sentinels; the ponies and oxen blinking stupidly as the flames stam-peded the shadows in which they were enveloped; and more weird than all, the buckskin-clad bullwhackers, squatted around the fire, their beards glowing red in its light, their faces drawn in strange black and yellow lines, while the spiked grasses shot tall and sword-like over them.

It was wonderful—that first night of the "boy extra."

But Will discovered that life on the plains is not all a supper under the stars when the sparks fly upward; it has its hardships and privations. There were days, as the wagons dragged their slow lengths along, when the clouds obscured the sky and the wind whistled dismally; days when torrents fell and swelled the streams that must be crossed, and when the mud lay ankle-deep; days when the cattle stampeded, and the round-up meant long, extra hours of heavy work; and, hardest but most needed work of all, the eternal vigil 'gainst an Indian attack.

Will did not share the anxiety of his companions. To him a brush with Indians would prove that boyhood's dreams sometimes come true, and in imagination he anticipated the glory of a first encounter with the "noble red man," after the fashion of the heroes in the hair-lifting Western tales he had read. He was soon to learn, as many another has learned, that the Indian of real life is vastly different from the Indian of fiction. He refuses to "bite the dust" at sight of a paleface, and a dozen of them have been known to hold their own against as many white men.

Some twenty miles west of Fort Kearny a halt was made for dinner at the bank of a creek that emptied into the Platte River. No signs of Indians had been observed, and there was no thought of special danger. Nevertheless, three men were constantly on guard. Many of the trainmen were asleep under the wagons while waiting dinner, and Will was watching the maneuvers of the cook in his mess. Suddenly a score of shots rang out from the direction of a neighboring thicket, succeeded by a chorus of savage yells.

Will saw the three men on the lookout drop in their

tracks, and saw the Indians divide, one wing stampeding the cattle, the other charging down upon the camp.

The trainmen were old frontiersmen, and although taken wholly by surprise, they lined up swiftly in battle array behind the wagons, with the bosses, Bill and Frank McCarthy, at their head, and the "boy extra" under the direction of the wagon master.

A well-placed volley of rifle-balls checked the Indians, and they wheeled and rode away, after sending in a scattering cloud of arrows, which wounded several of the trainmen. The decision of a hasty council of war was that a defensive stand would be useless, as the Indians outnumbered the whites ten to one, and red reinforcements were constantly coming up, until it seemed to Will as if the prairie were alive with them. The only hope of safety lay in the shelter of the creek's high bank, so a run was made for it. The Indians charged again, with the usual accompaniment of whoops, yells, and flying arrows; but the trainmen had reached the creek, and from behind its natural breastwork maintained a rifle fire that drove the foe back out of range.

To follow the creek and river to Fort Kearny was not accounted much of a chance for escape, but it was the only avenue that lay open; so, with a parting volley to deceive the besiegers into thinking that the fort was still held, the perilous and difficult journey was begun.

The Indians quickly penetrated the ruse, and another charge had to be repulsed. Besides the tiresome work of wading, there were wounded men to help along, and a ceaseless watch to keep against another rush of the reds. It was a trying ordeal for a man, doubly so for a boy like Will; but he was encouraged to coolness and endurance by a few words from Frank McCarthy, who remarked admiringly, "Well, Billy, you didn't scare worth a cent."

After a few miles of wading the little party issued out

upon the Platte River. By this time the wounded men were so exhausted that a halt was called to improvise a raft. On this the sufferers were placed, and three or four men detailed to shove it before them. In consideration of his youth, Will was urged to get upon the raft, but he declined, saying that he was not wounded, and that if the stream got too deep for him to wade, he could swim. This was more than some of the men could do, and they, too, had to be assisted over the deep places.

Thus wore the long and weary hours away, and though the men, who knew how hard a trip it was, often asked, "How goes it, Billy?" he uttered no word of complaint.

But half a day's wading, without rest or food, gradually weighted his heels, and little by little he lagged behind his companions. The moon came out and silvered tree and river, but the silent, plodding band had no eyes for the glory of the landscape.

Will had fallen behind some twenty rods, but in a moment fatigue was forgotten, the blood jumped in his veins, for just ahead of him the moonlight fell upon the feathered head-dress of an Indian chief, who was peering over the bank. Motionless, he watched the head, shoulders, and body of the brave come into view. The Indian supposed the entire party ahead, and Will made no move until the savage bent his bow.

Then he realized, with a thumping heart, that death must come to one of his comrades or the Indian.

Even in direst necessity it is a fearful thing to deliberately take a human life, but Will had no time for hesitation. There was a shot, and the Indian rolled down the bank into the river.

His expiring yell was answered by others. The reds were not far away. Frank McCarthy, missing Will, stationed guards, and ran back to look for him. He found the lad hauling the dead warrior ashore, and seizing his hand, cried out: "Well done, my boy; you've killed your first Indian, and done it like a man!"

Will wanted to stop and bury the body, but being assured that it was not only an uncustomary courtesy, but in this case quite impossible, he hastened on. As they came up with the waiting group, McCarthy called out:

"Pards, little Billy has killed his first redskin!"

The announcement was greeted with cheers, which grated on Will's ears, for his heart was sick and the cheers seemed strangely out of place.

Little time, however, was afforded for sentiment of any sort. Enraged at the death of their scout, the Indians made a final charge, which was repulsed, like the others, and after this Bill McCarthy took the lead, with Frank at the rear, to prevent further straggling of the forces.

It was a haggard-faced band that came up to Fort Kearny with the dawn. The wounded men were left at the post, while the others returned to the wrecked bull-train under escort of a body of troops. They hoped to make some salvage, but the cattle had either been driven away or had joined one of the numerous herds of buffalo; the wagons and their freight had been burned, and there was nothing to do but bury the three pickets, whose scalped and mutilated bodies were stretched where they had fallen.

Then the troops and trainmen parted company, the former to undertake a bootless quest for the red marauders, the latter to return to Leavenworth, their occupation gone. The government held itself responsible for the depredations of its wards, and the loss of the wagons and cattle was assumed at Washington.

CHAPTER 6

Family Defender and Household Tease

The fame to which Byron woke one historic morning was no more unexpected to him than that which now greeted Will. The trainmen had not been over-modest in their accounts of his pluck; and when a newspaper reporter lent the magic of his imagination to the plain narrative, it became quite a story, headed in display type, "The Boy Indian Slayer."

But Will was speedily concerned with other than his own affairs, for as soon as his position with the freighters was assured, mother engaged a lawyer to fight the claim against our estate. This legal light was John C. Douglass, then unknown, unhonored, and unsung, but talented and enterprising notwithstanding. He had just settled in Leavenworth, and he could scarcely have found a better case with which to storm the heights of fame—the dead father, the sick mother, the helpless children, and relentless persecution, in one scale; in the other, an eleven-year-old boy doing a man's work to earn the money needed to combat the family's enemies. Douglass put his whole strength into the case.

He knew as well as we that our cause was weak; it hung by a single thread—a missing witness, Mr. Barnhart. This man had acted as bookkeeper when the bills were paid, but he had been sent away, and the prosecution—or persecution—had thus far succeeded in keeping his whereabouts a secret. To every place where he was likely to be, Lawyer Douglass had written; but we were as much in the dark as ever when the morning for the trial of the suit arrived.

The case had excited much interest, and the court-room was crowded, many persons having been drawn thither by a curiosity to look upon "The Boy Indian Slayer." There was a cheerful unanimity of opinion upon the utter hopelessness of the Cody side of the case. Not only were prominent and wealthy men arrayed against us, but our young and inexperienced lawyer faced the heaviest legal guns of the Leavenworth bar. Our only witnesses were a frail woman and a girl of eighteen, though by their side, with his head held high, was the family protector, our brave young brother. Against us were might and malignity; upon our side, right and the high courage with which Christianity steels the soul of a believer. Mother had faith that the invisible forces of the universe were fighting for our cause.

She and Martha swore to the fact that all the bills had been settled; and after the opposition had rested its case, Lawyer Douglass arose for the defense. His was a magnificent plea for the rights of the widow and the orphan, and was conceded to be one of the finest speeches ever heard in a Kansas court-room; but though all were moved by our counsel's eloquence—some unto tears by the pathos of it—though the justice of our cause was freely admitted throughout the court-room, our best friends feared the verdict.

But the climax was as stunning to our enemies as it was unexpected. As Lawyer Douglass finished his last ringing period, the missing witness, Mr. Barnhart, hurried into the court-room. He had started for Leavenworth upon the first intimation that his presence there was needed, and had reached it just in time. He took the stand, swore to his certain knowledge that the bills in question had been paid, and the jury, without leaving their seats, returned a verdict for the defense.

Then rose cheer upon cheer, as our friends crowded about us and offered their congratulations. Our home was saved, and Lawyer Douglass had won a reputation for eloquence and sterling worth that stood undimmed through all his long and prosperous career.

The next ripple on the current of our lives was sister Martha's wedding day. Possessed of remarkable beauty, she had become a belle, and as young ladies were scarce in Kansas at that time, she was the toast of all our country round. But her choice had fallen on a man unworthy of her. Of his antecendents we knew nothing; of his present life little more, save that he was fair in appearance and seemingly prosperous. In the sanction of the union Will stood aloof. Joined to a native intuition were the sharpened faculties of a lad that lived beyond his years. Almost unerring in his insight, he disliked the object of our sister's choice so thoroughly that he refused to be a witness of the nuptials. This dislike we attributed to jealousy, as brother and sister worshiped each other, but the sequel proved a sad corroboration of his views.

Nature seemed to join her protest to Will's silent antagonism. A terrific thunder-storm came up with the noon hour of the wedding. So deep and sullen were the clouds that we were obliged to light the candles. When the wedding pair took their places before Hymen's altar, a crash of thunder rocked the house and set the casements rattling.

The couple had their home awaiting them in Leavenworth, and departed almost immediately after the ceremony.

The cares and responsibilities laid upon our brother's shoulders did not quench his boyish spirits and love of fun. Not Buffalo Bill's! He gave us a jack-o'lantern scare once upon a time, which I don't believe any of us will ever forget. We had never seen that weird species of pumpkin, and Will embroidered a blood-and-thunder narrative.

"The pumpkins all rise up out of the ground," said he, "on fire, with the devil's eyes, and their mouths open, like blood-red lions, and grab you, and go under the earth. You better look out!"

"That ain't so!" all of little girls cried; "you know it's a fib. Ain't it, mother?" and we ran as usual to mother.

"Will, you musn't tell the children such tales. Of course they're just fibs," said mother.

"So there!" we cried, in triumph. But Will had a "so there" answer for us a few nights later. We were coming home late one evening, and found the gate guarded by mad-looking yellow things, all afire, and grinning hideously like real live men in the moon dropped down from the sky.

"Jac-o'-lanterns!" screamed Eliza, grabbing May by the hand, and starting to run. I began to say my prayers, of course, and cry for mother. All at once the heads moved! Even Turk's tail shot between his legs, and he howled in fright. We saw the devil's eyes, the blood-red lion's mouths, and all the rest, and set up such a chorus of wild yells that the whole household rushed to our rescue. While we were panting out our story, we heard Will snickering behind the door.

"So there, smarties! You'll believe what I tell you next time. You bet—ter—had!"

But he liked best to invade our play-room and "work magic" on our dolls. Mother had set aside one apartment in our large log house for a playroom, and here each one of our doll families dwelt in peace and harmony, when Will wasn't around. But there was tragedy whenever he came near. He would scalp the mother dolls, and tie their babies to the bedposts, and would storm into their paste-board-box houses at night, after we had fixed them all in order, and put the families to standing on their heads. He was a dreadful tease. It was in this play-room that the germ of his Wild West took life. He formed us into a regular little company—Turk and the baby, too—and would start us in marching order for the woods. He made us stick horses and wooden tomahawks, spears, and horsehair strings, so that we could be cowboys, Indians, bullwhackers, and cavalrymen. All the scenes of his first freighting trip were acted out in the woods of Salt Creek Valley. We had stages, robbers, "hold-ups," and most ferocious Indian battles.

Will was always the "principal scalper," however, and we had few of our feathers left after he was on the warpath. We were so little we couldn't reach his feathers. He always wore two long shiny ones, which had been the special pride of our black rooster, and when he threw a piece of an old blanket gotten from the Leavenworth barracks around his shoulders, we considered him a very fine general indeed.

All of us were obedient to the letter on "show days," and scarcely ever said, "Now, stop," or "I'll tell mother on you!" But during one of these exciting performances Will came to a short stop.

"I believe I'll run a show when I get to be a man," said he.

"That fortune lady said you'd got to be President of the United States," said Eliza.

"How could ze presiman won a show?" asked Mary.

"How could that old fortune-teller know what I'm going to be?" Will would answer, disdainfully. "I rather guess I can have a show, in spite of all the fortune-tellers in the country. I'll tell you right now, girls, I don't propose to be President, but I do mean to have a show!"

Such temerity in disputing one's destiny was appalling;

and though our ideas of destiny were rather vague, we could grasp one dreadful fact: Will had refused to be President of the United States! So we ran crying to mother, and burying our faces in her lap, sobbed out: "Oh, mother! Will says he ain't going to be President. Don't he have to be?"

Still, in spite of Will's fine scorn of fortune-tellers, the prophecy concerning his future must have been sometimes in his mind. This was shown in an episode that the writer is in duty bound, as a veracious chronicler, to set down.

Our neighbor, Mr. Hathaway, had a son, Eugene, of about Will's age, and the two were fast friends. One day, when Will was visiting at Eugene's house, the boys introduced themselves to a barrel of hard cider. Temperance sentiment had not progressed far enough to bring hard cider under the ban, and Mr. Hathaway had lately pressed out a quantity of the old-fashioned beverage. The boys, supposing it a harmless drink, took all they desired—much more than they could carry. They were in a deplorable condition when Mr. Hathaway found them; and much distressed, the good old man put Eugene to bed and brought Will home.

The family hero returned to us with a flourish of trumpets. He stood up in the wagon and sang and shouted; and when Mr. Hathaway reproved him, "Don't talk to me," was his lofty rejoinder. "You forget that I am to be President of the United States."

There is compensation for everything. Will never touched cider again; and never again could he lord it over his still admiring but no longer docile sisters. If he undertook to boss or tease us more than to our fancy, we would subdue him with an imitation of his grandiloquent, "You forget that I am to be President of the United States." Indeed, so severe was this retaliation that we seldom saw him the rest of the day.

But he got even with us when "preacher day" came around.

Like "Little Breeches' " father, Will never did go in much on religion, and when the ministers assembled for "quarterly meeting" at our house, we never knew what to expect from him. Mother was a Methodist, and as our log house was larger than the others in the valley, it fell to our lot to entertain the preachers often. We kept our preparations on the quiet when Will was home, but he always managed to find out what was up, and then trouble began. His first move was to "sick" Turk on the yellow-legged chickens. They were our best ones, and the only thing we had for the ministers to eat. Then Will would come stalking in:

"Say, mother, just saw all the yellow-legged chickens a-scooting up the road. Methodist preachers must be in the wind, for the old hens are flying like sixty!"

"Now, Will you call Turk off, and round up those chickens right away."

"Catch meself!" And Will would dance around and tease so he nearly drove us all distracted. It was with the greatest difficulty that mother could finally prevail upon him to round up the chickens. That done, he would tie up the pump-handle, milk the cows dry, strew the path to the gate with burrs and thistles, and stick up a sign, "Thorney is the path and stickery the way that leedith unto the kingdom of heaven. Amen!"

Then when mother had put a nice clean valance, freshly starched and ruffled, around the big four-poster bed in the sitting-room, Will would daub it up with smearcase, and just before the preachers arrived, sneak in under it, and wait for prayers.

Mother always desired us to file in quietly, but we couldn't pass the bed without our legs being pinched; so we "hollered," but were afraid to tell mother the reason before the ministers. We had to bear it, but we snickered ourselves when the man called "Elder Green Persimmon," because when he prayed his mouth went inside out, came mincing into the room, and as he passed the valance and got a pinch, jerked out a sour-grape sneeze:

"Mercy on us! I thought I was bitten by that fierce dog of yours, Mrs. Cody; but it must have been a burr."

Then the "experiences" would begin. Will always listened quietly, until the folks began telling how wicked they had been before they got religion; then he would burst in with a vigorous "Amen!"

The elders did not know Will's voice; so they would get warmed up by degree as the amens came thicker and faster. When he had worked them all up to a red-hot pitch, Will would start that awful snort of his that always made us double up with giggles, and with a loud cockle-doodle-doo! would bolt from the bed like a lightning flash and make for the window.

So "preacher day," as Will always called it, became the torment of our lives.

To tell the truth, Will always was teasing us, but if he crooked his finger at us we would bawl. We bawled and squalled from morning til night. Yet we fairly worshiped him, and cried harder when he went away than when he was home.

CHAPTER 7

Indian Encounter and School-Day Incidents

Will was not long at home. The Mormons, who were settled in Utah, rebelled when the government, objecting to the quality of justice meted out by Brigham Young, sent a federal judge to the territory. Troops, under the command of General Albert Sidney Johnson, were dispatched to quell the insurrection, and Russell, Majors & Waddell contracted to transport stores and beef cattle to the army massing against the Mormons in the fall of 1857. The train was a large one, better prepared against such an attack as routed the McCarthy brothers earlier in the summer; yet its fate was the same.

Will was assigned to duty as "extra" under Lew Simpson, an experienced wagon-master, and was subject to his orders only. There was the double danger of Mormons and Indians, so the pay was good. Forty dollars a month in gold looked like a large sum to an eleven-year-old.

Will's second departure was quite as tragic as the first. We girls, as before, were loud in our wailings, and offered to forgive him the depredations in the doll-house and all his teasings, if only he would not go away and be scalped by the Indians. Mother said little, but her anxious look, as she recalled the perils of the former trip, spoke volumes. He carried with him the memory of the open-mouthed admiration of little Charlie, to whom "Brother Will" was the greatest hero in the world. Turk's grief at the parting was not a whit less than ours, and the faithful old fellow seemed to realize that in Will's absence the duty of the family protector devolved on him; so he made no attempt to follow Will beyond the gate.

The train made good progress, and more than half the journey to Fort Bridger was accomplished without a setback. When the Rockies were reached, a noon halt was made near Green River, and here the men were surrounded and overcome by a large force of Danites, the "Avenging Angels" of the Mormon Church, who had "stolen the livery of the court of heaven to serve the devil in." These were responsible for the atrocious Mountain Meadow Massacre, in June of this same year, though the wily "Saints" had planned to place the odium of an unprovoked murder of innocent women and children upon the Indians, who had enough to answer for, and in this instance were but the tools of the Mormon Church. Brigham Young repudiated his accomplice, and allowed John D. Lee to become the scapegoat. The dying statement of this man is as pathetic as Cardinal Wolsey's arraignment of Henry VIII.

"A victim must be had," said he, "and I am that victim. For thirty years I studied to make Brigham Young's will my law. See now what I have come to this day. I have been sacrificed in a cowardly, dastardly manner. I do not fear death. I cannot go to a worse place than I am now in."

John D. Lee deserved his fate, but Brigham Young was none the less a coward.

The Danites spared the lives of the trainmen, but they made sad havoc of the supplies. These they knew to be intended for the use of the army opposed to Brigham Young. They carried off all the stores they could handle, drove with them or stampeded the cattle, and burned the wagons. The trainmen were permitted to retain one wagon and team, with just enough supplies to last them to army headquarters.

It was a disheartened, discomfited band that reached Fort Bridger. The information that two other trains had been destroyed added to their discouragement, for that meant that they, in common with the other trainmen and the soldiers at the fort, must subsist on short rations for the winter. There were nearly four hundred of these trainmen, and it was so late in the season that they had no choice but to remain where they were until spring opened.

It was an irksome winter. The men at the fort hauled their firewood two miles; as the provisions dwindled, one by one the oxen were slaughtered, and when this food supply was exhausted, starvation reared its gaunt form. Happily the freighters got word of the situation, and a relief team reached the fort before the spring was fairly opened.

As soon as practicable the return journey was undertaken. At Fort Laramie two large trains were put in charge of Lew Simpson, as brigade wagon-master, and Will was installed as courier between the two caravans, which traveled twenty miles apart—plenty of elbow room for camping and foraging.

One morning, Simpson, George Woods, and Will, who were in the rear train, set out for the forward one, mounted upon mules, and armed, as the trainmen always were, with rifle, knife, and a brace of revolvers. About half of the twenty miles had been told off when the trio saw a band of Indians emerge from a clump of trees half a mile away and sweep toward them. Flight with the mules was useless; resistance promised hardly more success, as the Indians numbered a full half-hundred; but surrender was death and mutilation.

"Shoot the mules, boys!" ordered Simpson, and five minutes later two men and a boy looked grimly over a still palpitating barricade.

The defense was simple; rifles at range, revolvers for

close quarters, knives at the last. The chief, easily distinguished by his feathered head-dress, was assigned to
Will. Already his close shooting was the pride of the frontiersmen. Simpson's coolness steadied the lad, who realized that the situation was desperate.

The Indians came on with the rush and scream of the
March wind. "Fire!" said Simpson, and three ponies
galloped riderless as the smoke curled from three rifle
barrels.

Dismayed by the fall of their chief, the redskins
wheeled and rode out of range. Will gave a sigh of relief.

"Load up again, Billy!" smiled Simpson. "They'll soon
be back."

"They've only three or four rifles," said Woods. There
had been little lead in the cloud of arrows.

"Here they come!" warned Simpson, and the trio ran
their rifles out over the dead mules.

Three more riderless ponies; but the Indians kept on,
supposing they had drawn the total fire of the whites. A
revolver fusillade undeceived them, and the charging
column wavered and broke for cover.

Simpson patted Will on the shoulder as they reloaded.
"You're a game one, Billy!" said he.

"You bet he is," echoed Woods, cooly drawing an arrow from his shoulder. "How is that, Lew—poisoned?"

Will waited breathless for the decision, and his relief
was as great as Wood's when Simpson, after a critical
scrutiny, answered "No."

The wound was hastily dressed, and the little company gave an undivided attention to the foe, who were cir-
cling around their quarry, hanging to the off sides of their
ponies and firing under them. With a touch of the grim
humor that plain life breeds, Will declared that the mules
were veritable pincushions, so full of arrows were they
stuck.

The besieged maintained a return fire dropping pony after pony, and occasionally a rider. This proved expensive sport to the Indians, and the whole party finally withdrew from range.

There was a long breathing spell, which the trio improved by strengthening their defense, digging up the dirt with their knives and piling it upon the mules. It was tedious work, but preferable to inactivity and cramped quarters.

Two hours went by, and the plan of the enemy was disclosed. A light breeze arose, and the Indians fired the prairie. Luckily the grass near the trail was short, and though the heat was intense and the smoke stifling, the barricade held off the flame. Simpson had kept a close watch, and presently gave the order to fire. A volley went through the smoke and blaze, and the yell that followed proved that it was not wasted. This last ruse failing, the Indians settled down to their favorite game—waiting.

A thin line of them circled out of range; ponies were picketed and tents pitched; night fell, and the stars shot out.

As Woods was wounded, he was excused from guard duty, Will and Simpson keeping watch in turn. Will took the first vigil, and, tired though he was, experienced no difficulty in keeping awake, but he went soundly to sleep the moment he was relieved. He was awakened by a dream that Turk was barking to him, and vaguely alarmed, he sat up to find Simpson sleeping across his rifle.

The midnight hush was unbroken, and the darkness lay thick upon the plain, but shapes blacker than night hovered near, and Will laid his hand on Simpson's shoulder.

The latter was instantly alive, and Woods was awakened. A faint click went away on the night breeze, and a moment later three jets of flame carried warning to the up-creeping foe that the whites were both alive and on the alert.

There was no more sleep within the barricade. The dawn grew into day, and anxious eyes scanned the trail for reinforcements—coming surely, but on what heavy and slow-turning wheels!

Noon came and passed. The anxious eyes questioned one another. Had the rear train been overcome by a larger band of savages? But suddenly half a dozen of the Indians were seen to spring up with gestures of excitement, and spread the alarm around the circle.

"They hear the cracking of the bull-whips," said Simpson.

The Indians who had seen the first team pass, and had assumed that Simpson and his companions were straggling members of it, did not expect another train so soon. There was "mounting in hot haste," and the Indians rode away in one bunch for the distant foothills, just as the first ox-team broke into view.

And never was there fairer picture to more appreciative eyes than those same lumbering, clumsy animals, and never sweeter music than the harsh staccato of the bull-whips.

When hunger was appeased, and Woods's wound properly dressed, Will, for the second time, found himself a hero among the plainsmen. His nerve and coolness were dwelt upon by Simpson, and to the dream that waked him in season was ascribed the continued life on earth of the little company. Will, however, was disposed to allow Turk the full credit for the service.

The remainder of the trip was devoid of special incident, and as Will neared home he hurried on in advance of the train. His heart beat high as he thought of the dear faces awaiting him, unconscious that he was so near.

But the home toward which he was hastening with beating heart and winged heels was shadowed by a great grief. Sister Martha's married life, though brief, had amply justified her brother's estimate of the man into whose hands she had given her life. She was taken suddenly ill, and it was not until several months later that Will learned that the cause of her sickness was the knowledge that had come to her of the faithless nature of her husband. The revelation was made through the visit of one of Mr. C——'s creditors, who, angered at a refusal to liquidate a debt, accused Mr. C—— of being a bigamist, and threatened to set the law upon him. The blow was fatal to one of Martha's pure and affectionate nature, already crushed by neglect and cruelty. All that night she was delirious, and her one thought was "Willie," and the danger he was in—not alone the physical danger, but the moral and spiritual peril that she feared lay in association with rough and reckless men. She moaned and tossed, and uttered incoherent cries; but as the morning broke the storm went down, and the anxious watchers fancied that she slept. Suddenly she sat up, the light of reason again shining in her eyes, and with a joyous cry, "Tell mother Willie's saved! Willie's saved!" she fell back on her pillow, and her spirit passed away. On her face was the peace that the world can neither give nor take away. The veil of the Unknown had been drawn aside for a peace. She had "sent her soul through the Invisible," and it had found the light that lit the last weary steps through the Valley of the Shadow.

Mr. C—— had moved from Leavenworth to Johnson County, twenty-five miles away, and as there were neither telegraph nor mail facilities, he had the body sent home, himself accompanying it. Thus our first knowledge of Martha's sickness came when her lifeless clay was borne across our threshold, the threshold that, less than a year before, she had crossed a bright and bonny bride. Dazed by the shock, we longed for Will's return before we must lay his idolized sister forever in her narrow cell.

All of the family, Mr. C—— included, were gathered in the sitting-room, sad and silent, when Turk suddenly raised his head, listened a second, and bounded out of doors.

"Will is coming!" cried mother, and we all ran to the door. Turk was racing up the long hill, at the top of which was a moving speck that the dog knew to be his master. His keen ears had caught the familiar whistle half a mile away.

When Turk had manifested his joy at the meeting, he prepared Will for the bereavement that awaited him; he put his head down and emitted a long and repeated wail. Will's first thought was for mother, and he fairly ran down the hill. The girls met him some distance from the house, and sobbed out the sad news.

And when he had listened, the lad that had passed unflinchingly through two Indian fights, broke down, and sobbed with the rest of us.

"Did that rascal, C——, have anything to do with her death?" he asked, when the first passion of grief was over.

Julia, who knew no better at the time, replied that Mr. C—— was the kindest of husbands, and was crushed with sorrow at his loss; but spite of the assurance, Will, when he reached the house, had neither look nor word for him. He just put his arms about mother's neck, and mingled his grief with her words of sympathy and love.

Martha was shortly after laid by father's side, and as we stood weeping in that awful moment when the last spadeful of earth complete the sepulture, Will, no longer master of himself, stepped up before Mr. C——:

"Murderer," he said, "one day you shall answer to me for the death of her who lies there!"

When Will next presented himself at Mr. Major's office, he was told that his services had been wholly satisfactory, and that he could have work at any time he desired. This was gratifying, but a sweeter pleasure was to lay his winter's wages in mother's lap. Through his help, and her business ability, our pecuniary affairs were in good condition. We were comfortably situated, and as Salt Creek Valley now boasted of a schoolhouse, mother wished Will to enter school. He was so young when he came West that his school-days had been few; nor was the prospect of adding to their number alluring. After the excitement of life on the plains, going to school was dull work; but Will realized that there was a world beyond the prairie's horizon, and he entered school, determined to do honest work.

Our first teacher was of the good, old-fashioned sort. He taught because he had to live. He had no love for his work, and knew nothing of children. The one motto he lived up to was, "Spare the rod and spoil the child." As Will was a regular Tartar in the schoolroom, he, more than all the other scholars, made him put his smarting theory into practice. Almost every afternoon was attended with the dramatic attempt to switch Will. The schoolroom was separated into two grand divisions, "the boys on teacher's side," and those "on the Cody side." The teacher would send his pets out to get switches, and part of our division—we girls, of course—would begin to weep; while those who had spunk would spit on their hands, clench their fists, and "dare 'em to bring them switches in!" Those were hot times in old Salt Creek Valley!

One morning Turk, too, was seized with educational ambition, and accompanied Will to school. We tried to drive him home, but he followed at a distance, and as we entered the schoolhouse, he emerged from the shrubbery by the roadside and crept under the building.

Alas for the scholars, and alas for the school! Another ambitious dog reposed beneath the temple of learning.

Will, about that time, was having a bad quarter of an hour. An examination into his knowledge, or lack of it, was under way, and he was hard pressed. Had he been asked how to strike a trail, locate water, or pitch a tent, his replies would have been full and accurate, but the teacher's queries seemed as foolish as the "Reeling and Writhing, Ambition, Distraction, Uglification, and Derision" of the Mock Turtle in "Alice in Wonderland."

Turk effected an unexpected rescue. Snarls were heard beneath the schoolhouse; then savage growls and yelps, while the floor resounded with the whacks of the canine combatants. With a whoop that would not have disgraced an Indian, Will was out of doors, shouting, "Eat him up, Turk! Eat him up!"

The owner of the opposing dog was one Steve Gobel. 'Twixt him and Will a good-size feud existed. Steve was also on the scene, with a defiant, "Sic 'em, Nigger!" and the rest of the school followed in his wake.

Of the twisting, yelping bundle of dog-flesh that rolled from under the schoolhouse it was difficult to say which was Turk and which Nigger. Eliza and I called to Turk, and wept because he would not hear. The teacher ordered the children back to their studies, but they were as deaf as Turk; where at the enraged pedagogue hopped wildly about, flourishing a stick and whacking every boy that stayed within reach of it.

Nigger soon had enough of the fight, and striking his tail-colors fled yelping from the battleground. His master, Steve Gobel, a large youth of nineteen or twenty years, pulled off his coat to avenge upon Will the dog's defeat, but the teacher effected a Solomon-like compromise by whipping both boys for bringing their dogs to school, after which the interrupted session was resumed.

But Gobel nursed his wrath, and displayed his enmity in a thousand small ways. Will paid no attention to him, but buckled down to his school work. Will was a born "lady's man," and when Miss Mary Hyatt complicated the feud 'twixt him and Steve, it hurried to its climax. Mary was older than Will, but she plainly showed her preference for him over Master Gobel. Steve had never distinguished himself in an Indian fight; he was not a hero, but just a plain boy.

Now, indeed, was Will's life unendurable; "patience had had its perfect work." He knew that a boy of twelve, however strong and sinewy, was not a match for an almost full-grown man; so, to balance matters, he secreted on his person an old bowie-knife. When next he met Steve, the latter climaxed his bullying tactics by striking the object of his resentment; but he was unprepared for the sudden leap that bore him backward to the earth. Size and strength told swiftly in the struggle that succeeded, but Will, with a dextrous thrust, put the point of the bowie into the fleshy part of Steve's lower leg, a sport where he knew the cut would not be serious.

The stricken bully shrieked that he was killed; the children gathered round, and screamed loudly at the sight of blood. "Will Cody has killed Steve Gobel!" was the wailing cry, and Will, though he knew Steve was but pinked, began to realize that frontier styles of combat were not esteemed in communities given up to the soberer pursuits of spelling, arithmetic, and history. Steve, he knew, was more frightened than hurt; but the picture of the prostrate, ensanguined youth, and the group of awe-stricken children, bore in upon his mind the truth that his act was an infraction of the civil code; that even in self-defense, he had no right to use a knife unless his life was threatened.

The irate pedagogue was hastening to the scene, and after one glance at him, Will, incontinently fled. At the road he came upon a wagon train, and with a shout of joy recognized in the "boss" John Willis, a wagon-master employed by Russell, Majors & Waddell, and a great friend of the "boy extra." Will climbed up behind Willis on his horse, and related his escapade to a close and sympathetic listener.

"If you say so, Billy," was his comment, "I'll go over and lick the whole outfit, and stampede the school."

"No, let the school alone," replied Will; "but I guess I'll graduate, if you'll let me go along with you this trip."

Willis readily agreed, but insisted upon returning to the schoolhouse. "I'm not going," said he, "to let you be beaten by a bully of a boy, and a Yankee school-teacher, with a little learning, but not a bit of sand." His idea of equalizing forces was that he and "Little Billy" should fight against the pedagogue and Steve.

Will consented, and they rode back to the school-house, on the door of which Willis pounded with his revolver butt, and when the door was opened he invited Gobel and the "grammar man" to come forth and do battle. But Steve had gone home, and the teacher, on seeing the two gladiators, fled, while the scholars, dismissing themselves, ran home in a fright.

That night mother received a note from the teacher.

He was not hired, he wrote, to teach desperadoes; therefore Will was dismissed. But Will had already dismissed himself, and had rejoined the larger school whose walls are the blue bowl called the sky. And long after was his name used by the pedagogue to conjure up obedience in his pupils; unless they kissed the rod, they, too, might go to the bad, and follow in Will Cody's erring footsteps.

Willis and Will had gone but a piece on the road when horsemen were seen approaching.

"Mr. Gobel and the officers are after me," said Will.

"Being after you and gittin' you are two different things," said the wagon-master. "Lie low, and I'll settle the men."

Mr. Gobel and his party rode up with the information that they had come to arrest Will; but they got no satisfaction from Willis. He would not allow them to search the wagons, and they finally rode away. That night, when the camp was pitched, the wagon-master gave Will a mule, and accompanied him home. We were rejoined to see him, especially mother, who was much concerned over his escapade.

"Oh, Will, how could you do such a thing?" she said, sorrowfully. "It is a dreadful act to use a knife on any one."

Will disavowed any homicidal intentions; but his explanations made little headway against mother's disapproval and her disappointment over the interruption of his school career. As it seemed the best thing to do, she consented to his going with the wagon train under the care of John Willis, and the remainder of the night was passed in preparations for the journey.

CHAPTER 8

Death and Burial of Turk

This trip of Will's covered only two months, and was succeeded by another expedition, to the new post at Fort Wallace, at Cheyenne Pass.

Meanwhile mother had decided to improve the opportunity afforded by her geographical position, and under her supervision "The Valley Grove House" was going up.

The hotel commanded a magnificent prospect. Below lay the beautiful Salt Creek Valley. It derived its name from the saline properties of the little stream that rushed along its pebbly bed to empty its clear waters into the muddy Missouri. From the vantage-ground of our location Salt Creek looked like a silver thread, winding its way through the rich verdure of the valley. The region was dotted with fertile farms; from east to west ran the government road, known as the Old Salt Lake Trail, and back of us was Cody Hill, named for my father. Our house stood on the side hill, just above the military road, and between us and the hilltop lay the grove that gave the hotel its name. Government hill, which broke the eastern sky-line, hid Leavenworth and the Missouri River, culminating to the south in Pilot Knob, the eminence on which my father was buried, also beyond our view.

Mother's business sagacity was justified in the hotel venture. The trail began its half-mile ascent of Cody Hill just below our house, and at this point the expedient known as "doubling" was employed. Two teams hauled a wagon up the steep incline, the double team returning for the wagon left behind. Thus the progress of a wagon train, always slow, became a very snail's pace, and the hotel was insured a full quota of hungry trainmen.

Will found that his wages were of considerable aid to mother in the large expense incurred by the building of the hotel; and the winter drawing on, forbidding further freighting trips, he planned an expedition with a party of trappers. More money was to be made at this business during the winter than at any other time.

The trip was successful, and contained only one adventure spiced with danger, which, as was so often the case, Will twisted to his own advantage by coolness and presence of mind.

One morning, as he was making the round of his traps, three Indians appeared on the trail, each leading a pony laden with pelts. One had a gun; the others carried bows and arrows. The odds were three to one, and the brave with the gun was the most to be feared.

This Indian dropped his bridle-rein and threw up his rifle; but before it was at his shoulder Will had fired, and he fell forward on his face. His companions bent their bows, one arrow passing through Will's hat and another piercing his arm—the first wound he ever received. Will swung his cap about his head.

"This way! Here they are!" he shouted to an imaginary party of friends at his back. Then with his revolver he wounded another of the Indians, who, believing reinforcements were at hand, left their ponies and fled.

Will took the ponies on the double-quick back to camp, and the trappers decided to pull up stakes at once. It had been a profitable season, and the few more pelts to be had were not worth the risk of an attack by avenging Indians; so they packed their outfit, and proceeded to Fort Laramie. Will realized a handsome sum from the sale of his captured furs, besides those of the animals he had himself trapped.

At the fort were two men bound east, and impatient to set out, and Will, in his haste to reach home, joined forces with them. Rather than wait for an uncertain wagon train, they decided to chance the dangers of the road. They bought three ponies and a pack-mule for the camp outfit, and sallied forth in high spirits.

Although the youngest of the party, Will was the most experienced plainsman, and was constantly on the alert. They reached the Little Blue River without sign of Indians, but across the stream Will espied a band of them. The redskins were as keen of eye, and straightway exchanged the pleasures of the chase for the more exciting pursuit of human game. But they had the river to cross, and this gave the white men a good start. The pursuit was hot, and grew hotter, but the kindly darkness fell, and under cover of it the trio got safely away. That night they camped in a little ravine that afforded shelter from both Indians and weather.

A look over the ravine disclosed a cave that promised a snug harbor, and therein Will and one of his companions spread their blankets and fell asleep. The third man, whose duty it was to prepare the supper, kindled a fire just inside the cave, and returned outside for a supply of fuel. When he again entered the cave the whole interior was revealed by the bright firelight, and after one look he gave a yell of terror, dropped his firewood, and fled.

Will and the other chap were on their knees instantly, groping for their rifles, in the belief that the Indians were upon them; but the sight that met their eyes was more terror-breeding than a thousand Indians. A dozen bleached and ghastly skeletons were gathered with them around the camp-fire, and seemed to nod and sway, and thrust their long-chilled bones toward the cherry blaze.

Ghastly as it was within the cave, Will found it more unpleasant in the open. The night was cold, and a storm threatened.

"Well, said he to his companions, "we know the worst that's in there now. Those old dead bones won't hurt us. Let's go back."

"Not if I know myself, sonny," returned one of the men decidedly, and the other heartily agreed with him, swearing that as it was, he should not be able to close his eyes for a week. So, after a hurried lunch upon the cold provisions, the party mounted their ponies and pushed on. The promised snowstorm materialized, and shortly became a young blizzard, and obliged to dismount and camp in the open prairie, they made a miserable night of it.

But it had an end, as all things have, and with the morning they resumed the trail, reaching Marysville, on the Big Blue, after many trials and privations.

From here the trail was easier, as the country was pretty well settled, and Will reached home without further adventure or misadventure. Here there was compensation for hardship in the joy of handing over to mother all his money, realizing that it would lighten her burdens— burdens borne that she might leave her children provided for when she could no longer repel the dread messenger, that in all those years seemed to hover so near that even our childish hearts felt its presence ere it actually crossed the threshold.

It was early in March when Will returned from his trapping expedition. Mother's business was flourishing, though she herself grew frailer with the passing of each day. The summer that came on was a sad one for us all, for it marked Turk's last days on earth. One evening he was lying in the yard, when a strange dog came up the road, bounded in, gave Turk a vicious bite, and went on. We dressed the wound, and thought little of it, until some horsemen rode up, with the inquiry, "Have you seen a dog pass here?"

We answered indignantly that a strange dog had passed, and had bitten our dog.

"Better look out for him, then," warned the men as they rode away. "The dog is mad."

Consternation seized us. It was dreadful to think of Turk going mad—he who had been our playmate from infancy, and who, through childhood's years, had grown more dear to us than many human beings could; but mother knew the matter was serious, and issued her commands. Turk must be shut up, and we must not even visit him for a certain space. And so we shut him up, hoping for the best; but it speedily became plain that the poison was working in his veins, and that the greatest kindness we could do him was to kill him.

That was a frightful alternative. Will utterly refused to shoot him, and the execution was delegated to the hired man, Will stipulating that none of his weapons should be used, and that he be allowed to get out of ear-shot.

Late that afternoon, just before sunset, we assembled in melancholy silence for the funeral. A grave had been dug on the highest point of the eastern extremity of Cody Hill, and decorated in black ribbons, we slowly filed up the steep path, carrying Turk's body on a pine board softened with moss. Will led the procession with his hat in his hand, and every now and then his fist went savagely at his eyes. When we reached the grave, we formed around it in a tearful circle, and Will, who always called me "the little preacher," told me to say the Lord's Prayer. The sun was setting, and the brilliant western clouds were shining round below us, and the sounds in the valley were muffled and indistinct.

"Our Father which art in heaven," I whispered softly, as all the children bent their heads, "Hallowed be Thy name. Thy kingdom come, Thy will be done in earth as it is in heaven." I paused, and the other children said the rest in chorus. The next day Will procured a large block of red bloodstone, which abounds in that country, squared it off, carved the name of Turk upon it in large letters, and we placed it at the head of the grave.

To us there had been no incongruity in the funeral ceremonials and burial. Turk had given us all that dog could give; we, for our part, gave him Christian sepulture. Our sorrow was sincere. We had lost an honest, loyal friend. For many succeeding days his grave was garlanded with fresh flowers, placed there by loving hands. Vale Turk! Would that our friends of the higher evolution were all as stanch as thou!

THE BURIAL OF TURK

Only a dog! but the tears fall fast
   As we lay him to rest underneath the green sod,
Where bountiful nature, the sweet summer through,
   Will deck him with daisies and bright goldenrod.

The loving thought of a boyish heart
   Marks the old dog's grave with a bloodstone red;
The name, carved in letters rough and rude,
   Keeps his memory green, though his life be sped.

For the daring young hero of wood and plain
   Like all who are generous, strong and brave,
Has a heart that is loyal and kind and true,
   And shames not to weep o'er his old friend's grave.

Only a dog, do you say? but I deem
   A dog who with faithfulness fills his trust,
More worthy than many a man to be given
   A tribute of love, when but ashes and dust.

An unusually good teacher now presided at the schoolhouse in our neighborhood, and Will was again persuaded into educational paths. He put in a hard winter's work; but with the coming of spring and its unrest, the swelling of buds and the springing of grass, the return of the birds and the twittering from myriad nests, the Spirits of the Plains beckoned to him, and he joined a party of gold-hunters on the long trail to Pike's Peak.

The gold excitement was at its apogee in 1860. By our house had passed the historic wagon bearing on its side the classic motto, "Pike's Peak or Bust!" Afterward, stranded by the wayside, a whole history of failure and disappointment, borne with grim humor, was told by the addition of the eloquent word, "Busted!"

For all his adventures, Will was only fourteen, and although tall for his age, he had not the physical strength that might have been expected from his hardy life. It was not strange that he should take the gold fever; less so that mother should dread to see him again leave home to face unknown perils; and it is not at all remarkable that upon reaching Auraria, now Denver, he should find that fortunes were not lying around much more promiscuously in a gold country than in any other.

Recent events have confirmed a belief that under the excitement of a gold craze men exercise less judgment than at any other time. Except in placer mining, which almost any one can learn, gold mining is a science. Now and again a nugget worth a fortune is picked up, but the average mortal can get a better livelihood, with half the work, in almost any other field of effort. To become rich a knowledge of ores and mining methods is indispensable.

But Will never reached the gold-fields. Almost the first person he met on the streets of Julesberg was George Chrisman, who had been chief wagonmaster for Russell, Majors & Waddell. Will had become well acquainted with

Chrisman on the various expeditions he had made for the firm.

This man was located at Julesberg as agent for the Pony Express line, which was in process of formation. This line was an enterprise of Russell, Majors & Waddell. Mr. Russell met in Washington the Senator from California. This gentleman knew that the Western firm of contractors was running a daily stagecoach from the Missouri River to Sacramento, and he urged upon Mr. Russell the desirability of operating a pony express line along the same route. There was already a line known as the "Butterfield Route," but this was circuitous, the fastest time ever made on it was twenty-one days.

Mr. Russell laid the matter before his partners. They were opposed to it, as they were sure it would be a losing venture; but the senior member urged the matter so strongly that they consented to try it, for the good of the country, with no expectation of profit. They utilized the stagecoach stations already established, and only about two months were required to put the Pony Express line in running order.

Riders received from a hundred and twenty to a hundred and twenty-five dollars a month, but they earned it. In order to stand the life great physical strength and endurance were necessary; in addition, riders must be cool, brave, and resourceful. Their lives were in constant peril, and they were obliged to do double duty in case the comrade that was to relieve them had been disabled by outlaws or Indians.

Two hundred and fifty miles was the daily distance that must be made; this constituted an average of a little over ten miles an hour. In the exceedingly rough country this average could not be kept up; to balance it, there were a few places in the route where the rider was expected to cover twenty-five miles an hour.

In making such a run, it is hardly necessary to say that no extra weight was carried. Letters were written on the finest tissue paper; the charge was at the rate of five dollars for half an ounce. A hundred of these letters would make a bulk not much larger than an ordinary writing-tablet.

The mail-pouches were never to carry more than twenty pounds. They were leather bags, impervious to moisture; the letters, as a further protection, were wrapped in oiled silk. The pouches were locked, sealed, and strapped to the rider's side. They were not unlocked during the journey from St. Joseph to Sacramento.

The first trip was made in ten days; this was a saving of eleven days over the best time ever made by the "Butter-field Route." Sometimes the time was shortened to eight days; but an average trip was made in nine. The distance covered in this time was nineteen hundred and sixty-six miles.

President Buchanan's last presidential message was carried in December, 1860, in a few hours over eight days. President Lincoln's inaugural, the following March, was transmitted in seven days and seventeen hours. This was the quickest trip ever made.

The Pony Express line made its worth at once felt. It would have become a financial success but that a telegraph line was put into operation over the same stretch of territory, under the direction of Mr. Edward Creighton. The first message was sent over the wires the 24th of October, 1861. The Pony Express line had outlived its usefulness, and was at once discontinued. But it had accomplished its main purpose, which was to determine whether the route by which it went could be made a permanent track for travel the year through. The cars of the Union Pacific road now travel nearly the same old trails as those followed by the daring riders of frontier days.

Mr. Chrisman gave Will a cordial greeting. He explained the business of the express line to his young friend, and stated that the company had nearly perfected its arrangements. It was now buying ponies and putting them into good condition, preparatory to beginning operations. He added, jokingly:

"It's a pity you're not a few years older, Billy. I would give you a job as Pony Express rider. There's good pay in it."

Will was at once greatly taken with the idea, and begged so hard to be given a trial that Mr. Chrisman consented to give him work for a month. If the life proved too hard for him, he was to be laid off at the end of that time. He had a short run of forty-five miles; there were three relay stations, and he was expected to make fifteen miles an hour.

The 3rd of April, 1860, Mr. Russell stood ready to receive the mail from a fast New York train at St. Joseph. He adjusted the letter-pouch on the pony in the presence of an excited crowd. Besides the letters, several large New York papers printed special editions on tissue paper for this inaugural trip. The crowd plucked hairs from the tail of the first animal to start on the novel journey, and preserved these hairs as talismans. The rider mounted, the moment for starting came, the signal was given, and off he dashed.

At the same moment Sacramento witnessed a similar scene; the rider of that region started on the two thousand mile ride eastward as the other started westward. All the way along the road the several riders were ready for their initial gallop.

Will looked forward eagerly to the day when the express lines should be set in motion, and when the hour came it found him ready, standing beside his horse, and waiting for the rider whom he was to relieve. There was a clatter of hoofs, and a horseman dashed up and flung him the saddle-bag. Will threw them upon the waiting pony, vaulted into the saddle, and was off like the wind.

The first relay station was reached on time, and Will changed with hardly a second's loss of time, while the panting, reeking animal he had ridden was left to the care of the stock-tender. This was repeated at the end of the second fifteen miles, and the last station was reached a few minutes ahead of time. The return trip was made in good order, and then Will wrote to us of his new position, and told us that he was in love with the life.

CHAPTER 9

Will as Pony Express Rider

After being pounded against a saddle three dashes daily for three months, to the tune of fifteen miles an hour, Will began to feel a little loose in his joints, and weary withal, but he was determined to "stick it out." Besides the daily pounding, the track of the Pony Express rider was strewn with perils. A wayfarer through that wild land was more likely to run across outlaws and Indians than to pass unmolested, and as it was known that packages of value were frequently dispatched by the Pony Express line, the route was punctuated by ambuscades.

Will had an eye out every trip for a hold-up, but three months went by before he added that novelty to his other experiences. One day, as he flew around a bend in a narrow pass, he confronted a huge revolver in the grasp of a man who manifestly meant business, and whose salutation was:

"Halt! Throw up your hands!"

Most people do, and Will's hands were raised reluctantly. The highwayman advanced, saying, not unkindly:

"I don't want to hurt you, boy, but I do want them bags."

Money packages were in the saddlebags, and Will was minded to save them if he could, so, as the outlaw reached for the booty, Will touched the pony with his foot, and the upshot was satisfactory to an unexpected degree. The plunge upset the robber, and as the pony swept over him he got a vicious blow from one hoof. Will wheeled for a revolver duel, but the foe was prostrate, stunned, and bleeding at the head. Will disarmed the fellow, and pinioned his arms behind him, and then tied up his broken head. Will surmised that the prisoner must have a horse hidden hard by, and a bit of a search disclosed it. When he returned with the animal, its owner had opened his eyes and was beginning to remember a few things. Will helped him to mount, and out of pure kindness tied him on; then he straddled his own pony, and towed the dismal outfit along with him.

It was the first time that he had been behind on his run, but by way of excuse he offered to Mr. Chrisman a broken-headed and dejected gentleman tied to a horse's back; and Chrisman, with a grin, locked the excuse up for future reference.

A few days after this episode Will received a letlet from Julia, telling him that mother was ill, and asking him to come home. He at once sought out Mr. Chrisman, and giving his reason, asked to be relieved.

"I'm sorry your mother's sick," was the answer, "but I'm glad something has occurred to make you quit this life. It's wearing you out, Billy, and you're too gritty to give it up without a good reason."

Will reached home to find mother slightly improved. For three weeks was he content to remain idly at home; then (it was November of 1860) his unquiet spirit bore him away on another trapping expedition, this time with a young friend named David Phillips.

They bought an ox-team and wagon to transport the traps, camp outfit, and provisions, and took along a large supply of ammunition, besides extra rifles. Their destination was the Republican River. It coursed more than a hundred miles from Leavenworth, but the country about it was reputed rich in beaver. Will acted as scout on the journey, going ahead to pick out trails, locate camping grounds, and look out for breakers. The information concerning the beaver proved correct; the game was indeed so plentiful that they concluded to pitch a permanent camp and see the winter out.

They chose a hollow in a sidehill, and enlarged it to the dimensians of a decent-sized room. A floor of logs was put in, and a chimney fashioned of stones, the open lower part doing double duty as cook-stove and heater; the bed was spread in the rear, and the wagon sheltered the entrance. A corral of poles was built for the oxen, and one corner of it protected by boughs. Although, they accounted their winter quarters thoroughly satisfactory and agreeable.

The boys had seen no Indians on their trip out, and were not concerned in that quarter, though they were too good plainsmen to relax their vigilance. There were other foes, as they discovered the first night in their new quarters. They were aroused by a commotion in the corral where the oxen were confined, and hurrying out with their rifles, they found a huge bear intent upon a feast of beef. The oxen were bellowing in terror, one of them dashing crazily about the inclosure, and the other so badly hurt that it could not get up.

Phillips, who was in the lead, fired first, but succeeded only in wounding the bear. Pain was now added to the savagery of hunger, and the infuriated monster rushed upon Phillips. Dave leaped back, but his foot slipped on a bit of ice, and he went down with a thud, his rifle flying from his hand as he struck.

But there was a cool young head and a steady hand behind him. A ball from Will's rifle entered the distended mouth of the onrushing bear and pierced the brain, and the huge mass fell lifeless almost across Dave's body.

Phillips nerves loosened with a snap, and he laughed for very relief as he seized Will's hands.

"That's the time you saved my life, old fellow!" said he. "Perhaps I can do as much for you sometime."

"That's the first bear I ever killed," said Will, more interested in that topic than in the one Dave held forth on.

One of the oxen was found to be mortally hurt, and a bullet ended its misery. Will then took his first lesson in the gentle art of skinning a bear.

Dave's chance to square his account with Will came a fortnight later. They were chasing a bunch of elk, when Will fell, and discovered that he could not rise.

"I'm afraid I've broken my leg," said he, as Dave ran to him.

Phillips had once been a medical student, and he examined the leg with a professional eye. "You're right, Billy; the leg's broken," he reported.

Then he went to work to improvise splints and bind up the leg; and this done, he took Will on his back and bore him to the dugout. Here the leg was stripped, and set in carefully prepared splints, and the whole bound up securely.

The outlook was unpleasant, cheerfully as one might regard it. Living in the scoop of a sidehill when one is strong and able to get about and keep the blood coursing is one thing; living there pent up through a tedious winter is quite another. Dave medicated as he worked away at the pair of crutches.

"Tell you what I think I'd better do," said he. "The nearest settlement is some hundred miles away, and I can get there and back in twenty days. Suppose I make the trip, get a team for our wagon, and come back for you?"

The idea of being left alone and well-nigh helpless struck dismay to Will's heart, but there was no help for it, and he assented. Dave put matters into shipshape, piled wood in the dugout, cooked a quantity of food and put it where Will could reach it without rising, and fetched several days' supply of water. Mother, ever mindful of Will's education, had put some school-books in the wagon, and Dave placed these besides the food and water. When Phillips finally set out, driving the surviving ox before him, he left behind a very lonely and homesick boy.

During the first day of his confinement Will felt too desolate to eat, much less to read; but as he grew accustomed to solitude he derived real pleasure from the companionship of books. Perhaps in all his life he never extracted so much benefit from study as during that brief period of enforced idleness, when it was his sole means of making the dragging hours endurable. Dave, he knew, could not return in less than twenty days, and one daily task, never neglected, was to cut a notch in the stick that marked the humdrum passage of the days. Within the week he could hobble about on his crutches for a short distance; after that he felt more secure.

A fortnight passed. And one day, weary with his studies, he fell asleep over his books. Some one touched his shoulder, and looking up, he saw an Indian in war paint and feathers.

"How?" asked Will, with a show of friendliness, though he knew the brave was on the warpath.

Half a score of bucks followed at the heels of the first, squeezing into the little dugout until there was barely room for them to sit down.

With a sinking heart Will watched them enter, but he plucked up spirit again when the last, a chief, pushed in, for in this warrior he recognized an Indian that he had once done a good turn.

Whatever Lo's faults, he never forgets a kindness any more than he forgets an injury. The chief, who went by the name of Rain-in-the-Face, at once recognized Will, and asked him what he was doing in that place. Will displayed his bandages, and related the mishap that had made them necessary, and refreshed the chief's memory of a certain occasion when a blanket and provisions had drifted his way. Rain-in-the-Face replied, with proper gravity, that he and his chums were out after scalps, and confessed to designs upon Will's, but in consideration of Auld Lang Syne he would spare the paleface boy.

Auld Lang Syne however did not save the blankets and provisions and the bedizened crew stripped the dugout almost bare of supplies; but Will was thankful enough to see the back of the last of them.

Two days later a blizzard set in. Will took an inventory, and found that, economy considered, he had food for a week; but as the storm would surely delay Dave, he put himself on half rations.

Three weeks were now gone, and he looked for Dave momentarily; but as night followed day and day grew into night again, he was given over to keen anxiety. Had Phillips lost his way? Had he failed to locate the snow-covered dugout? Had he perished in the storm? Had he fallen victim to Indians? These and like questions haunted the poor lad continually. Study became impossible, and he lost his appetite for what food there was left; but the tally on the stick was kept.

The twenty-ninth day dawned. Starvation stalked into the dugout. The wood, too, was nigh gone. But great as was Will's physical suffering, his mental distress was greater. He sat before a handful of fire, shivering and hungry, wretched and despondent.

Hark! Was that his name? Choking with emotion, unable to articulate, he listened intently. Yes; it was his name, and Dave's familiar voice, and with all his remaining energy he made an answering call.

His voice enabled Phillips to locate the dugout, and a

passage was cleared through the snow. And when Will saw the door open, the tensions on his nerves let go, and he wept—"like a girl," as he afterward told us.

"God bless you, Dave!" he cried, as he clasped his friend around the neck.

CHAPTER 10

Echoes from Sumter

The guns that opened on Fort Sumter set the country all ablaze. In Kansas, where blood had already been shed, the excitement reached an extraordinary pitch. Will desired to enlist, but mother would not listen to the idea.

My brother had never forgotten the vow made in the post-trader's, and now with the coming of war his opportunity seemed ripe and lawful; he could at least take up arms against father's old-time enemies, and at the same time serve his country. This aspect of the case was presented to mother in glowing colors, backed by most eloquent pleading; but she remained obdurate.

"You are too young to enlist, Willie," she said. "They would not accept you, and if they did, I could not endure it. I have only a little time to live; for my sake, then, wait till I am no more before you enter the army."

This request was not to be disregarded, and Will promised that he would not enlist while mother lived.

Kansas had long been the scene of bitter strife between the two parties, and though there was a preponderance of the Free-Soil element when it was admitted to the Union in 1861, we were fated to see some of the horrors of slavery. Suffering makes one wondrous kind; mother had suffered so much herself that the misery of others ever vibrated a chord of sympathy in her breast, and our house became a station on "the underground railway."

Many a fugitive slave did we shelter, many here received food and clothing, and, aided by mother, a great number reached safe harbors.

One old man, named Uncle Tom, became so much attached to us that he refused to go on. We kept him as help about the hotel. He was with us several months, and we children grew very fond of him. Every evening when supper was over, he sat before the kitchen fire and told a breathless audience strange stories of the days of slavery. And one evening, never to be forgotten, Uncle Tom was sitting in his accustomed place, surrounded by his juvenile listeners, when he suddenly sprang to his feet with a cry of terror. Some men had entered the hotel sitting-room, and the sound of their voices drove Uncle Tom to his own little room, and under the bed.

"Mrs. Cody," said the unwelcome visitors, "we understand that you are harboring our runaway slaves. We propose to search the premises; and if we find our property, you cannot object to our removing it."

Mother was sorely distressed for the unhappy Uncle Tom, but she knew objection would be futile. She could only hope that the old colored man had made good his escape.

But no! Uncle Tom lay quaking under his bed, and there his brutal master found him. It is not impossible that there were slaveholders kind and humane, but the bitter curse of slavery was the open door it left for brutality and inhumanity; and never shall I forget the barbarity displayed by the owner of Uncle Tom before our horrified eyes. The poor slave was so old that his hair was wholly white; yet a rope was tied to it, and, despite our pleadings, he was dragged from the house, every cry he uttered evoking only a savage kick from a heavy riding-boot. When he was out of sight, and his screams out of hearing, we wept bitterly on mother's loving breast.

Uncle Tom again escaped, and made his way to our house, but he reached it only to die. We sorrowed for the poor old slave, but thanked God that he had passed beyond the inhumanity of man.

Debarred from serving his country as a soldier, Will decided to do so in some other capacity, and accordingly took service with a United States freight caravan, transporting supplies to Fort Laramie. On this trip his frontier training and skill as a marksman were the means of saving a life.

In Western travel the perils from outlaws and Indians were so real that emigrants usually sought the protection of a large wagon-train. Several families of emigrants journeyed under the wing of the caravan to which Will was attached.

When in camp one day upon the bank of the Platte River, and the members of the company were busied with preparations for the night's rest and the next day's journey, Mamie Perkins, a little girl from one of the emigrant families, was sent to the river for a pail of water. A moment later a monster buffalo was seen rushing upon the camp. A chorus of yells and a fusillade from rifles and revolvers neither checked nor swerved him. Straight through the camp he swept, like a cyclone, leaping ropes and boxes, overturning wagons, and smashing things generally.

Mamie, the little water-bearer, had filled her pail and was returning in the track selected by the buffalo. Too terrified to move, she watched, with white face and parted lips, the maddened animal sweep toward her, head down and tail up, its hoofs beating a thunderous tattoo on the plain.

Will had been asleep, but the commotion brought him to his feet, and snatching up his rifle, he ran toward the little girl, aimed and fired at the buffalo. The huge animal lurched, staggered a few yards farther, then dropped within a dozen feet of the terrified child.

A shout of relief went up, and while a crowd of praising men gathered about the embryo buffalo-hunter, Mamie was taken to her mother. Will never relished hearing his praises sung, and as the camp was determined to pedestal him as a hero, he ran away and hid in his tent.

Upon reaching Fort Laramie, Will's first business was to look up Alf Slade, agent of the Pony Express line, whose headquarters were at Horse-shoe Station, twenty miles from the fort. He carried a letter of recommendation from Mr. Russell, but Slade demurred.

"You're too young for a Pony Express rider," said he.

"I rode three months a year ago, sir, and I'm much stronger now," said Will.

"Oh, are you the boy rider that was on Chrisman's division?"

"Yes, sir."

"All right; I'll try you. If you can't stand it, I'll give you something easier."

Will's run was from Red Buttes, on the North Platte, to Three Crossings, on the Sweetwater—seventy-six miles.

The wilderness was of the kind that is supposed to howl, and no person fond of excitement had reason to complain of lack of it. One day Will arrived at his last station to find that the rider on the next run had been mortally hurt by Indians. There being no one else to do it, he volunteered to ride the eighty-five miles for the wounded man. He accomplished it, and made his own return trip on time—a continuous ride of three hundred and twenty-two miles. There was no rest for the rider, but twenty-one horses were used on the run—the longest ever made by a Pony Express rider.

Shortly afterward Will fell in with California Joe, a remarkable frontier character. He was standing beside a group of boulders that edged the trail when Will first clapped eyes on him, and the Pony Express man instantly reached for his revolver. The stranger as quickly dropped his rifle, and held up his hands in token of friendliness. Will drew rein, and ran an interested eye over the man, who was clad in buckskin.

California Joe, who was made famous in General Custer's book, entitled "Life on the Plains," was a man of wonderful physique, straight and stout as a pine. His red-brown hair hung in curls below his shoulders; he wore a full beard, and his keen, sparkling eyes were of the brightest hue. He came from an Eastern family, and possessed a good education, somewhat rusty from disuse.

"Hain't you the boy rider I has heard of—the youngest rider on the trail?" he queried, in the border dialect. Will made an affirmative answer, and gave his name.

"Waal," said Joe, "I guess you've got some money on this trip. I was strikin' fer the Big Horn, and I found them two stiffs up yonder layin' fer ye. We had a little misunderstandin', and now I has 'em to plant."

Will thanked him warmly, and begged him not to risk the perils of the Big Horn; but California Joe only laughed, and told him to push ahead.

When Will reached his station he related his adventure, and the stock-tender said it was "good-by, California Joe." But Will had conceived a better opinion of his new friend, and he predicted his safe return.

This confidence was justified by the appearance of California Joe, three months later, in the camp of the Pony Riders on the Overland Trail. He received a cordial greeting, and was assured by the men that they had not expected to see him alive again. In return, he told them his story, and a very interesting story it was.

"Some time ago," said he (I shall not attempt to reproduce his dialect), "a big gang of gold-hunters went into the Big Horn country. They never returned, and the general sent me to see if I could get any trace of them. The country is full of Indians, and I kept my eye skinned for them, but I wasn't looking for trouble from white men. I happened to leave my revolver where I ate dinner one day, and soon discovering the loss I went back after the gun. Just as I picked it up I saw a white man on my trail. I smelled trouble, but turned and jogged along as if I hadn't seen anything. That night I doubled back over my trail until I came to the camp where the stranger belonged. As I expected, he was one of a party of three, but they had five horses. I'll bet odds, Pard Billy"—this to Will—"that the two pilgrims laying for you belonged to this outfit.

"They thought I'd found gold, and were going to follow me until I struck the mine, then do me up and take possession.

"The gold is there, too, lots of it. There's silver, iron, copper, and coal, too, but no one will look at them so long as gold is to be had; but those that go for gold will, many of them, leave their scalps behind.

"We kept the trail day after day; the men stuck right to me, the chap ahead keeping me in sight and marking out the trail for his pard. When we got into the heart of the Indian country I had to use every caution; I steered clear of every smoke that showed a village or camp, and didn't use my rifle on game, depending on the rations I had with me.

"At last I came to a spot that showed signs of a battle. Skulls and bones were strewn around, and after a look about I was satisfied beyond doubt that white men had been of the company. The purpose of my trip was accomplished; I could safely report that the party of whites had been exterminated by Indians.

"The question now was, could I return without running

into Indians? The first thing was to give my white pursuers the slip.

"That night I crept down the bed of a small stream, passed their camp, and struck the trail a half mile or so below.

"It was the luckiest move I ever made. I had ridden but a short distance when I heard the familiar war-whoop, and knew that the Indians had surprised my unpleasant acquaintances and taken their scalps. I should have shared the same fate if I hadn't moved.

"But, boys, it is a grand and beautiful country, full of towering mountains, lovely valleys, and mighty trees."

About the middle of September the Indians became very troublesome along the Sweetwater. Will was ambushed one day, but fortunately he was mounted on one of the fleetest of the company's horses, and lying flat on the animal's back, he distanced the redskins. At the relay station he found the stock-tender dead, and as the horses had been driven off, he was unable to get a fresh mount; so he rode the same horse to Plontz Station, twelve miles farther.

A few days later the station boss of the line hailed Will with the information:

"There's Injun signs about; so keep your eyes open."

"I'm on the watch, boss," was Will's answer, as he exchanged ponies and dashed away.

The trail ran through a grim wild. It was darkened by mountains, overhung with cliffs, and fringed with monster pines. The young rider's every sense had been sharpened by frontier dangers. Each dusky rock and tree was scanned for signs of lurking foes as he clattered down the twilight track.

One large boulder lay in plain view far down the valley, and for a second he saw a dark object appear above it. He kept his course until within rifle-shot, and then suddenly swerved away in an oblique line. The ambush had failed; and a puff of smoke issued from behind the boulder. Two braves, in gorgeous war paint, sprang up, and at the same time a score of whooping Indians rode out of timber on the other side of the valley.

Before Will the mountains sloped to a narrow pass; could he reach that, he would be comparatively safe. The Indians at the boulder were unmounted, and though they were fleet of foot, he easily left them behind. The mounted reds were those to be feared, and the chief rode a very fleet pony. As they neared the pass Will saw that it was life against life. He drew his revolver, and the chief, for his part, fitted an arrow to his bow.

Will was a shade the quicker. His revolver cracked, and the warrior pitched dead from his saddle. His fall was the signal for a shower of arrows, one of which wounded the pony slightly; but the station was reached on time.

The Indians were now in evidence all the time. Between Split Rock and Three Crossings they robbed a stage, killed the driver and two passengers, and wounded Lieutenant Flowers, the assistant division agent. They drove the stock from the stations, and continually harassed the Pony Express riders and stage-drivers. So bold did the reds become that the Pony riders were laid off for six weeks, though stages were to make occasional runs if the business was urgent. A force was organized to search for missing stock. There were forty men in the party—stage-drivers, express-riders, stock-tenders, and ranchmen; and they were captained by a plainsman named Wild Bill, who was a good friend of Will for many years.

He had not earned the sobriquet through lawlessness. It merely denoted his dashing and daring. Physically he was well-nigh faultless—tall, straight, and symmetrical, with broad shoulders and splendid chest. He was handsome of face, with a clear blue eye, firm and well-shaped mouth, aquiline nose, and brown, curling hair, worn long upon his shoulders. Born of a refined and cultured family, he, like Will, seemingly inherited from some remote ancestor his passion for the wild, free life of the plains.

At this time Wild Bill was a well-known scout, and in this capacity served the United States to good purpose during the war.

CHAPTER 11

A Short but Dashing Indian Campaign

A s Will was one of the laid-off riders, he was allowed to join the expedition against the Indian depredators, though he was the youngest member of the company.

The campaign was short and sharp. The Indian trail was followed to Powder River, and thence along the banks of the stream the party traveled to within forty miles of the spot where old Fort Reno now stands; from here the trail ran westerly, at the foot of the mountains, and was crossed by Crazy Woman's Fork, a tributary of the Powder.

Originally this branch stream went by the name of the Big Beard, because of a peculiar grass that fringed it. On its bank had stood a village of the Crow Indians, and here a half-breed trader had settled. He bought the red man's furs, and gave him in return bright-colored beads and pieces of calico, paints, and blankets. In a short time he had all the furs in the village; he packed them on ponies, and said good-by to his Indian friends. They were sorry to see him go, but he told them he would soon return from the land of the paleface, bringing many gifts. Months passed; one day the Indian sentinels reported the approach of a strange object. The village was alarmed, for the Crows had never seen ox, horse, or wagon; but the excitement was allayed when it was found that the strange outfit was the property of the half-breed trader.

He had brought with him his wife, a white woman; she, too, was an object of much curiosity to the Indians.

The trader built a lodge of wood and stones, and exposed all his goods for sale. He had brought beads, ribbons, and brass rings as gifts for all the tribe.

One day the big chief visited the store; the trader led him into a back room, swore him to secrecy, and gave him a drink of black water. The chief felt strangely happy. Usually he was very dignified and stately; but under the influence of the strange liquid he sang and danced on the streets, and finally fell into a deep sleep, from which he could not be wakened. This performance was repeated day after day, until the Indians called a council of war. They said the trader had bewitched their chief, and it must be stopped, or they would kill the intruder. A warrior was sent to convey this intelligence to the trader; he laughed, took the warrior into the back room, swore him to secrecy, and gave him a drink of the black water. The young Indian, in his turn, went upon the street, and laughed and sang and danced, just as the chief had done. Surprised, his companions gathered around him and asked him what was the matter. "Oh, go to the trader and get some of the black water!" said he.

They asked for the strange beverage. The trader denied having any, and gave them a drink of ordinary water, which had no effect. When the young warrior awoke, they again questioned him. He said he must have been sick, and have spoken loosely.

After this the chief and warrior were both drunk every day, and all the tribe were sorely perplexed. Another council of war was held, and a young chief arose, saying that he had made a hole in the wall of the trader's house, and had watched; and it was true the trader gave their friends black water. The half-breed and the two unhappy Indians were brought before the council, and the young chief repeated his accusation, saying that if it were not true, they might fight him. The second victim of the black water yet denied the story, and said the young chief lied; but the trader had maneuvered into the position he desired, and he confessed. They bade him bring the water, that they might taste it; but before he departed the young chief challenged to combat the warrior that had said he lied. This warrior was the best spearsman of the tribe, and all expected the death of the young chief; but the black water had palsied the warrior's aim, his trembling hand could not fling true, and he was pierced to the heart at the first thrust. The tribe then repaired to the trader's lodge, and he gave them all a drink of the black water. They danced and sang, and then lay upon the ground and slept.

After two or three days the half-breed declined to provide black water free; if the warriors wanted it, they must pay for it. At first he gave them a "sleep," as they called it, for one robe or skin, but as the stock of black water diminished, two, then three, then many robes were demanded. At last he said he had none left except what he himself desired. The Indians offered their ponies, until the trader had all the robes and all the ponies of the tribe.

Now, he said, he would go back to the land of the paleface and procure more of the black water. Some of the warriors were willing he should do this; others asserted that he had plenty of black water left, and was going to trade with their enemy, the Sioux. The devil had awakened in the tribe. The trader's stores and packs were searched, but no black water was found. 'Twas hidden, then, said the Indians. The traders must produce it, or they would kill him. Of course he could not do this. He had sowed the wind; he reaped the whirlwind. He was scalped before the eyes of his horrified wife, and his body mutilated and mangled. The poor woman attempted to escape; a warrior struck her with his tomahawk, and she fell as if dead. The Indians fired the lodge. As they did so, a Crow squaw saw that the white woman was not dead. She took the wounded creature to her own lodge, bound up her wounds and nursed her back to strength. But the unfortunate woman's brain was crazed, and could not bear the sight of a warrior.

As soon as she could get around she ran away. The squaws went out to look for her, and found her crooning on the banks of the Big Beard. She would talk with the squaws, but if a warrior appeared, she hid herself till he was gone. The squaws took her food, and she lived in a covert on the bank of the stream for many months. One day a warrior, out hunting, chanced upon her. Thinking she was lost, he sought to catch her, to take her back to the village, as all Indian tribes have a veneration for the insane; but she fled into the hills, and was never seen afterward. The stream became known as the "Place of the Crazy Woman," or Crazy Woman's Fork, and has retained the name to this day.

A t this point, to return to my narrative, the signs indicated that reinforcements had reached the original body of Indians. The plainsmen were now in the heart of the Indian country, the utmost caution was required, and a sharp lookout was maintained. When Clear Creek, another tributary of the Powder, was come up with, an Indian camp, some three miles distant, was discovered on the farther bank.

A council of war was held. Never before had the white man followed the red so far into his domain, and 'twas plain the Indian was off his guard; not a scout was posted.

At Wild Bill's suggestion, the attack waited upon nightfall. Veiled by darkness, the company was to surprise the Indian camp and stampede the horses.

The plan was carried out without a hitch. The Indians outnumbered the white men three to one, but when the latter rushed cyclonically through the camp, no effort was made to repel them, and by the time the Indians had recovered from their surprise the plainsmen had driven off all the horses—those belonging to the reds as well as those that had been stolen. A few shots were fired, but the whites rode scathless away, and unpursued.

The line of march was now taken up for Sweetwater Bridge, and here, four days later, the plainsmen brought up, with their own horses and about a hundred Indian ponies.

This successful sally repressed the hostilities for a space. The recovered horses were put back on the road, and the stage-drivers and express-riders resumed their interrupted activity.

"Billy," said Mr. Slade, who had taken a great fancy to Will—"Billy, this is a hard life, and you're too young to stand it. You've done good service, and in consideration of it I'll make you a supernumerary. You'll have to ride only when it's absolutely necessary."

There followed for Will a period of *dolce far niente;* days when he might lie on his back and watch the clouds drift across the sky; when he might have an eye to the beauty of the woodland and the sweep of the plain, without the nervous strain of studying every tree and knoll that might conceal a lurking redskin. Winter closed in, and with it came the memories of the trapping season of 1860–61, when he had laid low his first and last bear. But there were other bears to be killed—the mountains were full of them; and one bracing morning he turned his horse's head toward the hills that lay down the Horseshoe Valley. Antelope and deer fed in the valley, the sage-hen and the jack-rabbit started up under his horse's hoofs, but such small game went by unnoticed.

Two o'clock passed without a sign of bear, save some tracks in the snow. The wintry air had put a keen edge on Will's appetite, and hitching his tired horse, he shot one of the lately scorned sage-hens, and broiled it over a fire that invited a longer stay than an industrious bear-hunter could afford. But nightfall found him and his quarry still many miles asunder, and as he did not relish the prospect of a chaffing from the men at the station, he cast about for the camping-place, finding one in an open spot on the bank of a little stream. Two more sage-hens were added to the larder, and he was preparing to kindle a fire when the whinnying of a horse caught his ear. He ran to his own horse to check the certain response, resaddled him, and disposed everything for flight, should it be necessary. Then, taking his rifle, he put forth on a reconnaissance.

He shortly came upon a bunch of horses, a dozen or more, around a crook of the stream. Above them, on the farther bank, shone a light. Drawing nearer, he saw that it came from a dugout, and he heard his own language spoken. Reassured, he walked boldly up to the door and rapped.

Silence—followed by a hurried whispering, and the demand:

"Who's there?"

"Friend and white man," answered Will.

The door opened reluctantly, and an ugly-looking customer bade him enter. The invitation was not responded to with alacrity, for eight such villainous-looking faces as the dugout held it would have been hard to match. Too late to retreat, there was nothing for it but a determined front, and let wit point the way of escape. Two of the men Will recognized as discharged teamsters from Lew Simpson's train, and from his knowledge of their long-standing weakness he assumed, correctly, that he had thrust his head into a den of horsethieves.

"Who's with you?" was the first query; and this answered, with sundry other information esteemed essential. "Where's your horse?" demanded the most striking portrait in the rogues' gallery.

"Down by the creek," said Will.

"All right, sonny; we'll go down and get him," was the obliging rejoinder.

"Oh, don't trouble yourself," said Will. "I'll fetch him and put up here over night, with your permission. I'll leave my gun here till I get back."

"That's right; leave your gun, you won't need it," said the leader of the gang, with a grin that was as near amiability as his rough, stern calling permitted him. "Jim and I will go down with you after the horse."

This offer compelled an acquiescence, Will consoling himself with the reflection that it is easier to escape from two men than from eight.

When the horse was reached, one of the outlaws obligingly volunteered to lead it.

"All right," said Will, carelessly. "I shot a couple of sage-hens here; I'll take them along. Lead away!"

He followed with the birds, the second horsethief bringing up the rear. As the dugout was neared he let fall one of the hens, and asked the chap following to pick it up, and as the obliging rear guard stopped, Will knocked him senseless with the butt of his revolver. The man ahead heard the blow, and turned, with his hand on his gun, but Will dropped him with a shot, leaped on his horse and dashed off.

The sextet in the dugout sprang to arms, and came running down the bank, and likely getting the particulars of the escape from the ruffian by the sage-hen, who was probably only stunned for the moment, they buckled warmly to the chase. The mountain-side was steep and rough, and men on foot were better than on horseback;

accordingly Will dismounted, and clapping his pony soundly on the flank, sent him clattering on down the declivity, and himself stepped aside behind a large pine. The pursuing party rushed past him, and when they were safely gone, he climbed back over the mountain, and made his way as best he could to the Horseshoe. It was a twenty-five mile plod, and he reached the station early in the morning, weary and footsore.

He woke the plainsmen, and related his adventure, and Mr. Slade at once organized a party to hunt out the bandits of the dugout. Twenty well-armed stock-tenders, stage-drivers, and ranchmen rode away at sunrise, and, notwithstanding his fatigue, Will accompanied them as guide.

But the ill-favored birds had flown; the dugout was deserted.

Will soon tired of this nondescript service, and gladly accepted a position as assistant wagon-master under Wild Bill, who had taken a contract to fetch a load of government freight from Rolla, Missouri.

He returned with a wagon-train to Springfield, in that state, and thence came home on a visit. It was a brief one, however, for the air was too full of war for him to endure inaction. Contented only when at work, he continued to work on government freight contracts, until he received word that mother was dangerously ill. Then he resigned his position and hastened home.

CHAPTER 12

The Mother's Last Illness

It was now autumn of 1863, and Will was a well-grown young man, tall, strong, and athletic, though not yet quite eighteen years old. Our oldest sister, Julia, had been married, the spring preceding, to Mr. J. A. Goodman.

Mother had been growing weaker from day to day; being with her constantly, we had not remarked the change for the worse; but Will was much shocked by the transformation which a few months had wrought. Only an indomitable will power had enabled her to overcome the infirmities of the body, and now it seemed to us as if her flesh had been refined away, leaving only the sweet and beautiful spirit.

Will reached home none too soon, for only three weeks after his return the doctor told mother that only a few hours were left to her, and if she had any last messages, it were best that she communicate them at once. That evening the children were called in, one by one, to receive her blessing and farewell. Mother was an earnest Christian character, but at that time I alone of all the children appeared religiously disposed. Young as I was, the solemnity of the hour when she charged me with the spiritual welfare of the family has remained with me through all the years that have gone. Calling me to her side, she sought to impress upon my childish mind, not the sorrow of death, but the glory of the resurrection. Then, as if she were setting forth upon a pleasant journey, she bade me good by, and I kissed her for the last time in life. When next I saw her face it was cold and quiet. The beautiful soul had forsaken its dwelling-place of clay, and passed on through the Invisible, to wait, a glorified spirit, on the farther shore for the coming of the loved ones whose life-story was as yet unfinished.

Julia and Will remained with her throughout the night. Just before death there came to her a brief season of long-lost animation, the last flicker of the torch before darkness. She talked to them almost continuously until the dawn. Into their hands was given the task of educating the others of the family, and on their hearts and consciences the charge was graven. Charlie, who was born during the early Kansas troubles, had ever been a delicate child, and he lay an especial burden on her mind.

"If," she said, "it be possible for the dead to call the living, I shall call Charlie to me."

Within the space of a year, Charlie, too, was gone; and who shall say that the yearning of a mother's heart for her child was not stronger than the influences of the material world?

Upon Will mother sought to impress the responsibilities of his destiny. She reminded him of the prediction of the fortune-teller, that "his name would be known the world over."

"But," said she, "only the names of them that are upright, brave, temperate, and true can be honorably known. Remember always that 'he that overcometh his own soul is greater than he who taketh a city.' Already you have shown great abilities, but remember that they carry with them grave responsibilities. You have been a good son to me. In the hour of need you have always aided me, so that I can die now feeling that my children are not unprovided for. I have not wished you to enlist in the war, partly because I knew you were too young, partly because my life was drawing near its close. But now you are nearly eighteen, and if when I am gone your country needs you in the strife of which we in Kansas know the bitterness, I bid you go as soldier in behalf of the cause for which your father gave his life."

She talked until sleep followed exhaustion. When she awoke she tried to raise herself in bed. Will sprang to aid her, and with the upward look of one that sees ineffable things, she passed away, resting in his arms.

Oh, the glory and the gladness
    Of a life without a fear;
Of a death like nature fading
    In the autumn of the year;
Of a sweet and dreamless slumber,
    In a faith triumphant borne,
Till the bells of Easter wake her
    On the resurrection morn!

Ah, for such a blessed falling
    Into quiet sleep at last,
When the ripening grain is garnered,
    And the toil and trial past;
When the red and gold of sunset
    Slowly changes, into gray;
Ah, for such a quiet passing,
    Through the night into the day!

The morning of the 22d day of November, 1863, began the saddest day of our lives. We rode in a rough lumber wagon to Pilot Knob Cemetery, a long, cold, hard ride; but we wished our parents to be united in death as they had been in life, so buried mother in a grave next to father's.

The road leading from the cemetery forked a short distance outside of Leavenworth, one branch running to the city, the other winding homeward along Government Hill. When we were returning, and reached this fork, Will jumped out of the wagon.

"I can't go home when I know mother is no longer there," said he. "I am going to Leavenworth to see Eugene Hathaway. I shall stay with him tonight."

We pitied Will—he and mother had been so much to each other—and raised no objection, as we should have done had we known the real purpose of his visit.

The next morning, therefore, we were much surprised to see him and Eugene ride into the yard, both clothed in the blue uniforms of United States soldiers. Overwhelmed with grief over mother's death, it seemed more than we could bear to see our big brother ride off to war. We threatened to inform the recruiting officers that he was not yet eighteen; but he was too thoroughly in earnest to be moved by our objections. The regiment in which he had enlisted was already ordered to the front, and he had come home to say good-by. He then rode away to the hardships, dangers, and privations of a soldier's life. The joy of action balanced the account for him, while we were obliged to accept the usual lot of girlhood and womanhood—the weary, anxious waiting, when the heart is torn with uncertainty and suspense over the fate of the loved ones who bear the brunt and burden of the day.

The order sending Will's regiment to the front was countermanded, and he remained for a time in Fort Leavenworth. His Western experiences were well known there, and probably for this reason he was selected as a bearer of military dispatches to Fort Larned. Some of our old pro-slavery enemies, who were upon the point of joining the Confederate army, learned of Will's mission, which they thought afforded them an excellent chance to gratify their ancient grudge against the father by murdering the son. The killing could be justified on the plea of service rendered to their cause. Accordingly, a plan was made to waylay Will and capture his dispatches at a creek he was obliged to ford.

He received warning of this plot. On such a mission the utmost vigilance was demanded at all times, and with an ambuscade ahead of him, he was alertness itself. His knowledge of Indian warfare stood him in good stead now. Not a tree, rock, or hillock escaped his keen glance. When he neared the creek at which the attack was expected, he left the road, and attempted to ford the stream four or five hundred yards above the common crossing, but found it so swollen by recent rains that he was unable to cross; so he cautiously picked his way back to the trail.

The assassins' camp was two or three hundred feet away from the creek. Darkness was coming on, and he took advantage of the shelter afforded by the bank, screening himself behind every clump of bushes. His enemies would look for his approach from the other direction, and he hoped to give them the slip and pass by unseen.

When he reached the point where he could see the little cabin where the men were probably hiding, he ran upon a thicket in which five saddle-horses were concealed.

"Five to one! I don't stand much show if they see me," he decided as he rode quietly and slowly along, his carbine in his hand ready for use.

"There he goes, boys! he's at the ford!" came a sudden shout from the camp, followed by the crack of a rifle. Two or three more shots rang out, and from the bound his horse gave Will knew one bullet had reached a mark. He rode into the water, then turned in his saddle and aimed like a flash at a man within range. The fellow staggered and fell, and Will put spurs to his horse, turning again only when the stream was crossed. The men were running toward the ford, firing as they came, and getting a warm return fire. As Will was already two or three hundred yards in advance, pursuers on foot were not to be feared, and he knew that before they could reach and mount their horses he would be beyond danger. Much depended on his horse. Would the gallant beast, wounded as he was, be able to long maintain the fierce pace he had set? Mile upon mile was put behind before the stricken creature fell. Will shouldered the saddle and bridle and continued on foot. He soon reached a ranch where a fresh mount might be procured, and was shortly at Fort Larned.

After a few hours' breathing-spell, he left for Fort Leavenworth with return dispatches. As he drew near the ford, he resumed his sharp lookout, though scarcely expecting trouble. The planners of the ambuscade had been so certain that five men could easily make away with one boy that there had been no effort at disguise, and Will had recognized several of them. He, for his part, felt certain that they would get out of that part of the country with all dispatch; but he employed none the less caution in crossing the creek, and his carbine was ready for business as he approached the camp.

The fall of his horse's hoofs evoked a faint call from one of the buildings. It was not repeated; instead there issued hollow moans.

It might be a trap; again, a fellow-creature might be at death's door. Will rode a bit nearer the cabin entrance.

"Who's there?" he called.

"Come in, for the love of God! I am dying here alone!" was the reply.

"Who are you?"

"Ed Norcross."

Will jumped from his horse. This was the man at whom he had fired. He entered the cabin.

"What is the matter?" he asked.

"I was wounded by a bullet," moaned Norcross, "and my comrades deserted me."

Will was now within range of the poor fellow lying on the floor.

"Will Cody!" he cried.

Will dropped on his knees beside the dying man, choking with the emotion that the memory of long years of friendship had raised.

"My poor Ed!" he murmured. "And it was my bullet that struck you."

"It was in defense of your own life, Will," said Norcross. "God knows, I don't blame you. Don't think too hard of me. I did everything I could to save you. It was I who sent you warning. I hoped you might find some other trail."

"I didn't shoot with the others," continued Norcross, after a short silence. "They deserted me. They said they would send help back, but they haven't."

Will filled the empty canteen lying on the floor, and re-arranged the blanket that served as a pillow; then he offered to dress the neglected wound. But the gray of death was already upon the face of Norcross.

"Never mind, Will," he whispered; "it's not worth while. Just stay with me till I die."

It was not a long vigil. Will sat beside his old friend, moistening his pallid lips with water. In a very short time the end came. Will disposed the stiffening limbs, crossing the hands over the heart, and with a last backward look went out of the cabin.

It was his first experience in the bitterness and savagery of war, and he set a grave and downcast face against the remainder of his journey.

As he neared Leavenworth he met the friend who had conveyed the dead man's warning message, and to him he committed the task of bringing home the body. His heaviness of spirit was scarcely mitigated by the congratulations of the commander of Fort Leavenworth upon his pluck and resources, which had saved both his life and the dispatches.

There followed another period of inaction, always irritating to a lad of Will's restless temperament. Meantime, we at home were having our own experiences.

We were rejoiced in great measure when sister Julia decided that we had learned as much as might be hoped for in the country school, and must thereafter attend the winter and spring terms of the school at Leavenworth. The dresses she cut for us, however, still followed the country fashion, which has regard rather to wear than to appearance, and we had not been a day in the city school before we discovered that our apparel had stamped "provincial" upon us in plain, large characters. In addition to this, our brother-in-law, in his endeavor to administer the estate economically, bought each of us a pair of coarse calfskin shoes. To these we were quite unused, mother having accustomed us to serviceable but pretty ones. The author of our "extreme" mortification, totally ignorant of the shy and sensitive nature of girls, only laughed at our protests, and in justice to him it may be said that he really had no conception of the torture he inflicted upon us.

We turned to Will. In every emergency he was our first thought, and here was an emergency that taxed his powers to an extent we did not dream of. He made answer to our letter that he was no longer an opulent trainman, but drew only the slender income of a soldier, and even that pittance was in arrears. Disappointment was swallowed up in remorse. Had we reflected how keenly he must feel his inability to help us, we would not have sent him the letter, which, at worst, contained only a sly suggestion of a fine opportunity to relieve sisterly distress. All his life he had responded to our every demand; now allegiance was due his country first. But, as was always the way with him, he made the best of a bad matter, and we were much comforted by the receipt of the following letter:

> "My Dear Sisters:
>
> "I am sorry that I cannot help you and furnish you with such clothes as you wish. At this writing I am so short of funds myself that if an entire Mississippi steamer could be bought for ten cents I couldn't purchase the smokestack. I will soon draw my pay, and I will send it, every cent, to you. So brave it out, girls, a little longer. In the meantime I will write to Al.
>
> > "Lovingly,
> >
> > > "Will."

We were comforted, yes; but my last hope was gone, and I grew desperate. I had never worn the obnoxious shoes purchased by my guardian, and I proceeded to dispose of them forever. I struck what I regarded as a famous bargain with an accommodating Hebrew, and came into possession of a pair of shiny morocco shoes, worth perhaps a third of what mine had cost. One would say they were designed for shoes, and they certainly looked like shoes, but as certainly they were not wearable. Still they were of service, for the transaction convinced my guardian that the truest economy did not lie in the purchasing of calfskin shoes for at least one of his charges. A little later he received a letter from Will, presenting our grievances and advocating our cause. Will also sent us the whole of his next month's pay as soon as he drew it.

In February, 1864, Sherman began his march through Mississippi. The Seventh Kansas regiment, known as "Jennison's Jayhawkers," was reorganized at Fort Leavenworth as veterans, and sent to Memphis, Tenn., to join

General A. J. Smith's command, which was to operate against General Forrest and cover the retreat of General Sturgis, who had been so badly whipped by Forrest at Cross-Roads. Will was exceedingly desirous of engaging in a great battle, and through some officers with whom he was acquainted, preferred a petition to be transferred to this regiment. The request was granted, and his delight knew no bounds. He wrote to us that his great desire was about to be gratified, that he should soon know what a real battle was like.

He was well versed in Indian warfare; now he was ambitious to learn, from experience, the superiority of civilized strife—rather, I should say, of strife between civilized people.

General Smith had acquainted himself with the record made by the young scout of the plains, and shortly after reaching Memphis he ordered Will to report to headquarters for special service.

"I am anxious," said the general, "to gain reliable information concerning the enemy's movements and position. This can only be done by entering the Confederate camp. You possess the need qualities—nerve, coolness, resource—and I believe you could do it."

"You mean," answered Will quietly, "that you wish me to go as a spy into the rebel camp."

"Exactly. But you must understand the risk you run. If you are captured, you will be hanged."

"I am ready to take the chances, sir," said Will; "ready to go at once, if you wish."

General Smith's stern face softened into a smile at the prompt response.

"I am sure, Cody," said he kindly, "that if any one can go through safely, you will. Dodging Indians on the plains was good training for the work in hand, which demands quick intelligence and ceaseless vigilance. I never require such service of any one, but since you volunteer to go, take these maps of the country to your quarters and study them carefully. Return this evening for full instructions."

During the few days his regiment had been in camp, Will had been on one or two scouting expeditions, and was somewhat familiar with the immediate environments of the Union forces. The maps were unusually accurate, showing every lake, river, creek, and highway, and even the by-paths from plantation to plantation.

Only the day before, while on a reconnaissance, Will had captured a Confederate soldier, who proved to be an old acquaintance named Nat Golden. Will had served with Nat on one of Russell, Majors & Waddell's freight trains, and at one time had saved the young man's life, and thereby earned his enduring friendship. Nat was born in the East, became infected with Western fever, and ran away from home in order to become a plainsman.

"Well, this is too bad," said Will, when he recognized his old friend. "I would rather have captured a whole regiment than you. I don't like to take you in as a prisoner. What did you enlist on the wrong side for, anyway?"

"The fortunes of war, Billy, my boy," laughed Nat. "Friend shall be turned against friend, and brother against brother, you know. You wouldn't have had me for a prisoner, either, if my rifle hadn't snapped; but I'm glad it did, for I shouldn't want to be the one that shot you."

"Well, I don't want to see you strung up," said Will; "so hand me over those papers you have, and I will turn you in as an ordinary prisoner."

Nat's face paled as he asked, "Do you think I'm a spy, Billy?"

"I know it."

"Well," was the reply, "I've risked my life to obtain these

papers, but I suppose they will be taken from me anyway; so I might as well give them up now, and save my neck."

Examination showed them to be accurate maps of the location and position of the Union army; and besides the maps, there were papers containing much valuable information concerning the number of soldiers and officers and their intended movements. Will had not destroyed these papers, and he now saw a way to use them to his own advantage. When he reported for final instructions, therefore, at General Smith's tent, in the evening, Will said to him:

"I gathered from a statement dropped by the prisoner captured yesterday, that a Confederate spy has succeeded in making out and carrying to the enemy a complete map of the position of our regiment, together with some idea of the projected plan of campaign."

"Ah," said the general; "I am glad that you have put me on my guard. I will at once change my position, so that the information will be of no value to them."

Then followed full instructions as to the duty required of the volunteer.

"When will you set out?" asked the general.

"To-night, sir. I have procured my uniform, and have everything prepared for an early start."

"Going to change your colors, eh?"

"Yes, for the time being, but not my principles."

The general looked approvingly at Will. "You will need all the wit, pluck, nerve, and caution of which you are possessed to come through this ordeal safely," said he. "I believe you can accomplish it, and I rely upon you fully. Good-by, and success go with you!"

After a warm hand-clasp, Will returned to his tent, and lay down for a few hours' rest. By four o'clock he was in the saddle, riding toward the Confederate lines.

CHAPTER 13

In the Secret Service

In common walks of life, to play the spy is an ignoble rôle; yet the work has to be done, and there must be men to do it. There always are such men—nervy fellows who swing themselves into the saddle when their commander lifts his hand, and ride a mad race, with Death at the horse's flank every mile of the way. They are the unknown heroes of every war.

It was with a full realization of the dangers confronting him that Will cantered away from the Union lines, his borrowed uniform under his arm. As soon as he had put the outposts behind him, he dismounted and exchanged the blue clothes for the gray. Life on the plains had bronzed his face. For aught his complexion could tell, the ardent Southern sun might have kissed it to its present hue. Then, if ever, his face was his fortune in good part; but there was, too, a stout heart under his jacket, and the light of confidence in his eyes.

The dawn had come up when he sighted the Confederate outposts. What lay beyond only time could reveal; but with a last reassuring touch of the papers in his pocket, he spurred his horse up to the first of the outlying sentinels. Promptly the customary challenge greeted him:

"Halt! Who goes there?"

"Friend."

"Dismount, friend! Advance and give the countersign!"

"Haven't the countersign," said Will, dropping from his

horse, "but I have important information for General Forrest. Take me to him at once."

"Are you a Confederate soldier?"

"Not exactly. But I have some valuable news about the Yanks, I reckon. Better let me see the general."

"Thus far," he added to himself, "I have played the part. The combination of 'Yank' and 'I reckon' ought to establish me as a promising candidate for Confederate honors."

His story was not only plausible, but plainly and fairly told; but caution is a child of war, and the sentinel knew his business. The pseudo-Confederate was disarmed as a necessary preliminary, and marched between two guards to headquarters, many curious eyes (the camp being now astir) following the trio.

When Forrest heard the report, he ordered the prisoner brought before him. One glance at the general's handsome but harsh face, and the young man steeled his nerves for the encounter. There was no mercy in those cold, piercing eyes. This first duel of wits was the one to be most dreaded. Unless confidence were established, his after work must be done at a disadvantage.

The general's penetrating gaze searched the young face before him for several seconds.

"Well, sir," said he, "what do you want with me?"

Yankee-like, the reply was another question:

"You sent a man named Nat Golden into the Union lines, did you not, sir?"

"And if I did, what then?"

"He is an old friend of mine. He tried for the Union camp to verify information that he had received, but before he started he left certain papers with me in case he should be captured."

"Ah!" said Forrest coldly. "And he was captured?"

"Yes, sir; but, as I happen to know, he wasn't hanged, for these weren't on him."

As he spoke, Will took from his pocket the papers he had obtained from Golden, and passed them over with the remark, "Golden asked me to take them to you."

General Forrest was familiar with the hapless Golden's handwriting, and the documents were manifestly genuine. His suspicion was not aroused.

"These are important papers," said he, when he had run his eye over them. "They contain valuable information, but we may not be able to use it, as we are about to change our location. Do you know what these papers contain?"

"Every word," was the truthful reply. "I studied them, so that in case they were destroyed you would still have the information from me."

"A wise thing to do," said Forrest approvingly. "Are you a soldier?"

"I have not as yet joined the army, but I am pretty well acquainted with this section, and perhaps could serve you as a scout."

"Um!" said the general, looking the now easy-minded young man over. "You wear our uniform."

"It's Golden's," was the second truthful answer. "He left it with me when he put on the blue."

"And what is your name?"

"Frederick Williams."

Pretty near the truth. Only a final "s" and a rearrangement of his given names.

"Very well," said the general, ending the audience; "you may remain in camp. If I need you, I'll send for you."

He summoned an orderly, and bade him make the volunteer scout comfortable at the courier's camp. Will breathed a sigh of relief as he followed at the orderly's heels. The ordeal was successfully passed. The rest was action.

Two days went by. In them Will picked up valuable information here and there, drew maps, and was prepared to depart at the first favorable opportunity. It was about time, he figured, that General Forrest found some scouting work for him. That was a passport beyond the lines, and he promised himself the outposts should see the cleanest pair of heels that ever left unwelcome society in the rear. But evidently scouting was a drug in the general's market, for the close of another day found Will impatiently awaiting orders in the couriers' quarters. This sort of inactivity was harder on the nerves than more tangible perils, and he about made up his mind that when he left camp it would be without orders, but with a hatful of bullets singing after him. And he was quite sure that his exit lay that way when, strolling past headquarters, he clapped eyes on the very last person that he expected or wished to see—Nat Golden!

And Nat was talking to an adjutant-general!

There were just two things to do, knock Golden on the head, or cut and run. Nat would not betray him knowingly, but unwittingly was certain to do so the moment General Forrest questioned him. There could be no choice between the two courses open; it was cut and run, and as a preliminary Will cut for his tent. First concealing his papers, he saddled his horse and rode toward the outposts with a serene countenance.

The same sergeant that greeted him when he entered the lines chanced to be on duty, and of him Will asked an unimportant question concerning the outer-flung lines. Yet as he rode along he could not forbear throwing an apprehensive glance behind.

No pursuit was making, and the farthest picket-line

was passed by a good fifty yards. Ahead was a stretch of timber.

Suddenly a dull tattoo of horses' hoofs caught his ear, and he turned to see a small cavalcade bearing down upon him at a gallop. He sank the spurs into his horse's side and plunged into the timber.

It was out of the frying-pan into the fire. He ran plump into a half-dozen Confederate cavalrymen, guarding two Union prisoners.

"Men, a Union spy is escaping!" shouted Will. "Scatter at once, and head him off. I'll look after your prisoners."

There was a ring of authority in the command; it came at least from a petty officer; and without thought of challenging it, the cavalrymen hurried right and left in search of the fugitive.

"Come," said Will, in a hurried but smiling whisper to the dejected pair of Union men. "I'm the spy! There!" cutting the ropes that bound their wrists. "Now ride for your lives!"

Off dashed the trio, and not a minute too soon. Will's halt had been brief, but it had been of advantage to his pursuers, who, with Nat Golden at their head, came on in full cry, not a hundred yards behind.

Here was a race with Death at the horse's flanks. The timber stopped a share of the singing bullets, but there were plenty that got by the trees, one of them finding lodgment in the arm of one of the fleeing Union soldiers. Capture meant certain death for Will; for his companions it meant Andersonville or Libby, at the worst, which was perhaps as bad as death; but Will would not leave them, though his horse was fresh, and he could easily have distanced them. Of course, if it became necessary, he was prepared to cut their acquaintance, but for the present he made one of the triplicate targets on which the galloping marksmen were endeavoring to score a bull's-eye.

The edge of the wood was shortly reached, and beyond—inspiring sight!—lay the outposts of the Union army. The pickets, at sight of the fugitives, sounded the alarm, and a body of blue-coats responded.

Will would have gladly tarried for the skirmish that ensued, but he esteemed it his first duty to deliver the papers he had risked his life to obtain; so, leaving friend and foe to settle the dispute as best they might, he put for the clump of trees where he had hidden his uniform, and exchanged it for the gray that had served its purpose and was no longer endurable. Under his true colors he rode into camp.

General Forrest almost immediately withdrew from that neighborhood, and after the atrocious massacre at Fort Pillow, on the 12th of April, left the state. General Smith was recalled, and Will was transferred, with the commission of guide and scout for the Ninth Kansas Regiment.

The Indians were giving so much trouble along the line of the old Santa Fé trail that troops were needed to protect the stagecoaches, emigrants, and caravans traveling that great highway. Like nearly all our Indian wars, this trouble was precipitated by the injustice of the white man's government of certain of the native tribes. In 1860 Colonel A. G. Boone, a worthy grandson of the immortal Daniel, made a treaty with the Comanches, Kiowas, Cheyennes, and Arapahoes, and at their request he was made agent. During his wise, just, and humane administration of all these savage nations were quiet, and held the kindliest feelings toward the whites. Any one could cross the plains without fear of molestation. In 1861 a charge of disloyalty was made against Colonel Boone by Judge Wright, of Indiana, and he succeeded in having the right man removed from the right place. Russell, Majors &

Waddell, recognizing his influence over the Indians, gave him fourteen hundred acres of land near Pueblo, Colorado. Colonel Boone moved there, and the place was named Booneville. Fifty chieftains from the tribes referred to visited Colonel Boone in the fall of 1862, and implored him to return to them. He told them that the President had sent him away. They offered to raise money, by selling their horses, to send him to Washington, to tell the Great Father what their agent was doing—that he stole their goods and sold them back again; and they bade the colonel say that there would be trouble unless some one were put in the dishonest man's place. With the innate logic for which the Indian is noted, they declared that they had as much right to steal from passing caravans as the agent had to steal from them.

No notice was taken of so trifling a matter as an injustice to the Indian. The administration had its hands more than full in the attempt to right the wrongs of the negro.

In the fall of 1863 a caravan passed along the trail. It was a small one, but the Indians had been quiet for so long a time that travelers were beginning to lose fear of them. A band of warriors rode up to the wagon-train and asked for something to eat. The teamsters thought they would be doing humanity a service if they killed a redskin, on the ancient principle that "the only good Indian is a dead one." Accordingly, a friendly, inoffensive Indian was shot.

The bullet that reached his heart touched that of every warrior in these nations. Every man but one in the wagon-train was slain, the animals driven off, and the wagons burned.

The fires of discontent that had been smoldering for two years in the red man's breast now burst forth with volcanic fury. Hundreds of atrocious murders followed, with wholesale destruction of property:

The Ninth Kansas Regiment, under the command of

Colonel Clark, was detailed to protect the old trail between Fort Lyon and Fort Larned, and as guide and scout
Will felt wholly at home. He knew the Indian and his
ways, and had no fear of him. His fine horse and glittering trappings were an innocent delight to him; and who
will not pardon in him the touch of pride—say vanity—
that thrilled him as he led his regiment down the Arkansas River?

During the summer there were sundry skirmishes with
Indians. The same old vigilance, learned in earlier days
on the frontier, was in constant demand, and there was
many a rough and rapid ride to drive the hostiles from the
trail. Whatever Colonel Clarke's men may have had to
complain of, there was no lack of excitement, no dull days,
in that summer.

In the autumn the Seventh Kansas was again ordered
to the front, and at the request of its officers Will was detailed for duty with his old regiment. General Smith's orders were that he should go to Nashville. Rosecrans was
then in command of the Union forces in Missouri. His
army was very small, numbering only about 6,500 men,
while the Confederate General Price was on the point of
entering the state with 20,000. This superiority of numbers was so great that General Smith received an order
countermanding the other, and remained in Missouri,
joining forces with Rosecrans to oppose Price. Rosecrans's entire force still numbered only 11,000, and he
deemed it prudent to concentrate his army around St.
Louis. General Ewing's forces and a portion of General
Smith's command occupied Pilot Knob. On Monday, the
24th of September, 1864, Price advanced against this position, but was repulsed with heavy losses. An adjacent fort
in the neighborhood of Ironton was assaulted, but the
Confederate forces again sustained a severe loss. This fort
held a commanding lookout on Shepherd Mountain,

which the Confederates occupied, and their well-directed fire obliged General Ewing to fall back to Harrison Station, where he made a stand, and some sharp fighting followed. General Ewing again fell back, and succeeded in reaching General McNeill, at Rolla, with the main body of his troops.

This was Will's first serious battle, and it so chanced that he found himself opposed at one point by a body of Missouri troops numbering many of the men who had been his father's enemies and persecutors nine years before. In the heat of the conflict he recognized more than one of them, and with the recognition came the memory of his boyhood's vow to avenge his father's death. Three of those men fell in that battle; and whether or not it was he who laid them low, from that day on he accounted himself freed of his melancholy obligation.

After several hard-fought battles, Price withdrew from Missouri with the remnant of his command—seven thousand where there had been twenty.

During this campaign Will received honorable mention "for most conspicuous bravery and valuable service upon the field," and he was shortly brought into favorable notice in many quarters. The worth of the tried veterans was known, but none of the older men was in more demand than Will. His was seemingly a charmed life. Often was he detailed to bear dispatches across the battlefield, and though horses were shot under him—riddled by bullets or torn by shells—he himself went scathless.

During this campaign, too, he ran across his old friend of the plains, Wild Bill. Stopping at a farm-house one day to obtain a meal, he was not a little surprised to hear the salutation:

"Well Billy, my boy, how are you?"

He looked around to see a hand outstretched from a coat-sleeve of Confederate gray, and as he knew Wild Bill

to be a staunch Unionist, he surmised that he was engaged upon an enterprise similar to his own. There was
an exchange of chaffing about gray uniforms and blue,
but more serious talk followed.

"Take these papers, Billy," said Wild Bill, passing over
a package. "Take 'em to General McNeill, and tell him
I'm picking up too much good news to keep away from
the Confederate camp."

"Don't take too many chances," cautioned Will, well
knowing that the only chances the other would take
would be the sort that were not visible.

Colonel Hickok, to give him his real name, replied, with
a laugh:

"Practice what you preach, my son. Your neck is of
more value than mine. You have a future, but mine is
mostly past. I'm getting old."

At this point the good woman of the house punctuated
the colloquy with a savory meal, which the pair discussed
with good appetite and easy conscience, in spite of their
hostess's refusal to take pay from Confederate soldiers.

"As long as I have a crust in the house," said she, "you
boys are welcome to it."

But the pretended Confederates paid her for her kindness
in better currency than she was used to. They withheld information concerning a proposed visit of her husband and
son, of which, during one spell of loquacity, she acquainted
them. The bread she cast upon the waters returned to her
speedily.

The two friends parted company, Will returning to the
Union lines, and Colonel Hickok to the opposing camp.

A few days later, when the Confederate forces were
closing up around the Union lines, and a battle was at
hand, two horsemen were seen to dart out of the hostile
camp and ride at full speed for the Northern lines. For a
space the audacity of the escape seemed to paralyze the

Confederates; but presently the bullets followed thick and fast, and one of the saddles was empty before the rescue party—of which Will was one—got fairly under way. As the survivor drew near, Will shouted:

"It's Wild Bill, the Union scout."

A cheer greeted the intrepid Colonel Hickok, and he rode into camp surrounded by a party of admirers. The information he brought proved of great value in the battle of Pilot Knob (already referred to), which almost immediately followed.

CHAPTER 14

A Rescue and a Betrothal

After the battle of Pilot Knob Will was assigned, through the influence of General Polk, to special service at military headquarters in St. Louis. Mrs. Polk had been one of mother's school friends, and the two had maintained a correspondence up to the time of mother's death. As soon as Mrs. Polk learned that the son of her old friend was in the Union army, she interested herself in obtaining a good position for him. But desk-work is not a Pony Express rush, and Will found the St. Louis detail about as much to his taste as clerking in a dry-goods store. His new duties naturally became intolerable, lacking the excitement and danger-scent which alone made him life worth while to him.

One event however, relieved the dead-weight monotony of his existence; he met Louise Frederici, the girl who became his wife. The courtship has been written far and wide with blood-and-thunder pen, attended by lariat-throwing and runaway steeds. In reality it was a romantic affair.

More than once, while out for a morning canter, Will had remarked a young woman of attractive face and figure, who sat her horse with the grace of Diana Vernon. Now, few things catch Will's eye more quickly than fine horsemanship. He desired to establish an acquaintance with the young lady, but as none of his friends knew her, he found it impossible.

At length a chance came. Her bridle-rein broke one

morning; there was a runaway, a rescue, and then acquaintance was easy.

From war to love, or from love to war, is but a step, and Will lost no time in taking it. He was somewhat better than an apprentice to Dan Cupid. If the reader remembers, he went to school with Steve Gobel. True, his opportunities to enjoy feminine society had not been many, which, perhaps, accounts for the promptness with which he embraced them when they did arise. He became the accepted suitor of Miss Louise Frederici before the war closed and his regiment was mustered out.

The spring of 1865 found him not yet twenty, and he was sensible of the fact that before he could dance at his own wedding he must place his worldly affairs upon a surer financial basis than falls to the lot of a soldier; so, much as he would have enjoyed remaining in St. Louis, fortune pointed to wider fields, and he set forth in search of remunerative and congenial employment.

First, there was the visit home, where the warmest of welcomes awaited him. During his absence the second sister, Eliza, had married a Mr. Myers, but the rest of us were at the old place, and the eagerness with which we awaited Will's home-coming was stimulated by the hope that he would remain and take charge of the estate. Before we broached this subject, however, he informed us of his engagement to Miss Frederici, which, far from awakening jealousy, aroused our delight, Julia voicing the sentiment of the family in the comment:

"When you're married, Will, you will have to stay at home."

This led to the matter of his remaining with us to manage the estate—and to the upsetting of our plans. The pay of a soldier in the war was next to nothing, and as Will had been unable to put any money by, he took the first chance that offered to better his fortunes.

This happened to be a job of driving horses from Leavenworth to Fort Kearny, and almost the first man he met after reaching the fort was an old plains friend, Bill Trotter.

"You're just the chap I've been looking for," said Trotter, when he learned that Will desired regular work. "I'm division station agent here, but stage-driving is dangerous work, as the route is infested with Indians and outlaws. Several drivers have been held up and killed lately, so it's not a very enticing job, but the pay's good, and you know the country. If any one can take the stage through, you can. Do you want the job?"

When a man is in love and the wedding-day has been dreamed of, if not set, life takes on an added sweetness, and to stake it against the markmanship of Indian or outlaw is not, perhaps, the best use to which it may be put. Will had come safely through so many perils that it seemed folly to thrust his head into another batch of them, and thinking of Louise and the coming wedding-day, his first thought was no.

But it was the old story, and there was Trotter at his elbow expressing confidence in his ability as a frontiersman—an opinion Will fully shared, for a man knows what he can do. The pay was good, and the sooner earned the sooner would the wedding be, and Trotter received the answer he expected.

The stage line was another of the Western enterprises projected by Russell, Majors & Waddell. When gold was discovered on Pike's Peak there was no method of traversing the great Western plain except by plodding ox-team, mule-pack, or stagecoach. A semi-monthly stage line ran from St. Joseph to Salt Lake City, but it was poorly equipped and very tedious, oftentimes twenty-one days being required to make this trip. The senior member of the firm, in partnership with John S. Jones, of Missouri, established a new line between the Missouri River and Denver, at that time a straggling mining hamlet. One thousand Kentucky mules were bought, with a sufficient number of coaches to insure a daily run each way. The trip was made in six days, which necessitated travel at the rate of a hundred miles a day.

The first stage reached Denver on May 17, 1859. It was accounted a remarkable achievement, and the line was pronounced a great success. In one way it was; but the expense of equipping it had been enormous, and the new line could not meet its obligations. To save the credit of their senior partner, Russell, Majors & Waddell were obliged to come to the rescue. They bought up all the outstanding obligations, and also the rival stage line between St. Joseph and Salt Lake City. They consolidated the two, and thereby hoped to put the Overland stage route on a paying basis. St. Joseph now became the starting-point of the united lines. From there the road went to Fort Kearny, and followed the old Salt Lake trail, already described in these pages. After leaving Salt Lake it passed through Camp Floyd, Ruby Valley, Carson City, Placerville, and Folsom, and ended in Sacramento.

The distance from St. Joseph to Sacramento by this old stage route was nearly nineteen hundred miles. The time required by mail contracts and the government schedule was nineteen days. The trip was frequently made in fifteen, but there were so many causes for detention that the limit was more often reached.

Each two hundred and fifty miles of road was designated a "division," and was in charge of an agent, who had great authority in his own jurisdiction. He was commonly a man of more than ordinary intelligence, and all matters pertaining to his division were entirely under his control. He hired and discharged employes, purchased horses, mules, harness, and food, and attended to their distribution at the different stations. He superintended the erection of all buildings, had charge of the water supply, and he was the paymaster.

There was also a man known as the conductor, whose route was almost coincident with that of the agent. He sat with the driver, and often rode the whole two hundred and fifty miles of his division without any rest or sleep, except what he could catch sitting on the top of the flying coach.

The coach itself was a roomy, swaying vehicle, swung on thoroughbraces instead of springs. It always had a six-horse or six-mule team to draw it, and the speed was nerve-breaking. Passengers were allowed twenty-five pounds of baggage, and that, with the mail, express, and the passengers themselves, was in charge of the conductor.

The Overland stagecoaches were operated at a loss until 1862. In March of that year Russell, Majors & Waddell transferred the whole outfit to Ben Holliday. Here was a typical frontiersman, of great individuality and character. At the time he took charge of the route the United States mail was given to it. This put the line on a sound financial basis, as the government spent $800,000 yearly in transporting the mail to San Francisco.

Will reported for duty the morning after his talk with Trotter, and when he mounted after his talk and gathered the reins over the six spirited horses, the passengers were assured of an expert driver.

His run was from Fort Kearny to Plum Creek. The country was sharply familiar. It was the scene of his first encounter with Indians. A long and lonely ride it was, and a dismal one when the weather turned cold; but it meant a hundred and fifty dollars a month, and each pay day brought him nearer to St. Louis.

Indian signs there had been right along, but they were only signs until one bleak day in November. He pulled out of Plum Creek with a sharp warning ringing in his ears. Indians were on the war-path, and trouble was more likely than not ahead. Lieutenant Flowers, assistant division agent, was on the box with him, and within the coach were six well-armed passengers.

Half the run had been covered, when Will's experienced eye detected the promised red men. Before him lay a stream which must be forded. The creek was densely fringed with underbrush, and along this the Indians were skulking, expecting to cut the stage off at the only possible crossing.

Perhaps this is a good place to say a word concerning the seemingly extraordinary fortune that has stood by Will in his adventures. Not only have his own many escapes been of the hairbreadth sort, but he has arrived on the scene of danger at just the right moment to rescue others from extinction. Of course, an element of luck has entered into these affairs, but for the most part they simply proved the old saying that an ounce of prevention is better than a pound of cure. Will had studied the plains as an astronomer studies the heavens. The slightest disarrangement of the natural order of things caught his eye. With the astronomer, it is a comet or an asteroid appearing upon a field whose every object has long since been placed and studied; with Will, it was a feathered headdress where there should have been but tree, or rock, or grass; a moving figure where nature should have been inanimate.

When seen, those things were calculated as the astronomer calculates the motion of the objects that he studies. A planet will arrive at a given place at a certain time; an Indian will reach a ford in a stream in about so many minutes. If there be time to cross before him, it is a matter of hard driving; if the odds are with the Indian, that is another matter.

A less experienced observer than Will would not have

seen the skulking redskins; a less skilled frontiersman
would not have apprehended their design; a less expert
driver would not have taken the running chance for life: a
less accurate marksman would not have picked off an Indian with a rifle while shooting from the top of a swinging,
jerking stagecoach.

Will did not hesitate. A warning shout to the passengers, and the whip was laid on, and off went the horses
full speed. Seeing that they had been discovered, the Indians came out into the open, and ran their ponies for the
ford, but the stage was there full five hundred yards before them. It was characteristic of their driver that the
horses were suffered to pause at the creek long enough to
get a swallow of water; then, refreshed, they were off at
full speed again.

The coach, creaking in every joint, rocked like a captive balloon, the unhappy passengers were hurled from
one side of the vehicle to the other, flung into one another's laps, and occasionally, when some uncommon obstacle sought to check the flying coach, their heads
collided with its roof. The Indians menaced them without, cracked skulls seemed their fate within.

Will plied the whip relentlessly, and so nobly did the
powerful horses respond that the Indians gained but
slowly on them. There were some fifty redskins in the
band, but Will assumed that if he could reach the relay
station, the two stock-tenders there, with himself, Lieutenant Flowers, and the passengers, would be more than a
match for the marauders.

When the pursuers drew within fair rifle range, Will
handed the reins to the lieutenant, swung round in his
seat, and fired at the chief.

"There," shouted one of the passengers, "that fellow
with the feathers is shot!" and another fusillade from the
coach interior drove holes in the air.

The relay station was now hard by, and attracted by the firing, the stock-tenders came forth to take a hand in the engagement. Disheartened by the fall of their chief, the Indians weakened at the sign of reinforcements, and gave up the pursuit.

Lieutenant Flowers and two of the passengers were wounded, but Will could not repress a smile at the excited assurance of one of his fares that they (the passengers) had "killed one Indian and driven the rest back." The stock-tender smiled also, but said nothing. It would have been too bad to spoil such a good story.

The gravest fears for the safety of the coach had been expressed when it was known that the reds were on the war-path; it was not thought possible that it could get through unharmed; and troops were sent out to scour the country. These, while too late to render service in the adventure just related, did good work during the remainder of the winter. The Indians were thoroughly subdued, and Will saw no more of them.

There was no other adventure of special note until February. Just before Will started on his run, Trotter took him to one side and advised him that a small fortune was going by the coach that day, and extra vigilance was urged, as the existence of the treasure might have become known.

"I'll do the best I can," said Will; and he had scarcely driven away when he suspected the two ill-favored passengers he carried. The sudden calling away of the conductor, whereby he was left alone, was a suspicious circumstance. He properly decided that it would be wiser for him to hold up his passengers than to let them hold up him, and he proceeded to take time by the forelock. He stopped the coach, jumped down, and examined the harness as if something was wrong; then he stepped to the coach door and asked his passengers to hand him a

rope that was inside. As they complied, they looked into
the barrels of two cocked revolvers.

"Hands up!" said Will.

"What's the matter with you!" demanded one of the
pair, as their arms were raised.

"Thought I'd come in first—that's all," was the answer.

The other was not without appreciation of humor.

"You're a cute one, youngster," said he, "but you'll find
more'n your match down the road, or I miss my guess."

"I'll look after that when I get to it," said Will. "Will
you oblige me by tying your friend's hands? Thank you.
Now throw out your guns. That's all? All right. Let me see
your hands."

When both outlaws had been securely trussed up and
proven to be disarmed, the journey was resumed. The remark dropped by one of the pair was evidence that they
were part of a gang. He must reach the relay station before
the attack. If he could do that, he had a plan for farther on.

The relay station was not far away, and was safely
reached. The prisoners were turned over to the stock-
tenders, and then Will disposed of the treasure against
future molestation. He cut open one of the cushions of the
coach, taking out part of the filling, and in the cavity thus
made stored everything of value, including his own watch
and pocketbook; then the filling was replaced and the hole
smoothed to a natural appearance.

If there were more in the gang, he looked for them at the
ford where the Indians had sought to cut him off, and he
was not disappointed. As he drew near the growth of willows that bordered the road, half a dozen men with menacing rifles stepped out.

"Halt, or you're a dead man!" was the conventional
salutation, in this case graciously received.

"Well, what do you want?" asked Will.

"The boodle you carry. Fork it over!"

"Gentlemen," said Will, smiling, "this is a case where it takes a thief to catch a thief."

"What's that?" cried one of the outlaws, his feelings outraged by the frank description.

"Not that I'm the thief," continued Will, "but your pals were one too many for you this time."

"Did they rob you?" howled the gang in chorus, shocked by such depravity on the part of their comrades.

"If there's anything left in the coach worth having, don't hesitate to take it," offered Will, pleasantly.

"Where's your strong-box?" demanded the outlaws, loath to believe there was no honor among thieves.

Will drew it forth and exposed its melancholy emptiness. The profanity that ensued was positively shocking.

"Where did they hold you up?" demanded the leader of the gang.

"Eight or nine miles back. You'll find some straw in the road. You can have that, too."

"Were there horses to meet them?"

"On foot the last I saw them."

"Then we can catch 'em boys," shouted the leader, hope upspringing in his breast. "Come, let's be off!"

They started for the willows on the jump, and presently returned, spurring their horses.

"Give them my regards!" shouted Will. But only the thud! thud! of horsehoofs answered him. Retribution was sweeping like a hawk upon its prey.

Will pushed along to the end of his run, and handed over his trust undisturbed. Fearing that his ruse might have been discovered, he put the "extra vigilance" urged by Trotter into the return trip, but the trail was deserted. He picked up the prisoners at the relay station and carried them to Fort Kearny. If their companions were to discover the sorry trick played upon them, they would have demanded his life as a sacrifice.

At the end of this exciting trip he found a letter from Miss Frederici awaiting him. She urged him to give up the wild life he was leading, return East, and find another calling. This was precisely what Will himself had in mind, and persuasion was not needed. In his reply he asked that the wedding-day be set, and then he handed Trotter his resignation from the lofty perch of a stage-driver.

"I don't like to let you go," objected Trotter.

"But," said Will, "I took the job only in order to save enough money to get married on."

"In that case," said Trotter, "I have nothing to do but wish you joy."

CHAPTER 15

Will as a Benedict

W hen Will reached home, he found another letter from Miss Frederici, who, agreeably to his request, had fixed the wedding-day, March 6, 1866.

The wedding ceremony was quietly performed at the home of the bride, and the large number of friends that witnessed it united in declaring that no handsomer couple ever bowed for Hymen's benediction.

The bridal journey was a trip to Leavenworth on a Missouri steamer. At that time there was much travel by these boats, and their equipment was first-class. They were sumptuously fitted out, the table was excellent, and except when sectional animosities disturbed the serenity of their decks, a trip on one of them was a very pleasant excursion.

The young benedict soon discovered, however, that in war times the "trail of the serpent" is liable to be over all things; even a wedding journey is not exempt from the baneful influence of sectional animosity. A party of excursionists on board the steamer manifested so extreme an interest in the bridal couple that Louise retired to a stateroom to escape their rudeness. After her withdrawal, Will entered into conversation with a gentleman from Indiana, who had been very polite to him, and asked him if he knew the reason for the insolence of the excursion party. The gentleman hesitated a moment, and then answered: "To tell the truth, Mr. Cody, these men are

Missourians, and say they recognize you as one of Jennison's Jayhawkers; that you were an enemy of the South,
and are, therefore, an enemy of theirs."

Will answered, steadily: "I was a soldier during the war,
and a scout in the Union army, but I had some experience
of Southern chivalry before that time." And he related to
the Indianian some of the incidents of the early Kansas
border warfare, in which he and his father had played so
prominent a part.

The next day the insolent behavior was continued. Will
was much inclined to resent it, but his wife pleaded so earnestly with him to take no notice of it that he ignored it.

In the afternoon, when the boat landed at a lonely
spot to wood up, the Missourians seemed greatly excited,
and all gathered on the guards and anxiously scanned the
river-bank.

The roustabouts were just about to make the boat fast,
when a party of armed horsemen dashed out of the woods
and galloped toward the landing. The captain thought
the boat was to be attacked, and hastily gave orders to back
out, calling the crew on board at the same time. These orders the negroes lost no time in obeying, as they often
suffered severely at the hands of these reckless marauders. The leader of the horsemen rode rapidly up, firing at
random. As he neared the steamer he called out, "Where
is that Kansas Jayhawker? We have come for him." The
other men caught sight of Will, and one of them cried,
"We know you, Bill Cody." But they were too late. Already the steamer was backing away from the shore,
dragging her gang-plank through the water; the negro
roustabouts were too much terrified to pull it in. When the
attacking party saw their plans were frustrated, and that
they were balked of their prey, they gave vent to their disappointment in yells of rage. A random volley was fired at

the retreating steamer, but it soon got out of range, and continued on its way up the river.

Will had prepared himself for the worst; he stood, revolver in hand, at the head of the steps, ready to dispute the way with his foes.

There was also a party of old soldiers on board, six or eight in number; they were dressed in civilians' garb, and Will knew nothing of them; but when they heard of their comrade's predicament, they hastily prepared to back up the young scout. Happily the danger was averted, and their services were not called into requisition. The remainder of the trip was made without unpleasant incident.

It was afterward learned that as soon as the Missourians became aware of the presence of the Union scout on board, they telegraphed ahead to the James and Younger brothers that Will was aboard the boat, and asked to have a party meet it at this secluded landing, and capture and carry off the young soldier. Will feared that Louise might be somewhat disheartened by such an occurrence on the bridal trip, but the welcome accorded the young couple on their arrival at Leavenworth was flattering enough to make amends for all unpleasant incidents. The young wife found that her husband numbered his friends by the score in his own home, and in the grand reception tendered them he was the lion of the hour.

Entreated by Louise to abandon the plains and pursue a vocation along more peaceful paths, Will conceived the idea of taking up the business in which mother had won financial success—that of landlord. The house she had built was purchased after her death by Dr. Cook, a surgeon in the Seventh Kansas Regiment. It was now for rent, which fact no doubt decided Will in his choice of an occupation. It was good to live again under the roof that had sheltered his mother in her last days; it was good to see the young wife amid the old scenes. So Will turned boniface, and invited May and me to make our home with him.

There was a baby in Julia's home, and it had so wound itself around May's heartstrings that she could not be enticed away; but there was never anybody who could supplant Will in my heart; so I gladly accepted his invitation.

Thoreau has somewhere drawn a sympathetic portrait of the Landlord, who is supposed to radiate hospitality as the sun throws off the heat—as its own reward—and who feeds and lodges men purely from a love of the creatures. Yet even such a landlord, if he is to continue long in business, must have an eye to profit, and make up in one corner what he parts with in another. Now, Will radiated hospitality, and his reputation as a lover of his fellowman got so widely abroad that travelers without money and without price would go miles out of their way to put up at his tavern. Socially, he was an irreproachable landlord; financially, his shortcomings were deplorable.

And then the life of an innkeeper, while not without its joys and opportunities to love one's fellowman, is somewhat prosaic, and our guests oftentimes remarked an absent, far-away expression in the eyes of Landlord Cody. He was thinking of the plains. Louise also remarked that expression, and the sympathy she felt for his yearnings was accentuated by an examination of the books of the hostelry at the close of the first six months' business. Half smiling, half tearful, she consented to his return to his Western life.

Will disposed of the house and settled his affairs, and when all the bills were paid, and Sister Lou and I cozily ensconced in a little home at Leavenworth, we found that Will's generous thought for our comfort through the winter had left him on the beach financially. He had planned a freighting trip on his own account, but the acquiring of a team, wagon, and the rest of the outfit presented a knotty problem when he counted over the few dollars left on hand.

For the first time I saw disappointment and discouragement written on his face, and I was sorely distressed, for he had never denied me a desire that he could gratify, and it was partly on my account that he was not in better financial condition. I was not yet sixteen; it would be two years more before I could have a say as to the disposition of my own money, yet something must be done at once.

I decided to lay the matter before Lawyer Douglass. Surely he could suggest some plan whereby I might assist my brother. I had a half-matured plan of my own, but I was assured that Will would not listen to it.

Mr. Douglass had been the legal adviser of the family since he won our first lawsuit, years before. We considered the problem from every side, and the lawyer suggested that Mr. Buckley, an old friend of the family, had a team and wagon for sale; they were strong and serviceable, and just the thing that Will would likely want. I was a minor, but if Mr. Buckley was willing to accept me as security for the property, there would be no difficulty in making the transfer.

Mr. Buckley proved entirely agreeable to the proposition. Will could have the outfit in return for his note with my indorsement.

That disposed of, the question of freight to put into the wagon arose. I thought of another old friend of the family, M. E. Albright, a wholesale grocer in Leavenworth. Would he trust Will for a load of supplies? He would.

Thus everything was arranged satisfactorily, and I hastened home to not the easiest task—to prevail upon Will to accept assistance at the hands of the little sister who, not so long ago, had employed his aid in the matter of a pair of shoes.

But Will could really do nothing save accept, and proud and happy, he sallied forth one day as an individual freighter, though not a very formidable rival of Russell, Majors & Waddell.

Alas for enterprises started on borrowed capital! How many of them end in disaster, leaving their projectors not only penniless, but in debt. Our young frontiersman, whose life had been spent in protecting the property of others, was powerless to save his own. Wagon, horses, and freight were all captured by Indians, and their owner barely escaped with his life. From a safe covert he watched the redskins plunge him into bankruptcy. It took him several years to recover, and he has often remarked that the responsibility of his first business venture on borrowed capital aged him prematurely.

The nearest station to the scene of this disaster was Junction City, and thither he tramped, in the hope of retrieving his fortunes. There he met Colonel Hickok, and in the pleasure of the greeting forgot his business ruin for a space. The story of his marriage and his stirring adventures as a landlord and lover of his fellowman were first to be related, and when these were commented upon, and his old friend had learned, too, of the wreck of the freighting enterprise, there came the usual inquiry:

"And now, do you know of a job with some money in it?"

"There isn't exactly a fortune in it," said Wild Bill, "but I'm scouting for Uncle Sam at Fort Ellsworth. The commandant needs more scouts, and I can vouch for you as a good one."

"All right," said Will, always quick in decision; "I'll go along with you, and apply for a job at once."

He was pleased to have Colonel Hickok's recommendation, but it turned out that he did not need it, as his own reputation had preceded him. The commandant of the fort was glad to add him to the force. The territory he had to scout over lay between Forts Ellsworth and Fletcher, and he alternated between those points throughout the winter.

It was at Fort Fletcher, in the spring of 1867, that he fell in with the dashing General Custer, and the friendship established between them was ended only by the death of the general at the head of his gallant three hundred.

This spring was an exceedingly wet one, and the fort, which lay upon the bank of Big Creek, was so damaged by floods that it was abandoned. A new fort was erected, some distance to the westward, on the south fork of the creek, and was named Fort Hayes.

Returning one day from an extended scouting trip, Will discovered signs indicating that Indians in considerable force were in the neighborhood. He at once pushed forward at all speed to report the news, when a second discovery took the wind out of his sails; the hostiles were between him and the fort.

At that moment a party of horsemen broke into view, and seeing they were white men, Will waited their approach. The little band proved to be General Custer and an escort of ten, en route from Fort Ellsworth to Fort Hayes.

Informed by Will that they were cut off by Indians, and that the only hopes of escape lay in a rapid flank movement, Custer's reply was a terse: "Lead on, scout, and we'll follow."

Will wheeled, clapped spurs to his horse, and dashed away, with the others close behind. All hands were sufficiently versed in Indian warfare to appreciate the seriousness of their position. They pursued a roundabout trail, and reached the fort without seeing a hostile, but learned from the reports of others that their escape had been a narrow one.

Custer was on his way to Larned, sixty miles distant, and he needed a guide. He requested that Will be assigned to the position, so pleased was he by the service already rendered.

"The very man I proposed to send with you, General," said the commandant, who knew well the keen desire of the Indians to get at "Yellow Hair," as they called Custer. "Cody knows this part of the country like a book; he is up to all the Indian games, and he is as full of resources as a nut is of meat."

At daybreak the start was made, and it was planned to cover the sixty miles before nightfall. Will was mounted on a mouse-colored mule, to which he was much attached, and in which he had every confidence. Custer, however, was disposed to regard the lowly steed in some disdain.

"Do you think, Cody, that mule can set the pace to reach Larned in a day?" he asked.

"When you get to Larned, General," smiled Will, "the mule and I will be with you."

Custer said no more for a while, but the pace he set was eloquent, and the mouse-colored mule had to run under "forced draught" to keep up with the procession. It was a killing pace, too, for the horses, which did not possess the staying power of the mule. Will was half regretting that he had ridden the animal, and was wondering how he could crowd on another pound or two of steam, when, suddenly glancing at Custer, he caught a gleam of mischief in the general's eye. Plainly the latter was seeking to compel an acknowledgment of error, but Will only patted the mouse-colored flanks.

Fifteen miles were told off; Custer's thoroughbred horse was still in fine fettle, but the mule had got the second of its three or four winds, and was ready for a century run.

"Can you push along a little faster, General?" asked Will slyly.

"If that mule of yours can stand it, go ahead," was the reply.

To the general's surprise, the long-eared animal did go ahead, and when the party got into the hills, and the traveling grew heavy, it set a pace that seriously annoyed the general's thoroughbred.

Fifteen miles more were pounded out, and a halt was called for luncheon. The horses needed the rest, but the mouse-colored mule wore an impatient expression. Having got its third wind, it wanted to use it.

"Well, General," said Will, when they swung off on the trail again, "what do you think of my mount?"

Custer laughed. "It's not very handsome," said he, "but it seems to know what it's about, and so does the rider. You're a fine guide, Cody. Like the Indian, you seem to go by instinct, rather than by trails and landmarks."

The praise of Custer was sweeter to the young scout than that of any other officer on the plains would have been.

At just four o'clock the mouse-colored mule jogged into Fort Larned and waved a triumphant pair of ears. A short distance behind rode Custer, on a thoroughly tired thoroughbred, while the escort was strung along the trail for a mile back.

"Cody," laughed the general, "that remarkable quadruped of yours looks equal to a return trip. Our horses are pretty well fagged out, but we have made a quick trip and a good one. You brought us 'cross country straight as the crow flies, and that's the sort of service I appreciate. Any time you're in need of work, report to me. I'll see that you're kept busy."

It was Custer's intention to remain at Fort Larned for some time, and Will, knowing that he was needed at

Hayes, tarried only for supper and a short rest before starting back.

When night fell, he proceeded warily. On the way out he had directed Custer's attention to signs denoting the near-by presence of a small band of mounted Indians.

Suddenly a distant light flashed into view, but before he could check his mule it had vanished. He rode back a few paces, and the light reappeared. Evidently it was visible through some narrow space, and the matter called for investigation. Will dismounted, hitched his mule, and went forward.

After he had covered half a mile, he found himself between two sand-hills, the pass leading into a little hollow, within which were a large number of Indians camped around the fire whose light he had followed. The ponies were in the background.

Will's position was somewhat ticklish, as, without a doubt, an Indian sentinel was posted in the pass; yet it was his duty, as he understood it, to obtain a measurably accurate estimate of the number of warriors in the band. Himself a very Indian in stealth, he drew nearer the camp-fire, when suddenly there rang out upon the night air—not a rifle-shot, but the unearthly braying of his mule.

Even in the daylight, amid scenes of peace and tranquillity, the voice of a mule falls short of the not enchanting music of the bagpipe. At night in the wilderness, when every nerve is keyed up to the snapping-point, the sound is simply appalling.

Will was startled, naturally, but the Indians were thrown into dire confusion. They smothered the camp-fire and scattered for cover, while a sentinel sprang up from behind a rock not twenty feet from Will, and was off like a deer.

The scout held his ground till he had made a good

guess at the number of Indians in the party; then he ran for his mule, whose voice, raised in seeming protest, guided him unerringly.

As he neared the animal he saw that two mounted Indians had laid hold of it, and were trying to induce it to follow them; but the mule, true to tradition and its master, stubbornly refused to budge a foot.

It was a comical tableau, but Will realized that it was but a step from farce to tragedy. A rifle-shot dropped one of the Indians, and the other darted off into the darkness.

Another bray from the mule, this time a pæan of triumph, as Will jumped into the saddle, with an arrow from the bow of the wounded Indian through his coat-sleeve. He declined to return the fire of the wounded wretch, and rode away into the timber, while all around the sound of Indians in pursuit came to his ears.

"Now, my mouse-colored friend," said Will, "if you win this race your name is Custer."

The mule seemed to understand; at all events, it settled down to work that combined the speed of a racer with the endurance of a buffalo. The Indians shortly abandoned the pursuit, as they could not see their game.

Will reached Fort Hayes in the early morning, to report the safe arrival of Custer at Larned and the discovery of the Indian band, which he estimated at two hundred braves. The mule received "honorable mention" in his report, and was brevetted a thoroughbred.

The colonel prepared to dispatch troops against the Indians, and requested Will to guide the expedition, if he were sufficiently rested, adding, with a smile:

"You may ride your mule if you like."

"No, thank you," laughed Will. "It isn't safe, sir, to hunt Indians with an animal that carries a brass-band attachment."

Captain George A. Armes, of the Tenth Cavalry, was to command the expedition, which comprised a troop of colored cavalry and a howitzer. As the command lined up for the start, a courier on a foam-splashed horse rode up with the news that the workmen on the Kansas Pacific Railroad had been attacked by Indians, six of them killed, and over a hundred horses and mules and a quantity of stores stolen.

The troops rode away, the colored boys panting for a chance at the redskins, and Captain Armes more than willing to gratify them.

At nightfall the command made camp near the Saline River, at which point it was expected to find the Indians. Before dawn they were in the saddle again, riding straight across country, regardless of trails, until the river was come up with.

Will's judgment was again verified by the discovery of a large camp of hostiles on the opposite bank of the stream. The warriors were as quick of eye, and as they greatly outnumbered the soldiers, and were emboldened by the success of their late exploit, they did not wait the attack, but came charging across the river.

They were nearly a mile distant, and Captain Armes had time to plant the howitzer on a little rise of ground. Twenty men were left to handle it. The rest of the command advanced to the combat.

They were just at the point of attack when a fierce yelling was heard in the rear, and the captain discovered that his retreat to the gun was cut off by another band of reds, and that he was between two fires. His only course was to repulse the enemy in front. If this were done, and the colored gunners did not flee before the overwhelming numbers, he might unite his forces by another charge.

The warriors came on with their usual impetuosity, whooping and screaming, but they met such a raking

fire from the disciplined troops that they fell back in disorder. Just then the men at the howitzer opened fire. The
effect of this field-piece on the children of the plains was
magical—almost ludicrous. A veritable stampede followed.

"Follow me!" shouted Captain Armes, galloping in
pursuit; but in their eagerness to give chase the troops fell
into such disorder that a bugle-blast recalled them before
any further damage was done the flying foe. The Indians
kept right along, however; they were pretty badly frightened.

Captain Armes was somewhat chagrined that he had
no prisoners, but there was consolation in taking back
nearly all the horses that had been stolen. These were
found picketed at the camp across the river, where likely
they had been forgotten by the Indians in their flight.

Shortly after this, Will tried his hand at land specula-
tion. During one of his scouting trips to Fort Harker, he
visited Ellsworth, a new settlement, three miles from the
fort. There he met a man named Rose, who had a grad-
ing contract for the Kansas Pacific Railroad, near Fort
Hayes. Rose had bought land at a point through which the
railroad was to run, and proposed staking it out as a town,
but he needed a partner in the enterprise.

The site was a good one. Big Creek was hard by, and it
was near enough to the fort to afford settlers reasonable
security against Indian raids. Will regarded the enterprise favorably. Besides the money sent home each
month, he had put by a small sum, and this he invested in
the partnership with Rose.

The town site was surveyed and staked off into lots; a
cabin was erected, and stocked with such goods as are
needed on the frontier, and the budding metropolis was
weighted with the classic name of Rome.

As an encouragement to settlers, a lot was offered to

any one that would agree to erect a building. The proprietors, of course, reserved the choicest lots.

Rome boomed. Two hundred cabins went up in less than sixty days. Mr. Rose and Will shook hands and complimented each other on their penetration and business sagacity. They were coming millionaries, they said. Alas! they were but babes in the woods.

One day Dr. W. E. Webb alighted in Rome. He was a gentleman of most amiable exterior, and when he entered the store of Rose & Cody they prepared to dispose of a large bill of goods. But Dr. Webb was not buying groceries. He chatted a while about the weather and Rome, and then suggested that the firm needed a third partner. But this was the last thing the prospective millionaires had in mind, and the suggestion of their visitor was mildly but firmly waived.

Dr. Webb was not a gentleman to insist upon a suggestion. He was locating towns for the Kansas Pacific Railroad, he said, and as Rome was well started, he disliked to interfere with it; but, really, the company must have a show.

Neither Mr. Rose nor Will had had experience with the power of a big corporation, and satisfied that they had the only good site for a town in that vicinity, they declared that the railroad could not help itself.

Dr. Webb smiled pleasantly, and not without compassion. "Look out for yourselves," said he, as he took his leave.

And within sight of Rome he located a new town. The citizens of Rome were given to understand that the railroad shops would be built at the new settlement, and that there was really nothing to prevent it becoming the metropolis of Kansas.

Rome became a wilderness. Its citizens stampeded to

the new town, and Mr. Rose and Will revised their estimate of their penetration and business sagacity.

Meantime, the home in Leavenworth had been gladdened by the birth of a little daughter, whom her father named Arta. As it was impossible for Will to return for some months, it was planned that the mother, the baby, and I should make a visit to the St. Louis home. This was accomplished safely; and while the grandparents were enraptured with the baby, I was enjoying the delight of a first visit to a large city.

While the new town of Rome was regarded as an assured success by Will, he had journeyed to St. Louis after his wife and little one. They proceeded with him to the cozy cabin home he had fitted up, while I went back to Leavenworth.

After the fall of Rome the little frontier home was no longer the desirable residence that Will's dream had pictured it, and as Rome passed into oblivion the little family returned to St. Louis.

CHAPTER 16

How the Sobriquet of "Buffalo Bill" Was Won

In frontier days a man had but to ask for work to get it. There was enough and to spare for every one. The work that paid best was the kind that suited Will, it mattered not how hard or dangerous it might be.

At the time Rome fell, the work on the Kansas Pacific Railroad was pushing forward at a rapid rate, and the junior member of the once prosperous firm of Rose & Cody saw a new field of activity open for him—that of buffalo-hunting. Twelve hundred men were employed on the railroad construction, and Goddard Brothers, who had undertaken to board the vast crew, were hard pressed to obtain fresh meat. To supply this indispensable, buffalo-hunters were employed, and as Will was known to be an expert buffalo-slayer, Goddard Brothers were glad to add him to their "commissary staff." His contract with them called for an average of twelve buffaloes daily, for which he was to receive five hundred dollars a month. It was "good pay," the desired feature, but the work was hard and hazardous. He must first scour the country for his game, with a good prospect always of finding Indians instead of buffalo; then, when the game was shot, he must oversee its cutting and dressing, and look after the wagons that transported it to the camp where the workmen messed. It was while working under this contract that he acquired the sobriquet of "Buffalo Bill." It clung to him ever after, and he wore it with more pride than he would

have done the title of prince or grand duke. Probably there
are thousands of people to-day who know him by that
name only.

At the outset he procured a trained buffalo-hunting
horse, which went by the unconventional name of
"Brigham," and from the government he obtained an improved breech-loading needle-gun, which, in testimony
of its murderous qualities, he named "Lucretia Borgia."

Buffaloes were usually plentiful enough, but there
were times when the camp supply of meat ran short.
During one of these dull spells, when the company was
pressed for horses, Brigham was hitched to a scraper.
One can imagine his indignation. A racer dragging a
street-car would have no more just cause for rebellion
than a buffalo-hunter tied to a work implement in the
company of stupid horses that never had a thought above
a plow, a hay-rake, or a scraper. Brigham expostulated,
and in such plain language, that Will, laughing, was on
the point of unhitching him, when a cry went up—the
equivalent of a whaler's: "There she blows!"—that a herd
of buffaloes was coming over the hill.

Brigham and the scraper parted company instantly,
and Will mounted him bareback, the saddle being at the
camp, a mile away. Shouting an order to the men to follow him with a wagon to take back the meat, he galloped
toward the game.

There were other hunters that day. Five officers rode
out from the neighboring fort, and joined Will while
waiting for the buffaloes to come up. They were recent
arrivals in that part of the country, and their shoulder-
straps indicated that one was a captain and the others
were lieutenants. They did not know "Buffalo Bill."
They saw nothing but a good-looking young fellow, in
the dress of a working man, astride a not handsome
horse, which had a blind bridle and no saddle. It was not a

formidable-looking hunting outfit, and the captain was disposed to be a trifle patronizing.

"Hello!" he called out. "I see you're after the same game we are."

"Yes, sir," returned Will. "Our camp's out of fresh meat."

The officer ran a critical eye over Brigham. "Do you expect to run down a buffalo with a horse like that?" said he.

"Why," said Will innocently, "are buffaloes pretty speedy?"

"Speedy? It takes a fast horse to overhaul those animals on the open prairie."

"Does it?" said Will; and the officer did not see the twinkle in his eye. Nothing amuses a man more than to be instructed on a matter that he knows thoroughly, and concerning which his instructor knows nothing. Probably every one of the officers had yet to shoot his first buffalo.

"Come along with us," offered the captain graciously. "We're going to kill a few for sport, and all we care for are the tongues and a chuck of the tenderloin; you can have the rest.

"Thank you," said Will. "I'll follow along."

There were eleven buffaloes in the herd, and the officers started after them as if they had a sure thing on the entire number. Will noticed that the game was pointed toward a creek, and understanding "the nature of the beast," started for the water, to head them off.

As the herd went past him, with the military quintet five hundred yards in the rear, he gave Brigham's blind bridle a twitch, and in a few jumps the trained hunter was at the side of the rear buffalo; Lucretia Borgia spoke, and the buffalo fell dead. Without even a bridle signal, Brigham was promptly at the side of the next buffalo, not ten feet away, and this, too, fell at the first shot. The maneuver was repeated until the last buffalo went down.

Twelve shots had been fired; then Brigham, who never wasted his strength, stopped. The officers had not had even a shot at the game. Astonishment was written on their faces as they rode up.

"Gentlemen," said Will, courteously, as he dismounted, "allow me to present you with eleven tongues and as much of the tenderloin as you wish."

"By Jove!" exclaimed the captain, "I never saw anything like that before. Who are you, anyway?"

"Bill Cody's my name."

"Well, Bill Cody, you know how to kill buffalo, and that horse of yours has some good running points, after all."

"One or two," smiled Will.

Captain Graham—as his name proved to be—and his companions were a trifle sore over missing even the opportunity of a shot, but they professed to be more than repaid for their disappointment by witnessing a feat they had not supposed possible in a white man—hunting buffalo without a saddle, bridle, or reins. Will explained that Brigham knew more about the business than most two-legged hunters. All the rider was expected to do was to shoot the buffalo. If the first shot failed, Brigham allowed another; if this, too, failed Brigham lost patience, and was as likely as not to drop the matter then and there.

It was this episode that fastened the name of "Buffalo Bill" upon Will, and learning of it, the friends of Billy Comstock, chief of scouts at Fort Wallace, filed a protest. Comstock, they said, was Cody's superior as a buffalo-hunter. So a match was arranged to determine whether it should be "Buffalo Bill" Cody or "Buffalo Bill" Comstock.

The hunting-ground was fixed near Sheridan, Kansas, and quite a crowd of spectators was attracted by the news of the contest. Officers, soldiers, plainsmen, and railroad-men took a day off to see the sport, and one excursion party, including many ladies, among them Louise, came up from St. Louis.

Referees were appointed to follow each man and keep a tally of the buffaloes slain. Comstock was mounted on his favorite horse, and carried a Henry rifle of large calibre. Brigham and Lucretia went with Will. The two hunters rode side by side until the first herd was sighted and the word given, when off they dashed to the attack, separating to the right and left. In this first trial Will killed thirty-eight and Comstock twenty-three. They had ridden miles, and the carcasses of the dead buffaloes were strung all over the prairie. Luncheon was served at noon, and scarcely was it over when another herd was sighted, composed mainly of cows with their calves. The damage to this herd was eighteen and fourteen, in favor of Cody.

In those days the prairies were alive with buffaloes, and a third herd put in an appearance before the rifle-barrels were cooled. In order to give Brigham a share of the glory, Will pulled off saddle and bridle, and advanced bareback to the slaughter.

That closed the contest. Score, sixty-nine to forty-eight. Comstock's friends surrendered, and Cody was dubbed "Champion Buffalo Hunter of the Plains."

The heads of the buffaloes that fell in this hunt were mounted by the Kansas Pacific Railroad Company, and distributed about the country, as advertisements of the region the new road was traversing. Meanwhile, Will continued hunting for the Kansas Pacific contractors, and during the year and a half that he supplied them with fresh meat he killed four thousand two hundred and eighty buffaloes. But when the railroad reached Sheridan it was decided to build no farther at that time, and Will was obliged to look for other work.

The Indians had again become so troublesome that a general war threatened all along the border, and General

P. H. Sheridan came West to personally direct operations. He took up his quarters at Fort Leavenworth, but the Indian depredations becoming more widespread, he transferred his quarters to Fort Hayes, then the terminus of the Kansas Pacific Railroad. Will was then in the employ of the quartermaster's department at Fort Larned, but was sent with an important dispatch to General Sheridan announcing that the Indians near Larned were preparing to decamp. The distance between Larned and Hayes was sixty-five miles, through a section infested with Indians, but Will tackled it, and reached the commanding General without mishap.

Shortly afterward it became necessary to send dispatches from Fort Hayes to Fort Dodge. Ninety-five miles of country lay between, and every mile of it was dangerous ground. Fort Dodge was surrounded by Indians, and three scouts had lately been killed while trying to get dispatches through, but Will's confidence in himself or his destiny was unshakable, and he volunteered to take the dispatches, as far, at least, as the Indians would let him.

"It is a dangerous undertaking," said General Sheridan, "but it is most important that the dispatches should go through; so, if you are willing to risk it, take the best horse you can find, and the sooner you start the better."

Within an hour the scout was in the saddle. At the outset Will permitted his horse to set his own pace, for in case of pursuit he should want the animal fresh enough to at least hold his own. But no pursuit materialized, and when the dawn came up he had covered seventy miles, and reached a station on Coon Creek, manned by colored troops. Here he delivered a letter to Major Cox, the officer in command, and after eating breakfast, took a fresh horse, and resumed his journey before the sun was above the plain.

Fort Dodge was reached, the dispatches delivered by

nine o'clock, and Will turned in for a needed sleep. When he awoke, he was assured by John Austin, chief of the scouts at Dodge, that his coming through unharmed from Fort Hayes was little short of a miracle. He was also assured that a journey to his own headquarters, Fort Larned, would be even more·ticklish than his late ride, as the hostiles were especially thick in that direction. But the officer in command at Dodge desired to send dispatches to Larned, and as none of the other scouts were willing to take them, Will volunteered his services.

"Larned's my headquarters," said he, "and I must go there anyway; so if you'll give me a good horse, I'll take your dispatches."

"We haven't a decent horse left," said the officer; "but you can take your pick of some fine government mules."

Will made a gesture of despair. Another race on mule-back with Indians was not an inviting prospect. There were very few mules like unto his quondam mouse-colored mount. But he succumbed to the inevitable, picked out the most enterprising looking mule in the bunch, and set forth. And neither he nor the mule guessed what was in store for each of them.

At Coon Creek Will dismounted for a drink of water, and the mule embraced the opportunity to pull away, and start alone on the wagon-trail to Larned. Will did not suspect that he should have any trouble in overtaking the capricious beast, but at the end of a mile he was somewhat concerned. He had threatened and entreated, raged and cajoled. 'Twas all wasted. The mule was as deaf to prayer as to objurgation. It browsed contentedly along the even tenor of its way, so near and yet so far from the young man, who, like "panting time, toil'd after it in vain." And Larned much more than twenty miles away.

What the poet calls "the golden exhalations of the dawn" began to warm the gray of the plain. The sun was in the roots of the grass. Four miles away the lights of Larned twinkled. The only blot on a fair landscape was the mule—in the middle distance. But there was a wicked gleam in the eye of the footsore young man in the foreground.

Boom! The sunrise gun at the fort. The mule threw back its head, waved its ears, and poured forth a song of triumph, a loud, exultant bray.

Crack! Will's rifle. Down went the mule. It had made the fatal mistake of gloating over its villainy. Never again would it jeopardize the life of a rider.

It had been a thirty-five mile walk, and every bone in Will's body ached. His shot alarmed the garrison, but he was soon on the ground with the explanation; and after turning over his dispatches, he sought his bed.

During the day General Hazen returned, under escort, from Fort Harker, with dispatches for Sheridan, and Will offered to be the bearer of them. An army mule was suggested, but he declined to again put his life in the keeping of such an animal. A good horse was selected, and the journey made without incident.

General Sheridan was roused at daylight to receive the scout's report, and praised Will warmly for having undertaken and safely accomplished three such long and dangerous rides.

"In all," says General Sheridan, in his Memoirs, "Cody rode three hundred and fifty miles in less than sixty hours, and such an exhibition of endurance and courage was more than enough to convince me that his services would be extremely valuable in the campaign; so I retained him at Fort Hayes until the battalion of Fifth Cavalry arrived, and then made him chief of scouts for that regiment."

CHAPTER 17

Satanta, Chief of the Kiowas

Within plain view of Fort Larned lay a large camp of Kiowas and Comanches. They were not yet bedaubed with war paint, but they were as restless as panthers in a cage, and it was only a matter of days when they would whoop and howl with the loudest.

The principal chief of the Yiowas was Satanta, a powerful and resourceful warrior, who, because of remarkable talents for speech-making, was called "The Orator of the Plains." Satanta was short and bullet-headed. Hatred for the whites swelled every square inch of his breast, but he had the deep cunning of his people, with some especially fine points of treachery learned from dealings with dishonest agents and traders. There probably never was an Indian so depraved that he could not be corrupted further by association with a rascally white man.

When the Kiowas were friendly with the government, Satanta received a guest with all the magnificence the tribe afforded. A carpet was spread for the white man to sit upon, and a folding board was set up for a table. The question of expense never intruded.

Individually, too, Satanta put on a great deal of style. Had the opportunity come to him, he would have worn a silk hat with a sack-coat, or a dress suit in the afternoon. As it was, he produced some startling effects with blankets and feathers.

It was part of General Hazen's mission to Fort Larned

to patch up a treaty with the outraged Kiowas and Comanches, if it could be brought about. On one warm
August morning, the general set out for Fort Zarah, on a
tour of inspection. Zarah was on the Arkansas, in what is
now Baton County, Kansas. An early start was made, as it
was desired to cover the thirty miles by noon. The general rode in a four-mule army ambulance, with an escort
of ten foot soldiers, in a four-mule escort wagon.

After dinner at Zarah the general went on to Fort
Harker, leaving orders for the scout and soldiers to return
to Larned on the following day. But as there was nothing
to do at Fort Zarah, Will determined to return at once; so
he trimmed the sails of his mule-ship, and squared away
for Larned.

The first half of the journey was without incident, but
when Pawnee Rock was reached, events began to crowd
one another. Some forty Indians rode out from behind the
rock and surrounded the scout.

"How? How?" they cried, as they drew near, and offered their hands for the white man's salutation.

The braves were in war paint, and intended mischief;
but there was nothing to be lost by returning their greeting, so Will extended his hand.

One warrior seized it and gave it a violent jerk; another
caught the mule's bridle; a third pulled the revolvers
from the holsters; a fourth snatched the rifle from across
the saddle; while a fifth, for a climax, dealt Will a blow on
the head with a tomahawk that nearly stunned him.

Then the band started for the Arkansas River, lashing
the mule, singing, yelling, and whooping. For one supposed to be stolid and taciturn, the Indian makes a good
deal of noise at times.

Across the river was a vast throng of warriors, who had
finally decided to go on the war-path. Will and his captors forded the shallow stream, and the prisoner was

conducted before the chiefs of the tribe, with some of whom he was acquainted.

His head throbbed from the tomahawking, but his wits were still in working order, and when asked by Satanta where he had been, he replied that he had been out searching for "whoa-haws."

He knew that the Indians had been promised a herd of "whoa-haws," as they termed cattle, and he knew, too, that the herd had not arrived, and that the Indians had been out of meat for several weeks; hence he hoped to enlist Satanta's sympathetic interest.

He succeeded. Satanta was vastly interested. Where were the cattle? Oh, a few miles back. Will had been sent forward to notify the Indians that an army of sirloin steaks was advancing upon them.

Satanta was much pleased, and the other chiefs were likewise interested. Did General Hazen say the cattle were for them? Was there a chance that the scout was mistaken?

Not a chance; and with becoming dignity Will demanded a reason for the rough treatment he had received.

Oh, that was all a joke, Satanta explained. The Indians who had captured the white chief were young and frisky. They wished to see whether he was brave. They were simply testing him. It was sport—just a joke.

Will did not offer to argue the matter. No doubt an excellent test of a man's courage is to hit him over the head with a tomahawk. If he lives through it, he is brave as Agamemnon. But Will insisted mildly that it was a rough way to treat friends; whereupon Satanta read the riot act to his high-spirited young men, and bade them return the captured weapons to the scout.

The next question was, were there soldiers with the cattle? Certainly, replied Will; a large party of soldiers were escorting the succulent sirloins. This intelligence necessitated another consultation. Evidently hostilities must be postponed until after the cattle had arrived. Would Will drive the cattle to them? He would be delighted to. Did he desire that the chief's young men should accompany him? No, indeed. The soldiers, also, were high-spirited, and they might test the bravery of the chief's young men by shooting large holes in them. It would be much better if the scout returned alone.

Satanta agreed with him, and Will recrossed the river without molestation; but, glancing over his shoulder, he noted a party of ten or fifteen young braves slowly following him. Satanta was an extremely cautious chieftain.

Will rode leisurely up the gentle slope of the river's bank, but when he had put the ridge between him and the Indian camp he pointed his mule westward, toward Fort Larned, and set it going at its best pace. When the Indians reached the top of the ridge, from where they could scan the valley, in which the advancing cattle were supposed to be, there was not a horn to be seen, and the scout was flying in an opposite direction.

They gave chase, but the mule had a good start, and when it got its second wind—always necessary in a mule—the Indian ponies gained but slowly. When Ash Creek, six miles from Larned, was reached, the race was about even, but two miles farther on, the Indians were uncomfortably close behind. The sunset gun at the fort boomed a synical welcome to the man four miles away, flying toward it for his life.

At Pawnee Fork, two miles from the fort, the Indians had crept up to within five hundred yards. But here, on the farther bank of the stream, Will came upon a government wagon containing half a dozen soldiers and Denver Jim, a well-known scout.

The team was driven among the trees, and the men hid themselves in the bushes, and when the Indians came along they were warmly received. Two of the reds were killed; the others wheeled and rode back in safety.

In 1868 General Sheridan had taken command of all the troops in the field. He arranged what is known as the winter expeditions against the Kiowas, Comanches, Southern Cheyennes, and Arapahoes. He personally commanded the expedition which left Fort Dodge, with General Custer as chief of cavalry. General Penrose started for Fort Lyon, Colorado, and General Eugene A. Carr was ordered from the Republican River country, with the Fifth Cavalry, to Fort Wallace, Kansas. Will at this time had a company of forty scouts with General Carr's command. He was ordered by General Sheridan, when leaving Fort Lyon, to follow the trail of General Penrose's command until it was overtaken. General Carr was to proceed to Fort Lyon, and follow on the trail of General Penrose, who had started from there three weeks before, when, as Carr ranked Penrose, he would take command of both expeditions. It was the 21st of November when Carr's expedition left Fort Lyon. The second day out they encountered a terrible snowstorm and blizzard in a place they christened "Freeze Out Cañon," by which name it is still known. As Penrose had only a pack-train and no heavy wagons, and the ground was covered with snow, it was a very difficult matter to follow his trail. But taking his general course, they finally came up with him on the south fork of the Canadian River, where they found him and his soldiers in a sorry plight, subsisting wholly on buffalo-meat. Their animals had all frozen to death.

General Carr made what is known as a supply camp, leaving Penrose's command and some of his own disabled stock therein. Taking with him the Fifth Cavalry and the best horses and pack-mules, he started south toward the main fork of the Canadian River, looking for the Indians. He was gone from the supply camp thirty days, but could not locate the main band of Indians, as they were farther to the east, where General Sheridan had located them, and had sent General Custer in to fight them, which he did, in what is known as the great battle of Wichita.

They had a very severe winter, and returned in March to Fort Lyon, Colorado.

In the spring of 1869, the Fifth Cavalry, ordered to the Department of the Platte, took up the line of march for Fort McPherson, Nebraska.

It was a large command, including seventy-six wagons for stores, ambulance wagons, and pack-mules. Those chief in authority were Colonel Royal (afterward superseded by General Carr), Major Brown, and Captain Sweetman.

The average distance covered daily was only ten miles, and when the troops reached the Solomon River there was no fresh meat in camp. Colonel Royal asked Will to look up some game.

"All right, sir," said Will. "Will you send a couple of wagons along to fetch in the meat?"

"We'll send for the game, Cody, when there's some game to send for," curtly replied the colonel.

That settled the matter, surely, and Will rode away, a trifle ruffled in temper.

He was not long in rounding up a herd of seven buffaloes, and he headed them straight for camp. As he drew near the lines, he rode alongside his game, and brought down one after another, until only an old bull remained. This he killed in almost the center of the camp.

The charge of the buffaloes had nearly stampeded the picketed horses, and Colonel Royal, who, with the other officers, had watched the hunt, demanded, somewhat angrily:

"What does this mean, Cody?"

"Why," said Will, "I thought, sir, I'd save you the trouble of sending after the game."

The colonel smiled, though perhaps the other officers enjoyed the joke more than he.

At the north fork of the Beaver, Will discovered a large and fresh Indian trail. The tracks were scattered all over the valley, showing that a large village had recently passed that way. Will estimated that at least four hundred lodges were represented; that would mean from twenty-five hundred to three thousand warriors, squaws, and children.

When General Carr (who had taken the command) got the news, he followed down a ravine to Beaver Creek, and here the regiment went into camp. Lieutenant Ward and a dozen men were detailed to accompany Will on a reconnoissance. They followed Beaver Creek for twelve miles, and then the lieutenant and the scout climbed a knoll for a survey of the country. One glance took in a large Indian village some three miles distant. Thousands of ponies were picketed out, and small bands of warriors were seen returning from the hunt, laden with buffalo-meat.

"I think, Lieutenant," said Will, "that we have important business at camp."

"I agree with you," said Ward. "The quicker we get out of here, the better."

When they rejoined the men at the foot of the hill, Ward dispatched a courier to General Carr, the purpose of the lieutenant being to follow slowly and meet the troops which he knew would be sent forward.

The courier rode away at a gallop, but in a few moments came riding back, with three Indians at his horse's heels. The little company charged the warriors, who turned and fled for the village.

"Lieutenant," said Will, "give me that note." And as it

was passed over, he clapped spurs to his horse and started for the camp.

He had proceeded but a short distance when he came upon another party of Indians, returning to the village with buffalo-meat. Without stopping, he fired a long-range shot at them, and while they hesitated, puzzled by the action, he galloped past. The warriors were not long in recovering from their surprise, and cutting loose their meat, followed; but their ponies were tired from a long hunt, and Will's fresh horse ran away from them.

When General Carr received the lieutenant's dispatch, he ordered the bughler to sound the inspiring "Boots and Saddles," and, while two companies remained to guard the wagons, the rest of the troops hastened against the Indians.

Three miles out they were joined by Lieutenant Ward's company, and five miles more brought them within sight of a huge mass of mounted Indians advancing up the creek. These warriors were covering the retreat of their squaws, who were packing up and getting ready for hasty flight.

General Carr ordered a charge on the red line. If it were broken, the cavalry was to continue, and surround the village. The movement was successfully executed, but one officer misunderstood the order, and, charging on the left wing of the hostiles, was speedily hemmed in by some three hundred redskins. Reinforcements were dispatched to his relief, but the plan of battle was spoiled, and the remainder of the afternoon was spent in contesting the ground with the Indians, who fought for their lodges, squaws, and children with desperate and dogged courage. When night came on, the wagon-trains, which had been ordered to follow, had not put in an appearance, and, though the regiment went back to look for them, it was nine o'clock before they were reached.

Camp was broken at daybreak, and the pursuit began,

but not an Indian was in sight. All the day the trail was followed. There was evidence that the Indians had abandoned everything that might hinder their flight. That night the regiment camped on the banks of the Republican, and the next morning caught a distant glimpse of the foe.

About eleven o'clock a charge was made by three hundred mounted warriors, but they were repulsed with considerable loss, and when they discovered that defeat was certain, they evaded further pursuit by breaking up into companies and scattering to all points of the compass. A large number of ponies were collected as trophies of this expedition.

CHAPTER 18

Will Made Chief of Scouts

In due time the Fifth Cavalry reached Fort McPherson, which became its headquarters while they were fitting out a new expedition to go into the Republican River country. At this time General Carr recommended to General Augur, who was in command of the Department, that Will be made chief of scouts in the Department of the Platte.

Will's fancy had been so taken by the scenery along the line of march that he proceeded to explore the country around McPherson, the result being a determination to make his future home in the Platte Valley.

Shortly after reaching the fort, the scouts' division of the Fifth Cavalry was reinforced by Major Frank North and three companies of the celebrated Pawnee scouts. These became the most interesting and amusing objects in camp, partly on account of their race, but mainly because of the bizarre dress fashions they affected. My brother, in his autobiography, describes the appearance presented by these scouts during a review of the command by Brigadier-General Duncan.

The regiment made a fine showing, the men being well drilled and thoroughly versed in tactics. The Pawnees also showed up well on drill, but their full-dress uniforms were calculated to excite even the army horses to laughter. Regular cavalry suits had been furnished them, but no two of the Pawnees seemed to agree as to the correct manner in which the various articles should be worn. As they lined up for dress parade, some of them wore heavy overcoats, others discarded even pantaloons, content with a breech-clout. Some wore large black hats, with brass accouterments, others were bareheaded. Many wore the pantaloons, but declined the shirts, while a few of the more original cut the seats from the pantaloons, leaving only leggins. Half of them were without boots or moccasins, but wore the clinking spurs with manifest pride.

They were a quaint and curious lot, but drilled remarkably well for Indians, and obeyed orders. They were devoted to their white chief, Major North, who spoke Pawnee like a native, and they were very proud of their position in the United States army. Good soldiers they made, too—hard riders, crack shots, and desperate fighters.

At the close of the parade and review referred to, the officers and the ladies attended an Indian dance, given by the Pawnees, which climaxed a rather exciting day.

The following morning an expedition moved back to the Republican River, to curb the high spirits of a band of Sioux, who had grown boldly troublesome. This was the sort of service the Pawnees welcomed, as they and the Sioux were hereditary enemies.

At the journey's end, camp was made at the mouth of the Beaver, and the Sioux were heard from within the hour. A party of them raided the mules that had been taken to the river, and the alarm was given by a herder, who dashed into camp with an arrow sticking in his shoulder.

Will did not wait to saddle his horse, but the Pawnees were as quick as he, and both of them rather surprised the Sioux, who did not expect such a swift response. Especially were they surprised to find themselves confronted by their tribal foe, the Pawnee, and they fell back hastily, closely pressed by Will and his red allies. A running fight was kept up for fifteen miles, and when many of the Sioux had been stretched upon the plain and the others scattered, the pursuing party returned to camp.

Will himself, on a fine horse, had been somewhat chagrined at being passed in the chase by a Pawnee on an inferior-looking steed. Upon inquiring of Major North, he found that the swifter horse was, like his own, government property. The Pawnee was much attached to his mount, but he was also fond of tobacco, and a few pieces of that commodity, supplemented by some other articles, induced him to exchange horses. Will named his new charge "Buckskin Joe," and rode him for four years. Joe proved a worthy successor to Brigham for speed, endurance, and intelligence.

This was the first adventure that Will and the Pawnees had pursued together, and they emerged with an increased esteem for each other. Not long afterward, Will's skill as a buffalo-hunter raised the admiration of the Indians to enthusiasm.

Twenty Pawnees that circled around one herd of buffaloes killed only twenty-two, and when the next herd came in view Will asked Major North to keep the Indians in the background while he showed them a thing or two. Buckskin Joe was a capital buffalo-hunter, and so well did he perform his part that Will brought down thirty-six, about one at every shot.

The Pawnees were delighted. They held it considerable of an achievement to kill two or three of the monarchs of the plains at a single run, and Will's feat dazzled them. He was at once pronounced a great chief, and ever after occupied a high place in their regard.

Moving up the Republican River, the troops went into camp on Black Tail Deer Fork. Scarcely were the tents pitched when a band of Indians were seen sweeping toward them at full speed, singing, yelling, and waving lances. The camp was alive in an instant, but the Pawnees, instead of preparing for defense, began to sing and yell in unison with the advancing braves. "Those are some of our own Indians," said Major North; "they've had a fight, and are bringing in the scalps."

And so it proved. The Pawnees reported a skirmish with the Sioux, in which a few of the latter had been killed.

The next day the regiment set forth upon the trail of the Sioux. They traveled rapidly, and plainly gained ground.

At every camp the print of a woman's shoe was noted among the tracks of mocassined feet. The band evidently had a white captive in tow, and General Carr, selecting the best horses, ordered a forced march, the wagon-trains to follow as rapidly as possible. Will, with six Pawnees, was to go ahead and locate the hostiles, and send back word, so that a plan of attack might be arranged before the Indian village was reached.

This village the scouts discovered among the sandhills at Summit Springs, a few miles from the South Platte River; and while the Pawnees remained to watch, Will returned to General Carr with the news.

There was suppressed excitement all along the line, as officers and men prepared for what promised to be a lively scrimmage. The troops moved forward by a circuitous route, and reached a hill overlooking the hostile camp without their presence being dreamed of by the red men.

The bugler was ordered to sound the charge, but he was trembling with excitement, and unable to blow a note.

"Sound the charge, man!" ordered General Carr a second time; but the unhappy wight could scarcely hold his horn, much less blow it. Quartermaster Hays snatched the instrument from the flustered man's hands, and as the call rang out loud and clear the troops rushed to the attack.

Taken wholly by surprise, the Indian village went to pieces in a twinkling. A few of the Sioux mounted and rode forward to repel the assault, but they turned back in half a minute, while those that were not mounted scattered for the foothills hard by. The cavalry swept through the village like a prairie fire, and pursued the flying Indians until darkness put an end to the chase.

By the next morning the bughler had grown calm enough to sound "Boots and Saddles!" and General Carr split his force into companies, as it was discovered that the Indians had divided. Each company was to follow a separate trail.

Will made one of a band of two hundred, and for two days they dogged the red man's footsteps. At sunrise of the third day the trail ran into another, showing that the Sioux had reunited their forces. This was serious for the little company of regulars, but they went ahead, eager for a meeting with the savages.

They had not long to wait. The sun was scarcely an hour high when some six hundred Sioux were espied riding in close ranks along the bank of the Platte. The Indians discovered the troops at the same moment, and at once gave battle. The Indian is not a coward, though he frequently declines combat if the odds are not largely in his favor.

In this engagement the Sioux outnumbered the soldiers three to one, and the latter fell back slowly until they reached a ravine. Here they tethered their horses and waited the course of Indian events, which, as usual, came in circular form. The Sioux surrounded the regulars, and finding them comparatively few in number, made a gallant charge.

But bows and arrows are futile against powder and ball, and the warriors reeled back from a scathing fire, leaving a score of their number dead.

Another charge, another repulse; and then a council of war. This lasted an hour, and evidently evolved a brilliant stratagem, for the Sioux divided into two bands, and while one made a show of withdrawing, the other circled around and around the position where the soldiers lay.

At a point in this revolving belt of redskins rode a well-mounted, handsome warrior, plainly a chief. It had been Will's experience that to lay low a chief was half the battle when fighting Indians, but this particular mogul kept just out of rifle-shot. There are, however, as many ways of killing an Indian as of killing a cat; so Will crawled on hands and knees along the ravine to a point which he thought would be within range of the chief when next he swung around the circle.

The calculation was close enough, and when the warrior came loping along, slacking his pace to cross the ravine, Will rose and fired.

It was a good four hundred yards, but the warrior pitched from his seat, and his pony ran down the ravine into the ranks of the soldiers, who were so elated over the success of the shot that they voted the animal to Will as a trophy.

The fallen warrior was Tall Bull, one of the ablest chiefs the Sioux ever had. His death so disheartened his braves that they at once retreated.

A union of General Carr's scattered forces followed, and a few days later an engagement took place in which three hundred warriors and a large number of ponies were captured. Some white captives were released, and several hundred squaws made prisoners.

Among these latter was the amiable widow of Tall Bull, who, far from cherishing animosity against Will as the slayer of her spouse, took pride in the fact that he had fallen under the fire of so great a warrior as "Pa-has-ka," Long-haired Chief, by which name our scout was known among the Indians.

CHAPTER 19

Army Life at Fort M'Pherson

I n the spring of 1870 Will proceeded to put into effect the determination of the previous year—to establish a home in the lovely country of the westerly Platte. After preparing quarters wherein his family might be comfortable, he obtained a leave of absence and departed for St. Louis to fetch his wife and daughter, Arta, now a beautiful child of three.

The fame of "Buffalo Bill" had extended far beyond the plains, and during his month's sojourn in St. Louis he was the object of a great deal of attention. When the family prepared to depart for the frontier home, my sister-in-law wrote to me to ask if I did not wish to accompany them. I should have been delighted to accept the invitation, but at that especial time there were strong attractions for me in my childhood's home; besides, I felt that sister May, who had not enjoyed the pleasure of the St. Louis trip, was entitled to the Western jaunt.

So May made a visit to McPherson, and a delightful time she had, though she was at first inclined to quarrel with the severe discipline of army life. Will ranked with the officers, and as a result May's social companions were limited to the two daughters of General Augur, who were also on a visit to the fort. To compensate for the shortage of feminine society, however, there were a number of young unmarried officers.

Every day had its curious or enlivening incident, and

May's letters to me were filled with accounts of the gayety of life at an army post. After several months I was invited to join her. She was enthusiastic over a proposed buffalo-hunt, as she desired to take part in one before her return to Leavenworth, and wished me to enjoy the sport with her.

In accepting the invitation I fixed a certain day for my arrival at McPherson, but I was delayed in my journey, and did not reach the fort until three days after the date set. May was much disturbed. She had allowed me three days for recuperation from the journey, and I had arrived on the eve of the buffalo-hunt. Naturally, I was too fatigued to rave over buffaloes, and I objected to joining the hunt; and I was encouraged in my objecting by the discovery that my brother was away on a scouting trip.

"You don't think of going buffalo-hunting without Will, do you?" I asked May.

"Why," said she, "we can never tell when he will be in camp and when away; he's off scouting nearly all the time. And we can't get up a buffalo-hunt on five minutes' notice; we must plan ahead. Our party is all ready to start, and there's a reporter here from an Omaha paper to write it up. We can't put it off, and you must go."

After that, of course, there was nothing more to be said, and when the hunting-party set forth I made one of it.

A gay party it was. For men, there were a number of officers, and the newspaper man, Dr. Frank Powell, now of La Crosse; for women, the wives of two of the officers, the daughters of General Augur, May, and myself. There was sunshine, laughter, and incessant chatter, and when one is young and fond of horseback-riding, and a handsome young officer rides by one's side, physical fatigue is apt to vanish for a time.

The fort was soon nothing but a break in the sky-line, and with a sense almost of awe I looked for the first time upon the great American desert. To our left, as we rode eastward, ran the swift and shallow Platte, dotted with green-garbed islands. This river Washington Irving called "the most magnificent and the most useless of streams." "The islands," he wrote, "have the appearance of a labyrinth of groves floating on the waters. Their extraordinary position gives an air of youth and loveliness to the whole scene. If to this be added the undulations of the river, the waving of the verdure, the alternations of light and shade, and the purity of the atmosphere, some idea may be formed of the pleasing sensations which the traveler experiences on beholding a scene that seems to have started fresh from the hands of the Creator."

In sharp contrast was the sandy plain over which we rode. On this grew the short, stubby buffalo-grass, the dust-colored sage-brush, and cactus in rank profusion. Over to the right, perhaps a mile away, a long range of foothills ran down to the horizon, with here and there the great cañons, through which entrance was effected to the upland country, each cañon bearing a historical or legendary name.

To my eyes the picture was as beautiful as it was novel. As far as one could see there was no sign of human habitation. It was one vast, untenanted waste, with the touch of infinity the ocean wears.

As we began to get into the foothills, one of our equestriennes narrowly escaped a fall. Her horse dropped a foot into a prairie-dog's hole, and came to an abrupt stop. The foot was extricated, and I was instructed in the dangers that beset the prairie voyager in these blind traps of the plain.

The trail had been ascending at a gentle grade, and we had a slight change of scene—desert hill instead of desert plain. The sand-hills rose in tiers before us, and I was informed that they were formed ages ago by the action of water. What was hard, dry ground to our horses' hoofs was once the bottom of the sea.

I was much interested in the geology of my environments; much more so than I should have been had I been told that those strange, weird hills were the haunt of the red man, who was on the war-path, and looking constantly for scalps. But these unpleasant facts were not touched upon by the officers, and in blissful ignorance we pursued the tenor of our way.

We were obliged to ride a great distance before we sighted any game, and after twenty miles had been gone over, my temporarily forgotten weariness began to reassert itself. Dr. Powell proposed that the ladies should do the shooting, but my interest in the hunt had waned. It had been several years since I had ridden a horse, and after the first few miles I was not in a suitable frame of mind or body to enjoy the most exciting hunt.

A herd of buffaloes finally came into view, and the party was instantly alive. One old bull was a little apart from the others of the herd, and was singled out for the first attack. As we drew within range, a rifle was given to May, with explicit directions as to its handling. The buffalo has but one vulnerable spot, and it is next to impossible for a novice to make a fatal shot. May fired, and perhaps her shot might be called a good one, for the animal was struck; but it was only wounded and infuriated, and dropping its shaggy head, it rushed toward us. The officers fusilladed the mountain flesh, succeeding only in rousing it to added fury. Another rifle was handed to May, and Dr. Powell directed its aim; but terrified by the near presence of the charging bull, May discharged it at random.

Although this is strictly a narrative of facts, exercising the privilege of the novelist, we leave our present heroine in her perilous position, and return, for a space, to the fort.

Will returned from his scouting trip shortly after the departure of the hunting party, and his first query was:

"Is Nellie here?"

"Come and gone," replied his wife; and she informed him of the manner in which I had been carried off on the long-talked-of buffalo-hunt. Whereupon Will gave way to one of his rare fits of passion. The scouting trip had been long and arduous, he was tired and hungry, but also keenly anxious for our safety. He knew what we were ignorant of—that should we come clear of the not insignificant dangers attendant upon a buffalo-hunt, there remained the possibility of capture by Indians.

"I must go after them at once," said he; and off he went, without thought of rest or food. He did take time, however, to visit the officers' quarters and pour a vial of wrath upon the bewildered head of the inferior who occupied the place of the absent commandant.

"Didn't you know," cried Will, "that my continued absence meant danger in the air? Fine idea, to let a party of ladies go beyond the fort on such a foolhardy expedition before I had assured you it was safe to do so! Understand, if any harm comes to my sisters, I'll hold the government responsible!"

With which tremendous threat he mounted the swiftest horse in camp and rode away before the astonished officer had recovered from his surprise.

He was able to track us over the sand-hills, and reached us, in accepted hero fashion, in the very nick of time. The maddened bull buffalo was charging on May, unchecked by a peppering fire from the guns of the officers. All hands were so absorbed by the intense excitement of the moment that the sound of approaching hoof-beats was unnoted. But I heard, from behind us, the crack of a rifle, and saw the buffalo fall dead almost at our feet.

The ill-humor of our rescuer dampened the ardor of

the welcome we gave him. The long ride on an empty stomach had not smoothed a ripple of his ruffled temper, and we were all properly lectured. We were ordered back to the fort at once, and the command was of such a nature that no one thought of disputing it. The only question was, whether we could make the fort before being cut off by Indians. There was no time to be wasted, even in cutting meat from the tongue of the fallen buffalo. Will showed us the shortest cut for home, and himself zigzagged ahead of us, on the watch for a danger signal.

For my part, I was so worn out that I would as soon be captured by Indians, if they would agree to provide me a wigwam wherein I might lie down and rest; but no Indians appeared. Five miles from the fort was the ranch of a wealthy bachelor, and at May's request a halt was here called. It was thought that the owner of the ranch might take pity upon my deplorable condition, and provide some sort of vehicle to convey the ladies the remainder of the journey.

We were heartily welcomed, and our bachelor host made us extremely comfortable in his cozy apartments, while he ordered supper for the party. Will considered that we were within the safety zone, so he continued on to the fort to obtain his postponed rest; and after supper the ladies rode to the fort in a carriage.

The next day's Omaha paper contained an account of the hunt from Dr. Powell's graphic pen, and in it May Cody received all the glory of the shot that laid the buffalo low. Newspaper men are usually ready to sacrifice exact facts to an innate sense of the picturesque.

At this time the fort was somewhat concerned over numerous petty crimes among the civilians, and General Emory, now chief in authority at the post, requested the county commissioners to appoint Will a justice of the peace. This was done, much to the dismay of the new justice, who, as he phrased it, "knew no more of law than a mule knows of singing." But he was compelled to bear the blushing honors thrust upon him, and his sign was posted in a conspicuous place:

WILLIAM F. CODY,
JUSTICE OF THE PEACE

Almost the first thing he was called upon to do in his new capacity was to perform a wedding ceremony. Cold sweat stood upon his brow as he implored our aid in this desperate emergency. The big law book with which he had been equipped at his installation was ransacked in vain for the needed information. The Bible was examined more diligently, perhaps, than it had ever been by him before, but the Good Book was as unresponsive as the legal tome. "Remember your own wedding ceremony," was our advice. "Follow that as nearly as possible." But he shook his head despondently. The cool-headed scout and Indian fighter was dismayed, and the dignity of the law trembled in the balance.

To put an edge on the crisis, nearly the entire fort attended the wedding. All is well, said we, as we watched the justice take his place before the bridal pair with not a sign of trepidation. At the outset his conducting of the ceremony was irreproachable, and we were secretly congratulating ourselves upon his success, when our ears were startled by the announcement:

"Whom God and Buffalo Bill hath joined together, let no man put asunder."

So far as I am informed, no man has attempted it.

Before May returned home, Will became the very proud father of a son. He had now three children, a second daughter, Orra, having been born two years before. The first boy of the family was the object of the undivided interest of the post for a time, and names by the dozen were suggested. Major North offered Kit Carson as an appropriate name for the son of a great scout and buffalo-hunter, and this was finally settled on.

My first touch of real anxiety came with an order to Will to report at headquarters for assignment to duty. The county was alive with Indians, the officers in command informed him, and this intelligence filled me with dread. My sister-in-law had grown accustomed to her husband's excursions into danger-land, and accepted such sallies as incidents of his position. Later, I too, learned this stoical philosophy, but at first my anxiety was so keen that Will laughed at me.

"Don't worry," said he; "the Indians won't visit the fort to-night. There's no danger of them scalping you."

"But," said I, "it is for you, not for myself, that I am afraid. It is horrible to think of you going out alone among those foothills, which swarm with Indians."

The fort was on the prairie, but the distant foothills stretched away interminably, and these furnished favorite lurking-places for the redskins. Will drew me to a window and pointed out the third tier of hills, some twelve or fifteen miles away.

"I would advise you," said he, "to go to bed and sleep, but if you insist on keeping awake and worrying, I will kindle a blaze on top of that hill at midnight. Watch closely. I can send up only one flash, for there will be Indian eyes unclosed as well as yours."

One may imagine with what a beating heart I stared into the darkness when the hour of twelve drew on. The night was a veil that hid a thousand terrors, but a gauzy veil, to my excited fancy, behind which passed a host of shadowy horsemen with uptossing lances. How could a

man ride alone into such a gloomy-terror-haunted domain? The knights of old, who sallied forth in search of
dismal ogres and noxious dragons, were not of stouter
heart, and they breasted only fancied perils.

Twelve o'clock! The night had a thousand eyes, but
they did not pierce the darkness of the foothills.

Ah! A thin ribbon of light curled upward for an instant,
then vanished. Will was safe thus far. But there were
many hours—and the darkest—before the dawn, and I
carried to my bed the larger share of my forebodings.

Next day the scout came home to report the exact location of the hostile Sioux. The troops, ready for instant
action, were hurled against them, and the Indians were
thoroughly thrashed. A large number of chiefs were captured, among them "Red Shirt," an interesting redskin,
who afterward traveled with the "Wild West."

Captive chiefs were always esteemed of great interest
by the ladies of the fort. To me the braves taken in the last
raid were remarkable mainly for economy of apparel and
sulkiness of demeanor.

This same fall the fort was visited by a gentleman introduced as Colonel Judson, though the public knows
him better as "Ned Buntline," the story-writer. He desired
to accompany the scouts on a certain proposed trip, and
Major Brown informed Will that the ulterior motive of the
author was to project Buffalo Bill into a novel as hero.

"Now, I'd look pretty in a novel, wouldn't I?" said Will
sarcastically and blushingly.

"Yes, I think you would," returned the major, eyeing
the other's splendid proportions critically.

Whereupon the scout blushed again, and doffed his
sombrero in acknowledgment of the compliment, for—

> " 'Tis pleasant, sure, to see one's name in print;
> A book's a book, although there's nothing in't."

A retired naval officer, Ned Buntline wore a black undress military suit. His face was bronzed and rugged, determined yet kindly; he walked with a slight limp, and carried a cane. He shook Will's hand cordially when they were introduced, and expressed great pleasure in the meeting. This was the genesis of a friendship destined to work great changes in Buffalo Bill's career.

During the scouting expedition that followed, the party chanced upon an enormous bone, which the surgeon pronounced the femur of a human body. Will understood the Indian tongues well enough to be in part possession of their traditions, and he related the Sioux legend of the flood.

It was taught by the wise men of this tribe that the earth was originally peopled by giants, who were fully three times the size of modern men. They were so swift and powerful that they could run alongside a buffalo, take the animal under one arm, and tear off a leg, and eat it as they ran. So vainglorious were they because of their own size and strength that they denied the existence of a Creator. When it lighted, they proclaimed their superiority to the lightning; when it thundered, they laughed.

This displeased the Great Spirit, and to rebuke their arrogance he sent a great rain upon the earth. The valleys filled with water, and the giants retreated to the hills. The water crept up the hills, and the giants sought safety on the highest mountains. Still the rain continued, the waters rose, and the giants, having no other refuge, were drowned.

The Great Spirit profited by his former mistake. When the waters subsided, he made a new race of men, but he made them smaller and less strong.

This tradition has been handed down from Sioux father to Sioux son since earliest ages. It shows, at least, as the legends of all races do, that the story of the Deluge is history common to all the world.

Another interesting Indian tradition bears evidence of a later origin. The Great Spirit, they say, once formed a man of clay, and he was placed in the furnace to bake, but he was subjected to the heat too long a time, and came out burnt. Of him came the negro race. At another trial the Great Spirit feared the second clay man might also burn, and he was not left in the furnace long enough. Of him came the paleface man. The Great Spirit was now in a position to do perfect work, and the third clay man was left in the furnace neither too long nor too short a time; he emerged a masterpiece, the *ne plus ultra* of creation— the noble red man.

CHAPTER 20

Pa-has-ka, the Long-Haired Chief

Although the glory of killing the buffalo on our hunt was accredited to sister May, to me the episode proved of much more moment. In the spring of 1871 I was married to Mr. Jester, the bachelor ranchman at whose place we had tarried on our hurried return to the fort. His house had a rough exterior, but was substantial and commodious, and before I entered it, a bride, it was refitted in a style almost luxurious. I returned to Leavenworth to prepare for the wedding, which took place at the home of an old friend, Thomas Plowman, his daughter Emma having been my chum in girlhood.

In our home near McPherson we were five miles "in the country." Nature in primitive wildness encompassed us, but life's song never ran into a monotone. The prairie is never dull when one watches it from day to day for signs of Indians. Yet we were not especially concerned, as we were near enough to the fort to reach it on short notice, and besides our home there was another house where the ranchmen lived. With these I had little to do. My especial factotum was a negro boy, whose chief duty was to saddle my horse and bring it to the door, attend me upon my rides, and minister to my comfort generally. Poor little chap! He was one of the first of the Indians' victims.

Early one morning John, as he was called, was sent out alone to look after the cattle. During breakfast the clatter of hoofs was heard, and Will rode up to inform us that the Indians were on the war-path and massed in force just beyond our ranch. Back of Will were the troops, and we were advised to ride at once to the fort. Hastily packing a few valuables, we took refuge at McPherson, and remained there until the troops returned with the news that all danger was over.

Upon our return to the ranch we found that the cattle had been driven away, and poor little John was picked up dead on the skirts of the foothills. The redskins had apparently started to scalp him, but had desisted. Perhaps they thought his wool would not make a desirable trophy, perhaps they were frightened away. At all events, the poor child's scalp was left to him, though the mark of the knife was plain.

Shortly after this episode, some capitalists from the East visited my husband. One of them, Mr. Bent, owned a large share in the cattle-ranches. He desired to visit this ranch, and the whole party planned a hunt at the same time. As there were no banking facilities on the frontier, drafts or bills of exchange would have been of no use; so the money designed for Western investment had been brought along in cash. To carry this on the proposed trip was too great a risk, and I was asked banteringly to act as banker. I consented readily, but imagine my perturbation when twenty-five thousand dollars in bank-notes were counted out and left in my care. I had never had the responsibility of so large a sum of money before, and compared to me the man with the elephant on his hands had a tranquil time of it. After considering various methods for secreting the money, I decided for the hair mattress on my bed. This I ripped open, inserted the envelope containing the bank-notes, and sewed up the slit. No one was aware of my trust, and I regarded it safe.

A few mornings later I ordered my pony and rode

away to visit my nearest neighbor, a Mrs. Erickson, purposing later to ride to the fort and spend the day with Lou, my sister-in-law. When I reached Mrs. Erickson's house, that good woman came out in great excitement to greet me.

"You must come right in, Mrs. Jester!" said she. "The foothills are filled with Indians on the war-path."

She handed me her field-glass, and directed my gaze to the trail below our ranch, over which buffaloes, cattle, and Indians passed down to the Platte. I could plainly see the warriors tramping along Indian-file, their head-feathers waving in the breeze and their blankets flapping about them as they walked. Instantly the thought of the twenty-five thousand dollars intrusted to my care flashed across my mind.

"Oh, Mrs. Erickson," I exclaimed, "I must return to the ranch immediately!"

"You must not do so, Mrs. Jester; it's as much as your life is worth to attempt it," said she.

But I thought only of the money, and notwithstanding warning and entreaty, mounted my horse and flew back on the homeward path, not even daring to look once toward the foothills. When I reached the house, I called to the overseer:

"The Indians are on the war-path, and the foothills are full of them! Have two or three men ready to escort me to the fort by the time I have my valise packed."

"Why, Mrs. Jester," was the reply, "there are no Indians in sight."

"But there are," said I. "I saw them as plainly as I see you, and the Ericksons saw them, too."

"You have been the victim of a mirage," said the overseer. "Look! there are no Indians now in view."

I scanned the foothills closely, but there was no sign of a warrior. With my field-glasses I searched the entire rim of the horizon; it was tranquillity itself. I experienced a great relief, nevertheless. My nerves were so shaken that I could not remain at home; so I packed a valise, taking along the package of bank-notes, and visited another neighbor, a Mrs. McDonald, a dear friend of many years' standing, who lived nearer the fort.

This excellent woman was an old resident of the frontier. After she had heard my story, she related some of her own Indian experiences. When she first settled in her present home, there was no fort to which she could flee from Indian molestation, and she was often compelled to rely upon her wits to extricate her from dangerous situations. The story that especially impressed me was the following:

"One evening when I was alone," said Mrs. McDonald, "I became conscious that eyes were peering at me from the darkness outside my window. Flight was impossible, and my husband would not likely reach home for an hour or more. What should I do? A happy thought came to me. You know, perhaps, that Indians, for some reason, have a strange fear of a drunken woman, and will not molest one. I took from a closet a bottle filled with a dark-colored liquid, poured out a glassful and drank it. In a few minutes I repeated the dose, and then seemingly it began to take effect. I would try to walk across the room, staggering and nearly falling. I became uproariously 'happy.' I flung my arms above my head, lurched from side to side, sang a maudlin song, and laughed loudly and foolishly. The stratagem succeeded. One by one the shadowy faces at the window disappeared, and by the time my husband and the men returned there was not an Indian in the neighborhood. I became sober immediately. Molasses and water is not a very intoxicating beverage."

I plucked up courage to return to the ranch that evening, and shortly afterward the hunting-party rode up.

When I related the story of my fright, Mr. Bent complimented me upon what he was pleased to call my courage.

"You are your brother's own sister," said he, "We'll make you banker again."

"Thank you, but I do not believe you will," said I. "I have had all the experience I wish for in the banking business in this Indian country."

Upon another occasion Indians were approaching the fort from the farther side, but as we were not regarded as in danger, no warning was sent to us. The troops sallied out after the redskins, and the cunning warriors described a circle. To hide their trail they set fire to the prairie, and the hills about us were soon ablaze. The flames spread swiftly, and the smoke rolled upon us in suffocating volume. We retreated to the river, and managed to exist by dashing water upon our faces. Here we were found by soldiers sent from the fort to warn settlers of their peril, and at their suggestion we returned to the ranch, saddled horses, and rode through the dense smoke five miles to the fort. It was the most unpleasant ride of my life.

In the preceding chapter mention was made of the finding of a remarkable bone. It became famous, and in the summer of 1871, Professor March, of Yale College, brought out a party of students to search for fossils. They found a number, but were not rewarded by anything the most credulous could torture into a human relic.

This summer also witnessed an Indian campaign somewhat out of the common in several of its details. More than one volume would be required to record all the adventures Scout Cody had with the Children of the Plains, most of which had so many points in common that it is necessary to touch upon only those containing incidents out of the ordinary.

An expedition, under command of General Duncan,

was fitted out for the Republican River country. Duncan was a jolly officer and a born fighter. His brother officers had a story that once on a time he had been shot in the head by a cannon-ball, and that while he was not hurt a particle, the ball glanced off and killed one of the toughest mules in the army.

Perhaps it was because the Pawnees spoke so little English, and spoke that little so badly, that General Duncan insisted upon their repeating the English call, which would be something like this: "Post Number One. Nine o'clock. All's well." The Pawnee effort to obey was so ludicrous, and provocative of such profanity (which they could express passing well), that the order was countermanded.

One afternoon Major North and Will rode ahead of the command to select a site for the night's camp. They ran into a band of some fifty Indians, and were obliged to take the back track as fast as their horses could travel. Will's whip was shot from his hand and a hole put through his hat. As they sighted the advance-guard of the command, Major North rode around in a circle—a signal to the Pawnees that hostiles were near. Instantly the Pawnees broke ranks and dashed pell-mell to the relief of their white chief. The hostiles now took a turn at retreating, and kept it up for several miles.

The troops took up the trail on the following day, and a stern chase set in. In passing through a deserted camp the troops found an aged squaw, who had been left to die. The soldiers built a lodge for her, and she was provided with sufficient rations to last her until she reached the Indian heaven, the happy hunting-grounds. She was in no haste, however, to get to her destination, and on their return the troops took her to the fort with them. Later she was sent to the Spotted Tail agency.

In September of 1871 General Sheridan and a party of

friends arrived at the post for a grand hunt. Between him and Will existed a warm friendship, which continued to the close of the general's life. Great preparations were made for the hunt. General Emory, now commander of the fort, sent a troop of cavalry to meet the distinguished visitors at the station and escort them to the fort. Besides General Sheridan, there were in the party Leonard and Lawrence Jerome, Carroll Livingstone, James Gordon Bennett, J. G. Heckscher, General Fitzhugh, Schuyler Crosby, Dr. Asch, Mr. McCarthy, and other well-known men. When they reached the post they found the regiment drawn up on dress parade; the band struck up a martial air, the cavalry were reviewed by General Sheridan, and the formalities of the occasion were regarded as over.

It was Sheridan's request that Will should act as guide and scout for the hunting-party. One hundred troopers under Major Brown were detailed as escort, and the commissary department fairly bulged. Several ambulances were also taken along, for the comfort of those who might weary of the saddle.

Game was abundant, and rare sport was had. Buffalo, elk, and deer were everywhere, and to those of the party who were new to Western life the prairie-dog villages were objects of much interest. These villages are often of great extent. They are made up of countless burrows, and so honeycombed is the country infested by the little animals that travel after nightfall is perilous for horses. The dirt is heaped around the entrance to the burrows a foot high, and here the prairie-dogs, who are sociability itself, sit on their hind legs and gossip with one another. Owls and rattlesnakes share the underground homes with the rightful owners, and all get along together famously.

When the hunting-party returned to McPherson, its members voted Will a veritable Nimrod—a mighty hunter, and he was abundantly thanked for his masterly guidance of the expedition.

That winter a still more distinguished party visited the post—the Grand Duke Alexis and his friends. As many of my readers will recall, the nobleman's visit aroused much enthusiasm in this country. The East had wined and dined him to satiety, but wining and dining are common to all nations, and the Grand Duke desired to see the wild life of America—the Indian in his tepee and the prairie monarch in his domain, as well as the hardy frontiersman, who feared neither savage warrior nor savage beast.

The Grand Duke had hunted big game in Eastern lands, and he was a capital shot. General Sheridan engineered this expedition also, and, as on the previous occasions, he relied upon Will to make it a success. The latter received word to select a good camp on Red Willow Creek, where game was plentiful, and to make all needed arrangements for the comfort and entertainment of the noble party. A special feature suggested by Sheridan for the amusement and instruction of the continental guests was an Indian war-dance and Indian buffalo-hunt. To procure this entertainment it was necessary to visit Spotted Tail, chief of the Sioux, and persuade him to bring over a hundred warriors. At this time there was peace between the Sioux and the government, and the dance idea was feasible; nevertheless, a visit to the Sioux camp was not without its dangers. Spotted Tail himself was seemingly sincere in a desire to observe the terms of the ostensible peace between his people and the authorities, but many of the other Indians would rather have had the scalp of the Long-haired Chief than a century of peace.

Will so timed his trip as to reach the Indian camp at dusk, and hitching his horse in the timber, he wrapped his blanket closely about him, so that in the gathering darkness he might easily pass for a warrior. Thus invested, he entered the village, and proceeded to the lodge of Spotted Tail.

The conference with the distinguished redskin was made smooth sailing by Agent Todd Randall, who happened to be on hand, and who acted as interpreter. The old chief felt honored by the invitation extended to him, and readily promised that in "ten sleeps" from that night he, with a hundred warriors, would be present at the white man's camp, which was to be pitched at the point where the government trail crossed Red Willow Creek.

As Spotted Tail did not repose a great amount of confidence in his high-spirited young men, he kept Will in his own lodge through the night. In the morning the chief assembled the camp, and presenting his guest, asked if his warriors knew him.

"It is Pa-has-ka, the Long-haired Chief!" they answered.

Whereupon Spotted Tail informed them that he had eaten bread with the Long-haired Chief, thus establishing a bond of friendship, against violating which the warriors were properly warned.

After that Will was entirely at his ease, although there were many sullen faces about him. They had long yearned for his scalp, and it was slightly irritating to find it so near and yet so far.

CHAPTER 21

The Hunt of the Grand Duke Alexis

A special train brought the Grand Duke Alexis and party to North Platte on January 12, 1872. Will was presented to the illustrious visitor by General Sheridan, and was much interested in him. He was also pleased to note that General Custer made one of the party.

Will had made all the arrangements, and had everything complete when the train pulled in. As soon as the Grand Duke and party had breakfasted, they filed out to get their horses or to find seats in the ambulances. All who were mounted were arranged according to rank. Will had sent one of his guides ahead, while he was to remain behind to see that nothing was left undone. Just as they were to start, the conductor of the Grand Duke's train came up to Will and said that Mr. Thompson had not received a horse. "What Thompson?" asked Will. "Why, Mr. Frank Thompson, who has charge of the Grand Duke's train." Will looked over the list of names sent him by General Sheridan of those who would require saddle-horses, but failed to find that of Mr. Thompson. However, he did not wish to have Mr. Thompson or any one else left out. He had following him, as he always did, his celebrated warhorse, "Buckskin Joe." This horse was not a very prepossessing "insect." He was buckskin in color, and rather a sorry-looking animal, but he was known all over the frontier as the greatest long-distance and best buffalo-horse living. Will had never allowed any one but

himself to ride this horse, but as he had no other there at
the time, he got a saddle and bridle, had it put on old
Buckskin Joe, and told Mr. Thompson he could ride him
until he got where he could get him another. This horse
looked so different from the beautiful animals the rest of
the party were supplied with that Mr. Thompson thought
it rather discourteous to mount him in such fashion.
However, he got on, and Will told him to follow up, as he
wanted to go ahead to where the general was. As Mr.
Thompson rode past the wagons and ambulances he noticed the teamsters pointing at him, and thinking the men
were guying him, rode up to one of them, and said, "Am I
not riding this horse all right?" Mr. Thompson felt some
personal pride in his horsemanship, as he was a Pennsylvania fox-hunter.

The driver replied, "Yes, sir; you ride all right."

"Well, then," said Thompson, "it must be this horse you
are guying."

The teamster replied:

"Guying that horse? Not in a thousand years!"

"Well, then, why am I such a conspicuous object?"

"Why, sir, are you not the king?"

"The king? Why did you take me for the king?"

"Because you are riding that horse. I guess you don't
know what horse you are riding, do you? Nobody gets to
ride that horse but Buffalo Bill. So when we all saw you
riding him we supposed that of course you were the
king, for that horse, sir, is Buckskin Joe."

Thompson had heard General Sheridan telling about
Buckskin Joe on the way out, and how Buffalo Bill had
once run him eighty miles when the Indians were after
him. Thompson told Will afterward that he grew about
four feet when he found out that he was riding that most
celebrated horse of the plains. He at once galloped
ahead to overtake Will and thank him most heartily for

allowing him the honor of such a mount. Will told him that he was going to let the Grand Duke kill his first buffalo on Buckskin Joe. "Well," replied Thompson, "I want to ask one favor of you: Let me also kill a buffalo on this horse." Will replied that nothing would afford him greater pleasure. Buckskin Joe was covered with glory on this memorable hunt, as both the Grand Duke of Russia and Mr. Frank Thompson, later president of the Pennsylvania Railroad, killed their first buffalo mounted on his back, and my brother ascribes to old Joe the acquisition of Mr. Frank Thompson's name to his list of life friendships. This hunt was an unqualified success, nothing occurring to mar one day of it.

Spotted Tail was true to his promise. He and his hundred braves were on hand, shining in the full glory of war paint and feathers, and the war-dance they performed was of extraordinary interest to the Grand Duke and his friends. The outlandish contortions and grimaces of the Indians, their leaps and crouchings, their fiendish yells and whoops, made up a barbaric jangle of picture and sound not soon to be forgotten. To the European visitors the scene was picturesque rather than ghastly, but it was not a pleasing spectacle to the old Indian fighters looking on. There were too many suggestions of bloodshed and massacre in the past, and of bloodshed and massacre yet to come.

The Indian buffalo-hunt followed the Terpsichorean revelry, and all could enjoy the skill and strength displayed by the red huntsmen. One warrior, Two-Lance by name, performed a feat that no other living Indian could do: he sent an arrow entirely through the body of a bull running at full speed.

General Sheridan desired that the Grand Duke should carry away with him a knowledge of every phase of life on the frontier, and when the visitors were ready to drive to the railroad station, Will was requested to illustrate, for their edification, the manner in which a stagecoach and six were driven over the Rocky Mountains.

Will was delighted at the idea; so was Alexis at the outset, as he had little idea of what was in store for him. The Grand Duke and the general were seated in a closed carriage drawn by six horses, and were cautioned to fasten their hats securely on their heads, and to hang onto the carriage; then Will climbed to the driver's seat.

"Just imagine," said he to his passengers, "that fifty Indians are after us." And off went the horses, with a jump that nearly spilled the occupants of the coach into the road.

The three miles to the station were covered in just ten minutes, and the Grand Duke had the ride of his life. The carriage tossed like a ship in a gale, and no crew ever clung to a life-line with more desperate grip than did Will's passengers to their seats. Had the fifty Indians of the driver's fancy been whooping behind, he would not have plied the whip more industriously, or been deafer to the groans and ejaculations of his fares. When the carriage finally drew up with another teeth-shaking jerk, and Will, sombrero in hand, opened the coach door to inquire of his Highness how he had enjoyed the ride, the Grand Duke replied, with suspicious enthusiasm:

"I would not have missed it for a large sum of money; but rather than repeat it, I would return to Russia via Alaska, swim Bering Strait, and finish my journey on one of your government mules."

This ride completed a trip which the noble party pronounced satisfactory in every detail. The Grand Duke invited Will into his private car, where he received the thanks of the company for his zeal and skill as pilot of a hunting-party. He was also invited by Alexis to visit him at his palace, should he ever make a journey to Russia, and was, moreover, the recipient of a number of valuable souvenirs.

At that time Will had very little thought of crossing the seas, but he did decide to visit the East, whither he had more than once journeyed in fancy. The Indians were comparatively quiet, and he readily obtained a leave of absence.

The first stopping-place was Chicago, where he was entertained by General Sheridan; thence he went to New York, to be kindly received by James Gordon Bennett, Leonard and Lawrence Jerome, J. G. Heckscher, and others, who, it will be recalled, were members of the hunting-party of the preceding year. Ned Buntline also rendered his sojourn in the metropolis pleasant in many ways. The author had carried out his intention of writing a story of Western life with Scout Cody for the hero, and the result, having been dramatized, was doing a flourishing business at one of the great city's theatres. Will made one of a party that attended a performance of the play one evening, and it was shortly whispered about the house that "Buffalo Bill" himself was in the audience. It is customary to call for the author of a play, and no doubt the author of this play had been summoned before the footlights in due course, but on this night the audience demanded the hero. To respond to the call was an ordeal for which Will was unprepared; but there was no getting out of it, and he faced a storm of applause. The manager of the performance, enterprising like all of his profession, offered Will five hundred dollars a week to remain in New York and play the part of "Buffalo Bill," but the offer was declined with thanks.

During his stay in the city Will was made the guest of honor at sundry luncheons and dinners given by his wealthy entertainers. He found considerable trouble in keeping his appointments at first, but soon caught on to the, to him, unreasonable hours at which New Yorkers dined, supped, and breakfasted. The sense of his social obligations lay so heavily on his mind that he resolved to balance accounts with a dinner at which he should be the host. An inventory of cash on hand discovered the sum of fifty dollars that might be devoted to playing Lucullus. Surely that would more than pay for all that ten or a dozen men could eat at one meal. "However," he said to himself, "I don't care if it takes the whole fifty. It's all in a lifetime, anyway."

In all confidence he hied him to Delmonico's, at which famous restaurant he had incurred a large share of his social obligations. He ordered the finest dinner that could be prepared for a party of twelve, and set as date the night preceding his departure for the West. The guests were invited with genuine Western hospitality. His friends had been kind to him, and he desired to show them that a man of the West could not only appreciate such things, but return them.

The dinner was a thorough success. Not an invited guest was absent. The conversation sparkled. Quip and repartee shot across the "festive board," and all went merry as a dinner-bell. The host was satisfied, and proud withal. The next morning he approached Delmonico's cashier with an air of reckless prodigality.

"My bill, please," said he, and when he got it, he looked hard at it for several minutes. It dawned on him gradually that his fifty dollars would about pay for one plate. As he confided to us afterward, that little slip of paper frightened him more than could the prospect of a combat single-handed with a whole tribe of Sioux Indians.

Unsophisticated Will! There was, as he discovered, a wonderful difference between a dinner at Delmonico's and a dinner on the plains. For the one, the four corners of the earth are drawn upon to provide the bill of fare; for

the other, all one needs is an ounce of lead and a charge
of powder, a bundle of fagots and a match.

But it would never do to permit the restaurant cashier to
suspect that the royal entertainer of the night before was
astonished at his bill; so he requested that the account be
forwarded to his hotel, and sought the open air, where he
might breathe more freely.

There was but one man in New York to whom he felt
he could turn in his dilemma, and that was Ned Buntline.
One who could invent plots for stories, and extricate his
characters from all sorts of embarrassing situations,
should be able to invent a method of escape from so
comparatively simple a perplexity as a tavern bill. Will's
confidence in the wits of his friend was not unfounded.
His first great financial panic was safely weathered, but
how it was done I do not know to this day.

One of Will's main reasons for visiting the East was to
look up our only living relatives on mother's side—
Colonel Henry R. Guss and family, of Westchester,
Pennsylvania. Mother's sister, who had married this gentleman, was not living, and we had never met him or any
of his family. Ned Buntline accompanied Will on his trip
to Westchester.

To those who have passed through the experience of
waiting in a strange drawing-room for the coming of relatives one has never seen, and of whose personality one
has but the vaguest idea, there is the uncertainty of the
reception. Will it be frank and hearty, or reserved and
doubtful? During the few minutes succeeding the giving
of his and Buntline's cards to the servant, Will rather
wished that the elegant reception-room might be meta-
morphosed into the Western prairie. But presently the entrance to the parlor was brightened by the loveliest girl
he had ever looked upon, and following her walked a
courtly, elegant gentleman. These were Cousin Lizzie

and Uncle Henry. There was no doubt of the quality of the welcome; it was most cordial, and Will enjoyed a delightful visit with his relatives. For his cousin he conceived an instant affection. The love he had held for his mother—the purest and strongest of his affections—became the heritage of this beautiful girl.

CHAPTER 22

Theatrical Experiences

T he Fifth Cavalry at Fort McPherson had been ordered to Arizona, and was replaced by the Third Cavalry under command of General Reynolds. Upon Will's return to McPherson he was at once obliged to take the field to look for Indians that had raided the station during his absence and carried off a considerable number of horses. Captain Meinhold and Lieutenant Lawson commanded the company dispatched to recover the stolen property. Will acted as guide, and had as an assistant T. B. Omohundro, better known by his frontier name of "Texas Jack."

Will was not long in finding Indian tracks and accompanied by six men, he went forward to locate the redskin camp. They had proceeded but a short distance when they sighted a small party of Indians, with horses grazing. There were just thirteen Indians—an unlucky number—and Will feared that they might discover the scouting party should it attempt to return to the main command. He had but to question his companions to find them ready to follow wheresoever he might lead, and they moved cautiously toward the Indian camp.

At the proper moment the seven rushed upon the unsuspecting warriors, who sprang for their horses and gave battle. But the rattle of the rifles brought Captain Meinhold to the scene, and when the Indians saw the reinforcements coming up they turned and fled. Six of their number were dead on the plain, and nearly all of the stolen horses were recovered. One soldier was killed, and this was one of the few occasions when Will received a wound.

And now once more was the versatile plainsman called upon to enact a new rôle. Returning from a long scout in the fall of 1872, he found that his friends had made him a candidate of the Nebraska legislature from the twenty-sixth district. He had never thought seriously of politics, and had a well-defined doubt of his fitness as a law-maker. He made no campaign, but was elected by a flattering majority. He was now privileged to prefix the title "Honorable" to his name, and later this was supplanted by "Colonel"—a title won in the Nebraska National Guard, and which he claims is much better suited to his attainments.

Will, unlike his father, had no taste for politics or for political honors. I recall one answer—so characteristic of the man—to some friends who were urging him to enter the political arena. "No," said he, "politics are by far too deep for me. I think I can hold my own in any fair and no foul fight; but politics seems to me all foul and no fair. I thank you, my friends, but I must decline to set out on this trail, which I know has more cactus burs to the square inch than any I ever followed on the plains."

Meantime Ned Buntline had been nurturing an ambitious project. He had been much impressed by the fine appearance made by Will in the New York theater, and was confident that a fortune awaited the scout if he would consent to enter the theatrical profession. He conceived the idea of writing a drama, entitled "The Scout of the Plains," in which Will was to assume the title rôle and shine as the star of the first magnitude. The bait he dangled was that the play should be made up entirely of frontier scenes, which would not only entertain the public, but instruct it.

The bait was nibbled at, and finally swallowed, but

there was a proviso that Wild Bill and Texas Jack must first be won over to act as "pards" in the enterpise. He telegraphed his two friends that he needed their aid in an important business matter, and went to Chicago to meet them. He was well assured that if he had given them an inkling of the nature of the "business matter," neither would put in an appearance; but he relied on Ned Buntline's persuasive powers, which were well developed.

There had never been a time when Wild Bill and Texas Jack declined to follow Will's lead, and on a certain morning the trio presented themselves at the Palmer House in Chicago for an interview with Colonel Judson.

The author could scarcely restrain his delight. All three of the scouts were men of fine physique and dashing appearance. It was very possible that they had one or two things to learn about acting, but their inexperience would be more than balanced by their reputation and personal appearance, and the knowledge that they were enacting on the stage mock scenes of what to them had oft been stern reality.

"Don't shoot, pards!" began Will, when the conference opened. "I guess, Judson," he continued, after vainly trying to find a diplomatic explanation, "you'd better tell them what we want."

Buntline opened with enthusiasm, but he did not kindle Wild Bill and Texas Jack, who looked as if they might at any moment grab their sombreros and stampede for the frontier. Will turned the scale.

"We're bound to make a fortune at it," said he. "Try it for a while, anyway."

The upshot of a long discussion was that the scouts gave a reluctant consent to a much-dreaded venture. Will made one stipulation.

"If the Indians get on the rampage," said he, "we must be allowed leave of absence to go back and settle them."

"All right, boys," said Buntline; "that shall be put in the contract. And if you're called back into the army to fight redskins, I'll go with you."

This reply established the author firmly in the esteem of the scouts. The play was written in four hours (most playwrights allow themselves at least a week), and the actor-scouts received their "parts." Buntline engaged a company to support the stellar trio, and the play was widely advertised.

When the critical "first night" arrived, none of the scouts knew a line of his part, but each had acquired all the varieties of stage fright known to the profession. Buntline had hinted to them the possibility of something of the sort, but they had not realized to what a condition of abject dismay a man may be reduced by the sight of a few hundred inoffensive people in front of a theater curtain. It would have done them no good to have told them (as is the truth) that many experienced actors have touches of stage fright, as well as the unfortunate novice. All three declared that they would rather face a band of war-painted Indians, or undertake to check a herd of stampeding buffaloes, than face the peaceful-looking audience that was waiting to criticise their Thespian efforts.

Like almost all amateurs, they insisted on peering through the peep-holes in the curtain, which augmented their nervousness, and if the persuasive Colonel Judson had not been at their elbows, reminding them that he, also, was to take part in the play, it is more than likely they would have slipped quietly out at the stage door and bought railway passage to the West.

Presently the curtain rolled up, and the audience applauded encouragingly as three quaking six-footers, clad in buckskin, made their first bow before the footlights.

I have said that Will did not know a line of his part, nor did he when the time to make his opening speech arrived. It had been faithfully memorized, but oozed from his mind like the courage from Bob Acres's fingertips. "Evidently," thought Buntline, who was on the stage with him, "he needs time to recover." So he asked carelessly:

"What have you been about lately, Bill?"

This gave "The Scout of the Plains" an inspiration. In glancing over the audience, he had recognized in one of the boxes a wealthy gentleman named Milligan, whom he had once guided on a big hunt near McPherson. The expedition had been written up by the Chicago papers, and the incidents of it were well known.

"I've been out on a hunt with Milligan," replied Will, and the house came down. Milligan was quite popular, but had been the butt of innumerable jokes because of his alleged scare over the Indians. The applause and laughter that greeted the sally stocked the scout with confidence, but confidence is of no use if one has forgotten his part. It became manifest to the playwright-actor that he would have to prepare another play in place of the one he had expected to perform, and that he must prepare it on the spot.

"Tell us about it, Bill," said he, and the prompter groaned.

One of the pleasures of frontier life consists in telling stories around the camp-fire. A man who ranks as a good frontiersman is pretty sure to be a good raconteur. Will was at ease immediately, and proceeded to relate the story of Milligan's hunt in his own words. That it was amusing was attested by the frequent rounds of applause. The prompter, with a commendable desire to get things running smoothly, tried again and again to give Will his cue, but even cues had been forgotten.

The dialogue of that performance must have been delightfully absurd. Neither Texas Jack nor Wild Bill was able to utter a line of his part during the entire evening. In the Indian scenes, however, they scored a great success; here was work that did not need to be painfully memorized, and the mock red men were slain at an astonishing rate.

Financially the play proved all that its projectors could ask for. Artistically—well, the critics had a great deal of fun with the hapless dramatist. The professionals in the company had played their parts acceptably, and, oddly enough, the scouts were let down gently in the criticisms; but the critics had no means of knowing that the stars of the piece had provided their own dialogue, and poor Ned Buntline was plastered with ridicule. It had got out that the play was written in four hours, and in mentioning this fact, one paper wondered, with delicate sarcasm, what the dramatist had been doing all that time. Buntline had played the part of "Gale Durg," who met death in the second act, and a second paper, commenting on this, suggested that it would have been a happy consummation had the death occurred before the play was written. A third critic pronounced it a drama that might be begun in the middle and played both ways, or played backward, quite as well as the way in which it had been written.

However, nothing succeeds like success. A number of managers offered to take hold of the company, and others asked for entrance to the enterprise as partners. Ned Buntline took his medicine from the critics with a smiling face, for "let him laugh who wins."

The scouts soon got over their stage fright, in the course of time were able to remember their parts, and did fully their share toward making the play as much of a success artistically as it was financially. From Chicago the company went to St. Louis, thence to Cincinnati and other large cities, and everywhere drew large and appreciative houses.

When the season closed, in Boston, and Will had made his preparations to return to Nebraska, an English gentleman named Medley, presented himself, with a request that the scout act as guide on a big hunt and camping trip through Western territory. The pay offered was liberal— a thousand dollars a month and expenses—and Will accepted the offer. He spent that summer in his old occupation, and the ensuing winter continued his tour as a star of the drama. Wild Bill and Texas Jack consented again to "support" him, but the second season proved too much for the patience of the former, and he attempted to break through the contract he had signed for the season. The manager, of course, refused to release him, but Wild Bill conceived the notion that under certain circumstances the company would be glad to get rid of him.

That night he put his plan into execution by discharging his blank cartridges so near the legs of the dead Indians on the stage that the startled "supers" came to life with more realistic yells than had accompanied their deaths. This was a bit of "business" not called for in the playbook, and while the audience was vastly entertained, the management withheld its approval.

Will was delegated to expostulate with the reckless Indian-slayer; but Wild Bill remarked calmly that he "hadn't hurt the fellows any," and he continued to indulge in his innocent pastime.

Severe measures were next resorted to. He was informed that he must stop shooting the Indians after they were dead, or leave the company. This was what Wild Bill had hoped for, and when the curtain went up on the next performance he was to be seen in the audience, enjoying the play for the first time since he had been mixed up with it.

Will sympathized with his former "support," but he had a duty to perform, and faithfully endeavored to persuade the recreant actor to return to the company. Persuasion went for nothing, so the contract was annulled, and Wild Bill returned to his beloved plains.

The next season Will removed his family to Rochester, and organized a theatrical company of his own. There was too much artificiality about stage life to suit one that had been accustomed to stern reality, and he sought to do away with this as much as possible by introducing into his own company a band of real Indians. The season of 1875–76 opened brilliantly; the company played to crowded houses, and Will made a large financial success.

One night in April, when the season was nearing its close, a telegram was handed to him, just as he was about to step upon the stage. It was from his wife, and summoned him to Rochester, to the bedside of his only son, Kit Carson Cody. He consulted with his manager, and it was arranged that after the first act he should be excused that he might catch the train.

The first act was a miserable experience, though the audience did not suspect that the actor's heart was almost stopped by fear and anxiety. He caught his train, and the manager, John Burke, an actor of much experience, played out the part.

It was, too, a miserable ride to Rochester, filled up with the gloomiest of forebodings, heightened by memories of every incident in the precious little life now in danger.

Kit was a handsome child, with striking features and curly hair. His mother always dressed him in the finest clothes, and tempted by these combined attractions, gypsies had carried him away the previous summer. But Kit was the son of a scout, and his young eyes were sharp. He marked the trail followed by his captors, and at the first opportunity gave them the slip and got safely home, exclaiming as he toddled into the sobbing family circle, "I tumed back adain, mama; don't cry." Despite his anxiety, Will smiled at the recollection of the season when his little son had been a regular visitor at the theater. The little fellow knew that the most important feature of a dramatic performance, from a management's point of view, is a large audience. He watched the seats fill in keen anxiety, and the moment the curtain rose and his father appeared on the stage, he would make a trumpet of his little hands, and shout from his box, "Good house, papa!" The audience learned to expect and enjoy this bit of by-play between father and son. His duty performed, Kit settled himself in his seat, and gave himself up to undisturbed enjoyment of the play.

When Will reached Rochester he found his son still alive, though beyond the reach of medical aid. He was burning up with fever, but still conscious, and the little arms were joyfully lifted to clasp around his father's neck. He lingered during the next day and into the night, but the end came, and Will faced a great sorrow of his life. He had built fond hopes for his son, and in a breath they had been swept away. His boyhood musings over the prophecy of the fortune-teller had taken a turn when his own boy was born. It might be Kit's destiny to become President of the United States; it was not his own. Now, hope and fear had vanished together, the fabric of the dream had dissolved, and left "not a rack behind."

Little Kit was laid to rest in Mount Hope Cemetery, April 24, 1876. He is not dead, but sleeping; not lost, but gone before. He has joined the innumerable company of the white-souled throng in the regions of the blest. He has gone to aid my mother in her mission unfulfilled—that of turning heavenward the eyes of those that loved them so dearly here on earth.

CHAPTER 23

The Government's Indian Policy

Very glad was the sad-hearted father that the theatrical season was so nearly over. The mummeries of the stage life were more distasteful to him than ever when he returned to his company with his crushing grief fresh upon him. He played nightly to crowded houses, but it was plain that his heart was not in his work. A letter from Colonel Mills, informing him that his services were needed in the army, came as a welcome relief. He canceled his few remaining dates, and disbanded his company with a substantial remuneration.

This was the spring of the Centennial year. It has also been called the "Custer year," for during that summer the gallant general and his heroic Three Hundred fell in their unequal contest with Sitting Bull and his warriors.

Sitting Bull was one of the ablest chiefs and fighters the Sioux nation ever produced. He got his name from the fact that once when he had shot a buffalo he sprang astride of it to skin it, and the wounded bull rose on its haunches with the Indian on its back. He combined native Indian cunning with the strategy and finesse needed to make a great general, and his ability as a leader was conceded alike by red and white man. A dangerous man at best, the wrongs his people had suffered roused all his Indian cruelty, vindictiveness, hatred, and thirst for revenge.

The Sioux war of 1876 had its origin, like most of its predecessors and successors, in an act of injustice on the part of the United States government and a violation of treaty rights.

In 1868 a treaty had been made with the Sioux, by which the Black Hills country was reserved for their exclusive use, no settling by white men to be allowed. In 1874 gold was discovered, and the usual gold fever was followed by a rush of whites into the Indian country. The Sioux naturally resented the intrusion, and instead of attempting to placate them, to the end that the treaty might be revised, the government sent General Custer into the Black Hills with instructions to intimidate the Indians into submission. But Custer was too wise, too familiar with Indian nature, to adhere to his instructions to the letter. Under cover of a flag of truce, a council was arranged. At this gathering coffee, sugar, and bacon were distributed among the Indians, and along with those commodities Custer handed around some advice. This was to the effect that it would be to the advantage of the Sioux if they permitted the miners to occupy the gold country. The coffee, sugar, and bacon were accepted thankfully by Lo, but no nation, tribe, or individual since the world began has ever welcomed advice. It was thrown away on Lo. He received it with such an air of indifference and in such a stoical silence that General Custer had no hope his mission had succeeded.

In 1875 General Crook was sent into the Hills to make a farcical demonstration of the government's desire to maintain good faith, but no one was deceived, the Indians least of all. In August, Custer City was laid out, and in two weeks its population numbered six hundred. General Crook drove out the inhabitants, and as he marched triumphantly out of one end of the village the people marched in again at the other.

The result of this continued bad faith was inevitable; everywhere the Sioux rose in arms. Strange as it might

seem to one who has not followed the government's remarkable Indian policy, it had dispensed firearms to the
Indians with a generous hand. The government's Indian
policy, condensed, was to stock the red man with rifles
and cartridges, and then provide him with a first-class
reason for using them against the whites. During May,
June, and July of that year the Sioux had received 1,120
Remington and Winchester rifles and 13,000 rounds of
patent ammunition. During that year they received several thousand stands of arms and more than a million
rounds of ammunition, and for three years before that
they had been regularly supplied with weapons. The
Sioux uprising of 1876 was expensive for the government. One does not have to go far to find the explanation.

Will expected to join General Crook, but on reaching
Chicago he found that General Carr was still in command
of the Fifth Cavalry, and had sent a request that Will return to his old regiment. Carr was at Cheyenne; thither
Will hastened at once. He was met at the station by Captain Charles King, the well-known author, and later
serving as brigadier-general at Manila, then adjutant of
the regiment. As the pair rode into camp the cry went up;
"Here comes Buffalo Bill!" Three ringing cheers expressed the delight of the troopers over his return to his
old command, and Will was equally delighted to meet his
quondam companions. He was appointed guide and chief
of scouts, and the regiment proceeded to Laramie. From
there they were ordered into the Black Hills country, and
Colonel Merritt replaced General Carr.

The incidents of Custer's fight and fall are so well
known that it is not necessary to repeat them here. It was a
better fight than the famous charge of the Light Brigade
at Balaklava, for not one of the three hundred came forth
from the "jaws of death." As at Balaklava, "some one

had blundered," not once, but many times, and Custer's command discharged the entire debt with their lifeblood.

When the news of the tragedy reached the main army, preparations were made to move against the Indians in force. The Fifth Cavalry was instructed to cut off, if possible, eight hundred Cheyenne warriors on their way to join the Sioux, and Colonel Wesley Merritt, with five hundred men, hastened to Hat, or War-Bonnet, Creek, purposing to reach the trail before the Indians could do so. The creek was reached on the 17th of July, and at daylight the following morning Will rode forth to ascertain whether the Cheyennes had crossed the trail. They had not, but that very day the scout discerned the warriors coming up from the south.

Colonel Merritt ordered his men to mount their horses, but to remain out of sight, while he, with his adjutant, Charles King, accompanied Will on a tour of observation. The Cheyennes came directly toward the troops, and presently fifteen or twenty of them dashed off to the west along the trail the army had followed the night before. Through his glass Colonel Merritt remarked two soldiers on the trail, doubtless couriers with dispatches, and these the Indians manifestly designed to cut off. Will suggested that it would be well to wait until the warriors were on the point of charging the couriers, when, if the colonel were willing, he would take a party of picked men and cut off the hostile delegation from the main body, which was just coming over the divide.

The colonel acquiesced, and Will, galloping back to camp, returned with fifteen men. The couriers were some four hundred yards away, and their Indian pursuers two hundred behind them. Colonel Merritt gave the word to charge, and Will and his men skurried toward the redskins.

In the skirmish that ensued three Indians were killed.

The rest started for the main band of warriors, who had halted to watch the fight, but they were so hotly pursued by the soldiers that they turned at a point half a mile distant from Colonel Merritt, and another skirmish took place.

Here something a little out of the usual occurred—a challenge to a duel. A warrior, whose decorations and war-bonnet proclaimed him a chief, rode out in front of his men, and called out in his own tongue, which Will could understand:

"I know you, Pa-has-ka! Come and fight me, if you want to fight!"

Will rode forward fifty yards, and the warrior advanced a like distance. The two rifles spoke, and the Indian's horse fell; but at the same moment Will's horse stumbled into a gopher-hole and threw its rider. Both duelists were instantly on their feet, confronting each other across a space of not more than twenty paces. They fired again simultaneously, and though Will was unhurt, the Indian fell dead.

The duel over, some two hundred warriors dashed up to recover the chieftain's body and to avenge his death. It was now Colonel Merritt's turn to move. He dispatched a company of soldiers to Will's aid, and then ordered the whole regiment to the charge. As the soldiers advanced, Will swung the Indian's topknot and war-bonnet which he had secured, and shouted, "The first scalp for Custer!"

The Indians made a stubborn resistance, but as they found this useless, began a retreat toward Red Cloud agency, whence they had come. The retreat continued for thirty-five miles, the troops following into the agency. The fighting blood of the Fifth was at fever heat, and they were ready to encounter the thousands of warriors at the agency should they exhibit a desire for battle. But they manifested no such desire.

Will learned that the name of the chief he had killed

that morning was "Yellow Hand." He was the son of "Cut Nose," a leading spirit among the Cheyennes. This old chieftain offered Will four mules if he would return the war-bonnet and accouterments worn by the young warrior and captured in the fight, but Will did not grant the request, much as he pitied Cut Nose in his grief.

The Fifth Calvary on the following morning started on its march to join General Crook's command in the Big Horn Mountains. The two commands united forces on the 3rd of August, and marched to the confluence of the Powder River with the Yellowstone. Here General Mills met them, to report that no Indians had crossed the stream.

No other fight occurred; but Will made himself useful in his capacity of scout. There were many long, hard rides, carrying dispatches that no one else would volunteer to bear. When he was assured that the fighting was all over, he took passage, in September, on the steamer "Far West," and sailed down the Missouri.

People in the Eastern States were wonderfully interested in the stirring events on the frontier, and Will conceived the idea of putting the incidents of the Sioux war upon the stage. Upon his return to Rochester he had a play written for his purpose, organized a company, and opened his season. Previously he had paid a flying visit to Red Cloud agency, and induced a number of Sioux Indians to take part in his drama.

The red men had no such painful experience as Wild Bill and Texas Jack. All they were expected to do in the way of acting was what came natural to them. Their part was to introduce a bit of "local color," to give a war-dance, take part in a skirmish, or exhibit themselves in some typical Indian fashion.

At the close of this season Will bought a large tract of land near North Platte, and started a cattle-ranch. He already owned one some distance to the northward, in partnership with Major North, the leader of the Pawnee scouts. Their friendship had strengthened since their first meeting, ten years before.

In this new ranch Will takes great pride. He has added to its area until it now covers seven thousand acres, and he has developed its resources to the utmost. Twenty-five hundred acres are devoted to alfalfa and twenty-five hundred sown to corn. One of the features of interest to visitors is a wooded park, containing a number of deer and young buffaloes. Near the park is a beautiful lake. In the center of the broad tract of land stands the picturesque building known as "Scout's Rest Ranch," which, seen from the foothills, has the appearance of an old castle.

The ranch is one of the most beautiful spots that one can imagine, and is, besides, an object-lesson in the value of scientific investigation and experiment joined with persistence and perseverance. When Will bought the property he was an enthusiastic believer in the possibilities of Nebraska development. His brother-in-law, Mr. Goodman, was put in charge of the place.

The whole Platte Valley formed part of the district once miscalled the Great American Desert. It was an idea commonly accepted, but, as the sequel proved, erroneous, that lack of moisture was the cause of lack of vegetation. An irrigating ditch was constructed on the ranch, trees were planted, and it was hoped that with such an abundance of moisture they would spring up like weeds. Vain hope! There was "water, water everywhere," but not a tree would grown.

Will visited his old Kansas home, and the sight of tall and stately trees filled him with a desire to transport some of this beauty to his Nebraska ranch.

"I'd give five hundred dollars," said he, "for every tree I had like that in Nebraska!"

Impressed by the proprietor's enthusiasm for arboreal development, Mr. Goodman began investigation and experiment. It took him but a short time to acquire a knowledge of the deficiencies of the soil, and this done, the bigger half of the problem was solved.

Indian legend tells us that this part of our country was once an inland sea. There is authority for the statement that to-day it is a vast subterranean reservoir, and the conditions warrant the assertion. The soil in all the region has a depth only of from one to three feet, while underlying the shallow arable deposit is one immense bedrock, varying in thickness, the average being from three to six feet. Everywhere water may be tapped by digging through the thin soil and boring through the rock formation. The country gained its reputation as a desert, not from lack of moisture, but from lack of soil. In the pockets of the foot-hills, where a greater depth of soil had accumulated from the washings of the slopes above, beautiful little groves of trees might be found, and the islands of the Platte River were heavily wooded. Everywhere else was a treeless waste.

The philosophy of the transformation from sea to plain is not fully understood. The most tenable theory yet advanced is that the bedrock is an alkaline deposit, left by the waters in a gradually widening and deepening margin. On this the prairie wind sifted its accumulation of dust, and the rain washed down its quota from the bank above. In the slow process of countless years the rock formation extended over the whole sea; the alluvial deposit deepened; seeds lodged in it, and the buffalo-grass and sage-brush began to grow, their yearly decay adding to the ever-thickening layer of soil.

Having learned the secret of the earth, Mr. Goodman devoted himself to the study of the trees. He investigated those varieties having lateral roots, to determine which would flourish best in a shallow soil. He experimented, he failed, and he tried again. All things come round to him who will but work. Many experiments succeeded the first, and many failures followed in their turn. But at last, like Archimedes, he could cry "Eureka! I have found it!" In a very short time he had the ranch charmingly laid out with rows of cottonwoods, box-elder, and other members of the tree family. The ranch looked like an oasis in the desert, and neighbors inquired into the secret of the magic that had worked so marvelous a transformation. The streets of North Platte are now beautiful with trees, and adjoining farms grow many more. It is "Scout's Rest Ranch," however, that is pointed out with pride to travelers on the Union Pacific Railroad.

Mindful of his resolve to one day have a residence in North Platte, Will purchased the site on which his first residence was erected. His family had sojourned in Rochester for several years, and when they returned to the West the new home was built according to the wishes and under the supervision of the wife and mother. To the dwelling was given the name "Welcome Wigwam."

CHAPTER 24

Literary Work

It was during this period of his life that my brother's first literary venture was made. As the reader has seen, his school-days were few in number, and as he told Mr. Majors, in signing his first contract with him, he could use a rifle better than a pen. A life of constant action on the frontier does not leave a man much time for acquiring an education; so it is no great wonder that the first sketch Will wrote for publication was destitute of punctuation and short of capitals in many places. His attention was directed to these shortcomings, but Western life had cultivated a disdain for petty things.

"Life is too short," said he, "to make big letters when small ones will do; and as for punctuation, if my readers don't know enough to take their breath without those little marks, they'll have to lose it, that's all."

But in spite of his jesting, it was characteristic of him that when he undertook anything he wished to do it well. He now had leisure for study, and he used it to such good advantage that he was soon able to send to the publishers a clean manuscript, grammatical, and well spelled, capitalized, and punctuated. The publishers appreciated the improvement, though they had sought after his work in its crude state, and paid good prices for it.

Our author would never consent to write anything except actual scenes from border life. As a sop to the Cerberus of sensationalism, he did occasionally condescend to heighten his effects by exaggeration. In sending one story to the publisher he wrote:

"I am sorry to have to lie so outrageously in this yarn. My hero has killed more Indians on one war-trail than I have killed in all my life. But I understand this is what is expected in border tales. If you think the revolver and bowie-knife are used too freely, you may cut out a fatal shot or stab wherever you deem it wise."

Even this story, which one accustomed to border life confessed to be exaggerated, fell far short of the sensational and blood-curdling tales usually written, and was published exactly as the author wrote it.

During the summer of 1877 I paid a visit to our relatives in Westchester, Pennsylvania. My husband had lost all his wealth before his death, and I was obliged to rely upon my brother for support. To meet a widespread demand, Will this summer wrote his autobiography. It was published at Hartford, Connecticut, and I, anxious to do something for myself, took the general agency of the book for the state of Ohio, spending a part of the summer there in pushing its sale. But I soon tired of a business life, and turning over the agency to other hands, went from Cleveland to visit Will at his new home in North Platte, where there were a number of other guests at the time.

Besides his cattle-ranch in the vicinity of North Platte, Will had another ranch on the Dismal River, sixty-five miles north, touching the Dakota line. One day he remarked to us:

"I'm sorry to leave you to your own resources for a few days, but I must take a run up to my ranch on Dismal River."

Not since our early Kansas trip had I had an experience in camping out, and in those days I was almost too young to appreciate it; but it had left me with a keen desire to try it again.

"Let us all go with you, Will," I exclaimed. "We can camp out on the road."

Our friends added their approval, and Will fell in with the suggestion at once.

"There's no reason why you can't go if you wish to," said he. Will owned numerous conveyances, and was able to provide ways and means to carry us all comfortably. Lou and the two little girls, Arta and Orra, rode in an open phaëton. There were covered carriages, surreys, and a variety of turnouts to transport the invited guests. Several prominent citizens of North Platte were invited to join the party, and when our arrangements were completed we numbered twenty-five.

Will took a caterer along, and made ample provisions for the inner man and woman. He knew, from long experience, that a camping trip without an abundance of food is rather a dreary affair.

All of us except Will were out for pleasure solely, and we found time to enjoy ourselves even during the first day's ride of twenty-five miles. As we looked around at the new and wild scenes while the tents were pitched for the night, Will led the ladies of the party to a tree, saying:

"You are the first white women whose feet have trod this region. Carve your names here, and celebrate the event."

After a good night's rest and a bounteous breakfast, we set out in high spirits, and were soon far out in the foothills.

One who has never seen these peculiar formations can have but little idea of them. On every side, as far as the eye can see, undulations of earth stretch away like the waves of the ocean, and on them no vegetation flourishes save buffalo-grass, sage-brush, and the cactus, blooming but thorny.

The second day I rode horseback, in company with

Will and one or two others of the party, over a constant succession of hill and vale; we mounted an elevation and descended its farther side, only to be confronted by another hill. The horseback party was somewhat in advance of those in carriages.

From the top of one hill Will scanned the country with his field-glass, and remarked that some deer were headed our way, and that we should have fresh venison for dinner. He directed us to ride down into the valley and tarry there, so that we might not startle the timid animals, while he continued part way up the hill and halted in position to get a good shot at the first one that came over the knoll. A fawn presently bounded into view, and Will brought his rifle to his shoulder; but much to our surprise, instead of firing, dropped the weapon to his side. Another fawn passed him before he fired, and as the little creature fell we rode up to Will and began chaffing him unmercifully, one gentleman remarking:

"It is difficult to believe we are in the presence of the crack shot of America, when we see him allow two deer to pass by before he brings one down."

But to the laughing and chaffing Will answered not a word, and recalling the childish story I had heard of his buck fever, I wondered if, at this late date, it were possible for him to have another attack of that kind. The deer was handed over to the commissary department, and we rode on.

"Will, what was the matter with you just now?" I asked him privately. "Why didn't you shoot that first deer; did you have another attack like you had when you were a little boy?"

He rode along in silence for a few moments, and then turned to me with the query:

"Did you ever look into a deer's eyes?" And as I replied that I had not, he continued:

"Every one has his little weakness; mine is a deer's eye. I don't want you to say anything about it to your friends, for they would laugh more than ever, but the fact is I have never yet been able to shoot a deer if it looked me in the eye. With a buffalo, or a bear, or an Indian, it is different. But a deer has the eye of a trusting child, soft, gentle, and confiding. No one but a brute could shoot a deer if he caught that look. The first that came over the knoll looked straight at me; I let it go by, and did not look at the second until I was sure it had passed me."

He seemed somewhat ashamed of his soft-heartedness; yet to me it was but one of many little incidents that revealed a side of his nature the rough life of the frontier had not corrupted.

Will expected to reach the Dismal River on the third day, and at noon of it he remarked that he had better ride ahead and give notice of our coming, for the man who looked after the ranch had his wife with him, and she would likely be dismayed at the thought of preparing supper for so large a crowd on a minute's notice.

Sister Julia's son, Will Goodman, a lad of fifteen, was of our party, and he offered to be the courier.

"Are you sure you know the way?" asked his uncle.

"Oh, yes," was the confident response; "you know I have been over the road with you before, and I know just how to go."

"Well, tell me how you would go."

Young Will described the trail so accurately that his uncle concluded it would be safe for him to undertake the trip, and the lad rode ahead, happy and important.

It was late in the afternoon when we reached the ranch, and the greeting of the overseer was:

"Well, well; what's all this?"

"Didn't you know we were coming?" asked Will quickly.

"Hasn't Will Goodman been here?" The ranchman shook his head.

"Haven't seen him, sir," he replied, "since he was here with you before."

"Well, he'll be along," said Will, quietly; but I detected a ring of anxiety in his voice. "Go into the house and make yourselves comfortable," he added. "It will be some time before a meal can be prepared for such a supper party." We entered the house, but he remained outside, and mounting the stile that served as a gate, examined the nearer hills with his glass. There was no sign of Will, Jr.; so the ranchman was directed to dispatch five or six men in as many directions to search for the boy, and as they hastened away on their mission Will remained on the stile, running his fingers every few minutes through the hair over his forehead—a characteristic action with him when worried. Thinking I might reassure him, I came out and chided him gently for what I was pleased to regard as his needless anxiety. It was impossible for Willie to lose his way very long, I explained, without knowing anything about my subject. "See how far you can look over these hills. It is not as if he were in the woods," said I.

Will looked at me steadily and pityingly for a moment. "Go back in the house, Nell," said he, with a touch of impatience; "you don't know what you are talking about."

That was true enough, but when I returned obediently to the house I repeated my opinion that worry over the absent boy was needless, for it would be difficult, I declared, for one to lose himself where the range of vision was so extensive as it was from the top of one of these foothills.

"But suppose," said one of the party, "that you were in the valley behind one of the foothills—what then?"

This led to an animated discussion as to the danger of

getting lost in this long-range locality, and in the midst of it Will walked in, his equanimity quite restored.

"It's all right," said he; "I can see the youngster coming along."

We flocked to the stile, and discovered a moving speck in the distance. Looked at through the field-glasses, it proved to be the belated courier. Then we appealed to Will to settle the question that had been under discussion.

"Ladies and gentlemen," he answered impressively, "if one of you were lost among these foothills, and a whole regiment started out in search of you, the chances are ten to one that you would starve to death, to say the least, before you could be found."

To find the way with ease and locate the trail unerringly over an endless and monotonous succession of hills identical in appearance is an ability the Indian possesses, but few are the white men that can imitate the aborigine. I learned afterward that it was accounted one of Will's great accomplishments as a scout that he was perfectly at home among the frozen waves of the prairie ocean.

When the laggard arrived, and was pressed for particulars, he declared he had traveled eight or ten miles when he found that he was off the trail. "I thought I was lost," said he; "but after considering the matter I decided that I had one chance—that was to go back over my own tracks. The marks of my horse's hoofs led me out on the mail trail, and your tracks were so fresh that I had no further trouble."

"Pretty good," said Will, patting the boy's shoulder. "Pretty good. You have some of the Cody blood in you, that's plain."

The next day was passed in looking over the ranch, and the day following we visited, at Will's solicitation, a spot that he had named "The Garden of the Gods." Our thoughtful host had sent ranchmen ahead to prepare the place for our reception, and we were as surprised and delighted as he could desire. A patch on the river's brink was filled with tall and stately trees and luxuriant shrubs, laden with fruits and flowers, while birds of every hue nested and sang about us. It was a miniature paradise in the midst of a desert of sage-brush and buffalo-grass. The interspaces of the grove were covered with rich green grass, and in one of these nature-carpeted nooks the workmen, under Will's direction, had put up an arbor, with rustic seats and table. Herein we ate our luncheon, and every sense was pleasured.

As it was not likely that the women of the party would ever see the place again, so remote was it from civilization, belonging to the as yet uninhabited part of the Western plains, we decided to explore it, in the hope of finding something that would serve as a souvenir. We had not gone far when we found ourselves out of Eden and in the desert that surrounded it, but it was the desert that held our great discovery. On an isolated elevation stood a lone, tall tree, in the topmost branches of which reposed what seemed to be a large package. As soon as our imaginations got fairly to work the package became the hidden treasure of some prairie bandit, and while two of the party returned for our masculine forces the rest of us kept guard over the cachet in the treetop. Will came up with the others, and when we pointed out to him the supposed chest of gold he smiled, saying that he was sorry to dissipate the hopes which the ladies had built in the tree, but that they were not gazing upon anything of intrinsic value, but on the open sepulchre of some departed brave. "It is a wonder," he remarked laughingly, "you women didn't catch on to the skeleton in that closet."

As we retraced our steps, somewhat crestfallen, we listened to the tale of another of the red man's superstitions.

When some great chief, who particularly distinguishes himself on the war-path, loses his life on the battle-field without losing his scalp, he is regarded as especially favored by the Great Spirit. A more exalted sepulchre than mother earth is deemed fitting for such a warrior. Accordingly, he is wrapped in his blanket-shroud, and, in his war paint and feathers and with his weapons by his side, he is placed in the top of the highest tree in the neighborhood, the spot thenceforth being sacred against intrusion for a certain number of moons. At the end of that period messengers are dispatched to ascertain if the remains have been disturbed. If they have not, the departed is esteemed a spirit chief, who, in the happy hunting-grounds, intercedes for and leads on to sure victory the warriors who trusted to his leadership in the material world.

We bade a reluctant adieu to the idyllic retreat, and threw it many a backward glance as we took our way over the desert that stretched between us and the ranch. Here another night was passed, and then we set out for home. The brief sojourn "near to Nature's heart" had been a delightful experience, holding for many of us the charm of novelty, and for all recreation and pleasant comradeship.

With the opening of the theatrical season Will returned to the stage, and his histrionic career continued for five years longer. As an actor he achieved a certain kind of success. He played in every large city of the United States, always to crowded houses, and was everywhere received with enthusiasm. There was no doubt of his financial success, whatever criticisms might be passed on the artistic side of his performance. It was his personality and reputation that interested his audiences. They did not expect the art of Sir Henry Irving, and you may be sure that they did not receive it.

Will never enjoyed this part of his career; he endured it simply because it was the means to an end. He had not forgotten his boyish dream—his resolve that he would one day present to the world an exhibition that would give a realistic picture of life in the Far West, depicting its dangers and privations, as well as its picturesque phases. His first theatrical season had shown him how favorably such an exhibition would be received, and his long-cherished ambition began to take shape. He knew that an enormous amount of money would be needed, and to acquire such a sum he lived for many years behind the footlights.

I was present in a Leavenworth theatre during one of his last performances—one in which he played the part of a loving swain to a would-be charming lassie. When the curtain fell on the last act I went behind the scenes, in company with a party of friends, and congratulated the star upon his excellent acting.

"Oh, Nellie," he groaned, "don't say anything about it. If heaven will forgive me this foolishness, I promise to quit it forever when this season is over."

That was the way he felt about the stage, so far as his part in it was concerned. He was a fish out of water. The feeble pretensions to a stern reality, and the mock dangers exploited, could not but fail to seem trivial to one who had lived the very scenes depicted.

CHAPTER 25

First Visit to the Valley of the Big Horn

My brother was again bereaved in 1880 by the death of his little daughter, Orra. At her own request, Orra's body was interred in Rochester, in beautiful Mount Hope Cemetery, by the side of little Kit Carson.

But joy follows upon sadness, and the summer before Will spent his last season on the stage was a memorable one for him. It marked the birth of another daughter, who was christened Irma. This daughter is the very apple of her father's eye; to her he gives the affection that is her due, and round her clings the halo of the tender memories of the other two that have departed this life.

This year, 1882, was also the one in which Will paid his first visit to the valley of the Big Horn. He had often traversed the outskirts of that region, and heard incredible tales from Indians and trappers of its wonders and beauties, but he had yet to explore it himself. In his early experience as Pony Express rider, California Joe had related to him the first story he had heard of the enchanted basin, and in 1875, when he was in charge of a large body of Arapahoe Indians that had been permitted to leave their reservation for a big hunt, he obtained more details.

The agent warned Will that some of the Indians were dissatisfied, and might attempt to escape, but to all appearances, though he watched them sharply, they were entirely content. Game was plentiful, the weather fine, and nothing seemed omitted from the red man's happiness.

One night about twelve o'clock Will was aroused by an Indian guide, who informed him that a party of some two hundred Arapahoes had started away some two hours before, and were on a journey northward. The red man does not wear his heart upon his sleeve for government daws to peck at. One knows what he proposes to do after he has done it. The red man is conspicuously among the things that are not always what they seem.

Pursuit was immediately set on foot, and the entire body of truant warriors were brought back without bloodshed. One of them, a young warrior, came to Will's tent to beg for tobacco. The Indian—as all know who have made his acquaintance—has no difficulty in reconciling begging with his native dignity. To work may be beneath him, to beg is a different matter, and there is frequently a delightful hauteur about his mendicancy. In this respect he is not unlike some of his white brothers. Will gave the young chief the desired tobacco, and then questioned him closely concerning the attempted escape.

"Surely," said he, "you cannot find a more beautiful spot than this. The streams are full of fish, the grazing is good, the game is plentiful, and the weather is fine. What more could you desire?"

The Indian drew himself up. His face grew eager, and his eyes were full of longing as he answered, by the interpreter:

"The land to the north and west is the land of plenty. There the buffalo grows larger, and his coat is darker. There the buy-yu (antelope) comes in droves, while here there are but few. There the whole region is covered with the short, curly grass our ponies like. There grow the wild plums that are good for my people in summer and winter. There are the springs of the Great Medicine Man, Tel-ya-ki-y. To bathe in them gives new life; to drink them cures every bodily ill.

"In the mountains beyond the river of the blue water there is gold and silver, the metals that the white man loves. There lives the eagle, whose feathers the Indian must have to make his war-bonnet. There, too, the sun shines always.

"It is the Ijis (heaven) of the red man. My heart cries for it. The hearts of my people are not happy when away from the Eithity Tugala."

The Indian folded his arms across his breast, and his eyes looked yearningly toward the country whose delights he had so vividly pictured; then he turned and walked sorrowfully away. The white man's government shut him out from the possession of his earthly paradise. Will learned upon further inquiry that Eithity Tugala was the Indian name of the Big Horn Basin.

In the summer of 1882 Will's party of exploration left the cars at Cheyenne, and struck out from this point with horses and pack-mules. Will's eyes becoming inflamed, he was obliged to bandage them, and turn the guidance of the party over to a man known as "Reddy." For days he traveled in a blinded state, and though his eyes slowly bettered, he did not remove the bandage until the Big Horn Basin was reached. They had paused for the midday siesta, and Reddy inquired whether it would not be safe to uncover the afflicted eyes, adding that he thought Will "would enjoy looking around a bit."

Off came the bandage, and I shall quote Will's own words to describe the scene that met his delighted gaze:

"To my right stretched a towering range of snow-capped mountains, broken here and there into minarets, obelisks, and spires. Between me and this range of lofty peaks a long irregular line of stately cottonwoods told me a stream wound its way beneath. The rainbow-tinted carpet under me was formed of innumerable brilliant-hued wild flowers; it spread about me in every direction, and sloped gracefully to the stream. Game of every kind played on the turf, and bright-hued birds flitted over it. It was a scene no mortal can satisfactorily describe. At such a moment a man, no matter what his creed, sees the hand of the mighty Maker of the universe majestically displayed in the beauty of nature; he becomes sensibly conscious, too, of his own littleness. I uttered no word for very awe; I looked upon one of nature's masterpieces.

"Instantly my heart went out to my sorrowful Arapahoe friend of 1875. He had not exaggerated; he had scarcely done the scene justice. He spoke of it as the Ijis, the heaven of the red man. I regarded it then, and still regard it, as the Mecca of all appreciative humanity."

To the west of the Big Horn Basin, Hart Mountain rises abruptly from the Shoshone River. It is covered with grassy slopes and deep ravines; perpendicular rocks of every hue rise in various places and are fringed with evergreens. Beyond this mountain, in the distance, towers the hoary head of Table Mountain. Five miles to the southwest the mountains recede some distance from the river, and from its bank Castle Rock rises in solitary grandeur. As its name indicates, it has the appearance of a castle, with towers, turrets, bastions, and balconies.

Grand as is the western view, the chief beauty lies to the south. Here the Carter Mountain lies along the entire distance, and the grassy spaces on its side furnish pasturage for the deer, antelope, and mountain sheep that abound in this favored region. Fine timber, too, grows on its rugged slopes; jagged, picturesque rock-forms are seen in all directions, and numerous cold springs send up their welcome nectar.

It is among the foothills nestling at the base of this mountain that Will has chosen the site of his future permanent residence. Here there are many little lakes, two of which are named Irma and Arta, in honor of his daughters. Here he owns a ranch of forty thousand acres, but the home proper will comprise a tract of four hundred and eighty acres. The two lakes referred to are in this tract, and near them Will proposes to erect a palatial residence. To him, as he has said, it is the Mecca of earth, and thither he hastens the moment he is free from duty and obligation. In that enchanted region he forgets for a little season the cares and responsibilities of life.

A curious legend is told of one of the lakes that lie on the border of this valley. It is small—half a mile long and a quarter wide—but its depth is fathomless. It is bordered and shadowed by tall and stately pines, quaking-asp and birch trees, and its waters are pure and ice-cold the year round. They are medicinal, too, and as yet almost unknown to white men. Will heard the legend of the lake from the lips of an old Cheyenne warrior.

"It was the custom of my tribe," said the Indian, "to assemble around this lake once every month, at the hour of midnight, when the moon is at its full. Soon after midnight a canoe filled with the specters of departed Cheyenne warriors shot out from the eastern side of the lake and crossed rapidly to the western border; there it suddenly disappeared.

"Never a word or sound escaped from the specters in the canoe. They sat rigid and silent, and swiftly plied their oars. All attempts to get a word from them were in vain.

"So plainly were the canoe and its occupants seen that the features of the warriors were readily distinguished, and relatives and friends were recognized."

For years, according to the legend, the regular monthly trip was made, and always from the eastern to the western border of the lake. In 1876 it suddenly ceased, and the Indians were much alarmed. A party of them camped on the bank of the lake, and watchers were appointed for every night. It was fancied that the ghostly boatman had changed the date of their excursion. But in three months there was no sign of canoe or canoeists, and this was regarded as an omen of evil.

At a council of the medicine men, chiefs, and wise-acres of the tribe it was decided that the canoeing trip had been a signal from the Great Spirit—the canoe had proceeded from east to west, the course always followed by the red man. The specters had been sent from the Happy Hunting-Grounds to indicate that the tribe should move farther west, and the sudden disappearance of the monthly signal was augured to mean the extinction of the race.

Once when Will was standing on the border of this lake a Sioux warrior came up to him. This man was unusually intelligent, and desired that his children should be educated. He sent his two sons to Carlisle, and himself took great pains to learn the white man's religious beliefs, though he still clung to his old savage customs and superstitions. A short time before he talked with Will large companies of Indians had made pilgrimages to join one large conclave, for the purpose of celebrating the Messiah, or "Ghost Dance." Like all religious celebrations among savage people, it was accompanied by the grossest excesses and most revolting immoralities. As it was not known what serious happening these large gatherings might portend, the President, at the request of many people, sent troops to disperse the Indians. The Indians resisted, and blood was spilled, among the slain being the sons of the Indian who stood by the side of the haunted lake.

"It is written in the Great Book of the white man," said the old chief to Will, "that the Great Spirit—the Nan-tan-in-chor—is to come to him again on earth. The white men in the big villages go to their council-lodges (churches) and talk about the time of his coming. Some say one time, some say another, but they all know the time will come, for it is written in the Great Book. It is to the great and good among the white men that go to these council-lodges, and those that do not go say, 'It is well; we believe as they believe; He will come.' It is written in the Great Book of the white man that all the human beings on earth are the children of the one Great Spirit. He provides and cares for them. All he asks in return is that his children obey him, that they be good to one another, that they judge not one another, and that they do not kill or steal. Have I spoken truly the words of the white man's Book?"

Will bowed his head, somewhat surprised at the tone of the old chief's conversation. The other continued:

"The red man, too, has a Great Book. You have never seen it; no white man has ever seen it; it is hidden here." He pressed his hand against his heart. "The teachings of the two books are the same. What the Great Spirit says to the white man, the Nan-tan-in-chor says to the red man. We, too, go to our council-lodges to talk of the second coming. We have our ceremony, as the white man has his. The white man is solemn, sorrowful; the red man is happy and glad. We dance and are joyful, and the white man sends soldiers to shoot us down. Does their Great Spirit tell them to do this?

"In the big city (Washington) where I have been, there is another big book (the Federal Constitution), which says the white man shall not interfere with the religious liberty of another. And yet they come out to our country and kill us when we show our joy to Nan-tan-in-chor.

"We rejoice over his second coming; the white man mourns, but he sends his soldiers to kill us in our rejoicing. Bah! The white man is false. I return to my people, and to the customs and habits of my forefathers. I am an Indian!"

The old chief strode away with the dignity of a red Cæsar, and Will, alone by the lake, reflected that every question has two sides to it. The one the red man has held in the case of the commonwealth versus the Indian has ever been the tragic side.

CHAPTER 26

Tour of Great Britain

It was not until the spring of 1883 that Will was able to put into execution his long-cherished plan—to present to the public an exhibition which should delineate in throbbing and realistic color, not only the wild life of America, but the actual history of the West, as it was lived for, fought for, died for, by Indians, pioneers, and soldiers.

The wigwam village; the Indian war-dance; the chant to the Great Spirit as it was sung over the plains; the rise and fall of the famous tribes; the "Forward, march!" of soldiers, and the building of frontier posts; the life of scouts and trappers; the hunt of the buffalo; the coming of the first settlers; their slow, perilous progress in the prairie schooners over the vast and desolate plains; the period of the Deadwood stage and the Pony Express; the making of homes in the face of fire and Indian massacre; United States cavalry on the firing-line, "Death to the Sioux!"—these are the great historic pictures of the Wild West, stirring, genuine, heroic.

It was a magnificent plan on a magnificent scale, and it achieved instant success. The adventurous phases of Western life never fail to quicken the pulse of the East.

An exhibition which embodied so much of the historic and picturesque, which resurrected a whole half-century of dead and dying events, events the most thrilling and dramatic in American history, naturally stirred up the interest of the entire country. The actors, too, were historic characters—no weakling imitators, but men of sand and grit, who had lived every inch of the life they pictured.

The first presentation was given in May, 1883, at Omaha, Nebraska, the state Will had chosen for his home. Since then it has visited nearly every large city on the civilized globe, and has been viewed by countless thousands—men, women, and children of every nationality. It will long hold a place in history.

The "grand entrance" alone has never failed to chain the interest of the onlooker. The furious galloping of the Indian braves—Sioux, Arapahoe, Brulé, and Cheyenne, all in war paint and feathers; the free dash of the Mexicans and cowboys, as they follow the Indians into line at break-neck speed; the black-bearded Cossacks of the Czar's light cavalry; the Riffian Arabs on their desert thoroughbreds; a cohort from the "Queen's Own" Lancers; troopers from the German Emperor's bodyguard; chasseurs and cuirassiers from the crack cavalry regiments of European standing armies; detachments from the United States cavalry and artillery; South American gauchos; Cuban veterans; Porto Ricans; Hawaiians; again frontiersmen, rough riders, Texas rangers—all plunging with dash and spirit into the open, each company followed by its chieftain and its flag; forming into a solid square, tremulous with color; then a quicker note of music; the galloping hoofs of another horse, the finest of them all, and "Buffalo Bill," riding with the wonderful ease and stately grace which only he who is "born to the saddle" can ever attain, enters under the flash of the lime-light, and sweeping off his sombrero, holds his head high, and with a ring of pride in his voice, advances before his great audience and exclaims:

"Ladies and Gentlemen, permit me to introduce to you a congress of the rough riders of the world."

As a child I wept over his disregard of the larger sphere

predicted by the soothsayer; as a woman, I rejoice that he was true to his own ideals, for he sits his horse with a natural grace much better suited to the saddle than to the Presidential chair.

From the very beginning the "Wild West" was an immense success. Three years were spent in traveling over the United States; then Will conceived the idea of visiting England, and exhibiting to the mother race the wild side of the child's life. This plan entailed enormous expense, but it was carried out successfully.

Still true to the state of his adoption, Will chartered the steamer "State of Nebraska," and on March 31, 1886, a living freight from the picturesque New World began its voyage to the Old.

At Gravesend, England, the first sight to meet the eyes of the watchers on the steamer was a tug flying American colors. Three ringing cheers saluted the beautiful emblem, and the band on the tug responded with "The Star-Spangled Banner." Not to be outdone, the cowboy band on the "State of Nebraska" struck up "Yankee Doodle." The tug had been chartered by a company of Englishmen for the purpose of welcoming the novel American combination to British soil.

When the landing was made, the members of the Wild West company entered special coaches and were whirled toward London. Then even the stolidity of the Indians was not proof against sights so little resembling those to which they had been accustomed, and they showed their pleasure and appreciation by frequent repetition of the red man's characteristic grunt.

Major John M. Burke had made the needed arrangements for housing the big show, and preparations on a gigantic scale were rapidly pushed to please an impatient London public. More effort was made to produce spectacular effects in the London amphitheater than is possible where a merely temporary staging is erected for one day's exhibition. The arena was a third of a mile in circumference, and provided accommodation for forty thousand spectators. Here, as at Manchester, where another great amphitheater was erected in the fall, to serve as winter quarters, the artist's brush was called on to furnish illusions.

The English exhibited an eager interest in every feature of the exhibition—the Indian war-dances, the bucking broncho, speedily subjected by the valorous cowboy, and the stagecoach attacked by Indians and rescued by United States troops. The Indian village on the plains was also an object of dramatic interest to the English public. The artist had counterfeited the plains successfully.

It is the hour of dawn. Scattered about the plains are various wild animals. Within their tents the Indians are sleeping. Sunrise, and a friendly Indian tribe comes to visit the wakening warriors. A friendly dance is executed, at the close of which a courier rushes in to announce the approach of a hostile tribe. These follow almost at the courier's heels, and a sham battle occurs, which affords a good idea of the barbarity of Indian warfare. The victors celebrate their triumphs with a wild war-dance.

A Puritan scene follows. The landing of the Pilgrims is shown, and the rescue of John Smith by Pocahontas. This affords opportunity for delineating many interesting Indian customs on festive celebrations, such as weddings and feast-days.

Again the prairie. A buffalo-lick is shown. The shaggy monsters come down to drink, and in pursuit of them is "Buffalo Bill," mounted on his good horse "Charlie." He has been acting as guide for an emigrant party, which soon appears. Campfires are lighted, supper is eaten, and the camp sinks into slumber with the dwindling of the

fires. Then comes a fine bit of stage illusion. A red glow is
seen in the distance, faint at first, but slowly deepening
and broadening. It creeps along the whole horizon, and
the camp is awakened by the alarming intelligence that
the prairie is on fire. The emigrants rush out, and hero-
ically seek to fight back the rushing, roaring flames.
Wild animals, driven by the flames, dash through the
camp, and a stampede follows. This scene was extremely
realistic.

A cyclone was also simulated, and a whole village
blown out of existence.

The "Wild West" was received with enthusiasm, not
only by the general public, but by royalty. Gladstone
made a call upon Will, in company with the Marquis of
Lorne, and in return a lunch was tendered to the "Grand
Old Man" by the American visitors. In an after-dinner
speech, the English statesman spoke in the warmest
terms of America. He thanked Will for the good he was
doing in presenting to the English public a picture of the
wild life of the Western continent, which served to illustrate the difficulties encountered by a sister nation in its
onward march of civilization.

The initial performance was before a royal party, com-
prising the Prince and Princess of Wales and suite. At the
close of the exhibition the royal guests, at their own request, were presented to the members of the company.
Unprepared for this contingency, Will had forgotten to
coach the performers in the correct method of saluting
royalty, and when the girl shots of the company were presented to the Princess of Wales, they stepped forward in
true democratic fashion and cordially offered their hands
to the lovely woman who had honored them.

According to English usage, the Princess extends the
hand, palm down, to favored guests, and these rever-
ently touch the finger-tips and lift the hand to their lips.

Perhaps the spontaneity of the American girls' welcome was esteemed a pleasing variety to the established custom. At all events, her Highness, true to her breeding, appeared not to notice any breach of etiquette, but took the proffered hands and shook them cordially.

The Indian camp was also visited, and Red Shirt, the great chief, was, like every one else, delighted with the Princess. Through an interpreter the Prince expressed his pleasure over the performance of the braves, headed by their great chief, and the Princess bade him welcome to England. Red Shirt had the Indian gift of oratory, and he replied, in the unimpassioned speech for which the race is noted, that it made his heart glad to hear such kind words from the Great White Chief and his beautiful squaw.

During the round the Prince stopped in at Will's private quarters, and took much interest in his souvenirs, being especially pleased with a magnificent gold-hilted sword, presented to Will by officers of the United States army in recognition of his services as scout.

This was not the only time the exhibition was honored by the visit of royalty. That the Prince of Wales was sincere in his expression of enjoyment of the exhibition was evidenced by the report that he carried to his mother, and shortly afterward a command came from Queen Victoria that the big show appear before her. It was plainly impossible to take the "Wild West" to court; the next best thing was to construct a special box for the use of her Majesty. This box was placed upon a dais covered with crimson velvet trimmings, and was superbly decorated. When the Queen arrived and was driven around to the royal box, Will stepped forward as she dismounted, and doffing his sombrero, made a low courtesy to the sovereign lady of Great Britain. "Welcome, your Majesty," said he, "to the Wild West of America!"

One of the first acts in the performance is to carry the flag to the front. This is done by a soldier, and is introduced to the spectators as an emblem of a nation desirous of peace and friendship with all the world. On this occasion it was borne directly before the Queen's box, and dipped three times in honor of her Majesty. The action of the Queen surprised the company and the vast throng of spectators. Rising, she saluted the American flag with a bow, and her suite followed her example, the gentleman removing their hats. Will acknowledged the courtesy by waving his sombrero about his head, and his delighted company with one accord gave three ringing cheers that made the arena echo, assuring the spectators of the healthy condition of the lungs of the American visitors.

The Queen's complaisance put the entire company on their mettle, and the performance was given magnificently. At the close Queen Victoria asked to have Will presented to her, and paid him so many compliments as almost to bring a blush to his bronzed cheek. Red Shirt was also presented, and informed her Majesty that he had come across the Great Water solely to see her, and his heart was glad. This polite speech discovered a streak in Indian nature that, properly cultivated, would fit the red man to shine as a courtier or politician. Red Shirt walked away with the insouciance of a king dismissing an audience, and some of the squaws came to display papooses to the Great White Lady. These children of nature were not the least awed by the honor done them. They blinked at her Majesty as if the presence of queens was an incident of their everyday existence.

A second command from the Queen resulted in another exhibition before a number of her royal guests. The kings of Saxony, Denmark, and Greece, the Queen of the Belgians, and the Crown Prince of Austria, with others of lesser rank, illumined this occasion.

The Deadwood coach was peculiarly honored. This is a coach with a history. It was built in Concord, New Hampshire, and sent to the Pacific Coast to run over a trail infested by road agents. A number of times was it held up and the passengers robbed, and finally both driver and passengers were killed and the coach abandoned on the trail, as no one could be found who would undertake to drive it. It remained derelict for a long time, but was at last brought into San Francisco by an old stagedriver and placed on the Overland trail. It gradually worked its way eastward to the Deadwood route, and on this line figured in a number of encounters with Indians. Again were driver and passengers massacred, and again was the coach abandoned. Will ran across it on one of his scouting expeditions, and recognizing its value as an adjunct to his exhibition, purchased it. Thereafter the tragedies it figured in were of the mock variety.

One of the incidents of the Wild West, as all remember, is an Indian attack on the Deadwood coach. The royal visitors wished to put themselves in the place of the traveling public in the Western regions of America; so the four potentates of Denmark, Saxony, Greece, and Austria became the passengers, and the Prince of Wales sat on the box with Will. The Indians had been secretly instructed to "whoop 'em up" on this interesting occasion, and they followed energetically the letter of their instructions. The coach was surrounded by a demoniac band, and the blank cartridges were discharged in such close proximity to the coach windows that the passengers could easily imagine themselves to be actual Western travelers. Rumor hath it that they sought refuge under the seats, and probably no one would blame them if they did; but it is only a rumor, and not history.

When the wild ride was over, the Prince of Wales, who

admires the American national game of poker, turned to
the driver with the remark:

"Colonel, did you ever hold four kings like that before?"

"I have held four kings more than once," was the
prompt reply; "but, your Highness, I never held four kings
and the royal joker before."

The Prince laughed heartily; but Will's sympathy went
out to him when he found that he was obliged to explain
his joke in four different languages to the passengers.

In recognition of this performance, the Prince of Wales
sent Will a handsome souvenir. It consisted of his feathered crest, outlined in diamonds, and bearing the motto
"Ich dien" worked in jewels underneath. An accompanying note expressed the pleasure of the royal visitors over
the novel exhibition.

Upon another occasion the Princess of Wales visited
the show incognito, first advising Will of her intention;
and at the close of the performance assured him that she
had spent a delightful evening.

The set performances of the "Wild West" were punctuated by social entertainments. James G. Blaine, Chauncey
M. Depew, Murat Halsted, and other prominent Americans were in London at the time, and in their honor Will
issued invitations to a rib-roast breakfast prepared in Indian style. Fully one hundred guests gathered in the "Wild
West's" dining-tent at nine o'clock of June 10, 1887. Besides the novel decorations of the tent, it was interesting
to watch the Indian cooks putting the finishing touches to
their roasts. A hole had been dug in the ground, a large
tripod erected over it, and upon this the ribs of beef were
suspended. The fire was of logs, burned down to a bed of
glowing coals, and over these the meat was turned
around and around until it was cooked to a nicety. This

method of open-air cooking over wood imparts to the meat a flavor that can be given to it in no other way.

The breakfast was unconventional. Part of the bill of fare was hominy, "Wild West" pudding, popcorn, and peanuts. The Indians squatted on the straw at the end of the dining-tables, and ate from their fingers or spread the meat with long white sticks. The striking contrast of table manners was an interesting object-lesson in the progress of civilization.

The breakfast was a novelty to the Americans who par-took of it, and they enjoyed it thoroughly.

Will was made a social lion during his stay in London, being dined and fêted upon various occasions. Only a man of the most rugged health could have endured the strain of his daily performances united with his social obligations.

The London season was triumphantly closed with a meeting for the establishment of a court of arbitration to settle disputes between America and England.

After leaving the English metropolis the exhibition visited Birmingham, and thence proceeded to its winter headquarters in Manchester. Arta, Will's elder daughter, accompanied him to England, and made a Continental tour during the winter.

The sojourn in Manchester was another ovation. The prominent men of the city proposed to present to Will a fine rifle, and when the news of the plan was carried to London, a company of noblemen, statesmen, and journalists ran down to Manchester by special car. In acknowledgment of the honor done him, Will issued invitations for another of his unique American entertainments. Boston pork and beans, Maryland fried chicken, hominy, and popcorn were served, and there were other distinctly American dishes. An Indian rib-roast was served on tin plates, and the distinguished guests enjoyed—or said they did—the novelty of eating it from their fingers, in true aboriginal fashion. This remarkable meal evoked the heartiest of toasts to the American flag, and a poem, a parody on "Hiawatha," added luster to the occasion.

The Prince of Wales was Grand Master of the Free Masons of England, which order presented a gold watch to Will during his stay in Manchester. The last performance in this city was given on May 1, 1887, and as a good-by to Will the spectators united in a rousing chorus of "For he's a jolly good fellow!" The closing exhibition of the English season occurred at Hull, and immediately afterward the company sailed for home on the "Persian Monarch." An immense crowd gathered on the quay, and shouted a cordial "bon voyage."

One sad event occurred on the homeward voyage, the death of "Old Charlie," Will's gallant and faithful horse. He was a half-blood Kentucky horse, and had been Will's constant and unfailing companion for many years on the plains and in the "Wild West."

He was an animal of almost human intelligence, extraordinary speed, endurance, and fidelity. When he was quite young Will rode him on a hunt for wild horses, which he ran down after a chase of fifteen miles. At another time, on a wager of five hundred dollars that he could ride him over the prairie one hundred miles in ten hours, he went the distance in nine hours and forty-five minutes.

When the "Wild West" was opened at Omaha, Charlie was the star horse, and held that position at all the exhibitions in this country and Europe. In London the horse attracted a full share of attention, and many scions of royalty solicited the favor of riding him. Grand Duke Michael of Russia rode Charlie several times in chase of the herd of buffaloes in the "Wild West," and became quite attached to him.

On the morning of the 14th Will made his usual visit to Charlie, between decks. Shortly after the groom reported him sick. He grew rapidly worse, in spite of all the care he received, and at two o'clock on the morning of the 17th he died. His death cast an air of sadness over the whole ship, and no human being could have had more sincere mourners than the faithful and sagacious old horse. He was brought on deck wrapped in canvas and covered with the American flag. When the hour for the ocean burial arrived, the members of the company and others assembled on deck. Standing alone with uncovered head beside the dead was the one whose life the noble animal had shared so long. At length, with choking utterance, Will spoke, and Charlie for the first time failed to hear the familiar voice he had always been so prompt to obey:

"Old fellow, your journeys are over. Here in the ocean you must rest. Would that I could take you back and lay you down beneath the billows of that prairie you and I have loved so well and roamed so freely; but it cannot be. How often at break of day, the glorious sun rising on the horizon has found us far from human habitation! Yet, obedient to my call, gladly you bore your burden on, little heeding what the day might bring, so that you and I but shared its sorrows and pleasures alike. You have never failed me. Ah, Charlie, old fellow, I have had many friends, but few of whom I could say that. Rest entombed in the deep bosom of the ocean! I'll never forget you. I loved you as you loved me, my dear old Charlie. Men tell me you have no soul; but if there be a heaven, and scouts can enter there, I'll wait at the gate for you, old friend."

On this homeward trip, Will made the acquaintance of

a clergyman returning from a vacation spent in Europe.
When they neared the American coast this gentleman prepared a telegram to send to his congregation. It read simply:
"2 John i. 12." Chancing to see it, Will's interest was
aroused, and he asked the clergyman to explain the significance of the reference, and when this was done he said: "I
have a religious sister at home who knows the Bible so well
that I will wire her that message and she will not need to
look up the meaning."

He duplicated to me, as his return greeting, the minister's telegram to his congregation, but I did not justify his
high opinion of my Biblical knowledge. I was obliged to
search the Scriptures to unravel the enigma. As there may
be others like me, but who have not the incentive I had
to look up the reference, I quote from God's word the
message I received: "Having many things to write unto
you, I would not write with paper and ink; but I trust to
come unto you, and speak face to face, that our joy may
be full."

CHAPTER 27

Return of the "Wild West" to America

When the "Wild West" returned to America from its first venture across seas, the sail up the harbor was described by the New York *World* in the following words:

"The harbor probably has never witnessed a more picturesque scene than that of yesterday, when the 'Persian Monarch' steamed up from quarantine. Buffalo Bill stood on the captain's bridge, his tall and striking figure clearly outlined, and his long hair waving in the wind; the gayly painted and blanketed Indians leaned over the ship's rail; the flags of all nations fluttered from the masts and connecting cables. The cowboy band played 'Yankee Doodle' with a vim and enthusiasm which faintly indicated the joy felt by everybody connected with the 'Wild West' over the sight of home."

Will had been cordially welcomed by our English cousins, and had been the recipient of many social favors, but no amount of foreign flattery could change him one hair from an "American of the Americans," and he experienced a thrill of delight as he again stepped foot upon his native land. Shortly afterward he was much pleased by a letter from William T. Sherman—so greatly prized that it was framed, and now hangs on the wall of his Nebraska home. Following is a copy:

"FIFTH AVENUE HOTEL, NEW YORK.

"COLONEL WM. F. CODY:

"*Dear Sir:* In common with all your countrymen, I want to let you know that I am not only gratified but proud of your management and success. So far as I can make out, you have been modest, graceful, and dignified in all you have done to illustrate the history of civilization on this continent during the past century. I am especially pleased with the compliment paid you by the Prince of Wales, who rode with you in the Deadwood coach while it was attacked by Indians and rescued by cowboys. Such things did occur in our days, but they never will again.

"As nearly as I can estimate, there were in 1865 about nine and one-half million of buffaloes on the plains between the Missouri River and the Rocky Mountains; all are now gone, killed for their meat, their skins, and their bones. This seems like desecration, cruelty, and murder, yet they have been replaced by twice as many cattle. At that date there were about 165,000 Pawnees, Sioux, Cheyennes, and Arapahoes, who depended upon these buffaloes for their yearly food. They, too, have gone, but they have been replaced by twice or thrice as many white men and women, who have made the earth to blossom as the rose, and who can be counted, taxed, and governed by the laws of nature and the civilization. This change has been salutary, and will go on to the end. You have caught one epoch of this country's history, and have illustrated it in the very heart of the modern world— London, and I want you to feel that on this side of the water we appreciate it.

"This drama must end; days, years, and centuries follow fast; even the drama of civilization must have an end. All I aim to accomplish on this sheet of paper is to assure you that I fully recognize your work. The presence of the Queen, the beautiful Princess of Wales, the Prince, and the British public are marks of favor which reflect back on America sparks of light which illuminate many a house and cabin in the land where once you guided me honestly and faithfully, in 1865–66, from Fort Riley to Kearny, in Kansas and Nebraska.

"Sincerely your friend,

"W. T. SHERMAN."

Having demonstrated to his satisfaction that the largest measure of success lay in a stationary exhibition of his show, where the population was large enough to warrant it, Will purchased a tract of land on Staten Island, and here he landed on his return from England. Teamsters for miles around had been engaged to transport the outfit across the Island to Erastina, the site chosen for the exhibition. And you may be certain that Cut Meat, American Bear, Flat Iron, and the other Indians furnished unlimited joy to the ubiquitous small boy, who was present by the hundreds to watch the unloading scenes.

The summer season at this point was a great success. One incident connected with it may be worth relating.

Teachers everywhere have recognized the value of the "Wild West" exhibition as an educator, and in a number of instances public schools have been dismissed to afford the children an opportunity of attending the entertainment. It has not, however, been generally recognized as a spur to religious progress, yet, while at Staten Island, Will was invited to exhibit a band of his Indians at a missionary meeting given under the auspices of a large mission Sunday-school. He appeared with his warriors, who were expected to give one of their religious dances as an object-lesson in devotional ceremonials.

The meeting was largely attended, and every one, children especially, waited for the exercises in excited curiosity and interest. Will sat on the platform with the superintendent, pastor, and others in authority, and close by sat the band of stolid-faced Indians.

The service began with a hymn and the reading of the Scriptures; then, to Will's horror, the superintendent requested him to lead the meeting in prayer. Perhaps the good man fancied that Will for a score of years had fought Indians with a rifle in one hand and a prayer-book in the other, and was as prepared to pray as to shoot. At least he surely did not make his request with the thought of embarrassing Will, though that was the natural result. However, Will held holy things in deepest reverence; he had the spirit of Gospel if not the letter; so, rising, he quietly and simply, with bowed head, repeated the Lord's Prayer.

A winter exhibition under roof was given in New York, after which the show made a tour of the principal cities of the United States. Thus passed several years, and then arrangements were made for a grand Continental trip. A plan had been maturing in Will's mind ever since the British season, and in the spring of 1889, it was carried into effect.

The steamer "Persian Monarch" was again chartered, and this time its prow was turned toward the shores of France. Paris was the destination, and seven months were passed in the gay capital. The Parisians received the show with as much enthusiasm as did the Londoners, and in Paris as well as in the English metropolis everything American became a fad during the stay of the "Wild West." Even American books were read—a crucial test of faddism; and American curios were displayed in all the shops. Relics from American plain and mountain—buffalo-robes, bearskins, buckskin suits embroidered with porcupine quills, Indian blankets, woven mats, bows and arrows, bead-mats, Mexican bridles and saddles—sold like the proverbial hot cakes.

In Paris, also, Will became a social favorite, and had he accepted a tenth of the invitations to receptions, dinners, and balls showered upon him, he would have been obliged to close his show.

While in this city Will accepted an invitation from Rose Bonheur to visit her at her superb chatêau, and in return for the honor he extended to her the freedom of the stables, which contained magnificent horses used for transportation purposes, and which never appeared in the public performance—Percherons, of the breed depicted by the famous artist in her well-known painting of "The Horse Fair." Day upon day she visited the camp and made studies, and as a token of her appreciation of the courtesy, painted a picture of Will mounted on his favorite horse, both horse and rider bedecked with frontier paraphernalia. This souvenir, which holds the place of honor in his collection, he immediately shipped home.

The wife of a London embassy attaché relates the following story:

"During the time that Colonel Cody was making his triumphant tour of Europe, I was one night seated at a banquet next to the Belgian Consul. Early in the course of the conversation he asked:

"'Madame, you haf undoubted been to see ze gr-rand Bouf-falo Beel?'

"Puzzled by the apparently unfamiliar name, I asked:

"'Pardon me, but whom did you say?'

"'Vy, Bouf-falo Beel, ze famous Bouf-falo Beel, zat gr-reat countryman of yours. You must know him.'

"After a moment's thought, I recognized the well-known showman's name in its disguise. I comprehended that the good Belgian thought his to be one of America's most eminent names, to be mentioned in the same breath with Washington and Lincoln."

After leaving Paris, a short tour of Southern France was made, and at Marseilles a vessel was chartered to transport the company to Spain. The Spanish grandees eschewed their favorite amusement—the bull-fight—long enough to give a hearty welcome to the "Wild West." Next followed a tour of Italy; and the visit to Rome was the most interesting of the experiences in this country.

The Americans reached the Eternal City at the time of Pope Leo's anniversary celebration, and, on the Pope's invitation Will visited the Vatican. Its historic walls have rarely, if ever, looked upon a more curious sight than was presented when Will walked in, followed by the cowboys in their buckskins and sombreros and the Indians in war paint and feathers. Around them crowded a motley throng of Italians, clad in the brilliant colors so loved by these children of the South, and nearly every nationality was represented in the assemblage.

Some of the cowboys and Indians had been reared in the Catholic faith, and when the Pope appeared they knelt for his blessing. He seemed touched by this action on the part of those whom he might be disposed to regard as savages, and, bending forward, extended his hands and pronounced a benediction; then he passed on, and it was with the greatest difficulty that the Indians were restrained from expressing their emotions in a wild whoop. This, no doubt, would have relieved them, but it would, in all probability, have stampeded the crowd.

When the Pope reached Will he looked admiringly upon the frontiersman. The world-known scout bent his head before the aged "Medicine Man," as the Indians call his reverence, the Papal blessing was again bestowed, and the procession passed on. The Thanksgiving Mass,

with its fine choral accompaniment, was given, and the
vast concourse of people poured out of the building.

This visit attracted much attention.

"I'll take my stalwart Indian braves
　　Down to the Coliseum,
And the old Romans from their graves
　　Will all arise to see 'em.
Prætors and censors will return
　　And hasten through the Forum;
The ghostly Senate will adjourn,
　　Because it lacks a quorum.

"And up the ancient Appian Way
　　Will flock the ghostly legions,
From Gaul unto Calabria,
　　And from remoter regions;
From British bay and wild lagoon,
　　And Libyan desert sandy,
They'll all come marching to the tune
　　Of 'Yankee Doodle Dandy.'

"Prepare triumphal cars for me,
　　And purple thrones to sit on,
For I've done more than Julius C.—
　　He could not down the Briton!
Cæsar and Cicero shall bow,
　　And ancient warriors famous,
Before the myrtle-wreathed brow
　　Of Buffalo Williamus.

"We marched, unwhipped, through history—
　　No bulwark can detain us—
And link the age of Grover C.

And Scipio Africanus.
I'll take my stalwart Indian braves
    Down to the Coliseum,
And the old Romans from their graves
    Will all arise to see 'em."

It may be mentioned in passing that Will had visited the Coliseum with an eye to securing it as an amphitheater for the "Wild West" exhibition, but the historic ruin was too dilapidated to be a safe arena for such a purpose, and the idea was abandoned.

The sojourn in Rome was enlivened by an incident that created much interest among the natives. The Italians were somewhat skeptical as to the abilities of the cowboys to tame wild horses, believing the bronchos in the show were specially trained for their work, and that the horse-breaking was a mock exhibition.

The Prince of Sermonetta declared that he had some wild horses in his stud which no cowboys in the world could ride. The challenge was promptly taken up by the daring riders of the plains, and the Prince sent for his wild steeds. That they might not run amuck and injure the spectators, specially prepared booths of great strength were erected.

The greatest interest and enthusiasm were manifested by the populace, and the death of two or three members of the company was as confidently looked for as was the demise of sundry gladiators in the "brave days of old."

But the cowboys laughed at so great a fuss over so small a matter, and when the horses were driven into the arena, and the spectators held their breath, the cowboys, lassos in hand, awaited the work with the utmost nonchalance.

The wild equines sprang into the air, darted hither and thither, and fought hard against their certain fate, but in less time than would be required to give the details, the cowboys had flung their lassos, caught the horses, and saddled and mounted them. The spirited beasts still resisted, and sought in every way to throw their riders, but the experienced plainsmen had them under control in a very short time; and as they rode them around the arena, the spectators rose and howled with delight. The display of horsemanship effectually silenced the skeptics; it captured the Roman heart, and the remainder of the stay in the city was attended by unusual enthusiasm.

Beautiful Florence, practical Bologna, and stately Milan, with its many-spired cathedral, were next on the list for the triumphal march. For the Venetian public the exhibition had to be given at Verona, in the historic amphitheater built by Diocletian, A. D. 290. This is the largest building in the world, and within the walls of this representative of Old World civilization the difficulties over which New World civilization had triumphed were portrayed. Here met the old and new; hoary antiquity and bounding youth kissed each other under the sunny Italian skies.

The "Wild West" now moved northward, through the Tyrol, to Munich, and from here the Americans digressed for an excursion on the "beautiful blue Danube." Then followed a successful tour of Germany.

During this Continental circuit Will's elder daughter, Arta, who had accompanied him on his British expedition, was married. It was impossible for the father to be present, but by cablegram he sent his congratulations and check.

CHAPTER 28

A Tribute to General Miles

In view of the success achieved by my brother, it is remarkable that he excited so little envy. Now for the first time in his life he felt the breath of slander on his cheek, and it flushed hotly. From an idle remark that the Indians in the "Wild West" exhibition were not properly treated, the idle gossip grew to the proportion of malicious and insistent slander. The Indians being government wards, such a charge might easily become a serious matter; for, like the man who beat his wife, the government believes it has the right to maltreat the red man to the top of its bent, but that no one else shall be allowed to do so.

A winter campaign of the "Wild West" had been contemplated, but the project was abandoned and winter quarters decided on. In the quaint little village of Benfield was an ancient nunnery and a castle, with good stables. Here Will left the company in charge of his partner, Mr. Nate Salisbury, and, accompanied by the Indians for whose welfare he was responsible, set sail for America, to silence his calumniators.

The testimony of the red men themselves was all that was required to refute the notorious untruths. Few had placed any belief in the reports, and friendly commenters were also active.

As the sequel proved, Will came home very opportunely. The Sioux in Dakota were again on the war-path, and his help was needed to subdue the uprising. He disbanded the warriors he had brought back from Europe, and each returned to his own tribe and people, to narrate around the camp-fire the wonders of the life abroad, while Will reported at headquarters to offer his services for the war. Two years previously he had been honored by the commission of Brigadier-General of the Nebraska National Guard, which rank and title were given to him by Governor Thayer.

The officer in command of the Indian campaign was General Nelson A. Miles, who has rendered so many important services to his country, and who, as Commander-in-Chief of our army, played so large a part in the recent war with Spain. At the time of the Indian uprising he held the rank of Brigadier-General.

This brilliant and able officer was much pleased when he learned that he would have Will's assistance in conducting the campaign, for he knew the value of his good judgment, cool head, and executive ability, and of his large experience in dealing with Indians.

The "Wild West," which had served as an educator to the people of Europe in presenting the frontier life of America, had quietly worked as important educational influences in the minds of the Indians connected with the exhibition. They had seen for themselves the wonders of the world's civilization; they realized how futile were the efforts of the children of the plains to stem the resistless tide of progress flowing westward. Potentates had delighted to do honor to Pa-has-ka, the Long-haired Chief, and in the eyes of the simple savage he was as powerful as any of the great ones of earth. To him his word was law; it seemed worse than folly for their brethren to attempt to cope with so mighty a chief, therefore their influence was all for peace; and the fact that so many tribes did not join in the uprising may be attributed, in part, to their good counsel and advice.

General Miles was both able and energetic, and managed the campaign in masterly fashion. There were one or two hard-fought battles, in one of which the great Sioux warrior, Sitting Bull, the ablest that nation ever produced, was slain. This Indian had traveled with Will for a time, but could not be weaned from his loyalty to his own tribe and a desire to avenge upon the white man the wrongs inflicted on his people.

What promised at the outset to be a long and cruel frontier war was speedily quelled. The death of Sitting Bull had something to do with the termination of hostilities. Arrangements for peace were soon perfected, and Will attributed the government's success to the energy of its officer in command, for whom he had a most enthusiastic admiration. He paid this tribute to him recently:

"I have been in many campaigns with General Miles, and a better general and more gifted warrior I have never seen. I served in the Civil War, and in any number of Indian wars; I have been under at least a dozen generals, with whom I have been thrown in close contact because of the nature of the services which I was called upon to render. General Miles is the superior of them all.

"I have known Phil Sheridan, Tecumseh Sherman, Hancock, and all of our noted Indian fighters. For cool judgment and thorough knowledge of all that pertains to military affairs, none of them, in my opinion, can be said to excel General Nelson A. Miles.

"Ah, what a man he is! I know. We have been shoulder to shoulder in many a hard march. We have been together when men find out what their comrades really are. He is a man, every inch of him, and the best general I ever served under."

After Miles was put in command of the forces, a dinner was given in his honor by John Chamberlin. Will was a guest and one of the speakers, and took the opportunity to eulogize his old friend. He dwelt at length on the respect in which the red men held the general, and in closing said:

"No foreign invader will ever set foot on these shores as long as General Miles is at the head of the army. If they should—just call on me!"

The speaker sat down amid laughter and applause.

While Will was away at the seat of war, his beautiful home in North Platte, "Welcome Wigwam," burned to the ground. The little city is not equipped with much of a fire department, but a volunteer brigade held the flames in check long enough to save almost the entire contents of the house, among which were many valuable and costly souvenirs that could never be replaced.

Will received a telegram announcing that his house was ablaze, and his reply was characteristic:

"Save Rosa Bonheur's picture, and the house may go to blazes."

When the frontier war was ended and the troops disbanded, Will made application for another company of Indians to take back to Europe with him. Permission was obtained from the government, and the contingent from the friendly tribes was headed by chiefs named Long Wolf, No Neck, Yankton Charlie, and Black Heart. In addition to these, a company was recruited from among the Indians held as hostages by General Miles at Fort Sheridan, and the leaders of these hostile braves were such noted chiefs as Short Bull, Kicking Bear, Lone Bull, Scatter, and Revenge. To these the trip to Alsace-Lorraine was a revelation, a fairy-tale more wonderful than anything in their legendary lore. The ocean voyage, with its seasickness, put them in an ugly mood, but the sight of the encampment and the cowboys dissipated their sullenness, and they shortly felt at home. The hospitality extended to all the members of the company by the inhabitants of the village in which they wintered was most cordial, and left them the pleasantest of memories.

An extended tour of Europe was fittingly closed by a brief visit to England. The Britons gave the "Wild West" as hearty a welcome as if it were native to their heath. A number of the larger cities were visited, London being reserved for the last.

Royalty again honored the "Wild West" by its attendance, the Queen requesting a special performance on the grounds of Windsor Castle. The requests of the Queen are equivalent to commands, and the entertainment was duly given. As a token of her appreciation the Queen bestowed upon Will a costly and beautiful souvenir.

Not the least-esteemed remembrance of this London visit was an illuminated address presented by the English Workingman's Convention. In it the American plainsman was congratulated upon the honors he had won, the success he had achieved, and the educational worth of his great exhibition. A banquet followed, at which Will presented an autograph photograph to each member of the association.

Notwithstanding tender thoughts of home, English soil was left regretfully. To the "Wild West" the complacent Briton had extended a cordial welcome, and manifested an enthusiasm that contrasted strangely with his usual disdain for things American.

A singular coincidence of the homeward voyage was the death of Billy, another favorite horse of Will's.

CHAPTER 29

The "Wild West" at the World's Fair

European army officers of all nationalities regarded my brother with admiring interest. To German, French, Italian, or British eyes he was a commanding personality, and also the representative of a peculiar and interesting phase of New World life. Recalling their interest in his scenes from his native land, so unlike anything to be found in Europe to-day, Will invited a number of these officers to accompany him on an extended hunting-trip through Western America.

All that could possibly do so accepted the invitation. A date was set for them to reach Chicago, and from there arrangements were made for a special train to convey them to Nebraska.

When the party gathered, several prominent Americans were of the number. By General Miles's order a military escort attended them from Chicago, and the native soldiery remained with them until North Platte was reached.

Then the party proceeded to "Scout's Rest Ranch," where they were hospitably entertained for a couple of days before starting out on their long trail.

At Denver ammunition and supplies were taken on board the train. A French chef was also engaged, as Will feared his distinguished guests might not enjoy camp-fare. But a hen in water is no more out of place than a French cook on a "roughing-it" trip. Frontier cooks, who understand primitive methods, make no attempts at a fashionable cuisine, and the appetites developed by open-air life are equal to the rudest, most substantial fare.

Colorado Springs, the Garden of the Gods, and other places in Colorado were visited. The foreign visitors had heard stories of this wonderland of America, but, like all of nature's masterpieces, the rugged beauties of this magnificent region defy an adequate description. Only one who has seen a sunrise on the Alps can appreciate it. The storied Rhine is naught but a story to him who has never looked upon it. Niagara is only a waterfall until seen from various viewpoints, and its tremendous force and transcendent beauty are strikingly revealed. The same is true of the glorious wildness of our Western scenery; it must be seen to be appreciated.

The most beautiful thing about the Garden of the Gods is the entrance known as the Gateway. Color here runs riot. The mass of rock in the foreground is white, and stands out in sharp contrast to the rich red of the sandstone of the portals, which rise on either side to a height of three hundred feet. Through these giant portals, which in the sunlight glow with ruddy fire, is seen mass upon mass of gorgeous color, rendered more striking by the dazzling whiteness of Pike's Peak, which soars upward in the distance, a hoary sentinel of the skies. The whole picture is limned against the brilliant blue of the Colorado sky, and stands out sharp and clear, one vivid block of color distinctly defined against the other.

The name "Garden of the Gods" was doubtless applied because of the peculiar shape of the spires, needles, and basilicas of rock that rise in every direction. These have been corroded by storms and worn smooth by time, until they present the appearance of half-baked images of clay molded by human hands, instead of sandstone rocks fashioned by wind and weather. Each grotesque and fantastic shape has received a name. One is here introduced to the "Washerwoman," the "Lady of the Garden," the "Siamese Twins," and the "Ute God," and besides these may be seen the "Wreck," the "Baggage Room," the "Eagle," and the "Mushroom." The predominating tone is everywhere red, but black, brown, drab, white, yellow, buff, and pink rocks add their quota to make up a harmonious and striking color scheme, to which the gray and green of clinging mosses add a final touch of picturesqueness.

At Flagstaff, Arizona, the train was discarded for the saddle and the buckboard. And now Will felt himself quite in his element; it was a never-failing pleasure to him to guide a large party of guests over plain and mountain. From long experience he knew how to make ample provision for their comfort. There were a number of wagons filled with supplies, three buckboards, three ambulances, and a drove of ponies. Those who wished to ride horseback could do so; if they grew tired of a bucking broncho, opportunity for rest awaited them in ambulance or buckboard. The French chef found his occupation gone when it was a question of cooking over a camp-fire; so he spent his time picking himself up when dislodged by his broncho. The daintiness of his menu was not a correct gauge for the daintiness of his language on these numerous occasions.

Through the Grand Cañon of the Colorado Will led the party, and the dwellers of the Old World beheld some of the rugged magnificence of the New. Across rushing rivers, through quiet valleys, and over lofty mountains they proceeded, pausing on the borders of peaceful lakes, or looking over dizzy precipices into yawning chasms.

There was no lack of game to furnish variety to their table; mountain sheep, mountain lions, wildcats, deer, elk, antelope, and even coyotes and porcupines, were shot, while the rivers furnished an abundance of fish.

It seemed likely at one time that there might be a hunt of bigger game than any here mentioned, for in crossing the country of the Navajos the party was watched and followed by mounted Indians. An attack was feared, and had the red men opened fire, there would have been a very animated defense; but the suspicious Indians were merely on the alert to see that no trespass was committed, and when the orderly company passed out of their territory the warriors disappeared.

The visitors were much impressed with the vastness and the undeveloped resources of our country. They were also impressed with the climate, as the thermometer went down to forty degrees below zero while they were on Buckskin Mountain. Nature seemed to wish to aid Will in the effort to exhibit novelties to his foreign guests, for she tried her hand at some spectacular effects, and succeeded beyond mortal expectation. She treated them to a few blizzards; and shut in by the mass of whirling, blinding snowflakes, it is possible their thoughts reverted with a homesick longing to the sunny slopes of France, the placid vales of Germany, or the foggy mildness of Great Britain.

On the summit of San Francisco Mountain, the horse of Major St. John Mildmay lost its footing, and began to slip on the ice toward a precipice which looked down a couple of thousand feet. Will saw the danger, brought out his ever-ready lasso, and dexterously caught the animal in time to save it and its rider—a feat considered remarkable by the onlookers.

Accidents happened occasionally, many adventures were met with, Indian alarms were given, and narrow were some of the escapes. On the whole, it was a remarkable trail, and was written about under the heading, "A Thousand Miles in the Saddle with Buffalo Bill."

At Salt Lake City the party broke up, each going his

separate way. All expressed great pleasure in the trip, and united in the opinion that Buffalo Bill's reputation as guide and scout was a well-deserved one.

Will's knowledge of Indian nature stands him in good stead when he desires to select the quota of Indians for the summer season of the "Wild West." He sends word ahead to the tribe or reservation which he intends to visit. The red men have all heard of the wonders of the great show; they are more than ready to share in the delights of travel and they gather at the appointed place in great numbers.

Will stands on a temporary platform in the center of the group. He looks around upon the swarthy faces, glowing with all the eagerness which the stolid Indian nature will permit them to display. It is not always the tallest nor the most comely men who are selected. The unerring judgment of the scout, trained in Indian warfare, tells him who may be relied upon and who are untrustworthy. A face arrests his attention—with a motion of his hand he indicates the brave whom he has selected; another wave of the hand and the fate of a second warrior is settled. Hardly a word is spoken, and it is only a matter of a few moments' time before he is ready to step down from his exalted position and walk off with his full contingent of warriors following happily in his wake.

The "Wild West" had already engaged space just outside the World's Fair grounds for an exhibit in 1893, and Will was desirous of introducing some new and striking feature. He had succeeded in presenting to the people of Europe some new ideas, and, in return, the European trip had furnished to him the much-desired novelty. He had performed the work of an educator in showing to Old World residents the conditions of a new civilization, and the idea was now conceived of showing to the world gathered at the arena in Chicago a representation of the cosmopolitan military force. He called it "A Congress of the Rough Riders of the World." It is a combination at once ethnological and military.

To the Indians and cowboys were added Mexicans, Cossacks, and South Americans, with regular trained cavalry from Germany, France, England, and the United States. This aggregation showed for the first time in 1893, and was an instantaneous success. Of it Opie Read gives a fine description:

"Morse made the two worlds touch the tips of their fingers together. Cody has made the warriors of all nations join hands.

"In one act we see the Indian, with his origin shrouded in history's mysterious fog; the cowboy— nerve-strung product of the New World; the American soldier, the dark Mexican, the glittering soldier of Germany, the dashing cavalryman of France, the impulsive Irish dragoon, and that strange, swift spirit from the plains of Russia, the Cossack.

"Marvelous theatric display, a drama with scarcely a word—Europe, Asia, Africa, America in panoramic whirl, and yet as individualized as if they had never left their own country."

In 1893 the horizon of my brother's interests enlarged. In July of that year I was married to Mr. Hugh A. Wetmore, editor of the Duluth *Press*. My steps now turned to the North, and the enterprising young city on the shore of Lake Superior became my home. During the long years of my widowhood my brother always bore toward me the attitude of guardian and protector; I could rely upon his support in any venture I deemed a promising one, and his considerate thoughtfulness did not fail when I remarried. He wished to see me well established in my new home; he desired to insure my happiness and prosperity, and with this end in view he purchased the Duluth *Press* plant, erected a fine brick building to serve as headquarters for the newspaper venture, and we became business partners in the untried field of press work.

My brother had not yet seen the Zenith City. So in January of 1894 he arranged to make a short visit to Duluth. We issued invitations for a general reception, and the response was of the genuine Western kind—eighteen hundred guests assembling in the new Duluth *Press* Building to bid welcome and do honor to the world-famed Buffalo Bill.

His name is a household word, and there is a growing demand for anecdotes concerning him. As he does not like to talk about himself, chroniclers have been compelled to interview his associates, or are left to their own resources. Like many of the stories told about Abraham Lincoln, some of the current yarns about Buffalo Bill are of doubtful authority. Nevertheless, a collection of those that are authentic would fill a volume. Almost every plainsman or soldier who met my brother during the Indian campaigns can tell some interesting tale about him that has never been printed. During the youthful season of redundant hope and happiness many of his ebullitions of wit were lost, but he was always beloved for his good humor, which no amount of carnage could suppress. He was not averse to church-going, though he was liable even in church to be carried away by the rollicking spirit that was in him. Instance his visit to the little temple which he had helped to build at North Platte.

His wife and sister were in the congregation, and this ought not only to have kept him awake, but it should have insured perfect decorum on his part. The opening hymn commenced with the words, "Oh, for a thousand tongues to sing," etc. The organist, who played "by ear," started the tune in too high a key to be followed by the choir and congregation, and had to try again. A second attempt ended, like the first, in failure. "Oh, for a thousand tongues to sing, my blest—" came the opening words for the third time, followed by a squeak from the organ, and a relapse into painful silence. Will could contain himself no longer, and blurted out: "Start it at five hundred, and mebbe some of the rest of us can get in."

Another church episode occurred during the visit of the "Wild West" to the Atlantic Exposition. A locally celebrated colored preacher had announced that he would deliver a sermon on the subject of Abraham Lincoln. A party of white people, including my brother, was made up, and repaired to the church to listen to the eloquent address. Not wishing to make themselves conspicuous, the white visitors took a pew in the extreme rear, but one of the ushers, wishing to honor them, insisted on conducting them to a front seat. When the contribution platter came around, our hero scooped a lot of silver dollars from his pocket and deposited them upon the plate with such force that the receptacle was tilted and its contents poured in a jingling shower upon the floor. The preacher left his pulpit to assist in gathering up the scattered treasure, requesting the congregation to sing a hymn of thanksgiving while the task was being performed. At the conclusion of the hymn the sable divine returned to the pulpit and supplemented his sermon with the following remarks:

"Brudderen an' sisters: I obsahve dat Co'nel and Gen'l Buflo Bill am present. [A roar of "Amens" and "Bless God's" arose from the audience.] You will wif-hold yuh Amens till I git froo. You all owes yuh free-dom to Abraham's bosom, but he couldn't hab went an' gone an' done it widout Buflo Bill, who he'ped him wid de sinnoose ob wah! Abraham Lincum was de brack man's fren'—Buflo Bill am de fren' ob us all. ["Amen!" screamed a sister.] Yes, sistah, he am yo' fren', moreova, an' de fren' ob every daughtah ob Jakup likewise. De chu'ch debt am a cross to us, an' to dat cross he bends his back as was prefigu'd in de scriptu's ob ol'. De sun may move, aw de sun mought stan' still but Buflo Bill nebba stan's still—he's ma'ching froo Geo'gia wid his Christian cowboys to sto'm de Lookout Mountain ob Zion. Deacon Green Henry Turner will lead us in prayah fo' Buflo Bill."

The following is one of Will's own stories: During the first years of his career as an actor Will had in one of his theatrical companies a Westerner named Broncho Bill. There were Indians in the troupe, and a certain missionary had joined the aggregation to look after the morals of the Indians. Thinking that Broncho Bill would bear a little looking after also, the good man secured a seat by his side at the dinner-table, and remarked pleasantly:

"This is Mr. Broncho Bill, is it not?"

"Yaas."

"Where were you born?"

"Near Kit Bullard's mill, on Big Pigeon."

"Religious parents, I suppose?"

"Yaas."

"What is your denomination?"

"My what?"

"Your denomination?"

"O—ah—yaas. Smith & Wesson."

While on his European tour Will was entertained by a great many potentates. At a certain dinner given in his honor by a wealthy English lord, Will met for the first time socially a number of blustering British officers, fresh from India. One of them addressed himself to the scout as follows: "I understand you are a colonel. You Americans are blawsted fond of military titles, don't cherneow. By gad, sir, we'll have to come over and give you fellows a good licking!"

"What, again?" said the scout, so meekly that for an instant his assailant did not know how hard he was hit, but he realized it when the retort was wildly applauded by the company.

Before closing these pages I will give an account of an episode which occurred during the Black Hills gold excitement, and which illustrates the faculty my hero possesses of adapting himself to all emergencies. Mr. Mahan, of West Superior, Wisconsin, and a party of adventurous gold-seekers were being chased by a band of Indians, which they had succeeded in temporarily eluding. They met Buffalo Bill at the head of a squad of soldiers who were looking for redskins. The situation was explained to the scout, whereupon he said:

"I am looking for that identical crowd. Now, you draw up in line, and I will look you over and pick out the men that I want to go back with me."

Without any questioning he was able to select the men who really wanted to return and fight the Indians. He left but two behind, but they were the ones who would have been of no assistance had they been allowed to go to the front. Will rode some distance in advance of his party, and when the Indians sighted him, they thought he was alone, and made a dash for him. Will whirled about and made his horse go as if fleeing for his life. His men had been carefully ambushed. The Indians kept up a constant firing, and when he reached a certain point Will pretended to be hit, and fell from his horse. On came the Indians, howling like a choir of maniacs. The next moment they were in a trap, and Will and his men opened fire on them, literally annihilating the entire squad. It was the Indian style of warfare, and the ten "good Indians" left upon the field, had they been able to complain, would have had no right to do so.

Will continued the march, and as the day was well advanced, began looking for a good place to camp. Arriving at the top of a ridge overlooking a little river, Will saw a spot where he had camped on a previous expedition; but, to his great disappointment, the place was in possession of a large village of hostiles, who were putting up their tepees, building camp fires, and making themselves comfortable for the coming night.

Quick as a flash Will decided what to do. "There are too many of them for us to whip in the tired condition of ourselves and horses," said our hero. Then he posted his men along the top of the ridge, with instructions to show themselves at a signal from him, and descended at once, solitary and alone, to the encampment of the hostiles. Gliding rapidly up to the chief, Will addressed him in his own dialect as follows:

"I want you to leave here right away, quick! I don't want to kill your women and children. A big lot of soldiers are following me, and they will destroy your whole village if you are here when they come."

As he waved his hand in the direction of the hilltop, brass buttons and polished gun-barrels began to glitter in the rays of the setting sun, and the chief ordered his braves to fold their tents and move on.

CHAPTER 30

Cody Day at the Omaha Exposition

Since 1893 the "Wild West" exhibitions have been restricted to the various cities of our own land. Life in "Buffalo Bill's Tented City," as it is called, is like life in a small village. There are some six hundred persons in the various departments. Many of the men have their families with them; the Indians have their squaws and papooses, and the variety of nationalities, dialects, and costumes makes the miniature city an interesting and entertaining one.

The Indians may be seen eating bundles of meat from their fingers and drinking tankards of iced buttermilk. The Mexicans, a shade more civilized, shovel with their knives great quantities of the same food in the capacious receptacles provided by nature. The Americans, despite what is said of their rapid eating, take time to laugh and crack jokes, and finish their repast with a product only known to the highest civilization—ice-cream.

When the "Wild West" visited Boston, one hot June day the parade passed a children's hospital on the way to the show-grounds. Many of the little invalids were unable to leave their couches. All who could do so ran to the open windows and gazed eagerly at the passing procession, and the greatest excitement prevailed. These more fortunate little ones described, as best they could, to the little sufferers who could not leave their beds the wonderful things they saw. The Indians were the special admiration of the children. After the procession passed, one wee lad, bedridden by spinal trouble, cried bitterly because he had not seen it. A kind-hearted nurse endeavored to soothe the child, but words proved unavailing. Then a bright idea struck the patient woman; she told him he might write a letter to the great "Buffalo Bill" himself and ask him for an Indian's picture.

The idea was taken up with delight, and the child spent an eager hour in penning the letter. It was pathetic in its simplicity. The little sufferer told the great exhibitor that he was sick in bed, was unable to see the Indians when they passed the hospital, and that he longed to see a photograph of one.

The important missive was mailed, and even the impatient little invalid knew it was useless to expect an answer that day. The morning had hardly dawned before a child's bright eyes were open. Every noise was listened to, and he wondered when the postman would bring him a letter. The nurse hardly dared to hope that a busy man like Buffalo Bill would take time to respond to the wish of a sick child.

"Colonel Cody is a very busy man," she said. "We must be patient."

At perhaps the twentieth repetition of this remark the door opened noiselessly. In came a six-foot Indian, clad in leather trousers and wrapped in a scarlet blanket. He wore a head-dress of tall, waving feathers, and carried his bow in his hand.

The little invalids gasped in wonder; then they shrieked with delight. One by one, silent and noiseless, but smiling, six splendid warriors followed the first. The visitors had evidently been well trained, and had received explicit directions as to their actions.

So unusual a sight in the orderly hospital so startled the nurse that she could not even speak. The warriors drew up in a line and saluted her. The happy children were shouting in such glee that the poor woman's fright was unnoticed.

The Indians ranged themselves in the narrow space between the cots, laid aside their gay blankets, placed their bows upon the floor, and waving their arms to and fro, executed a quiet war-dance. A sham battle was fought, followed by a song of victory. After this the blankets were again donned, the kindly red men went away, still smiling as benignly as their war paint would allow them to do. A cheer of gratitude and delight followed them down the broad corridors. The happy children talked about Buffalo Bill and the "Wild West" for weeks after this visit.

North Platte had long urged my brother to bring the exhibition there. The citizens wished to see the mammoth tents spread over the ground where the scout once followed the trail on the actual war-path; they desired that their famous fellow-citizen should thus honor his home town. A performance was finally given there on October 12, 1896, the special car bearing Will and his party arriving the preceding day, Sunday. The writer of these chronicles joined the party in Omaha, and we left that city after the Saturday night performance.

The Union Pacific Railroad had offered my brother every inducement to make this trip; among other things, the officials promised to make special time in running from Omaha to North Platte.

When we awoke Sunday morning, we found that in some way the train had been delayed, that instead of making special time we were several hours late. Will telegraphed this fact to the officials. At the next station double-headers were put on, and the gain became at once perceptible. At Grand Island a congratulatory telegram was sent, noting the gain in time. At the next station we passed the Lightning Express, the "flyer," to which usually everything gives way, and the good faith of the company was evidenced by the fact that this train was sidetracked to make way for Buffalo Bill's "Wild West" train. Another message was sent over the wires to the officials; it read as follows:

"Have just noticed that Lightning Express is sidetracked to make way for Wild West. I herewith promote you to top seat in heaven."

The trip was a continued ovation. Every station was thronged, and Will was obliged to step out on the platform and make a bow to the assembled crowds, his appearance being invariably greeted with a round of cheers. When we reached the station at North Platte, we found that the entire population had turned out to receive their fellow-townsman. The "Cody Guards," a band to which Will presented beautiful uniforms of white broadcloth trimmed with gold braid, struck up the strains of "See, the Conquering Hero Comes." The major attempted to do the welcoming honors of the city, but it was impossible for him to make himself heard. Cheer followed cheer from the enthusiastic crowd.

We had expected to reach the place some hours earlier, but our late arrival encroached upon the hour of church service. The ministers discovered that it was impossible to hold their congregations; so they were dismissed, and the pastors accompanied them to the station, one reverend gentleman humorously remarking:

"We shall be obliged to take for our text this morning 'Buffalo Bill and his Wild West,' and will now proceed to the station for the discourse."

Will's tally-ho coach, drawn by six horses, was in waiting for the incoming party. The members of his family seated themselves in that conveyance, and we passed through the town, preceded and followed by a band. As we arrived at the home residence, both bands united in a welcoming strain of martial music.

My oldest sister, Julia, whose husband is manager of "Scout's Rest Ranch," when informed that the "Wild West" was to visit North Platte, conceived the idea of making this visit the occasion of a family reunion. We had never met in an unbroken circle since the days of our first separation, but as a result of her efforts we sat thus that evening in my brother's home. The next day our mother-sister, as she had always been regarded, entertained us at "Scout's Rest Ranch."

The "Wild West" exhibition had visited Duluth for the first time that same year. This city has a population of 65,000. North Platte numbers 3,500. When he wrote to me of his intention to take the exhibition to Duluth, Will offered to make a wager that his own little town would furnish a bigger crowd than would the city of my residence. I could not accept any such inferred slur upon the Zenith City, so accepted the wager, a silk hat against a fur cloak.

October 12th, the date of the North Platte performance, dawned bright and cloudless. "To-day decides our wager," said Will. "I expect there will be two or three dozen people out on this prairie. Duluth turned out a good many thousands, so I suppose you think your wager as good as won."

The manager of the tents evidently thought the outlook a forlorn one. I shared his opinion, and was, in fancy, already the possessor of a fine fur cloak.

"Colonel, shall we stretch the full canvas?" asked the tent man.

"Every inch of it," as the prompt response. "We want to

show North Platte the capacity of the 'Wild West,' at any rate."

As we started for the grounds Will was evidently uncertain over the outcome, in spite of his previous boast of the reception North Platte would give him. "We'll have a big tent and plenty of room to spare in it," he observed.

But as we drove to the grounds we soon began to see indications of a coming crowd. The people were pouring in from all directions; the very atmosphere seemed populated; as the dust was nearly a foot deep on the roads, the moving populace made the air almost too thick for breathing. It was during the time of the county fair, and managers of the Union Pacific road announced that excursion trains would be run from every town and hamlet, the officials and their families coming up from Omaha on a special car. Where the crowds came from it was impossible to say. It looked as if a feat of magic had been performed, and that the stones were turned into men, or, perchance, that, as in olden tales, they came up out of the earth.

Accustomed though he is to the success of the show, Will was dumfounded by this attendance. As the crowds poured in I became alarmed about my wager. I visited the ticket-seller and asked how the matter stood.

"It's pretty close," he answered. "Duluth seems to be dwindling away before the mightiness of the Great American Desert."

This section of the country, which was a wilderness only a few years ago, assembled over ten thousand people to attend a performance of the "Wild West."

Omaha, where the opening performance of this exhibition was given, honored Will last year by setting apart one day as "Cody Day." August 31st was devoted to his reception, and a large and enthusiastic crowd gathered to do the Nebraska pioneer honor. The parade reached the fairgrounds at eleven o'clock, where it was fittingly received by one hundred and fifty mounted Indians from the encampment. A large square space had been reserved for the reception of the party in front of the Sherman gate. As it filed through, great applause was sent up by the waiting multitude, and the noise became deafening when my brother made his appearance on a magnificent chestnut horse, the gift of General Miles. He was accompanied by a large party of officials and Nebraska pioneers, who dismounted to seat themselves on the grand-stand. Prominent among these were the governor of the state, Senator Thurston, and Will's old friend and first employer, Mr. Alexander Majors. As Will ascended the platform he was met by General Manager Clarkson, who welcomed him in the name of the president of the exposition, whose official duties precluded his presence. Governor Holcomb was then introduced, and his speech was a brief review of the evolution of Nebraska from a wilderness of a generation ago to the great state which produced this marvelous exposition. Manager Clarkson remarked, as he introduced Mr. Majors: "Here is the father of them all, Alexander Majors, a man connected with the very earliest history of Nebraska, and the business father of Colonel Cody."

This old pioneer was accorded a reception only a shade less enthusiastic than that which greeted the hero of the day. He said:

"*Gentlemen, and My Boy, Colonel Cody:* [Laughter.] Can I say a few words of welcome? Friend Creighton and I came down here together to-day, and he thought I was not equal to the occasion. Gentlemen, I do not know whether I am equal to the occasion at this time, but I am going to do the best for you that I can. Give me your hand, Colonel. Gentlemen, forty-three years ago this day, this fine-looking physical specimen of manhood was brought to me by his mother—a little boy nine years old—and little did I think at that time that the boy that was standing before me, asking for employment of some kind by which I could afford to pay his mother a little money for his services, was going to be a boy of such destiny as he has turned out to be. In this country we have great men, we have great men in Washington, we have men who are famous as politicians in this country; we have great statesmen, we have had Jackson and Grant, and we had Lincoln; we have men great in agriculture and in stock-growing, and in the manufacturing business men who have made great names for themselves, who have stood high in the nation. Next, and even greater, we have a Cody. He, gentlemen, stands before you now, known the wide world over as the last of the great scouts. When the boy Cody came to me, standing straight as an arrow, and looked me in the face, I said to my partner, Mr. Russell, who was standing by my side, 'We will take this little boy, and we will pay him a man's wages, because he can ride a pony just as well as a man can.' He was lighter and could do service of that kind when he was nine years old. I remember when we paid him twenty-five dollars for the first month's work. He was paid in half-dollars, and he got fifty of them. He tied them up in his little handkerchief, and when he got home he untied the handkerchief and spread the money all over the table."

Colonel Cody—"I have been spreading it ever since."

A few remarks followed indicative of Mr. Major's appreciation of the exhibition, and he closed with the remark, "Bless your precious heart, Colonel Cody!" and sat down, amid great applause.

Senator Thurston's remarks were equally happy. He said:

"Colonel Cody, this is your day. This is your exposition. This is your city. And we all rejoice that Nebraska is your state. You have carried the fame of our country and of our state all over the civilized world; you have been received and honored by princes, by emperors, and by kings; the titled women in the courts of the nations of the world have been captivated by your charm of manner and your splendid manhood. You are known wherever you go, abroad or in the United States, as Colonel Cody, the best representative of the great and progressive West. You stand here to-day in the midst of a wonderful assembly. Here are representatives of the heroic and daring characters of most of the nations of the world. You are entitled to the honor paid you today, and especially entitled to it here. This people know you as a man who has carried this demonstration of yours to foreign lands, and exhibited it at home. You have been a great national and international educator of men. You have furnished a demonstration of the possibilities of our country that has advanced us in the opinion of all the world. But we who have been with you a third, or more than a third, of a century, we remember you more dearly and tenderly than others do. We remember that when this whole Western land was a wilderness, when these representatives of the aborigines were attempting to hold their own against the onward tide of civilization, the settler and the hardy pioneer, the women and the children, felt safe whenever Cody rode along the frontier; he was their protector and defender.

"Cody, this is your home. You live in the hearts of the people of our state. God bless you and keep you and prosper you in your splendid work."

Will was deeply touched by these strong expressions from his friends. As he moved to the front of the platform to respond, his appearance was the signal for a prolonged burst of cheers. He said:

"You cannot expect me to make adequate response for the honor which you have bestowed upon me today. You have overwhelmed my speaking faculties. I cannot corral enough ideas to attempt a coherent reply in response to the honor which you have accorded me. How little I dreamed in the long ago that the lonely path of the scout and the pony-express rider would lead me to the place you have assigned me to-day. Here, near the banks of the mighty Missouri, which flows unvexed to the sea, my thoughts revert to the early days of my manhood. I looked eastward across this rushing tide to the Atlantic, and dreamed that in that long-settled region all men were rich and all women happy. My friends, that day has come and gone. I stand among you a witness that nowhere in the broad universe are men richer in manly integrity, and women happier in their domestic kingdom, than here in our own Nebraska.

"I have sought fortune in many lands, but wherever I have wandered, the flag of our beloved state has been unfurled to every breeze from the Platte to the Danube, from the Tiber to the Clyde, the emblem of our sovereign state has always floated over the 'Wild West.' Time goes on and brings with it new duties and responsibilities, but we 'old men,' we who are called old-timers, cannot forget the trials and tribulations which we had to encounter while paving the path for civilization and national prosperity.

"The whistle of the locomotive has drowned the howl of the coyote; the barb-wire fence has narrowed the range of the cow-puncher; but no material evidence of prosperity can obliterate our contribution to Nebraska's imperial progress.

"Through your kindness to-day I have tasted the sweetest fruit that grows on ambition's tree. If you extend your kindness and permit me to fall back into the ranks as a high private, my cup will be full.

"In closing, let me call upon the 'Wild West, the Congress of Rough Riders of the World,' to voice their appreciation of the kindness you have shown them today."

At a given signal the "Wild West" gave three ringing cheers for Nebraska and the Trans-Mississippi Exposition. The cowboy band followed with the "Red, White, and Blue," and an exposition band responded with the "Star-Spangled Banner." The company fell into line for a parade around the grounds, Colonel Cody following on his chestnut horse, Duke. After him came the officials and invited guests in carriages; then came the Cossacks, Cubans, the German cavalry, the United States cavalry, the Mexicans, and representatives of twenty-five countries.

As the parade neared its end, my brother turned to his friends and suggested that as they had been detained long past the dinner-hour in doing him honor, he would like to compensate them by giving an informal spread. This invitation was promptly accepted, and the company adjourned to a café, where a tempting luncheon was spread before them. Never before had such a party of pioneers met around a banquet-table, and many were the reminiscences of early days brought out. Mr. Majors, the the originator of the Pony Express line, was there. The two Creighton brothers, who put through the first telegraph line, and took the occupation of the express riders from them, had seats of honor. A. D. Jones was introduced as the man who carried the first postoffice of Omaha around in his hat, and who still wore the hat. Numbers of other pioneers were there, and each contributed his share of racy anecdotes and pleasant reminiscences.

CHAPTER 31

The Last of the Great Scouts

The story of frontier days is a tale that is told. The "Wild West" has vanished like mist in the sun before the touch of the two great magicians of the nineteenth century—steam and electricity.

The route of the old historic Santa Fé trail is nearly followed by the Atchison, Topeka and Santa Fé Railroad, which was completed in 1880. The silence of the prairie was once broken by the wild war-whoop of the Indian as he struggled to maintain his supremacy over some adjoining tribe; the muffled roar caused by the heavy hoof-beats of thousands of buffaloes was almost the only other sound that broke the stillness. To-day the shriek of the engine, the clang of the bell, and the clatter of the car-wheels form a ceaseless accompaniment to the cheerful hum of busy life which everywhere pervades the wilderness of thirty years ago. Almost the only memorials of the struggles and privations of the hardy trappers and explorers, whose daring courage made the achievements of the present possible, are the historic landmarks which bear the names of some of these brave men. But these are very few in number. Pike's Peak lifts its snowy head to heaven in silent commemoration of the early traveler whose name it bears. Simpson's Rest, a lofty obelisk, commemorates the mountaineer whose life was for the most part passed upon its rugged slopes, and whose last request was that he should be buried on its summit. Another cloud-capped mountain-height bears the name of Fisher's Peak, and thereby hangs a tale.

Captain Fisher commanded a battery in the army engaged in the conquest of New Mexico. His command encamped near the base of the mountain which now bears his name. Deceived by the illusive effect of the atmosphere, he started out for a morning stroll to the supposed near-by elevation, announcing that he would return in time for breakfast. The day passed with no sign of Captain Fisher, and night lengthened into a new day. When the second day passed without his return, his command was forced to believe that he had fallen a prey to lurking Indians, and the soldiers were sadly taking their seats for their evening meal when the haggard and wearied captain put in an appearance. His morning stroll had occupied two days and a night; but he set out to visit the mountain, and he did it.

The transcontinental line which supplanted the Old Salt Lake trail, and is now known as the Union Pacific Railroad, antedated the Atchison, Topeka and Santa Fé by eleven years. The story of the difficulties encountered, and the obstacles overcome in the building of this road, furnishes greater marvels than any narrated in the Arabian Nights' Tales.

This railroad superseded the Pony Express line, the reeking, panting horses of which used their utmost endeavor and carried their relentless riders fifteen miles an hour, covering their circuit in eight days' time at their swiftest rate of speed. The iron horse gives a sniff of disdain, and easily traverses the same distance, from the Missouri line to the Pacific Coast, in three days.

Travelers who step aboard the swiftly moving, luxurious cars of to-day give little thought to their predecessors; for the dangers the early voyagers encountered they have no sympathy. The traveler in the stagecoach was beset by perils without from the Indians and the outlaws; he faced the equally unpleasant companionship of fatigue and discomfort within. The jolting, swinging coach bounced and jounced the unhappy passengers as the reckless driver lashed the flying horses. Away they galloped over mountains and through ravines, with no cessation of speed. Even the shipper pays the low rate of transportation asked to-day with reluctance, and forgets the great debt he owes this adjunct of our civilization.

But great as are the practical benefits derived from the railways, we cannot repress a sigh as we meditate on the picturesque phases of the vanished era. Gone are the bullwhackers and the prairie-schooners! Gone are the stagecoaches and their drivers! Gone are the Pony Express riders! Gone are the trappers, the hardy pioneers, the explorers, and the scouts! Gone is the prairie monarch, the shaggy, unkempt buffalo!

In 1869, only thirty years ago, the train on the Kansas Pacific road was delayed eight hours in consequence of the passage of an enormous herd of buffaloes over the track in front of it. But the easy mode of travel introduced by the railroad brought hundreds of sportsmen to the plains, who wantonly killed this noble animal solely for sport, and thousands of buffaloes were sacrificed for their skins, for which there was a widespread demand. From 1868 to 1881, in Kansas alone, there was paid out $2,500,000 for the bones of this animal, which were gathered up on the prairie and used in the carbon works of the country. This represents a total death-rate of 31,000,000 buffaloes in one state. As far as I am able to ascertain, there remains at this writing only one herd, of less than twenty animals, out of all the countless thousands that roamed the prairie so short a time ago, and this herd is carefully preserved in a private park. There may be a few isolated specimens in menageries and shows, but this wholesale slaughter has resulted in the practical extermination of the species.

As with the animal native to our prairies, so has it been with the race native to our land. We may deplore the wrongs of the Indian, and sympathize with his efforts to wrest justice from his so-called protectors. We may admire his poetic nature, as evidenced in the myths and legends of the race. We may be impressed by the stately dignity and innate ability as orator and statesman which he displays. We may preserve the different articles of his picturesque garb as relics. But the old, old drama of history is repeating itself before the eyes of this generation; the inferior must give way to the superior civilization. The poetic, picturesque, primitive red man must inevitably succumb before the all-conquering tread of his pitiless, practical, progressive white brother.

Cooper has immortalized for us the extinction of a people in the "Last of the Mohicans." Many another tribe has passed away, unhonored and unsung. Westward the "Star of Empire" takes its way; the great domain west of the Mississippi is now peopled by the white race, while the Indians are shut up in reservations. Their doom is sealed; their sun is set. "Kismet" has been spoken of them; the total extinction of the race is only a question of time. In the words of Rudyard Kipling:

"Take up the White Man's burden—
    Ye dare not stoop to less—
Nor call too loud on freedm
    To cloke your weariness.
By all ye will or whisper,
    By all ye leave or do,
The silent, sullen peoples
    Shall weigh your God and you."

Of this past epoch of our national life there remains but one well-known representative. That one is my brother. He occupies a unique place in the portrait gallery of famous Americans to-day. It is not alone his commanding personality, nor the success he has achieved along various lines, which gives him the strong hold he has on the hearts of the American people, or the absorbing interest he possesses in the eyes of foreigners. The fact that in his own person he condenses a period of national history is a large factor in the fascination he exercises over others. He may fitly be named the "Last of the Great Scouts." He has had great predecessors. The mantle of Kit Carson has fallen upon his shoulders, and he wears it worthily. He has not, and never can have, a successor. He is the vanishing-point between the rugged wilderness of the past in Western life and the vast achievement in the present.

When the "Wild West" disbands, the last vestige of our frontier life passes from the scene of active realities, and becomes a matter of history.

"Life is real, life is earnest," sings the poet, and real and earnest it has been for my brother. It has been spent in others' service. I cannot recall a time when he has not thus been laden with heavy burdens. Yet for himself he has won a reputation, national and international. A naval officer visiting in China relates that as he stepped ashore he was offered two books for purchase—one the Bible, the other a "Life of Buffalo Bill."

For nearly half a century, which comprises his childhood, youth, and manhood, my brother has been before the public. He can scarcely be said to have had a childhood, so early was he thrust among the rough scenes of frontier life, therein to play a man's part at an age when most boys think of nothing more than marbles and tops. He enlisted in the Union army before he was of age, and did his share in upholding the flag during the Civil War as ably as many a veteran of forty, and since then he has remained, for the most part, in his country's service, always ready to go to the front in any time of danger. He has achieved distinction in many and various ways. He is president of the largest irrigation enterprise in the world, president of a colonization company, of a town-site company, and of two transportation companies. He is the foremost scout and champion buffalo-hunter of America, one of the crack shots of the world, and its greatest popular entertainer. He is broad-minded and progressive in his views, inheriting from both father and mother a hatred of oppression in any form. Taking his mother as a standard, he believes the franchise is a birthright which should appertain to intelligence and education, rather than to sex. It is his public career that lends an interest to his private life, in which he has been a devoted and faithful son and brother, a kind and considerate husband, a loving and generous father. "Only the names of them that are upright, brave, and true can be honorably known," were the mother's dying words; and honorably known has his name become, in his own country and across the sea.

With the fondest expectation he looks forward to the hour when he shall make his final bow to the public and retire to private life. It is his long-cherished desire to devote his remaining years to the development of the Big Horn Basin, in Wyoming. He has visited every country in Europe, and has looked upon the most beautiful of Old World scenes. He is familiar with all the most splendid regions of his own land, but to him this new El Dorado of the West is the fairest spot on earth.

He has already invested thousands of dollars and given much thought and attention toward the accomplishment of his pet scheme. An irrigating ditch costing nearly a million dollars now waters this fertile region, and various other improvements are under way, to prepare a land flowing with milk and honey for the reception of thousands of homeless wanderers. Like the children of Israel, these would never reach the promised land but for the untiring efforts of a Moses to go on before; but unlike the ancient guide and scout of sacred history, my brother has been privileged to penetrate the remotest corner of his primitive land of Canaan. The log cabin he has erected there is not unlike the one of our childhood days. Here he finds his haven of rest, his health-resort, to which he hastens when the show season is over and he is free again for a space. He finds refreshment in the healthful, invigorating atmosphere of his chosen retreat; he enjoys sweet solace from the cares of life under the influence of its magnificent scenery.

And here, in the shadow of the Rockies, yet in the very "light of things," it is his wish to finish his days as he began them, in opening up for those who come after him the great regions of the still undeveloped West, and in poring over the lesson learned as a boy on the plains:

> "That nature never did betray
> The heart that loved her."

Zane Grey Adds the Finishing Touch to the Story
by Telling of the Last Days of the Last of
the Great Scouts

And now the last of the Great Scouts has crossed the Great Divide.

There is now only one left of that magnificent group of frontiersmen who opened up the west to civilization. And strange to relate, he shared a fame only second to Cody's, and a name somewhat similar. Buffalo Jones! I told his story in "The Last of the Plainsmen." Buffalo Bill and Buffalo Jones were life-long friends. Buffalo Bill earned his fame by killing thousands of buffalo. Buffalo Jones earned his by capturing and preserving buffalo calves to prevent the extinction of the species.

Here is what Buffalo Jones writes me about Buffalo Bill:

"About a half century ago I met Cody in Abaline, Kansas. He was city marshal. He said to me:

"'Young man, we have organized a law and order league. Are you with us or against us?'

"'I'm with you,' was my reply.

"'From that day to his death we were true friends. On that meeting he asked me to drink with him, and I refused. During the fifty years of our acquaintance I met him hundreds of times, all over the world, I might say, and he respected my temperance habit to the extent that he never asked me to drink again. The last time I met him was some years ago in Kansas City, where we three old-timers—Buffalo Bill, Pawnee Bill, and I—had our picture taken together.

"Buffalo Bill was a wonderful character and a great man."

The last performance of Buffalo Bill's "Wild West" took place in Denver about 1913. The show was attached for debts and was finally taken into the Sells-Floto circus. The Sells people advertised him as "Buffalo Bill Himself," and he appeared in the performances for some time, probably for nearly a year, and then he associated himself with the "101 Ranch." But he soon tired of this lessening tide in his fortunes, and particularly the show business. He went to Cody, Wyoming, to look after his private ranching interests, and there to try to recover his failing health. Nearly seventy years old, ill and broken, and almost penniless, he faced a new and strange trail. All his personal property had gone in the break-up of his "Wild West" show.

Cody went to Denver. He was planning another "Wild West" show. But there he broke down and went to the home of his youngest sister, Mrs. May Cody Decker. After a few weeks of slowly failing strength he died on January 10, 1917. It is the opinion of his close friends that his failing health and death were due to a broken heart.

Mr. Chauncey Thomas, the well-known writer of *Outdoor Life,* knew Cody personally and had the last interview with the great scout. I venture to predict that this interview will become historical; and I am indebted to Mr. Thomas for permission to quote him:

"The greatest thing Buffalo Bill ever did, a thing that few men throughout the ages have ever equalled, was to give a new game to the children of the world. And in that his fame will probably outlive Cæsar's, for when Cæsar and Napoleon have faded into oblivion Buffalo Bill will have become a legendary hero, known in the literature and the legends and the children's games of civilizations yet to come. At one time Cinderella, Sinbad, Robinson

Crusoe, Friday, and their kind undoubtedly lived in the flesh, but so long ago that the memory of man runneth not to the contrary. What Robin Hood was to England, so Buffalo Bill will probably be to America. . . .

"Buffalo Bill took the American frontier around the world. London, Paris, Berlin, people by the million the earth around saw with their own eyes, not an imitation, not a mere stage or theatrical effect, but the real thing. Here, before their own eyes, were the actual men, red and white, who rode the Western plains of America. No other man has ever done that, no other man now can do that. Buffalo Bill benefited, the West benefited, the whole world benefited by it, and no one lost. That our outdoor West is known all over the earth as in no other country, we owe to Buffalo Bill, and to no one else.

"But his last days were as quiet, calm and peaceful as his life had been active and brilliant. Mrs. May Cody Decker, in whose home he died, gave her brother every care and attention that love and admiration could bestow. May Cody was his youngest sister, and he often used to take her with him on the plains in the early days. Between the two was a life-long bond that few sisters know, and when his death drew near Buffalo Bill went to her home.

"When the doctors told him that he would never see another sunset, Buffalo Bill dropped his head on his breast for a moment, a long, still moment, then raised it, fearlessly and serene. Those eagle eyes, keen and kindly as ever they were, looked long at the mountains, snowy in the distance, then he quietly gave a few directions about his funeral, and then again became the knightly, genial man he had always been. The man was majestic.

"In the room were his two sisters, Mrs. May Cody Decker and Mrs. Julia Cody Goodman, and another relative, Miss Hazel Olive Bennet—who made this story possible, and to whose kindly influence and intelligent cooperation the world is indebted for this interview—myself, and that white, calm figure, William Frederick Cody.

"It was the End, and we all knew it. We talked at random, as all do, perhaps, at such times. I can make no attempt to put down here what was said, as if this were a stenographic report. The Grand Old American talked of this and of that, now of the early days on the Great Plains, now of the boyhood of the present King of England—and in the room was a personal message from that King, and another from the President of the United States, and from others of equal rank throughout the world. Buffalo Bill, Colonel Cody, Pa-has-ka, they came and went, but the center of that last group was 'Brother Will.'

"But his mind went back eagerly to the minor details of his earlier life and to the names of those he used to know, who long ago passed beyond the Great White Range. We talked of many of the old friends of my father's, W. R. Thomas, like Reno, Custer, Benteen, Captain Mix, Grant, Sheridan, Carr, Crook, and Sherman, and the few I had known when a boy—the soldiers, stage-drivers and scouts of the early days.

"Then I spoke of guns. 'Which gun was his favorite?'

"'Lucretia Borgia,' he smiled. That was the name of his favorite buffalo gun.

"'The old fifty-caliber Springfield needle-gun?' I asked.

"'No, forty-eight caliber. The muzzle loaders of the Civil War were fifty-two caliber, you remember'—I didn't because I was not born till after the war, and he laughed—'but they made the breech-loading Springfield forty-eight caliber. I liked it better than the Sharps, and with it I killed 4,250 buffalo one year—or 4,862 in eighteen months, besides deer and antelope—for the Union Pacific builders.'

"'Did you always use the same gun?'"

" 'Practically so. The barrel of Lucretia Borgia is now on the elk horns at the ranch, with the knife with which I killed Yellow Hand. I don't know where the stock is'—and here the white head drooped wearily, and some one took up the talk for a while.

" 'Yes,' he began again, 'I have killed over 40,000 buffalo, and most of them with that old gun. But not all of them, of course.'

" "That was your favorite gun, then?'

" 'It is now, but our term of service on the Plains covered so many years, and so many different kinds of guns came into use that we tried out this one, then that one. The '73 Winchester was well liked, as was the Spencer carbine, especially on horseback, but they could not shoot alongside of the .48-caliber needle-gun. That carried 70 grains of powder and 470 grains of lead. "Shoot to-day!—kill tomorrow!" was what the Indians called it.'

" 'That was my father's rifle, and I love that gun.'

"I asked him about the old buffalo Sharps rifle, the .45-120-550 gun that weighed from sixteen to eighteen pounds, or the .44-caliber, bottle-neck, eleven-pound Sharps, like the one I own, my first rifle, and that were the usual favorites with the buffalo-killers, but he did not say much about them. To my surprise he did not seem interested in them at all. I presume the reason was that he usually hunted buffalo from horseback, and so did not use these heavy rifles, as did the men who killed from the ground.

"Then I learned how he killed his buffalo and how he got his name. He used to ride on the right-hand side of a herd as near to the front as he could get, and always shoot to the left hand, as a rifleman on horseback naturally would do. This method usually caused the herd soon to run in a solid circle, or to 'mill,' as the cattlemen call it, and this kept the herd in one place, running round and round and round like a wheel. Thus one could kill as many as were needed for that day, and have them all in the same spot, convenient for the skinners and the meat wagons.

"The other method—one he did not use so much as others did—was to 'get a stand' on a small herd and shoot down the animals that were inclined to break away and lead the herd out of range. From this method comes, I have no doubt, our present purely American word, 'to buffalo,' meaning to have some one confused, intimidated, bluffed and outgeneraled.

"But he did not consider this so much hunting as it was railroad building, opening the wilderness to civilization, and that the buffalo had to go as the first step in subduing the Indian; also because cattle-raising and farming, as every old-timer knows, was impossible where the buffalo were. The wild cattle (the buffalo), savage and untamable as the wolves that followed them, ruined fences and crops and killed all domestic cattle, for it is death for the domestic cow—due to the hump on the calf—to breed with the buffalo bull, and the buffalo bulls could easily run down and kill any domestic bull.

"The elimination of the buffalo was not wanton; it was necessary. In their place to-day are domestic cattle, less picturesque but far more valuable to mankind. I speak of this somewhat at length out of justice to Buffalo Bill. He never killed for slaughter's own sake. The more than forty thousand that fell to his rifle were killed for food, just as we kill to-day. He fed with wild meat the men who laid the first iron trail across the plains, who first linked the two oceans with a path of steel.

" 'Who was the best revolver shot you ever knew?' I asked.

" 'Frank North, white chief of the Pawnees. He was the best revolver shot, standing still, in the air, from horseback, or at running animals or men, that I ever saw,' and again those dark eagle eyes of the Old Scout lit up like an excited boy's. Then came his sister's lifted hand of caution behind his shoulder, and I changed the subject, for that great heart was liable to stop at any instant, and we had to avoid anything tending to excite him. But after a time I came back to the same subject.

" 'Was Wild Bill one of the quickest shots?' I ventured.

" 'Fair,' smiled Cody, and I too smiled to hear a man say that Wild Bill was a 'fair' shot. But this was Buffalo Bill speaking, and he spoke as one with authority.

" ' "Bill" was only a nickname we gave him, you know.' I didn't know, but nodded. 'His real name was James B. Hickox, and we got to calling him "Wild Bill" because when we were all boys together there were four "Bills" in the wagon train, and we had to sort them out somehow. Jim Hickox was always popping away at everything he saw move when on guard at night over the stock, so we sort of got to calling him "Wild" Bill, and that is how the name came to him. They called me "Buffalo" Bill because I had that buffalo contract with the U. P. and got down over 4,250 for meat. I have forgotten what became of the other two "Bills." ' "

" 'How did Hickox get so many men?' I asked.

" 'Well, Bill was a pretty good shot, but he could not shoot as quick as half a dozen men we all knew in those days. Nor as straight, either. But Bill was cool, and the men he went up against were rattled, I guess. Bill beat them to it. He made up his mind to kill the other man before the other man had finished thinking, and so Bill would just quietly pull his gun and give it to him. That was all there was to it. It is easy enough to beat the other man if you start first. Bill always shot as he raised his gun. That is, he was never in a hurry about it; he just pulled the gun from his hip and let it go as he was raising it; shoot on the up-raise, you might call it. Most men lifted the gun higher, then threw it down to cock it before firing. Bill cocked it with his thumb, I guess, as it was coming up into line with his man. That's how he did it. But he was not the quickest man by any means. He was just cool and quiet, and started first. Bill Hickox was not a bad man, as is often pictured. But he was a bad man to tackle. Always cool, kind, and cheerful, almost, about it. And he never killed a man unless that man was trying to kill him. That's fair.' It was, and so I agreed.

" 'Was any particular revolver, size, or caliber the favorite in the early days?'

" 'No, not particularly. Like the rifles, new kinds and sizes came in and put other kinds out. So we used all kinds, and sometimes any kind we could get. It was the cap-and-ball Colt, then the metallic cartridge six-guns came on the plains, and they saved us a lot of trouble, especially in wet weather, or on horseback. The only way we could load a cap-and-ball on horseback was to have extra cylinders, and change from an empty to a loaded one, and then reload all the empty cylinders when we had a chance. But with wet clothes, wet hands, and everything wet, that was often hard to do, and sometimes we could not reload at all. A muzzle-loading rifle or shot-gun was different, because we could keep the muzzle and the loading things covered better. So the metal cartridges were a great thing.'

" 'Was the .45 Colt or the .44-caliber preferred by most men?'

" 'It didn't make any difference. Just what we happened to have.'

" 'Was any kind of knife a special favorite on the plains?'

" 'No. Any kind that the owner liked, or could get. Such things as guns, revolvers and knives were just like any other kind of fashion or tools. Some kinds were favorites, maybe, in one place or at one time here and there, then other kinds. I used all of them, I guess. But for buffalo I liked best the .48-caliber Springfield. "Shoot to-day!—kill tomorrow!"

" 'What kind of a knife did you kill Yellow Hand with?'

" 'Just a big heavy bowie blade. For skinning and cutting up meat, of course, we used common butcher knives; no particular kind. Whatever we had or could get. Often we had to make such things ourselves. We were not particular, just so such things did their work.'

" 'Could the old-timers shoot better than the men of to-day?'

" 'No,' and a shadow of injured pride or regret, it seemed like, crossed the Old Scout's face. 'No, we could not shoot as good as you do to-day. We did not have as accurate guns, either in rifles or revolvers or loads. And we could not afford the ammunition with which to practice. I never saw such revolver shooting as Captain Hardy did one night over at his house, in that private shooting place he has down cellar.'

"But Hardy, one of the world's best shots, says that Buffalo Bill was the best shot from horseback that the world has ever seen.

" 'No; none of us, not even Frank North, could do such things. C. M. McCutchen can shoot a revolver far faster than any man I ever knew on the frontier; five hits on a man at ten yards in three-fifths of a second is more than twice as fast as we could do. He is probably the fastest man with a revolver who ever lived. All of them to-day— the best shots, I mean—can beat us old-timers every time. But we did the work all the same. We had to.'

"The voice was tired now, and the doctor came.

" 'Brother Will, it is time for him to go,' said Mrs. Goodman gently, and I arose. The Old Scout was in pajamas and slippers, and over them had been drawn a house coat. Instantly Buffalo Bill was on his feet, straight as an Indian, head up, as in days of old. The man recalled the Spanish cavalier, courtly as the prince he was in his kindly grace, all unaided by gorgeous trappings or picturesque surroundings, just the Man Himself standing there, waxen pale, his silver hair flowing down over his straight, square shoulders, his hand out in the last farewell. He asked for me afterwards, but the doctors said, 'No.' But as we all stood up in that little home room a silence fell. It was the last time. I knew it; he knew it; we all knew it. But on the surface not a sign.

"'Good-by.'"

The *Denver Post* of January 14, 1917, said in part:

WEST TO BID FAREWELL TO-DAY TO BUFFALO BILL AS THOUSANDS GATHER TO HONOR IDOL OF PLAINS
BODY TO LIE IN STATE AT CAPITOL THIS MORNING UNTIL NOON, WITH FORT LOGAN SOLDIERS FORMING GUARD OF HONOR AND ESCORT

Farewell, Pa-has-ka!

For to-day the good-bye must be said; the last glimpse taken of him who laid the foundations of the West, the last godspeed given by those who remain behind while he has gone on—on beyond the setting sun and the last frontier. For to-day Denver and the West, assembled, will pay homage to the memory of Col. William Frederick Cody—"Buffalo Bill." To-day an idol goes to his crypt in the eternal sleep. Few in Denver won't pass by his casket.

And few there will be of Denver's great population who will not pass beside the form of Colonel Cody as it lies in state in the capitol building to-day. Few will be those who will not gather on the streets to watch the procession as it travels from the state house to the Elks' home at Fourteenth and California streets for the eulogies and the song he loved. For Denver intends to say good-bye, from its school children to its most aged citizens—good-bye to the man who knew Denver when Denver was a weakling, who scouted the plains and fought the hostile Indians that the stagecoach might rock its tortuous way in and out of the "camp on Cherry Creek." Veterans, scouts, Indian fighters, dignitaries— every phase of Denver's population—will to-day walk in homage past the casket of Pa-has-ka to gaze for the last time upon the face of a man distinctive, whose niche in history never can be filled again. There was only one Buffalo Bill.

They buried Buffalo Bill on a promontory of Lookout Mountain, near Denver.

It was not the place he had hoped to go to his last sleep, but, nevertheless, it is indeed a fitting grave for the last of the great scouts. He would have chosen a lonelier grave, far from the crowd. In the years to come his resting place will be visited by thousands; and that will be well. The coming generations ought to have memorable appreciation of the man who so faithfully served the West.

Every hunter and plainsman and scout loved the solitude and loneliness of the wilds. That is what made them great.

The sunset, the descending twilight, the sweet silence of the hills, the brightening star, the lonely darkness of the night—these things Buffalo Bill loved. And these he will have. His life was full to the brim. He will not be forgotten. He represented the onward movement of a race. Surely he will rest in peace there on the rocky height where the wind will moan and the day will break solemn and grand and the night fall to the end of time.

—ZANE GREY
November, 1917